TENDER WARRIOR

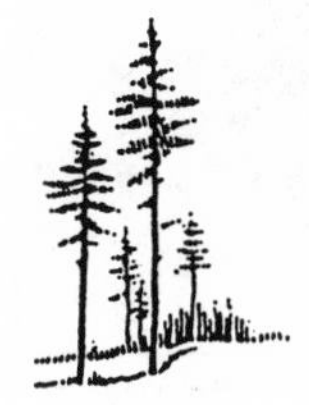

Also by Fern Michaels
in Thorndike Large Print®

Texas Heat
Texas Rich
Texas Fury
Texas Sunrise
To Have and to Hold
Desperate Measures

This Large Print Book carries the
Seal of Approval of N.A.V.H.

TENDER WARRIOR

Fern Michaels

Thorndike Press • Thorndike, Maine

Published in 1995 by arrangement with Ballantine Books, a division of Random House, Inc.

Thorndike Large Print ® Romance Series.

The tree indicium is a trademark of Thorndike Press.

The text of this Large Print edition is unabridged.
Other aspects of the book may vary from the original edition.

Set in 16 pt. News Plantin by Juanita Macdonald.

Printed in the United States on permanent paper.

Library of Congress Cataloging in Publishing Data

Michaels, Fern.
Tender warrior / Fern Michaels.
p. cm.
ISBN 0-7862-0497-4 (lg. print : hc)
1. Cid, ca. 1043–1099 — Fiction. 2. Spain — History — 711–1516 — Fiction. 3. Heroes — Spain — Fiction.
I. Title.
[PS3563.I27T43 1995]
813′.54—dc20 95-17739

AUTHOR'S NOTE

Immortalized in ballad, play, and film, the life of Rodrigo Ruy Diaz — El Cid, Compeador — has fascinated storytellers through the centuries. There is, in fact, no tangible trace of the Cid today, except for one or two old parchments that name him; but he lives in legend and history.

In spite of painstaking historical researches that have been in progress for hundreds of years, old fallacies die hard. Historian Ramón Menéndez Pidal was successful in separating much of the fiction from fact, yet the Cid is still described in many Spanish references as "semi-mythical."

A whole library has grown around his name, but the Cid did live and die between the years 1043 and 1099. Relating to his life are records written in his lifetime and still in existence. The *Poema de mio Cid*, written within forty years of his death, so closely relates to Spanish and Arab history that it may be considered documentary.

After a century or two, however, the romantic bent of minstrels and balladeers thought to improve on history and take poetic license. A number of ballads, such as *Mocedadez*, were told and retold, often recounting adventures of Cid's youth with people who were long dead before he was born. The fiction also included the episode of the duel and death of the imaginary Count Gomez Lozano and Cid's subsequent marriage to the count's orphan daughter, Jimena, who was also fictional. However, Cid did marry a member of the royal house of Asturias whose name was Himena (Ximena).

It is the undocumented years of Ruy Diaz's life that fascinated me and tempted my imagination. Especially when I learned it is believed he enjoyed a loving relationship with the daughter of an Islamic ruler. No actual evidence supported the idea that Cid's marriage to Himena was founded on love. To the contrary, it would seem it was a politically advantageous move on both their parts. Three daughters were born into this marriage, but the known movements of the Cid and their respective dates of birth do not always correspond and give credence that he was their father. It is known that daughters had little worth except for alliances through their marriages, and it would be quite possible — were any of Himena's children sons and heirs —

that the Cid might have protested that he was their father.

In researching this material my flights of fancy took me toward the romantic notion that Ruy Diaz would have loved the woman he chose for himself, rather than the woman politics chose for him.

FERN MICHAELS

PROLOGUE

Through the high narrow windows of their bed chamber the midnight sky seemed a tapestry of lights, the stars appearing so close that one might reach up to touch them. The sheer curtains billowed inward from the early autumn breezes, bringing the faint, heady aroma of fallen leaves, damp earth, and the crispness of snow from the nearby mountaintops.

Mirjana curled her body against his, more for love than for warmth. Her head rested lightly on his shoulder, her arm wrapped around his naked chest. This was the best place to be, she had told him often, sighing with satisfaction as she nestled against him. And it was, he knew. Having her beside him this way, feeling each light beat of her heart, each stirring of her breath, was in its own way his heaven.

She fit so neatly against him, her full breasts pressed to him, her thigh thrown so intimately over his. There was a new contour to add to her beauty, the swelling of their child who grew within her. His hand grazed lovingly down the length of her, careful not to disturb her sleep. The incredible softness of her skin was warm and vibrant beneath his touch. The slope of her back, the curve of her hip, the perfume of her hair were potent aphrodisiacs to his prowess. He had made love to her not an hour before and yet, if she invited him, he would take her again.

Mirjana. His Mirjana. Soft, gray eyes half-closed in passion, pouting lips that murmured his name. She had given him the precious gift of her love and with each wonderful expression of it he was renewed. Tenderly, he pressed closer to her, wanting her again, knowing he would never have enough of her.

Sensing his wakefulness, her eyes opened, smiling up at him in the half light from the dying fire in the hearth. She welcomed his touch to the sensitive skin of her breasts and sighed contentedly when his hand slipped lower, grazing along her velvet haunches to the downy soft triangle between her thighs. She knew his need for her and it was echoed in her everlasting desire for him.

No other man existed for her, only Ruy. He knew every inch of her body, every curve and hollow, and claimed them for his own with a tenderness born of love. He caressed her gently with his warrior's hands, taking command of her senses and control of her passions.

He was a masterful lover, demanding and urgent, heating her responses to a fiery blaze. And he was soft with her when she needed him to be soft, provoking her passions and teasing her to a wanton pitch. He filled her, this man she loved, replenishing her soul with himself, saturating her heart with his love and sating her desires and lusty hungers with his own throbbing urgencies.

He would take her again and it would be no less glorious than the last. He covered her with his body, fitting himself between her thighs, searching for her center and invading it with his flesh. Cradled together in a loving embrace they knew a sense of coming home, where love burned the fires of passion brighter than any they had ever known.

CHAPTER 1

When the early morning sun reflected the heavenly colors of pink and mauve against the towering white spires of the Mosque on the far side of the city, she could imagine the mythical Unicorn prancing with high-stepping grace from his sanctuary in the clouds to rejoice in the blessing of another day. His equine hooves, flashing with rainbows, seemed to scrape the cerulean blue sky above the glimmering skyline of buildings and facades created by the hands of the world's most artistic craftsmen. Seville lay before her, jewel of the western world, center of learning and culture and art, built on the southern rolling plains of Spain that were known by Muslim and Christian alike as al-Andalus.

Within sight of the brilliantly tiled exterior of the Great Mosque stood the palace of Mútadid, where visiting dignitaries came to discuss diplomatic policies, and scholars from the world over brought their newest and most startling discoveries. Artisans and poets were welcome to fill the halls with their crafts, music, and manuscripts while seeking financial support and patronage for which Mútadid was famously generous.

Mirjana, first daughter of Mútadid by his second wife, stood on the balcony overlooking the tiled courtyard where armed guardsmen supervised the packing of precious gifts that were to complement the caravan through the wild plains outside Seville to the Taifa Kingdom of Granada. She kept her smoky gray eyes on the horizon of the city, immersing herself in her daydreams of the Unicorn, dreading the sight that was taking place beneath her balcony. She knew that casks and crates crammed with precious silks and silver plateware and golden chalices were stacked beside bolts of imported velvets embroidered with golden threads and coffers of costly spices and perfumes. Her full, sensuous mouth puckered into a grim line. Thick, golden tipped lashes fluttered against her smooth ivory cheeks. The caravan was being assembled to take her to Granada, to leave her there in the harem of Yusuf, emir of that kingdom, where she was expected to take her place as Yusuf's third wife.

Mirjana's hands clasped over her breasts, as if trying to quell the furious beating of her heart. A silent cry swelled in her throat and her eyes squeezed shut in misery. To leave Seville, her beloved home, to leave her family and friends to make a place for herself in Yusuf's already too crowded harem. It was unthinkable, unbearable.

A fist banged against the rail of the balcony. It would not be! It could not! Regardless of what preparations were made for the trek to Granada, regardless of her father's orders and the pact he had made with Yusuf, when the time came for the caravan to leave, it would leave without her. To leave Seville was an intolerable thought. Here was the place of her youth, of her very existence. To leave it would mean the death of her soul, of her heart. It would mean the end of all that mattered to her, of her life. She would never see Omar again. The thought stabbed her with a furious sharp dagger. Never to see Omar again! Never to sit beside him while he read to her from his manuscripts, sharing his dreams with her, looking down at her with his dark, glowing gaze, that smile she had come to love softening the curve of his mouth. She could not leave him! She wouldn't!

"Do you hear me, Tanige?" Mirjana clamored to her servant who was folding masses of her mistress's garments in preparation for the caravan. "I will not leave Seville, and that is my final word!"

Tanige backed away from Mirjana's determination, her eyes downcast, head bobbing to show she had indeed understood her mistress's distress.

Whirling about, Mirjana entered the cathedral proportions of her suite, stepping over and onto her belongings which were scattered about the room, kicking them into further disarray, undoing Tanige's work. "Get these things out of my sight. Put them away. I intend to see my father and settle this lunacy once and for all!" She propelled herself toward the doorway, kicking sundry items out of her path, her ivory complexion flushed with anger.

Tanige watched Mirjana leave the suite in search of the emir, her father. The soft apricot silk gown rustled with the angry hiss of a viper with each step her mistress took, and the sound birthed hope in Tanige's scrawny breast. At last her mistress was going to speak her mind and throw herself on Mútadid's mercy, begging him to cancel this marriage contract to Emir Yusuf, allowing them both to remain here in Seville.

Mirjana was less than ten years old when Tanige had been selected to become her handmaiden. Older than her mistress by almost two years, Tanige had been grateful for the opportunity to escape the drudgery of the cavernous kitchens in the lower regions of the palace where her mother still worked. She had been blessed by the winking eye of Allah, her mother was always quick to remind her whenever she had cause to complain. As a personal handmaiden, she was responsible for laundry and other personal duties to Princess Mirjana, a station that carried responsibility and dignity. To be shut into the kitchens sweating over braziers and stoves and constant scrubbing was a life much closer to hell than to be surrounded by luxury and refinement. That Mirjana was a considerate and kind mistress was a double blessing.

Tanige carefully folded a delicate face veil, a yashmak of gossamer sheer fabric, and placed it on Mirjana's bed which was draped in pale blue silk. The entire suite was decorated in shades of blue with the softest of ivory accents. It was a serene atmosphere, cool and refined, like Mirjana herself. The only flash of colors to disrupt the eye were the occasional pillows and tapestries of crimson and burnt ocher. Tanige smiled, knowing these accent colors could be said to represent her mistress's sudden flares of temper and rebellion. Like the suite's accessories, these bouts of temper were few and far between, but added life and boldness to an otherwise complacent personality.

Tanige reminded herself that when Mirjana decided to make herself heard, the entire palace was forced to sit up and listen. This was what she was counting upon now. Mútadid just *had* to listen to his daughter; he *had* to take pity on her! Tanige's own fate, along with Mirjana's, depended upon it!

Outside the ornately carved and Mozarabic arched door leading to Mútadid's private chamber, Mirjana encountered an armed sentry from the palace guard. "Step aside, I wish to see my father." Her tone sizzled with authority and her gray eyes glowered with such ferocity the guardsman almost obeyed her. Then, remembering his duty, he extended his arm across the doorway, barring her entrance.

"Princess Mirjana, Emir Mútadid has not yet risen."

"Stand back," she ordered, pushing past him, banging on the door with her fist. "Father, are you awake? I'm coming in. I must see you!"

From behind the door came a sleepy grumble. "If you must." Mútadid sat up in his bed, pulling the covers up around his chest and smoothing his dark beard with his fingers. A vain man by nature, he disliked facing anyone before his morning ablutions and having the opportunity to dress and comb his beard. He had been expecting this meeting with his daughter, and he had also been taking pains to avoid it. Now, with her banging on his door, there was nothing to be done for it. It would be unseemly for him to deny his own child an audience and would no doubt set the entire palace speculating on his cowardice in refusing to see her. Mirjana's flights of temper were well advertised by any and all who had met the lash of her tongue.

"Father! I insist on seeing you, and this — this dolt refuses to allow me to enter!" Mirjana stood her ground outside the door, refusing to move or give an inch. The sentry was painfully aware of the fact that this was a royal princess who was wrestling with his barricading arm to gain entrance to the emir's apartments.

"Enter, I say!" Mútadid called again, raising his voice above the din outside his door. "Allow her to pass!" Allah be blessed, all this commotion at so early an hour.

Tripping past the sentry into the private chamber, Mirjana shot him one last look of triumph and purposefully slammed the door in his face. Once inside Mútadid's suite the audacity of her behavior struck her. Regardless of the fact he was her father, he was also her king! He demanded her respect as one of his subjects, daughter or no. Stubbornly holding fast to her conviction, she called to him again, her voice echoing off the high vaulted ceiling decorated with frescoes depicting a royal hunt. "Father!"

"My hearing is not impaired, Daughter. I insist you lower your voice before you have my entire household in an uproar." Mútadid stepped out from behind a faceted screen, fumbling with the belt on his robe.

Mirjana felt the force of his reproachful stare as he moved toward her. He was a huge man, tall of height and broad of girth, and beside him, she felt tiny and ineffectual. Summoning her nerve, she was determined to hold her ground and speak her mind. Then she would beg if she must, but he had to rescind his plans. He simply had to!

"It is rather early for a visit from my daughter, is it not?" Mútadid's voice seemed to fill the room, sending shivers up her spine. Mútadid may be many things, but of them, he was never a fool. He was quick to realize she had been neglecting to use his respectful title of "Emir," calling him by the familiar term of "father." Even as a royal princess, court etiquette demanded she always refer to him by his royal title.

"Your point is well taken, my emir. I was rude and beg forgiveness." She spoke softly in a tone that was almost a purr as her eyes narrowed like those of a cats as she faced him.

Mútadid almost shuddered. He could never quite decide which was worse — her shouting fury or her cat's purr. "Some day, Allah permit, I will understand why you were not born a son. You've the boldness of a man when it suits your needs."

"If I were born a son, I would be deemed valuable by my father, and I would never have to hear the pain of being sent away from my home and his household." Mirjana's eyes were downcast, a tremor in her voice.

So, he was correct, Mútadid thought. At last she had come to beg her way out of the marriage agreement with Yusuf. It was a pity, in this above all else, he could not give her her way. The contracts were signed and already gifts had been exchanged. There was no way to escape it without losing face. The territories and outlands between Seville and Granada had already given their tribute and taxes to Mútadid's treasury as was part of the arrangement with Yusuf. With the gold already sitting in his own coffers, Mútadid would disgrace himself if he withdrew from the agreement now. And it was unthinkable to return the tax tribute. Unthinkable!

Mirjana stood before her father, her eyes downcast, her heart sinking as though she could read his mind. She had mulled this over hundreds of times, and she knew Mútadid would consider it unthinkable to return the gold from his treasury to Yusuf. But it was also unthinkable for her to go to Granada to marry a man she could never love.

It was difficult for Mútadid to face his daughter. She was so comely, so feminine. The apricot silk gown she wore brought out the youthful blush on her cheeks and enhanced the golden lights in her burnished hair. Even her eyes, so like her mother's, seemed luminescent and fathomless, like the shadows in the forest, against the pale, warm color. Slim and graceful, taller than fashion dictated, she would be a welcome addition to Yusuf's household. A further pity that she would merely become Yusuf's third wife, never accomplishing the respected station that her wits and charm and education should have ensured her. Perhaps that was where he had wronged her, allowing her to become educated, tutored in mathematics and languages and philosophies. As a first daughter by his second wife, Cloe, Mirjana never could hope to enjoy the respect and station that the children by his first wife received. Ah, but that was the way of things. There was rank and distinction even within families. If only this one with the quick tongue and agile mind were a son! He would have raised her above all the others. Dolts, all of them! Allah be praised that he live long enough to see the day when any of his sons became responsible and clever enough to take the throne. Out of five sons there was not a one who was as quick or facile as Mirjana. Life could sometimes be difficult, even for the emir of a great province like Seville. This was no time, he told himself, to soften to Mirjana's desires or pleas.

Turning his back on his daughter, refusing to see the questions in her eyes, Mútadid stepped toward the doors of his balcony, opened them and entered the bright shaft of sunlight. "I have been a good father to you, Mirjana. Of all your brothers and sisters I have been most proud of you. Learning and culture were bred into you. Your own mother was a woman of letters and intelligence. Would that she would have lived long enough to give me a son! Instead, I have you. You have been a joy to me, my daughter. I have loved you. But as you know, daughters have their value through the marriages they make. As Yusuf's intended you have brought great sums into my treasury as well as gifts befitting a child of an emir. I assure you, Yusuf is a kindly man, clever and charming. Many of your own sisters would be glad to change places with you, but it was you for whom Yusuf asked, and I will not disappoint him!"

Mútadid kept his gaze directed to the gardens beneath his balcony and to the city beyond the palace walls. He could not bring himself to face Mirjana and see her breaking heart. Never would he allow himself to believe he was doing her a disservice by sending her to Yusuf. He would never allow that doubt to creep into his conscience.

"You will join the caravan and be on your way to Granada just as planned. Allow no harsh words to pass between us, Mirjana. I want us to part with joy for your forthcoming marriage to Yusuf." Mútadid felt no guilt. He had fulfilled his role of parent, more than fulfilled it by six years. Mirjana was nearly twenty years old, past the age when she should have been given in marriage.

"I humble myself to you, Father. You must reconsider and allow me to stay here in Seville. I beg you. I will make myself useful to you. I will teach the younger children —"

"Enough! I will hear no more! A man, even a man who is also a father, must have peace." Raising his dark gaze, Mútadid viewed his child. Gray eyes, alive with lights and shadows that always seemed to glimmer with untold secrets, stared back at him. They were lovely eyes; a man could lose himself in them, drown in them and welcome the fate he would find in those fathomless depths. Yet they were eyes that were lacking a woman's one saving grace — humility. This one, with her warm ivory skin and slender patrician nose, could never be humble. Looking at her, he could mourn his grief for her mother from whom Mirjana inherited this vibrant beauty, and knew that since the day she had entered this world he had been pleased she had displayed Cloe's Circassian blood rather than his own Berber heritage. He watched as Mirjana's lower lip trembled. It was on the tip of his tongue to tell her that if she cried he would bodily tie her to the caravan's lead horse and drive her from the city now, this moment. Oh, to be rid of her. To escape the indecision and conflict she was creating in him. He was old and ailing, and he had already sent priceless treasure to Yusuf to honor the forthcoming marriage. It wasn't that he was penurious, he excused himself, it was the principle of the matter. A man could not allow women to rule his life! If Mirjana was to have her way then he would be an open target for each of his other daughters to work their wiles on him. Rarely, if ever, did a woman bring a dowry to her husband that was as rich as the one he had granted. He could hold his head high and know he was sending Mirjana to Granada with monumental respectability.

Once Mirjana arrived in Granada at Yusuf's palace, Mútadid's obligation would be completed. And should Mirjana become sulky or complaining, these faults would fall on Yusuf's deaf ears — ears deafened by the clank of gold and jewels falling into his coffers from his third wife's marriage pledge.

"You know I love you, Daughter. As your father, I must see to your best interests. If your mother were here now, she would agree with me. She would be delighted that you are escaping the stain of spinsterhood, even at your advanced age, and that you will have children. It will be a new life, an adventure!"

Mirjana's carefully controlled fury broke. "A new life, is it? Have you considered that my children, your grandchildren, will be fathered by Yusuf? How proud will you be if they resemble their father? What if they have fish scales for skin and round, popping eyes? Has it occurred to you that the odious Yusuf of Granada will be touching my person?" Seeing the expression on Mútadid's face, she continued. "Aha, you hadn't thought of that, had you? I will gag! Is this what is expected of a daughter of the great Emir of Seville? How can you, my father, subject me to that . . . that fat fish who salivates at the mouth when be looks upon food and women? He's a pig!" she exhorted, condemning Yusuf to the worst of all epithets in Islam — a foul, unclean pig!

"Mirjana! I will not have revolt in my

household! You know nothing of which you speak, and I must hasten to remind you that I am your ruler, your emir, and as such I demand your respect." Gratified that Mirjana's demeanor instantly became deferential, he continued in a calm, fatherly tone. "You have not seen Yusuf since you were a child. I assure you he is a man of charm and eloquence, most fitting for a daughter of Mútadid. You wound me that you should believe I would send you to someone beneath your station. You speak as though I were casting you out among dogs, as though Yusuf were as barbarous as that one we called El Cid, who prowls and pillages the outlands of al-Andalus, who would ravage you and leave you to die amid the brambles."

Mirjana stood, thunderstruck. There was so much else she wanted to say. She wanted to stomp her feet, and rail and cry and curse the fates that were sending her away from Seville, from all she had ever known, from one she loved more than life itself. Mútadid had pulled himself to full height, squaring his shoulders, his dark eyes sparkling with challenge. She instinctively knew that if she continued with this rebellion, Mútadid would indeed tie her to the lead horse of the caravan and send her out from Seville this very instant.

In a voice that crackled with rancor, Mirjana faced her father. "Allah forgive you for what you are doing to me, my emir, my father, for I cannot."

For a long moment Mútadid looked into his daughter's face, feeling somehow humbled and at a loss by her last statement. She had never spoken to him this way; none of his children had ever spoken to him this way. The shock of it was like a dagger to the heart. An old man, Mútadid nodded his head, feeling as though each year of his life weighed heavily on his shoulders. His vainglorious pride and ego were injured. He had never thought to hear such a thing from a child of his loins. Mirjana was insolent and stubborn, forgetting her father's authority and the respect due him as her emir. If their parting was to be such, so be it. Anger could also be a balm to a guilty spirit.

"Leave me now, Mirjana. Through the centuries children have been known to rebel against their parents, and fate and Allah always seem to turn it around. Some day, child, you will again need my fatherly concern. As your emir, I assure you of it. As your father, you should know that *I* forgive *you.*"

Mirjana sat quietly in her rooms, exhausted by the confrontation with Mútadid. There was so much she should have said, so much she should have done. Her relationship with her father had never been one of close familial ties. There were too many children, too many wives, and all too many duties to cloud Mútadid's attentions to single out one child among many. Still, it rankled her that Mútadid always reminded her that she was nearly worthless as a female and yet, bearing the same intelligence and qualities, she would have been indispensable as a son.

Tanige, who had witnessed Mirjana's temper before this, had escaped for regions unknown, fearful of becoming the brunt of her mistress's fury. Reclining on her bed, Mirjana felt the cool satin pillow beneath her cheek. The day was almost done. She had been sulking here for hours, and now the sun was dipping behind the walls of the palace, its big, coppery hues burning a path to her bed and filling her suite with color.

Mirjana sighed. In her heart she had known Mútadid would not bend. Her fate had been arranged and now it was sealed. She was doomed to spend the rest of her life in Granada, third wife of Yusuf. "I should have told my father there is one here in the palace whom I love above all others. I should have spoken my heart." And now it was too late. Her hasty words had caused a rift between them that might never be bridged. She pounded her fist into the pillow, squeezing her eyes shut against the sudden image of Omar, beautiful Omar, whose liquid dark gaze burned with fervor and passion. Perhaps Mútadid would have weakened if she had been honest. If her father truly loved her, surely he would admit there was no better husband for her than the gentle Persian poet, Omar Khayyám.

No, she comforted herself. Mútadid was a man of power sitting on the Islamic throne of Seville. Emirs' daughters did not marry poets. Theirs was a destiny dictated by policies and political obligations. No matter what she would have said to Mútadid, the outcome would have remained the same.

Stunned by the pain of regret, Mirjana buried her face into the damp pillow. Omar didn't think it awful that she was nearly twenty years of age and still unmarried. "He could love me," she cried out in her loneliness. "I know he could. And if he doesn't, I have enough love for the two of us. We could spend our days beneath the acacia trees while he reads his works to me." Sweet Omar. How could she bear to leave him? If only she could hold his hand and press it to her cheek and feel the comfort of his gentleness. She needed to fall under the gaze of his beautiful dark eyes that seemed to look into the depths of her soul. It was Omar she should be marrying, not some middle-aged despot who would take her for his third wife, impregnate her and forget she was alive. A sob rose in her throat and was born upon the stillness surrounding her. How would she live without Omar's kind and gentle words? How would she rise and face the day knowing that his beautiful face would not greet her at some point in the day? "I can't leave you," she sobbed, "I would rather die!"

Perhaps when Omar learned she had been unsuccessful in her pleas to Mútadid he would then go himself to the emir and plead Mirjana's case. Would he weep at her departure? Would he beg for her hand in marriage?

Mirjana sat up, gulping back her tears and frustration. It was a foolish thought. All along, for months, she had talked of nothing else but her resolution not to leave Seville, regardless of Mútadid's commands. Omar had looked at her with his suffering eyes and spoken to her, soothing her fears and calming her indignation. The words he had used were not those she wished to hear but they were beautiful all the same. He had never truly spoken his heart to her.

A horrible thought struck Mirjana. Was it possible Omar did not return her love? Was she merely the daughter of the emir, his patron, and he was addressing his duty of tutoring her in her studies? Impossible. There was such emotion when he read love poems to her and when he detailed his theories on astronomy, Mirjana's heart ached for him. Nothing would do but to be near him, feel his gaze upon her and hear his wonderful, lyrical voice.

Omar had arrived in Seville two years earlier, his studies taking him from Persia to Damascus, across the deserts of North Africa, from palace to palace, hosted by the most powerful rulers in the world until he had discovered Seville. He was known for never staying in one place as long as he had remained here in Mútadid's palace. Surely there must be a reason. Certainly it was because of her. It must be!

Mirjana wiped the tears from her face with the back of her hand. She must go to him, give him this last opportunity to speak his heart. If he agreed, she would run away with him, go with him anywhere, to the ends of the earth if need be. She wasn't behaving like a silly adolescent with romantic dreams. Her love for Omar was real. Her passions for him haunted her sleep when she would dream he would take her in his arms and teach her the secrets of the flesh that she had only read about in the words of the poets he so admired.

Less than an hour later, Mirjana quietly left her suite of rooms and entered the long marble hallway lighted by the warm glow of oil lamps which were suspended from the high arches supported by hundreds of slender columns decorated with mosaic tile work. She was freshly bathed and had changed into a gown of the softest blue wool, bound at the waist by a girdle of golden embroidered velvet. Her embroidered felt slippers carried her silently across the highly polished marble floors as she hurried along the gallery to the stairway leading below to Omar's quarters.

Timidly, she knocked on his closed door, and when there was no response, she knocked again. The door opened a crack and then wider, and there stood Omar, the light from the hall falling on his finely carved face, reflecting in the black depths of his eyes. Taller than she, his shoulders were broad and his waist tapered. There was a manliness about him, and yet there was a delicacy also. His innate gracefulness when he moved, the way his robes and tunics draped and swept the floor as he walked, the sudden blackness of his closely cropped beard against his refined features — all blended to make him the most attractive of men. There was romance in his soul, she believed, and it was shown in each movement, each spoken word. How beautiful he is, Mirjana marveled for the thousandth time. I can't leave him. I won't!

"Is something wrong, Mirjana?" How tender his voice, as though he were speaking to a frightened dove. She pretended a calmness she did not feel as she entered his apartment which also served as his study and classroom.

"Omar, you really must allow the servants to clean this room for you. You'll choke on this chalk dust. Here, let me help," she told him, searching for an excuse to hide her nervousness. Before he could protest, Mirjana had his chalks and quills in hand.

"Mirjana, you must not," he told her, taking the items from her hands. "It is not befitting a princess to tidy the clutter of a humble scholar. Something is troubling you. Do you want to talk about it?" Omar's brow drew together in concern for her, and she wanted nothing more than to throw herself into his arms and cry out her love for him.

"I spoke to my father this morning, begging him not to send me away to Granada to marry Yusuf. I told him I wanted to stay here in Seville. I — I . . ." Sudden tears sprang to her eyes; her voice was choked with emotion.

Seeing her distress, Omar led her to the divan near the brazier. Her hands were so cold and she was shaking. Tenderly, he seated her and knelt down before her, drying her tears with the hem of his sleeve. "You mustn't cry, Mirjana. Tell me what troubles you."

Gulping back her torment, Mirjana said, "I have told my father I must stay here in Seville. I — I want to continue my studies with you as my teacher. I can't bear to leave; I've grown so fond of you." Mirjana turned her gaze to Omar, begging him to read the meaning behind her words, begging him to admit his feelings for her.

"Your marriage has been arranged, little one. You cannot change your father's plans at this late hour. You'll grow to love Granada. I have heard it is as splendid as Seville."

"Omar, you are truly the poet." She managed a smile. "You see only good in everything. It is not Granada; it's not my love for Seville. It's my love for you!" There, she had said it. The words had tumbled out, and once said, she knew a lightening of the burden she had carried for too long.

Omar stared at the beautiful woman-child unable to believe his ears. What was she saying? How could she love someone such as himself, he who had no thought for anything or anyone save his work? He knew that she had spoken her heart, that she was serious. How had it happened? When? He must choose his words carefully, he must be kind and gentle, when he told her the only love he could ever know, the only commitment he would ever accept, was his work.

Mirjana was so young, so impressionable. Twenty years be damned, she was little more than a child, innocent and trusting. Believing herself to be in love with an impoverished poet past the age of thirty who had no other thought than for his art and the sciences. It seemed so long ago since he had come to Seville, and he recalled the long hours Mirjana would sit quietly near him, watching him work. Occasionally, he would look up, surprised that she was still there, and her face would shine with the light of a hundred lanterns beneath his notice.

As the weeks turned to months and the months to years, she had made herself more conspicuous, delighting in his verses, comprehending his philosophies, listening quietly as he expounded his mathematical theories. And then there were the long walks in the twilight where he again would whisper soft phrases written by the master poets, phrases as soft as the gray velvet evenings. A student, a friend, was what Mirjana had been to him these past two years. And now, he sighed deeply, knowing no matter what or how he said it, he was going to hurt her.

Mirjana's gaze devoured him as she waited for his response. Twilight was descending, casting his library into shadow. The meager light from the tall, narrow window fell on him, putting his delicately carved face into relief against the darkness behind him. His hair was as black as the narcissus bud, thick and curly, and free of the customary turban. She watched his long, slim fingers toy with the chalk he had been using, knowing that in her deepest dreams those sensitive hands had caressed her body and had combed through her hair. His mouth was wide and generous, full and tender of line; his nose, long and as poetic as his sonnets. But it was to his eyes that her gaze always returned. Dark, burning, with a shadow of suffering that melted a woman's heart and made her arms ache to hold him.

Prompted by her overwhelming need for him, Mirjana spoke. "I know you can love me, Omar. It's only that you've never tried." Her voice was a husky whisper, rife with anguish, desolate with yearning.

"Mirjana, heart of the tender rose, in my life there has never been a woman as dear to me as you." Even as he spoke her face lit with happiness. Suddenly, he was astounded by the loveliness before him — thick, red-gold curls arranged on the top of her head, only the wispiest of tendrils framing her face, haloing it; wide, smoky gray eyes that lent a coolness to her smooth, pale gold complexion; curving, sensuous mouth, smiling one moment, pouting with concentration the next. Mirjana of Seville, a beautiful woman, artfully crafted for a man's hand and eye to enjoy, to relish. And within her burned the fires of the spirit that could seduce a man's heart to beat for her alone. How had he never noticed the allure of this creature who was a vision of Allah's handiwork? How could he have spent long hours in her company, tutoring her in her studies and have never seen the spark that glowed within her that craved for a man's love to ignite it to a flame?

Something in his eyes, some thought, must have made itself known to her. Next he knew she was in his arms, clinging to him, her lips pressed close to his ear, breathing words of devotion and submission. He held her, intensely aware of her slim, supple form, knowing the fragrance of her perfume and the sweet power of her allure.

"Mirjana," he breathed, alarmed to hear his voice a trembling whisper. "You are so innocent, so loving, you don't know what you do to a man."

"No, Omar, I don't. Show me, teach me. Show me how love can be between a man and a woman. Show me what the poets and minstrels write about, sing about. Show me the caress that stirs a man's blood and takes him into oblivion where the pleasures of the flesh rule the logic of the mind. Show me, gentle teacher, show me . . ."

Her voice throbbed through him, exciting him as no woman ever had. She called him teacher, yet she held the answers. She had been his student, and now she was maestro, plucking at his emotions like the thrum of a thousand lutes, enticing him to gather her into his arms and seek her giving mouth with his own.

Mirjana's fingers played with the fastenings of his surplice and tunic, undoing them, sliding between fabric and skin in a slow, sensual exploration. The fine hairs on his chest teased her fingers, rubbing against her palm, bringing the knowledge that there was softness in the contact between the flesh of a man and the flesh of a woman.

Tendrils of fire licked her spine as his hands gripped her, holding her closer, allowing her access to the hidden mysteries of desire. Pulling her to her feet, he gazed down at her, his eyes mirroring dark shadows. Mirjana brazened his gaze, her mind and body receptive to him, willing him to again be her teacher, this time in a subject more worldly than the evocations of poetic writings.

Impatient, aware of herself as a woman and the fact that she wanted to give herself to him, *must* give herself to him, she tugged at the fastenings of her light woolen gown. Loosening the golden belt at her waist, she opened the garment, exposing her body to his eyes and his touch.

Omar watched her, unable to pull his gaze away from her busy fingers. Backing off a step, he looked at her with wide eyes and an unbidden smile on his lips. She stood before him, a goddess waiting for his touch, his approval, his love. Her body was trembling, her eyes pleading. Against all that was holy, he opened his arms to her, drawing her close against him, slowly helping her divest herself of her few remaining garments.

His smooth, gentle hands found her breasts and caressed them, lifting them, adoring them. When he saw her lips part and the tip of her tongue dart out to moisten them, he lowered his head, finding her mouth with his own, knowing unfound passion in her, Allah's garden of sensual delights.

Eager to be close to him, Mirjana's love knew no shame. Her fingers tore at his surplice and tunic, hurrying him with hushed whispers and moist kisses to remove them, to be naked against her, to teach her the secrets she had so long been denied.

His mouth sought hers, his arms locked her in a hard embrace. Wave after wave of desire coursed through her as she answered his kisses and inspired his caresses. Her tongue darted into the warm recesses of his mouth; her arms wound around him, making him her prisoner. Soft hands caressed and stroked her back, smoothing along the curve of her waist to the fullness of her hips and bottom, bringing her ever closer to her desires. Her breasts were taut and full beneath his hands as he gently lowered her to the mound of cushions atop his long divan. Soft moans of ecstasy escaped her parted lips as he aroused her to the heights of her passions, teaching her where the font of her femininity was centered, showing her the full expanse of her needs as a woman, and instructing her into the caresses and embraces that have been known to lovers since the beginning of time. He devoured her with his eyes, covered her with his lips, igniting her sensuality with teasing touches of his tongue against her fiery skin. His fingertips grazed the sleekness of her inner thighs, and helpless, she felt her body arch against his hand with a will of its own to aid in his explorations.

Mirjana's fingers wound through his hair, searching, finding his mouth with her own. She loved the feel of him, the touch of him, the way his lips evoked a cry in her throat, how his fingers learned and knew her body better than her own. He was tall, slim, hard muscled. Her greedy fingers could not touch him enough, her hungry mouth thirsted to taste every morsel of him. And always there were the words, beautiful and loving, praising her loveliness, adoring her passion, filling her head and warming her heart, throbbing through her and creating a need for him, the likes of which she had never dreamed possible.

His thighs twined with hers, and she was totally aware of his body and the desire he held for her. A deep wave of yearning spread through her belly, drawing up her knees, yielding herself closer, inviting the union between them.

Her eyes opened, bathing him with their silvery splendor. Every turn and curve of her body was a song sung to his poetry. And when she whispered lines from his favorite writings, her voice was deep and husky, reminding him she was a woman, that the girl-child had been left behind. The girl who had been sent to him by Mútadid as his pupil was now a woman.

Omar pulled himself away from Mirjana, leaving her feeling suddenly cold and bereft. Her arms opened to him, willing him to enter them again, to complete the loving that had left such yearning within her. Moving away, keeping his eyes averted, Omar picked up her gown and tossed it to her, covering her nudity with the lightly woven fabric, ignoring the heartrending sob that tore from her.

"Princess Mirjana —" His voice was thick with unquenched emotions. "— you must dress. You must leave before I lose whatever control I still possess."

Mirjana sat up on the divan, mindless that her gown had slipped to the floor, leaving her exposed. "Why, Omar?" she whispered, a tear streaking down her cheek. How could he do this to her? Where did he find the strength to leave her like this? Was she lacking? Had she done something to make him find her undesirable?

"Please dress, Mirjana," Omar entreated, already reaching for his surplice, careful to keep his distance from her entreating arms. "I have betrayed your father's trust in me. I have dishonored myself as a teacher."

Never taking her eyes from him, Mirjana stood and slipped into her gown. She felt as though she were paralyzed as she forced her clumsy fingers to work the fastenings. Her face flamed scarlet, her cheeks burned with rejection and shame. What had she done wrong? How could Omar have left her this way, abandoned her just when the breezes of passion were swirling into winds which promised her an ultimate fulfillment?

The very air in the room seemed still and oppressive. A part of her brain was demanding she run from here, cover her face with her trembling hands and run! Another part of her wanted to prolong this time spent with Omar regardless of the pain and misery she was feeling.

Pulling the ends of his belt tightly around his waist, as though somehow frightened that she would attack him, rip his garments from his body and seduce him against his will, Omar turned to her, his eyes bleak with compassion. "Mirjana," he whispered, his voice urgent, "you mustn't misunderstand what almost took place between us. You mustn't blame yourself. I accept full responsibility." He floundered for words, hearing himself sound like a pubescent schoolboy making untrue excuses to his teacher, knowing the lie he would tell was not to be believed. "I want you as I have never wanted any other woman. You stir my blood, cloud my brain, erasing all reason." This at least was true. Mirjana was the most desirable creature he had ever held in his arms. She was lovely beyond belief, and for the rest of his days he would remember her face as it was this evening, soft and sultry, glowing with passion's fire. Allah be blessed, where had he found the strength to remember his responsibilities to his work and to himself?

A single precious tear traced a lonely pattern over the curve of her cheek. The distance between them seemed charged with an unnamed power, like the air before a lightning storm, drawing her closer to him, ever aware of him and her need for his love.

"Don't cry, Mirjana. Neither for me nor yourself. You must understand that we would dishonor ourselves by indulging in the passions we feel for one another. You are my emir's daughter; your father has trusted me to be your teacher. I was employed to be your mentor, never your lover. I am unworthy of you." Omar spoke the words fervently, watching her face, reading her expression. He cared for Mirjana, but more for himself, and he never wanted her to hate him. Even the prophet had spoken of a woman's scorn and had said it was a fate more bitter than the taste of hell's ashes upon the tongue. As a princess, Mirjana was a member of royalty, and even though a woman, she carried great influence in the highest places. As a poet and a scholar, his very livelihood depended upon the charity and patronage of the ruling class. No, it would never do to have Mirjana, soon to be a wife of a powerful emir, as his enemy. He must tread very lightly, make her believe his rejection was out of duty and consideration for her future last act of nobility on his part and one of great sacrifice to himself. She must never realize that it was out of selfish concern for himself, his very life. Mútadid would have him beheaded if Yusuf should cast Mirjana out because she wasn't a virgin and it was learned that Omar was responsible.

Mirjana's heart flooded with pain; she felt she would stagger beneath the weight of the hollow ache. How like Omar to claim his unworthiness when it was she who was unworthy of him. "Omar, won't you come with me to see my father? He respects you, admires you. When you tell him how we love one another, his heart will soften and he'll bless us. I know he will!" Her words were piteous in the face of Omar's calculating selfishness, so full of ardor and emotion that even he felt shame.

Omar stepped forward, catching her in his embrace, holding her closely, aware of her trembling. He must be very careful, he warned himself, swallowing hard, mind racing to find the perfect words. "Sweet one, what have I, a lowly poet, to offer you? It would break my heart each day to know that because of our love you were deprived of the life Allah himself meant for you to live. Mútadid would never approve our match. Admit that you realize this. We would be forced to run away into the desert. Your marriage contract has been sworn in the eyes of Allah. To break it would condemn us to eternal damnation. If you would love me as I love you, spare me this. My hell would be found each day, thousands of times over, to know that because of me you will never again be recognized by your father or your family."

"I don't care about my family or my father. I only care about you!" Mirjana railed against his logic. Her fists pounded his chest, tears coursed down her cheeks, glistening like diamonds before falling onto her gown in heavy, mournful droplets.

"I care, Mirjana. A man wants to give to the woman he loves, not take from her. We are star-crossed and damned! I would rather die than see you suffer for one instant because of your love for me!" His voice was filled with desolation, his eyes moist with unshed tears. "You must go to Yusuf; you must fulfill your destiny. Ours waits for us beyond this life, in another time when Allah himself will smile upon our union. Please, if you love me, spare me. It would be better to lose you to Yusuf than to lose you day by day, minute by minute, because as outcasts we would be fugitives searching the ground for roots to sustain one another. That is not the life I want for you, dear one. I would rather die."

Mirjana's heart was breaking for him. She had never meant to bring him such pain. Even in her most secret dreams she had never realized the depth of his love for her, his nobility and his capacity for self-sacrifice that only made her love him the more. Leaning her head against his chest, she could hear the rapid drumbeat of his heart. "I will find a way, my darling. I will come back to you, I promise."

Omar pressed his lips against her perfumed hair to hide the relief he was feeling. Mirjana would go to Yusuf. As for her finding a way to return, he knew it was futile. As an emir's wife, childbearer for the throne, she would spend her life in the confinement of the harem. Pity prompted him to encourage her in what he knew was a useless cause. If hope in her heart could make leaving easier for her, who was he to deny it? "I will count the days until I am with you again, Mirjana. And when again we meet, nothing will keep me from you. We will share what was begun here this night."

A last kiss, an embrace, and he took her to his door, gently leading her into the hallway beyond, allowing an appropriate trace of misery tremoring in his voice as he whispered his farewell.

Before she could argue, tempt him into further argument, Omar escaped into the solitude of his apartment, grateful when the door was closed behind him. His fist banged against the solid stone wall in frustration for what he had almost found here tonight and for what he had lost. Still, his materialistic mind drew comfort from the fact that Mirjana would soon be leaving Seville, but until then, he would not enjoy an easy breath.

CHAPTER 2

Beneath the first rosy glow of dawn, the city of Seville awakened from its deep night's slumber. Before the sun climbed its fiery ladder in the sky to burn the plains and glance blindingly off the white stone walls of the city, merchants began to set up their stalls and chant their goods. Soldiers carrying their helmets in the crooks of their arms noisily greeted one another as they arrived at their posts near the palace of Mútadid. Scholars dressed in long, flowing robes hurried through the city for their destinations in the library or classrooms. Goatherds led their bleating flocks along the narrow byways, enjoying their privilege of traveling through the city. Although Seville was an Islamic city, Christian merchants were valuable to its economy; the masses must be fed. Fruits, wines, meats, cheeses, and breads were brought to the marketplace daily. And always the thought that would enter their minds whenever it was disclosed that he was nearby was the speculation of whether or not the infamous El Cid would choose this day to mark Seville as the next target for his army to spoil and pillage, leaving behind death and destruction.

The year, according to the Christian calendar, was 1071, and the provinces of Castile, Leona, and Galicia were in upheaval. King Ferdinando, who until his death six years ago had reigned over these northern territories, had divided his kingdom among his three sons, bequeathing them a political muddle. Sancho, the eldest, received Castile: Alphonso, the middle son, inherited Leona; and Galicia went to the third and youngest son, Garcia. The arguments between the princes began almost as soon as the funeral was over. Each son had inherited the right to collect tax money from one or more of the taifas, those Islamic cities in the south who paid tribute money, which was a delicate term for extortion.

Greed led to squabbles and distrust between the sons of Ferdinando. As a result, Rodrigo Ruy Diaz of Bivar, who had pledged himself to Sancho, had founded his reputation as a warrior par excellence. To settle the rivalry between Sancho and Alphonso, it was decided that the outcome of a battle should be judged the will of God and that the winner should take all.

The battle was fought at Llantada, and Alphonso lost miserably. Ruy Diaz was instrumental in the fall of Alphonso's armies. Dishonoring the pledge he had made, Alphonso refused to relinquish Leona to Sancho and was also fortunate to have the support of one of his taifa kings, Mamun of Toledo, and sought refuge with Mamun's brother-in-law who was the ruler of Badajoz.

Now, almost two years later, word had it that Alphonso was planning to leave asylum in Badajoz to take up the sword once again against Sancho. Reports told that Sancho's most valuable and noble vassal, Ruy Diaz, was on the border of Badajoz to discourage Alphonso and his army.

Badajoz was the Islamic kingdom just to the east, and it was quite natural for the citizens of Seville to be uneasy with the infamous warrior so close to their border. It was believed by Christian and Muslim alike that Ruy Diaz was unconquerable; he had never been injured in battle, and it was said that no enemy had ever touched him with his sword. The Muslims had begun to refer to him as al Said, "the Lord." The Spanish called him *Compeador*, the "Champion." It wasn't long before the Muslim and Castilian titles were combined and he became known as El Cid, Compeador — "the Lord Champion." Tales and fables were told and retold by both cultures, magnifying his image out of proportion. Diaz was enjoying the status of a legend even while he lived.

In Mútadid's palace across from the Great Mosque, in her blue and cream colored apartment which overlooked the expansive gardens and tiled courtyard, the first light of day touched Mirjana's soft cheek. Her thickly lashed, cinder-gray eyes fluttered open, narrowing slightly against the sun's glare. Turning on her side to avoid the light through the sheerly curtained balcony doors, she pressed her face into her pillow, determined to ignore the arrival of the day. All she wanted was to stay here, alone with her thoughts and dreams, and relive the moments of the evening before with Omar. Stretching her slim body beneath the silken coverlets, she relished and remembered the feel of Omar's gentle hands on her body. Her breasts seemed to tingle with the memory, and she became aware of a vague, aching need in the center of herself. Mirjana was certain that last evening was a prelude to the fulfillment she could find only in Omar's arms. Thoughts of Yusuf and her duty to her father banished her erotic musings. There must be a way to keep her promise to return to Seville. There simply must!

A soft rap sounded on the door before Tange, her handmaiden, let herself into Mirjana's suite. "You don't have to tiptoe, Tanige, I'm awake."

Tanige's sharp black eyes immediately surveyed the tangled bedcovers, the pillows strewn over the Persian-loomed carpet, and the dark circles under the princess's eyes. Tanige pursed her lips in disapproval, but the thought of leaving Seville was also preying on her own mind, and she was newly discouraged that the princess hadn't seemed to make much headway with Emir Mútadid. Gathering the assorted discarded pillows in her thin arms, she dumped them on the divan near the bedside.

Mirjana laughed, a scornful note in her tone. "You don't seem to have spent a much better night than I have. Have you looked at yourself in a mirror this morning?"

Tanige bristled. She would have liked to answer the princess in kind, but her position as a servant forced her into a respectful demeanor. "Would the princess like her own mirror?" she asked, bowing slightly, allowing only a bare shade of mockery to enter her voice.

"No, I haven't the stomach for it this morning. I know what devils robbed me of my sleep. What seems to be your problem?" Sitting up in bed and pulling the covers across her lap, Mirjana brushed the tangled threads of her bright hair away from her face.

"I suppose it was the same devils as your own. I don't want to leave Seville either." Tanige's glance sharpened, focusing on Mirjana, willing the princess to utter the words that would free her from traveling to Granada. One word, one simple word, and Tanige could be relieved of her duty to the princess, and some other servant could take her place to travel with Mirjana.

A small pout formed on Mirjana's lips. "Would you like me to allow you to stay behind? Yes, I can see you would. Put the thought out of your head, Tanige. If I must go, then so must you. What reason do you have for wanting to stay behind? We've been together for so many years. Would it be that simple for you to desert me now?"

Tanige lowered her head. "The princess knows that being separated from you would cause me great distress. It is my mother, my very own mother. She needs me. I'm all she has in this world. Her years are upon her and she's failing in health. Surely, the princess can understand a daughter's concern for her mother."

"Bah!" Mirjana cried in disbelief, throwing back the covers and rising from her bed. "You never gave your mother a moment's thought since the day you left her breast. It's only since you learned you were to accompany me to Granada that you've begun to show all this devotion. No, Tanige, I know you too well. You have some other reason for wanting to stay here in Seville." She turned, eyeing her handmaiden sharply. "Come to think of it, when did you defer to me by my title? As long as we've been together, since childhood, you've referred to me by my given name. Actually, Tanige, this obeisance doesn't become you. Are you going to tell me your real reason for wanting to remain in Seville?"

Nervously, Tanige made herself busy, straightening the bed and replacing the pillows. Mirjana was too quick, too clever, seeing beneath the lie too easily.

Mirjana was not discouraged by Tanige's silence. "Let me see," she muttered, knowing her servant's ears were trained on her words, "what would keep a young woman from embarking on an adventure? A man!" she cried triumphantly. "It must be a man! Who is he? Does he live here at the palace? How long have you been losing sleep over him?"

Tanige's complexion darkened and she stumbled over her own feet.

"Aha! I know it for the truth! It's a man!" Mirjana giggled, tossing her bright curls, her eyes lightening with laughter to the color of a dove's wing. She knew she was teasing Tanige unmercifully, but the girl looked so comical with her sharp, pointed face suffusing with color and her narrow shoulders hunching in a way that suggested she wanted nothing more than to hide from her mistress's ridicule. The very fact that Tanige wasn't bristling with her usual self-righteousness told Mirjana that she had targeted the truth. Tanige was feisty and stubborn and could stand up for herself. It was one of the reasons Mirjana liked her so well, in fact considered her her best friend. Tanige had spirit and could give as good as she got.

"I have no idea what you mean, Mirjana. You keep me so busy running here and there, doing this and that, when would I find time to think about a man? And just look at this apartment! One would think a herd of camels found a new caravan route —"

"Oh, no, you will not get off so easily. Come, bring the tea and a cup for yourself. You can tell me all about him while I breakfast."

Tanige obeyed, knowing it was useless to protest. She would join Mirjana for a cup of tea, but wild horses would never drag the truth from her. It was never wise to have one's mistress know too much about oneself. Besides, Tanige scowled, in truth, there was little to tell. Abdul, the handsome soldier who was assigned to post himself at the kitchen gate, had never shown the slightest interest in her, aside from appreciating the delicacies she pilfered from the kitchens for him. Tanige emitted an audible sigh. To Abdul, she was nothing more than a proffered pastry or sweetmeat. It was not the cravings of his stomach Tanige wanted to inspire, it was a stirring in his loins she was aiming at. If only she weren't so homely, if only her feet weren't the size of barge boats, she knew Abdul would fall in love with her. Even as she thought it, she knew it was a lie. Abdul was a handsome devil, tall and broad, with shining black hair and dancing dark eyes. He could have his choice of women. Why should he content himself with such a one as herself? Why should she expect him to see behind the mouse-colored hair that always escaped its bindings to hang in strings around her face? Her skin was good, she knew, clear and smooth, not pockmarked like so many other women who had suffered pubescent blemishes and other afflictions. Good skin hardly compensated for a figure that was reed thin and seemed to consist of bony protrusions and sharp angles. Men liked women with flesh on their bones and soft curves and rounded breasts, and Abdul was no different. Why should he settle for a woman whose breasts were practically nonexistent and whose hips were so narrow and boyish? Abdul couldn't care that she was possessed of a keen mind and a honed wit. The entertainment he sought with a woman had little to do with mental gymnastics. Still, there was a hunger within her that cried for a man's love and an impatience that prompted a fervent hope that she would not go to her grave a dry and wasted spinster.

Raising the fragile porcelain teacup to her lips and sipping the bracing brew, Mirjana recognized the frustration in Tanige's dun-colored eyes. There was a man, she was certain of it, and leaving for Granada would dash all of Tanige's dreams. How often she had seen that same look of desperation in her own reflection when she thought of leaving Omar. "It seems neither of us wishes to leave Seville."

Peering over the rim of her teacup, Tanige saw Mirjana's hopelessness. Still smarting from her mistress's quick deduction that there was a man somewhere whom she hated to leave, Tanige sparred with a deduction of her own. "Do you think Omar Khayyám will follow you to Granada?"

Mirjana's eyes widened. She nearly choked on a swallow of tea. "Omar! Granada!" Immediately, she controlled herself, pretending an indifference she would never feel. "Why should my tutor come to Granada? Why would I want him to? There are tutors in Granada."

"But none with eyes so black and a heart so pure and arms so strong —"

Mirjana gasped. How long had Tanige known her secret? Had her emotions been all that obvious?

"You keep your secrets well, Mirjana, but you must remember how well I know you. I've seen the look on your face and the softness in your eyes whenever you walk with him in the gardens. And I see the way you read those poems he gives you to study. Even a fool would know you have given your heart to Khayyám."

All color drained from Mirjana's face. "And who else knows this besides yourself? Have you been discussing me with anyone? Do you share my secrets with this man you've lost your head over? Tell me, Tanige, it is most important."

"I discuss you with no one. Not even my own mother. My own fate is too closely knit with yours to betray you to anyone. I only want to know why you haven't used your head and devised some way to keep us here in Seville. Yesterday, when you stormed out of here to see your father, I hoped that at last you were taking our futures into your own hands."

"I see no way to stay here in Seville, Tanige.

But I have made a promise to return as soon as possible. Now, the problem is to find a way to keep that promise."

Tanige drew her thin upper lip into a sneer. "It is as I thought. You will do nothing. There is nothing you can do. You disappoint me, Mirjana. I always thought you had a brain or two in that pretty head."

"And what would you have me do? Quick Tanige, give me your solution to the problem," Mirjana said hotly. "You're so very clever, what should I do?"

"You could pretend to be ill. You could make yourself displeasing to Yusuf. You could throw yourself on your father's mercy and beg him not to send you. You could do any number of things, and so far, you have done nothing."

"Stupid. I've already thought of everything and also the consequences. Nothing will work. Nothing. Mútadid is committed to Yusuf, and if he had to send me on my deathbed, he would do it to keep his treasury filled. No, there is nothing to do but to leave for Granada and find my way back from there."

"If we ever reach Granada, you mean," Tanige said sourly. "Everyone is talking about al Said being camped almost on Seville's doorstep. A caravan like the one taking us to Granada would be a great temptation for him."

"What do I care for al Said? Let him take the caravan. Let him take everything if it meant I would not reach Granada and could come home." Her own words suddenly penetrated her head; she felt a sudden surge of hope in her breast. "Tanige, who is talking? Where is al Said camped?"

"Everyone is talking. The marketplace is filled with news about him. Al Said is camped on the border between Badajoz and Seville to keep Alphonso from staging another attack on his brother, Sancho. When I was getting your breakfast, the kitchens were filled with news brought back from the market."

Dove-gray eyes seemed to be shot with crystal lights, a calculating smile turned up the corners of Mirjana's mouth. "Tell me everything you've heard about al Said," she said impatiently, an idea already taking shape in her mind. "Everything!"

Tanige blinked at this sudden change in her mistress. "I only know what I have already told you. Al Said is on the march between Seville and Badajoz holding Alphonso back. What else can I know?"

Mirjana clicked a fingernail against her teeth. Her eyes narrowed in concentration. Her mind flew in wild directions. Her situation was desperate, as she saw it, and it called for desperate measures. The only power greater than Mútadid's and Yusuf's was that of the Christian warrior, al Said.

Tanige watched her mistress with a growing sense of horror. Something was taking form inside her head, and Tanige knew she would not like it. All this talk about Granada and weddings and men and, finally, al Said. No, Tanige decided, she would not like it at all.

"Tanige, I want you to go into the city for me — now, just as soon as I've written a missive. You will take it directly to the priest at the Christian monastery."

Reacting as though all the air had been punched out of her, Tanige gasped. "I — I couldn't . . . I wouldn't . . ."

"You will! You want to come back to Seville, don't you? Have you already given up on this man you are so secretive about? And what of your poor, sick, aged mother? Shouldn't she have your comfort in her old age?" Mirjana's eyes challenged her servant, and a flush of color stained Tanige's cheekbones. "It is impossible for me to leave the palace unnoticed, but you could always pretend to be going into the marketplace on an errand for me. I will prepare the letter while you make yourself ready. Hurry now, desperate straits call for desperate measures!"

"I pray you know what you're about, Mirjana," Tanige told her somberly, the edges of fear making her voice thin and reedy. "Since my fate is so closely wrapped with your own, I would like to know what your plan is."

"Go, get ready. By the time you return, I'll have written the missive. You will take it to the abbot at the monastery. From there, it is out of our hands."

"Your hands, you mean," Tanige grumbled, stepping toward the door. She would have to change her felt slippers for leather sandals, and change her dress. At least, Tanige told herself, she would leave by the kitchen gate and have another opportunity to see Abdul.

When the door closed behind her handmaiden, Mirjana flew into action. She must act on her impulse, for if she allowed herself to think of what she was about to do and its repercussions, she would change her mind. Her arm swept across the table, spilling tea and cups and honeyed breads onto the carpet. Sitting down with paper and quill, she began to compose her epistle. She doubted that a barbarian like al Said would be able to read the script she carefully lettered in Latin, the universal language; but he, like all warriors, would travel with a priest in his ranks who would be educated and who would read the missive to him.

Her hand shook with her daring to make contact with the infamous al Said. Surely, she must be mad! She was actually *inviting* him to plunder the caravan which would take her to Granada! Actually describing the route it would take! Her hand hesitated; suddenly afraid. It was insane to place herself into al Said's hands for even an instant, but it was the only chance she had of returning to Seville and buying more time to persuade Mútadid that she could not marry Yusuf. She must do it! If not for herself, then for Omar.

If al Said attacked her caravan, then she *must* return to Seville. All the gifts that had been so carefully acquired for her wedding would be gone, and Mútadid would never want her to arrive in Granada without the proper accoutrements her rank demanded.

Returning to Mirjana's apartment, Tanige's narrow face was pinched and disapproving. She had discarded her soft felt slippers for thick-soled leather sandals, and was carrying a coarse, dark cloak that would cover her from head to toe. Seeing her, Mirjana laughed, "You take no chances on being discovered in a Benedictine monastery, I see."

"It's not to my liking to associate with Christian monks, Mirjana — especially since I am ignorant of what I will be doing there," Tanige sniffed, clearly showing that this errand was not to her liking and definitely beneath her station.

"It's to your liking to live out your days in Seville with your mystery man, is it not? Then you will do as I say and take this letter to the holy man at the monastery. Remember, you will speak to none other than the abbot himself. Understood?"

"No, I don't understand. What trick have you up your sleeve, Mirjana? Oh, I know my head will be severed from this poor, miserable body if I do as you want!"

"Save your dramatics, Tanige. Now, what do you think is ample payment for the abbot to relay this letter to al Said?"

"Al Said! Did you say al Said? Have you lost your mind? Do you mean to associate with that barbarian, that devil? No! I won't go! Instead, I'll go to the emir and tell him you've lost your mind —"

"Hush! Listen to me and I'll tell you my plan. This letter," Mirjana said, holding the crackling paper and waving it under Tanige's nose, "is our redemption. If anything can save us from going to Granada, this is it!" In it, I tell al Said of the route the caravan takes to Granada and of the riches we carry. I tell him it can all be his if he will only intercept us and see to it that I am sent back to Seville. My father would never allow me to proceed to Granada without my marriage gifts; it would dishonor him in Yusuf's eyes. Al Said will have the plunder and we, Tanige, will return to Seville."

"Only for as long as another caravan can be assembled," Tanige scoffed, clearly thinking her mistress mad.

"That can take weeks, months! And it will give me time to persuade my father that he does not want me to marry Yusuf. Whatever comes of it, it is a small price to pay for time." Mirjana spoke with such earnestness that Tanige almost believed she had struck on a remedy for their situation.

"How will you know if al Said agrees? We are to leave within the next few days. How will you know if al Said even receives your letter? Mirjana, this is the most foolish idea you have ever had. You can't trust that barbarian. You mustn't," Tanige pleaded.

"I may be foolish but I am also desperate. I have no other choice." Mirjana's voice quavered on the near edge of panic. Everything Tanige spoke was truth. "You will please not refer to al Said as 'that barbarian.' It is true he has earned a reputation for ruthlessness in battle and politics, but there is no reason to think him a barbarian."

Tanige bristled, taking exception with Mirjana's rebuke. "I have heard you call him a barbarian with my own ears. You know of the tales that he dresses in wolf skins and breastplate armor, and wears a necklace of bear teeth around his neck. It is said the sight of him is more terrifying than the threat of his sword. His eyes are red, like a rat's, and his hair is long to his waist, and vipers nest in it and writhe and spit —"

"Enough, Tanige! You repeat a child's nightmare. Al Said is vassal to King Sancho; he is accepted in a royal court. What you say is ridiculous!" All the while she was trying to abolish Tanige's fears, she was fighting with her own. She, too, had heard the tales of the great knight. In a tone that was absolute in its logic, she commanded her servant, "Our culture of Islam is ages older than the culture and civilization of these Castilians. It's natural we view them as barbarians. They are direct descendants of those ancient Visigoths, and their preoccupation has been making war while we have been concerned with music and the arts and a refinement of living. Omar Khayyám says that the lowliest of Muslims is more educated and lives in a more pleasing manner than the kings of Christendom. My tutor says that 'barbarian' is hardly descriptive of these Christians, 'unwashed' is closer to the truth." The picture she drew was little more pleasing to her than the tales Tanige already believed, and Mirjana's skin felt crawly when she thought of having direct dealings with the knight. How could she think to trust al Said? He was a Christian knight, and she was an Islamic princess. They were from worlds apart, and there was no reason whatever to believe he would help her — not even for the booty of the caravan. Yet, it was a chance she would take, for to do nothing and set her fate into the hands of Mútadid and Yusuf without so much as lifting a finger on her own behalf was intolerable to her. From the carved ivory coffer on her dressing table she fished through her assorted jewels, deciding on a gold and sapphire bracelet. "Here, Tanige, give this to the abbot when you deliver the letter. If he indicates this is not payment enough, tell him you will return with another. Hurry, and keep your cloak wrapped high over your face. You mustn't be recognized entering the church, else there will be questions to answer."

Like all Islamic cities, Seville boasted religious tolerance, and it was not unusual for a mosque of Islam to be under the same roof as a Christian church. Within all of al-Andalus there was a large element of Christians comprising the population, and they were considered to be a valuable and contributing part of Seville's economy. Still, it wouldn't do to have Tanige recognized. Questions of all sorts could be asked, and not to speak was better than to have to speak a lie.

Pushing Tanige toward the door, Mirjana shoved her into the corridor and slammed the door behind her. There was an uneasy cloying in the pit of her stomach, and her hands shook. Yet, there was a reborn hope in her heart. She would leave for Granada, but within days she would find herself back in Seville, back with Omar. Allah himself must be watching over her, she thought, to present the proximity of al Said just when he could be most useful. The Lord Champion would change the direction of her life, she was certain of it!

Hours had passed since Tanige left to deliver her mistress's letter to the abbot, and each moment had passed with agonizing deliberation for Mirjana. In some obscure way she felt as though she had sealed her fate.

Earlier, she had bathed and dressed in a pale olive caftan of the finest wool which was embroidered around the simple round neck and wide, flaring sleeves with garnet and carnelian threads. Beneath, she wore a simple shift of cream silk with long, slim sleeves which tapered to graceful points that covered the backs of her hands to the knuckles. A variation of the wimple, which was the formal headdress of Castilian women, was adapted to a softer, more flattering style that skimmed over the top of her bright red-gold curls and was held back from her face by ornate jeweled clasps. Her soft felt slippers matched her caftan and deadened the sound of her steps on the polished tiled floor as she paced back and forth waiting for Tanige's return.

She would have liked to spend these hours being distracted by Omar, but he was nowhere to be found. Shortly after the noon hour, when she knew he usually abandoned his work for a leisurely midday meal, Mirjana had gone down to his study, hoping to find him waiting for her. The study had been empty as had the paths in the gardens where he would sometimes go to read. She had questioned the guards and the servants, but no one seemed to know his whereabouts. This was such a departure from his usual routine that Mirjana was certain he was avoiding her. At first she was disconsolate, and then she realized that seeing her again and knowing that she must obey Mútadid and leave for Granada was so painful to him that he couldn't bear her company. She smiled. Poor Omar, dear Omar, so gentle, so considerate. Didn't he realize that each moment was also bittersweet to her, but that she would gladly suffer any pain just to look into his dark, passionate eyes?

A sound at her door caught her attention

away from her musings. Thinking it to be Tanige, she ran to the door herself and swung it open. Instead of Tanige it was one of Mútadid's servants.

"Princess Mirjana, the emir wishes to see you at once. Qadi Hassan also wishes your presence."

Mirjana searched the man's eyes, looking for a clue to this unexpected command. Hope, always eternal, prompted her to pray silently that Mútadid had changed his mind about sending her to Granada. Surely, Hassan's presence was significant. Being the firstborn son, Hassan would inherit Mútadid's throne. In preparation for his royal duties, Mútadid had made Hassan a *qadi,* a "civil judge." Yes, certainly Hassan's presence was significant. Remembering the letter Tanige was delivering to the abbot gave Mirjana a pang of dread as she followed the manservant to her father's suite. If there were no caravan to Granada and al Said should make inquiries, if her rash actions were discovered . . . No, she would not think about that now. She must clear her head and be receptive to Mútadid's summons. Beyond that, she could not think.

Entering the anteroom of Mútadid's bedchamber, Mirjana was faced with a congregation of family. Present were her father's three living wives and their children, some of them no more than babes in arms. There was Fatima, her twelve-year-old sister, whose dark eyes and soft brown hair were inherited from Sayyim, her mother; Abi Amir, her nine-year-old brother; and Hakam, their baby brother. Pulgar, second-living wife to Mútadid, sat near the balcony with her children Nasr, Almohad, and her daughter, Rahmana, who was still nursing at the breast. Baeza, the youngest of the wives, sat meekly on a long divan, her slender arms cradling her swollen, pregnant belly. And presiding over all was Hassan, tall and almost wretchedly thin, his beaklike nose protruding importantly from above his black beard.

"Mirjana," he greeted her informally, as though he had only been in her company yesterday when, in truth, she had not seen him for more than a year. "We are assembled here at our father's request. The others will arrive if the situation becomes desperate."

Mirjana's eyes widened. "Desperate?"

"Our father is unwell," Hassan told her, barely hiding the smile on his ungenerous mouth.

Glancing around the room again, Mirjana saw tears glistening on Baeza's smooth cheeks. Immediately, she felt pity for this girl who was younger than herself and married to an old man like Mútadid. Yet, it was a statement that the girl should cry for her husband. She, Mirjana, would never, ever cry for Yusuf. The weight of the situation suddenly descended upon her, and she pierced Hassan with a glance. "How is it that there has been time to alert my father's children who live outside Seville, and yet I, who keep my apartments in the same palace, have just now been called?"

Hassan appeared uneasy and his dislike for his half-sister was evident in his voice. "Because, Sister, it was the prudent decision. If our father should not survive then he should at least have the comfort of his children."

"That does not explain why I have been the last to be notified," she challenged. She had almost forgotten how much she disliked Hassan, hated him actually. Ever since achieving manhood, he had been too eager for the throne. His methods were deceitful and canny, and more than once when he was a boy, Mútadid had had to save him from disgrace. Then it had been tolerated as boyhood mischief, but Mirjana knew that Hassan had grown into a greedy, haughty man who aspired to greatness and yet would never recognize true greatness if it had teeth and bit him. His eyes never seemed to be content; they were always shifting, glancing into corners, looking over his shoulder. Even his voice was a kind of conspiratorial whisper as though what he spoke would not stand under the judgment of a third ear. Also, he had earned the reputation for being merciless in his duties as a civil judge, a position that was honorable and important. He was the representative of the justice of Seville and the voice for Mútadid himself. A more disappointing representation of Mútadid's wisdom Mirjana could not imagine.

"My sister," Hassan said between tight lips, "it was only through my intercession that you were called at all." Seeing her shock, he allowed a hint of a sneer to touch his mouth. "Yes, I know of your last audience with our father, and I must tell you he was quite distressed at your brashness and lack of duty. You said some very unpleasant things, didn't you?"

Mirjana shook her arm out of Hassan's grasp. "When I last saw my father it was I who was angry. This he understood and forgave. I had his word on it. At the last he told me he forgave my insolence. What are you trying to do, Hassan? Isn't ascending the throne of Seville good enough for you? Why is it your whole life you have tried everything you could to alienate my father from his children? Are you so insecure in his love because you know you are not worthy of it?"

Hassan's features hardened. Mirjana remembered too late that he was no longer a sly, resentful boy but a powerful man who one day would become emir of Seville, and to have him as an enemy would be unwise. When Hassan once again gripped her arm, she allowed it, even though his long, thin fingers were biting painfully into her flesh. Anything, she would withstand anything, to stay here in Seville with Omar. "When may I see my father?" she asked him, deferring to his importance, hiding her instinctive loathing of this man.

"Soon. When the physicians leave him. Do you think I should send word to Yusuf that your arrival will be delayed because of Mútadid's illness?"

Mirjana tried to hide her relief. She should have known that deceit and trickery were too familiar to Hassan to fool him. He instantly recognized her eagerness to delay leaving Seville. Before she could think of an appropriate answer, the double doors leading to Mútadid's bedchamber opened and one of the royal physicians stepped into the anteroom.

Everyone stood at attention, watchful for the man's reaction to the emir's illness. Giving no hint of his patient's condition, the man said simply, "The emir wishes to see Princess Mirjana."

Hassan was the quickest to act. Leaving

Mirjana, he crossed the room and confronted the physician. "*I* will go in to see my father," he said imperiously, "the others will wait."

Mirjana's temper flared, and it was with great control that she elevated her chin haughtily and modulated her voice. "I will see my father now." Squaring her shoulders and feeling the sting of Hassan's hatred scorch her back, she entered Mútadid's chamber.

She found her father sitting up in bed drinking tea. His beard was carefully combed and his hand was steady as he brought the cup to his lips. "Father," she cried with relief, "you have us all fearful for you and here you sit drinking your favorite tea!"

Flanked by his physicians, Mútadid waved them off, hearing their cautions about dosing himself with the herbs they left at his bedside. "Yes, yes," he told them impatiently, "I'll drink your bitter herbs and follow your advice. Leave me now with my daughter."

As they closed the doors behind them, Mirjana saw Hassan peering into the bedchamber, hungry for a glimpse of his father. "Hassan is pacing the anteroom, Father," she said abstractedly.

"Yes, I would think he would be. Each day he becomes hungrier for the power of the throne. I thought making him qadi would satisfy him for the time being," Mútadid sighed heavily. "I should have known that patience is not a quality that fits him. You Mirjana, should have been my firstborn son. Then I could close these weary eyes and find peace."

"What did your physicians prescribe for you?" she asked, sniffling at the powders and medicines left near her father's bed.

"Enematas for the most part."

Mirjana laughed, the color flushing her cheeks. "You mean to say that constipation was your complaint?" She laughed again, the sound merry and bringing an answering smile from Mútadid. Gasping for breath, she told him, "Hassan has sent word to all the family to put them on the alert for a funeral, and all because our father was having difficulty moving his royal bowels!"

Mútadid roared with laughter, wiping the tears from his eyes. "That young fool! I haven't given up the ghost yet, and he cannot come to terms with the fact that I am born of a long line of men who live into their nineties. Poor Hassen, poor, poor Hassan!" Another wave of laughter overtook him and the bed shook beneath his weight.

"Mirjana, you have always been good for me. I sent especially for you to mend the distance between us. Having you near me is like having your mother over again. You have always known that of all my wives, Cloe was the best loved. And of all my children, you —"

"Are the most trouble!" The voice was Hassan's. He had opened the doors and was striding into the bedchamber. His face was set in grim, hostile lines, and his dark eyes mirrored his jealousy.

Mirjana and Mútadid glanced at one another, wondering how much Hassan had overheard. "I was about to talk to Mirjana about leaving for Granada," Mútadid told his son. Something in the old man's demeanor changed right before Mirjana's eyes. Suddenly, he appeared less certain of himself; his eyes darted furtively from Hassan and back to his daughter.

Approaching the bedside, Hassan stood close to his father, almost looming over the old man. "I hope you voiced your regret that the circumstances surrounding her marriage to Yusuf cannot be altered."

Hassan's tone held authority and challenge. How dare he speak to his father in such a manner! How dare he challenge the word of his emir! Mirjana looked at both men — one tall and strong and menacing, the other enfeebled with illness and age. No, that was wrong. Mútadid was still a vital man! Baeza's pregnant belly was proof of that fact. Mútadid wasn't crippled by age or illness. This was something that went much deeper, right to the core of his authority as emir. She waited for her father to take up the challenge Hassan presented. Only a moment ago he had expressed pity for his son's greed for the throne, and yet, here in Hassan's presence, Mútadid seemed to cringe beneath his power.

"Mirjana would be a comfort to me," Mútadid said, his voice regaining some of its strength. "A man should have comfort in his declining years."

"That is so," Hassan agreed. "As emir there is also comfort in knowing the treasury has been made richer by Yusuf's generosity. There is also the comfort of all your children and your wives. And since I have been appointed qadi, have I not done all in my power to relieve you of your heaviest burdens?"

This last Hassan said with a slick, oily tone, and Mirjana realized the depth of his statement. As qadi, an important civil judge, and as inheritor of the throne, Hassan had found himself possessed of many allies who, looking to their own futures, could help him ascend the throne even before Mútadid's death. Mútadid would remain as figurehead while Hassan was the real power behind the throne, a state of affairs that had occurred before in history and would occur again and again wherever power and money were concerned.

"Hassan, go and call the others in to me.

I can hear Baeza's tears even from this distance. Sweet child, she should not be upset at a time like this." Mútadid carefully avoided Mirjana's eyes, unable to bear what he would find there. None knew better than he that he had betrayed her trust in him as her father. None knew better than he that when she left for Granada he would be totally at Hassan's mercy.

As though reading her father's thoughts, Mirjana was glad she had sent Tanige with the letter to the abbot. Not only would its results be expedient to her own motives, but it would also help Mútadid. It was enough to know that he had reconsidered sending her to Yusuf. When she returned to Seville under the guise of assembling another caravan and escort, the delay would serve to conspire with Mútadid to find a way to protect him from the greedy Hassan. Her future was almost assured. After making herself invaluable to Mútadid he would never send her away again.

The dust flew from beneath the wagon wheels, spraying out into a red plume. The stink of horseflesh sweating beneath the relentless sun seemed to choke her even through the curtains hanging on the carriage windows. On the barren March, the borderland between Seville and Granada, Mirjana's caravan traveled at a miserably slow pace. The sedan seats inside her carriage seemed to be padded with rocks. The constant swaying and jarring made every bone in her body ache. Each night when they broke for camp, Mirjana would swear to herself that she would rather die than climb into the carriage for still another day's ride.

Foot soldiers and guards on horseback flanked the caravan, keeping a wary eye open for bandits. Mules and packhorses followed in each other's steps, wheezing against the dust clouding around the hooves. Scrub brush and occasional trees broke the monotony of rocky ground and parched earth. As they continued their journey northward, the terrain seemed to turn a deeper green on the horizon.

It was the third day of the trek, and Mirjana's nerves were raw and tight. She snapped at the servants, barely giving them a chance to complete an order. She bounded from one side of her carriage to the other, parting the draperies to peer outside. Her ears strained for the sound of rushing hooves, and her eyes ached from watching the distant horizons for swirls of dust that would indicate a column of marching men. Hours that could have been put to use in other ways were instead wasted in anxious anticipation. Every bone in her body seemed to have a sharp edge which dug into muscle and flesh. Her head throbbed with the heat, and she thought her eyes held the sands of the Sudan.

Tanige, seated across from her mistress in the carriage, mirrored each of Mirjana's tortures. She had delivered the letter to the abbot, instructing that it be delivered to al Said. Snatching for the jeweled bracelet she had taken as payment for his troubles, the religious man had promised to send it forth immediately. That had been nearly seven days ago. The strain of anticipation pinched her features to an even greater degree. "When do you think?" she asked in a hushed whisper.

"Tanige, if you ask me that question one more time, I'll put you out of the carriage and you'll walk beside the mules. I don't know. You are certain the abbot understood —"

"Certainly I am certain!" Tanige rebuked. "Do you take me for an idiot? I have told you and told you. The abbot promised to send your letter by messenger. He was greedy enough for your bracelet, I can tell you that! When he snatched it out of my hand —"

"Enough! My ears are stopped and my poor head aches with your telling and retelling of what must have been your life's greatest adventure," Mirjana said wearily, rubbing her temples.

Tanige snapped her mouth shut, shooting reproving glances at her mistress. She didn't like this change in Mirjana, she did not like it at all. The princess had always been level-headed and steady of temper and manner, in every way a gentle lady. Her impending marriage to Emir Yusuf had altered her into a nervous shrew, discontented with the smallest geniality. "I was only trying to amuse the princess," Tanige said petulantly.

"The princess is not amused," Mirjana answered testily. "Were it not for the fact that we have been together since childhood, I swear I would not tolerate your abrasiveness and your lack of respect. Have you instructed the captain of the guard to seek a campsite near a stream where I can bathe? Take heart, Tanige, things will go as we planned them," she said when she saw the doubtful look on her servant's face and noticed the fidgeting of her skinny, nail-bitten fingers. "Soon you will be back in the arms of your mystery man and I will be back with Omar. You will see."

Several hours later the caravan stopped for evening camp. As instructed, the captain of the guard had chosen a small, shallow glade that was sheltered from the afternoon sun by wild acacia trees. The soldiers went about erecting tents and preparing cook fires at a comfortable distance from the princess's campsite in order to afford her privacy.

Through long practice, the tents went up

quickly. Mirjana's tent, the most opulent and spacious, was erected, and the light, colorful fabric billowed pleasantly in the breeze. From the wagons, rugs and pillows and most of the comforts of home were brought forth and put into her tent. Braziers to ward off the chill of evening, oil lamps, delicately scented with perfumes, and water jugs appeared and were carried inside the blue and white striped domicile.

Tanige approached Mirjana after being certain the servants were assigned to their duties. Her manner was restrained and conspicuously respectful. "I will walk with you to the stream, Princess Mirjana. While you bathe, I will see to our meal."

Realizing that Tanige's sudden correctness was a mockery intended to goad her mistress for the rebuke concerning her handmaiden's disrespect hours before, Mirjana considered herself properly chastised. "Tanige, my temper flares because of frustration. Please, this journey must not become a tournament of wits between us. If I hurt your feelings, I am sorry. Come with me; the water will be cool and we will both be better for it."

"And have the fish bite my toes? No thank you, Mirjana. I prefer to do my bathing directly out of the water jugs in the tent!"

Mirjana laughed. "Tanige, you have become spoiled by the comforts of the palace. Have it your own way, you always do somehow."

Freed from the imprisonment of the carriage, Mirjana's spirits lifted. The late afternoon sun was warm on her face, and the tall, knee-high grasses were soft underfoot. Crickets sang their songs and wild flowers bent obligingly in the gentle breeze. The banks of the stream were lined with tall, flowering acacia trees, their yellow buds ready to burst into huge, pungent-smelling splendor. The water held a mild current and was blue, reflecting the cloudless sky on its mirrored surface.

Tanige set a basket of soaps and perfumed oils on the grassy bank. "I will take your soiled garments back to the tent and bring fresh ones on my return."

The cool stream was inviting, and within seconds Mirjana was submerged to her neck, her arms waving through the water, making delicious currents that soothed her aches. It was a pleasant place, surrounded by trees and the softness of encroaching twilight. The camp seemed miles away, lost somewhere on the frontier, and she felt alone and at peace. There was no one who would intrude on the moment. It had taken more than ten minutes to walk the distance to this point of the winding stream, and she was assured of her privacy.

Sweetly scented soaps wrought their magic and were a balm to her anxiety. She was lost in a sensual bliss, forgetting her watchfulness and the anticipations which had plagued her journey. All was peace and she could revel in thoughts of Omar and how, if her plans were accomplished, she would soon be back in his arms.

She was losing herself in her thoughts when a hellish explosion of noise slashed through the stillness. Instead of frightening her, the sounds brought joy. Well, it was about time the tardy al Said made his appearance! Languishing in the water, her face beamed contentment. Within hours she would be on her way back to Seville. Thanks to her cleverness and, of course, to Allah's intervention. Playfully, she slipped beneath the water. How wonderful she felt; how sweet was life! Soon, she would be in Omar's arms — and to think all that was required were the riches of the caravan. A musical ripple of laughter pealed from her as she applauded her success and ingenuity.

CHAPTER 3

Trapped as she was in the stream, naked, Mirjana could only wait until Tanige came with garments to rescue her. The sky was darkening by the minute as she listened with heightened alarm at the sounds of a skirmish coming from over the ridge. The water was turning her limbs to ice; she was cold and trembling and frightened. She had never considered the consequences of her actions. She could hear the clash of iron upon iron and sounds of shouting men. The trees interfered with her vision, but she knew the reason for the sounds that echoed in the twilight. The continued clash of distant swords and the bleating cry of a war horn fixed her with terror. What a fool she had been! What a silly, self-serving idiot! She should have known that her guardsmen and soldiers would never give over the caravan without a fight. Never, in all her careful calculations and plans, had she dreamed there would be a battle. Her legs turned to jelly, her skin broke out in bumps. Fool! Fool! Men were losing their lives! The caravan's escort were soldiers of Mútadid's army, ordered to protect her and the emir's property from marauding brigands and attacks. She had been so preoccupied with her determination to return to Seville she had never considered the loss of lives that would be sacrificed to her selfishness. Frightened tears filled her eyes, and she hung her head in shame. Long tendrils of hair that had escaped its pins trailed over her naked shoulders and dipped onto the surface of the water. Beyond the shallow ridge that hid the carnage from her view men were being killed and wounded, and she alone was responsible. The thought was so devastating, so overwhelming, her legs collapsed under her, plunging her beneath the surface of the stream, hiding her from her shame.

When Mirjana came up to breathe, an armored knight stood before her on the bank. The stallion he rode was as black as the night and twice as huge as any horse she had ever seen. The destrier reared on his back quarters, his majestic head thrown back as his rider drew in on the reins. They were as one, the beast and the man — if he was a man. Mirjana knew that far to the north where the cold winds blew and the seas would choke with ice there were a breed of men who were more kin to the beasts of the forests than to mankind. This, then, must be such a one.

His hair was dark, ungroomed, shaggier than the wolfskins he wore over his massive shoulders, and was held back by a headband of rawhide that cut across his forehead and held a dull gray metal stud in its center. The stud, glinting in the late day's light, gave the appearance of a third eye, reminding her of the tales of ancient Cyclops. Unpolished breastplate armor covered his chest, molded and forged to suggest the muscular, brutish strength of a great bear. Dust-covered chausses clung to his legs, emphasizing the muscular play of his thighs as they pressed authoritatively into the black flanks of his steed. His beard, dark as his hair, covered most of his face, so it was into his eyes that she brazened herself to look, and she could feel their eagle's gaze focusing upon her, holding her nearly mesmerized within their power.

He slipped from his saddle, pulling the dun-colored cape he wore over his back from its fastenings, and offered it to her. "Allow me," he said in her own language, gallantly bowing low, an incredulous gesture of gallantry from one who more closely resembled a beast of the demon kind.

There was no way to hide her nakedness from him, and from the curious heated expression in his eyes, he would not have allowed it in any case. Wading from the water onto the rocky stream bed, Mirjana crossed her arms over her breasts and walked toward him. Refusing to show him her humiliation, she held her chin high, meeting his glance brazenly. Reaching for his cape, she wrapped it around her nakedness, deliberately taking her time, knowing that he saw the sun's last golden light glance off her slim, water-beaded body. Her eyes met and held with his, and there was small satisfaction to find he was embarrassed. Of course! From what she knew the Christians were secretive and ashamed of their bodies, rutting beneath covers and adhering to the ban the church had placed on bathing. How unlike her own people, the children of Allah, who considered the human body a miracle of nature.

He was tall, so tall she felt she was standing in a hole when she looked up at him. His appearance was more frightening close up than it had been at a distance. It was only when he smiled, showing good, strong teeth made whiter by his surrounding black beard, that she was certain he was human.

"I am Rodrigo Ruy Diaz de Bivar, and I believe you summoned my assistance. You may have heard me addressed as El Cid, Compeador!"

Annoyed by his vanity and by the apparent conceit he took in his harshly won title of "The Lord Champion," Mirjana bristled. Again, he had used her own tongue; and rather well, she was forced to admit, but his arrogant manner incensed her. How dare he think himself the only one who was versed in more than one language! "I know who you are!" she told him, the Castilian words rushing from her lips. "And I wish to say you took your time in getting here. I expected you three days ago. Now I must travel all that distance again to return to Seville. Chivalry, Don Rodrigo Diaz, is essential. However, I am prepared to overlook your lack of it just this once. All I need from you is my carriage and my garments and I will leave you to your plundering. If you will be good enough to escort me back to my encampment, I will be on my way."

El Cid threw back his head and roared with laughter. "You have the bite of a viper, Princesa Mirjana. And if I tell you I will not allow you to leave? What would you do then?"

"Kill you," Mirjana said coldly, forcing her bravado. Not for the world would she allow him to see her fear.

He seemed to find this exceedingly humorous as he laughed again, abrading her nerves.

"Beautiful lady, you are indeed worth a king's ransom. Two kings, if truth be known!" Again, he seemed to find amusement in baiting her, and his white teeth flashed.

"You devil! What do you mean?" Mirjana hissed.

"Simply, your father, Mútadid, will pay a hefty ransom for the safe return of his daughter. Yusuf of Granada will also pay for the safe return of his bride. Added to the wealth of the caravan, I can return home victorious!"

"You are a blackhearted swine if you think you can abduct me," Mirjana snarled in outrage. "Attempt it and you will seal your own death. I advise you to allow me safe conduct back to Seville."

"You don't understand, gentle lady," he mocked. "The services of the Compeador come high, much higher than you planned to pay." His gaze swept over her, searing her exposed flesh as though appraising her like a horse at auction. Mirjana's eyes widened, as she pulled the dusty cape closer about her. What price was he talking about, she wondered alarmed? The ransoms from Mútadid and Yusuf, or a price of a more personal nature?

"You will only return to Seville when I allow it," he continued. All humor had left his voice.

His power and authority were evident, sending waves of panic up her spine.

Mirjana refused to be cowed, regardless of her trembling inwards. A show of bravado was more to her character, and she refused to accede to him and his ruthlessness. "We had an agreement, Lord Champion," she nearly spit out his title. "You were to receive the contents of the caravan and I was to return to Seville. I had heard you were a barbarian, but even the lowest of the low respects a bargain once made." Tossing the hem of his cloak over her shoulder, she faced him, eyes flashing, voice steady. "You will live to regret this, and I advise you never to turn your back to me. For if you do . . ."

"Tell me, what if I do?" he grinned down at her.

"We are desert people, adept with a knife."

"But you don't have a knife," he taunted. "You have nothing but my meager cloak to hide your nakedness. Give me your hand, Princesa. You ride back to camp beside me."

Mirjana backed off. "Never!"

His tone was patient. "Better to reconsider. I rarely repeat my orders."

"I refuse to go anywhere with you, on or off that beast you ride. You — you smell . . . like a goat!" She wrinkled her nose in condemnation of his grooming.

Deep, mahogany eyes narrowed and burned through her with acid penetration. "Better a goat than a whore. You have used enough scent to make an honest man desire death to escape it."

"And you, Don Rodrigo Ruy Diaz, are not an honest man. You are a barbarian! A stinking one!" she spat as she turned and ran through the acacia trees, his cloak trailing behind her.

Hooves tore the soft earth, obscenities filled the air. One moment her feet were on the ground, and the next she was in the air and placed close to his hard, muscled body atop the destrier. "I told you I rarely repeat an order. If I have injured your dignity, it was deliberate. Do us both a mercy and keep your mouth closed else I'll fill it with stones. I have heard enough for one day."

The almighty strength of his arm around her body shocked Mirjana. He had picked her up and tucked her close against him as though she were a small child. Even his steed did not appear to notice he was bearing her additional weight. In spite of herself, Mirjana found she was clinging to al Said. The distance to the ground as it passed beneath the destrier's hooves seemed greater than that from her balcony at the palace to the gardens below. To terrify her, from time to time he would seem to lose his grip of her, making her gasp in fear and cling to him all the more. The tall grasses that had come to her knees seemed far below her, and with each movement of the animal they seemed to wave and bend beneath him like a roiling sea. At last she could see the pinnacled roofs of her encampment. It appeared abandoned. Where were her servants? Where was Tanige? Daring to stretch her neck to see beyond the ridge where her escort was camped, she could see nothing save the wispy smoke from the cook fires they had started in preparation for their evening meal.

Mirjana's heart seemed to stop within her breast. To be alone with this barbarian in wolfskins and to be dependent upon his obvious lack of mercy terrified her. Only the sight of Tanige running toward her brought a sudden comfort. Never had she thought she would be so relieved to see her thin, pinched face, even though her eyes were filled with accusations.

"Put me down! Put me down!" she cried, her dignity overcoming her fear as she squirmed and struggled against his grip.

Put her down he did, and when she landed she lay sprawling, the sharp, deadly hooves of the destrier prancing too close for comfort. The wind was almost knocked from her, and Tanige ran to her assistance. Recovering, Mirjana stood on her own feet and held his cloak tightly wrapped around her.

"I would suggest the princess return to her tent and dress," he told her. "There are men among us who have dreamed of a woman's arms for many months, and you make a fetching picture dressed only in my cloak."

Mirjana glared up at him, fire lighting her eyes to a cindery gray where the ashes of damnation seemed to burn. Nevertheless, she saw the wisdom in his words. She felt so vulnerable standing naked with only his cloak for covering — and so terribly frightened. Perhaps being dressed would restore at least a part of her courage.

"Come with me, Tanige," she ordered quietly. "Al Said has told me to dress and he rarely, if ever, repeats an order twice." Garnering all the dignity she could summon, she lifted her chin and strode toward her tent, Tanige quick on her heels.

Her tent was like a silken cocoon whose walls and roof billowed and moved gracefully in the light breezes, and it was with gratitude that she and Tanige sought sanctuary. "Quickly, Tanige, bring me something simple to wear, a light woolen, perhaps with a sturdy kirtle to wear beneath. No, not that one," Mirjana judged, "something more simple, less revealing. Yes, that one," she agreed to a slim-fitting caftan of apricot with a deeper shade for the underdress. “Now stockings, yes, those dark ones and slippers. No, no, sturdy ones. Little telling how long it will be before I am reacquainted with my wardrobe. I’ll need serviceable garments.”

Mirjana let down her hair and attacked it with her brushes, bending forward from the waist to pull it to the top of her head and wind it into a secure coil, and with Tanige’s help, fastening it to the top of her head. A lightly woven chemise, underdrawers, and the kirtle were quickly donned. She had little liking for the thought of al Said bursting into her tent and finding her naked again. The stockings were pulled up over her knees and held with garters. The shoes she had chosen were flat-heeled and held securely on her feet with leather bindings.

“Tanige, quickly prepare a bundle of what we will need most in an emergency. There is no telling what that barbarian has in mind for us. Roll everything into heavy robes, cloaks, anything. Only the essentials.”

Tanige looked around the tent and shrugged. There was so much that was essential to a princess. There were perfumes and garments, twenty pairs of shoes, her jewel box, the bedding, hairbrushes, undergarments and pillows . . . There was so much! Never would she be able to bundle it into a robe, much less carry it!

Seeing her handmaiden's quandary, Mirjana sprang forward, gathering an extra pair of shoes, a clean kirtle, and a bar of soap. "Do the same for yourself," she told Tanige. "Add to it any preserved or dried fruit we have brought along and a flask for carrying water."

"Why?" Tanige demanded, fear striking her. "Are we not returning immediately to Seville? Mirjana, I'm frightened out of my skin! What has come over you? Are we not returning to Seville?" Her voice quavered and her skinny shoulders began to shudder.

Answering the questions suddenly seemed to overwhelm Mirjana. She sank onto the top of one of her trunks and covered her face with her hands. When she at last faced Tanige, it was to see accusation and terror in her eyes. "Tanige. I am not certain what is to become of us. Surely, soon we will be allowed to return to Seville. But for the time being, we are al Said's prisoners. Instead of adhering to our bargain, the barbarian has devised a scheme of his own. He plans to ransom me, both to my father and to Yusuf."

Tanige's knees seemed to crumple under her as she sank to the floor. "I knew something would go wrong. I told you it would! I told you!" she moaned, rocking back and forth and holding her arms close to her chest as though for protection. Mirjana immediately went to Tanige and held her.

"No, no, you mustn't cry. You must not show weakness. It will all come right, Tanige, I promise you. It cannot take more than a few days for the ransoms to be arranged. Don't cry, Tanige. I promise to take care of you. I promise!" Mirjana tried to sound confident and soothing, but she actually felt anything but. In reality, she wanted to hide, like she had when she was a small child, hide and pray to Allah that the nightmare would go away and never return.

When Mirjana and Tanige stepped out of the tent, they found it was being guarded by a heavyset man with an amiable smile, dressed in Christian armor. Al Said was on the other side of the encampment talking to a few of his men. She was struck by the differences between the men and their leader. They, at least, seemed to have some sense of grooming, even though they were dirty and unkempt from campaigning at the borders of Badajoz. They were not dressed in wolfskins nor wearing horrifying, Visigothic breastplate armor. Their hair was cropped short and they were clean shaven, except for an occasional moustache — unlike al Said whose very image was like a demon from a nightmare. In the descending evening and the feeble light from the torches, his beard seemed even blacker. The studded headband that gave him the look of a Cyclops winked boldly, and the wolfskin tunic broadened his already massive shoulders and made him kin to the beasts of the forest, closer kin than to humankind.

Seeing her, he turned, leaving his men, and walked toward her. His quick eye took in the bundle Tanige was carrying. "What's this?" he asked, turning to Mirjana for his answer.

"Necessities. There is no telling what you plan to do with us, and we have prepared." It was difficult to speak when she was trying to keep her lips from curling into a sob. The thought of being left to die on the wild Marches filled her with dread. Poor Tanige, she had asked for none of this. This was all her own doing.

"You will not need it, Princesa," he told her. "You are my captive while we await the ransom. Do you think I would leave someone as valuable as yourself behind?"

"I have no idea what to think!" she exclaimed, fury and fear feeding on her better judgment. "I have never dealt with someone as irresponsible as yourself!"

This last seemed to set the spark to his temper. He glared down at her, moving his hands to his hips and taking a step closer. "If you were a man, I would beat you," he snarled.

"I, El Cid, Compeador, irresponsible? No, milady, it is soft little kittens like yourself who are the undoing. *You* are irresponsible! *You* are the one who lacks a sense of duty! If not, you would have followed your father's wishes and would have traveled unmolested to Granada to marry Yusuf. I have no liking for attacking women. I was on a solemn duty when I received your letter calling me from my post to take your caravan. Can I be blamed if I am an enterprising man? I saw there was much else to be gained than bridal gifts. When the ransom is made, you will be set free. This I promise you."

"Bah! How can a promise from an untrustworthy man be believed? I am a Princess, a child of the throne of Seville! You are a barbarian without loyalty or honesty!"

"And were you so honest and loyal, Princesa? Tell me, would your guardsmen and soldiers think their *princesa* so responsible if they knew how you had plotted to bring me here to help myself to your caravan?" His tone had lost its mocking flavor; he was shouting at her, railing against her, his dusky-brown eyes turning to lampblack in his fury. Without another word he seized her by the scruff of the neck and dragged her along beside him, forcing her to take three steps to one of his long-legged strides.

She was helpless to do anything but follow him across the encampment to the shallow ridge behind which her caravan was camped. Horses and wagons and mules stood, still carrying their packs and burdens, but now under different masters. Christian guardsmen and soldiers now held their tethers, surrounded by the carnage that always followed a battle. She saw the familiar uniforms of her father's soldiers, stained now with their life's blood. Several of the pack animals had been slaughtered in the foray and lay in odd and awkward positions where they had fallen, but none more awkward or horrible than the bodies of Mútadid's soldiers. *Her escort,* her people!

Mirjana's legs would not hold her and she fell to her knees. While standing in the stream she had been felled by the impact of what horror her plan had wrought. Nothing as terrible as the reality was imagined then; only in seeing it with her own eyes could she know. She remembered with soul-wrenching shame the first elation she had felt when she had heard the clash of swords and realized that al Said had finally come to her rescue. At what price? The cost of human life, the lives of her own people — soldiers, servants, caravan drivers.

"How?" she asked, tears of self-reproach swimming in her eyes before falling to scald her cheeks.

"That is how." He loomed over her, commanding her attention, pointing into the distance where she saw a column of marching men and signs they were attached to a contingent of cavalry. "Did you think I would come to take your caravan without my army? Just what did you expect, Princesa Mirjana?"

"Certainly not this." She made a feeble, helpless gesture that encompassed the battlefield. "There were so few of them, so many of you. And yet it would seem they fought bravely."

"Yes, bravely. More's the pity for the fools, thinking they were protection for the child of their king, their own Princesa Mirjana." She could hear the disgusted sneer in his tone; she need not look up into his face to see her own self-contempt mirrored there. "I have no liking for the waste of a good man. Were it not for the fact they were outnumbered ten to one, they would have gone on fighting to the last man. Fortunately, I was able to contact your captain of the guard, Abd il Addan. It was with him I sent the terms of your release to your father. Abd il Addan arranged for the same terms to be forwarded to Yusuf of Granada."

Fresh tears stung Mirjana's eyes, but she would not allow them to flow. It was sad, she thought, that al Said should know and remember the name of her captain of the guard while in the long days she had traveled with him and conversed with him she had never bothered to ask his name. She had never considered herself so selfish, so self-serving, that she had taken the names and personal knowledge of those who served her for granted. Now, here in the midst of the carnage her indulgence in her own desires had created, she knew it for the awful truth.

Mirjana extended her arm blindly, reaching for her captor. "Take me out of here, my lord. Please."

There was such sorrow in her voice, such self-condemnation on her lovely features, that the Christian knight was moved. He helped her to her feet and allowed her to turn her face from the scene he had forced her to witness. He was uneasy with his sudden impulse to show her what results her scheme had caused. She had acted upon a selfish whim when she had sent him her letter, and he had acted upon his greed. He truly believed she had had no idea what his intervention would cost. She, although a seemingly intelligent person, had never thought her plan through to the end. She was only a woman, after all, and could not be expected to know the ways of men and the military.

"It will not be long before Mútadid responds

to my demands," he told her. "The contingent of men who escaped death and wounds will make fast travel, unhampered by carriages and wagons."

Was she wrong, or had his attitude softened just a little? She turned suddenly and looked up at him. His black beard seemed to hide less of his face than she had thought; his eyes were the color of burnt almonds, and now he was smiling his consolation, and the flash of his strong, white teeth was somehow reassuring. She was confident for the first time that this ordeal would soon come to an end and she and Tanige would return to Seville unmolested. But, oh, what she would have given if she could turn back time and had never written that letter. Knowing what she now knew, she would have traveled on to Granada, become the bride of Yusuf, and kept thoughts of her dear Omar for her dreams. Anything, rather than to know she had cost these men their lives.

Mirjana paced the confines of her tent like a caged animal. From time to time she expressed her frustration and fears to Tanige who sat huddled near the opening of the tent. "I should be doing something. You should be doing something. It has been ten days since word was sent to my father and to Yusuf.

What is taking so long? Why don't we hear something? I don't think I can bear this confinement another day!"

Tanige had heard this so often she did not even glance up to acknowledge that she had been listening. Ten days had passed since they had first laid eyes upon the infamous al Said, who by this time they had come to think of as Don Ruy, as his captains called him. They were no longer camped near the stream where they were first accosted. Don Ruy had ordered they move their camp miles away, thinking that if Mútadid or Yusuf planned to forgo the ransom and rescue the *princesa* by force it would not be accomplished by a surprise attack. Runners and lookouts had been left at the former encampment to relay information when news did arrive from Seville or Granada. It was a risky business, Don Ruy knew, but it was not the first time a royal personage had been kidnapped for ransom, and he was certain it would not be the last. Also, he did not fear any political repercussions. Both Seville and Granada were taifa kingdoms, paying each year a hefty sum into the Christian coffers to be permitted to conduct their businesses and live in peace. Militarily, the Castilian armies far outnumbered and were more rigorously trained than any Muslim army. Over the centuries, the kingdoms of Islam had been made to relinquish more and more territory on the Spanish peninsula, and now holding the southern regions known as al-Andalus, there was nowhere to go but into the sea or back to the northern deserts of Africa. Also, Don Ruy wisely intended to share the ransoms with King Sancho, who would be glad for the unexpected boon to his treasuries.

For Mirjana and Tanige the time had dragged; each moment was imposed with anxious waiting and the fate of an uncertain future. At least they were comfortable. Along with the caravan, which now belonged to Don Ruy, all of their personal belongings had been brought along.

Tanige glanced outside the tent and wondered what in the name of Allah she was doing in this forsaken place. It made no difference to her that they were camped on a verdant plain just beyond the March of Seville, or that there was abundance of fresh water and wild game. To Tanige, it was the wilderness. There were no smooth palace floors or gossamer hangings or vibrantly colored tapestries. No fine dishes, no crystal or silver. Living so closely with the princess was denying her a certain personal freedom which she prized greatly. She could no longer pilfer a few drops of scented oil for her own bath — and she did love to go to bed smelling like the first flower of the summer. If caught, she knew Mirjana would scold but never beat her. Of late, she had become more brazen in helping herself to Mirjana's belongings — scarves and hair ornaments, and occasionally a pair of slippers the princess would never miss. Tanige would then prance through the servants' quarters in the palace, hoping to entice one of the grooms. To any who would ask, Tanige would praise the princess's generosity in making presents of such luxuries, fix her face into a smug smile, and pray they would never have occasion to mention it to Mirjana. Upon seeing Abdul, the guardsman at the kitchen gate, Tanige had become even more brazen, helping herself to earrings and jewelry which she would always return to Mirjana's jewel box. Almost always. There was a particular pair of earrings with deep green stones that Abdul admired, and Tanige couldn't bear to part with them. Homely and awkward as she was, even Allah could not blame her when she attempted anything which would make her attractive to a man. For years now, Allah had forgotten her, and she felt forced to take matters into her own hands and dare fate.

Another week was all she would have needed to seduce Abdul. She wanted to know what it was like to lay in a man's arms, any man! Abdul was a fair choice. He liked her, she knew he did. If only she could find a man who would want to marry her. Mirjana would surely give her her freedom, perhaps even a gift or two to take to her own household. The princess was generous and would never hold it against her that she would prefer to be in the service of a husband rather than a royal princess.

A man, Tanige sighed, feeling that special tingle that throbbed in her center whenever she dreamed of what it would be like to be loved by a man.

Seeing that Mirjana was once again immersed in one of the books Omar Khayyám had given her, Tanige slipped out of the tent. She smoothed the folds and creases out of her gown and covered the lower half of her face with the tail of her shawl. Stepping out into the sunshine, she looked about the camp. There were men — everywhere! Most of them were stripped down to their blouses and chausses, leaving behind their tunics and armor. Holding her back stiff and head high, Tanige walked among them. There were no admiring glances, no wicked winks for the eyes. Skinny as a broom and twice as bristly, Tanige continued with her awkward gait. Big feet on spindly legs made several of the men snicker behind her back as she tramped through the camp, daring to defy the advice of Don Ruy and his confessor, Padre Tomas. They had cautioned Mirjana and herself to keep close to their tent, or only walk about with an approved escort, which they would assign. The men had not been in the company of women for an overlong time, they explained.

Tanige heard the snickers, was aware of the laughter and the disinterest they showed her. If it were Mirjana who walked alone through the camp, the reaction would have been much different, she knew, and felt a familiar pang of jealousy. At last, unable to bear the ridicule another moment, she halted abruptly and swiveled to hiss at her tormentors. A long, bony finger shot out. "From this moment on the curse of a three-toed devil is upon you! I, Tanige, declare it!"

Loud guffaws floated around her as she stalked back to the tent. Absently, she bent to pick a handful of brilliant field flowers, and in doing so, realized where her mindless footsteps had taken her — to Don Ruy's tent. And he was inside talking to his captains. Cautiously, she looked about to see if anyone had noticed her, and then she scuttled behind the tent away from any watchful eye.

Tanige dropped to her knees, pretending to pick herbs and flowers. Her face took on a glowing expression of anticipation of what she could overhear. Mirjana would be so proud of her when she returned with any information concerning their futures. She might even give her a small token of appreciation, something Tanige would have stolen sooner or later.

She blinked and swallowed hard when she heard al Said's voice through the thin fabric of the tent. He sounded as though he were right beside her, his deep basso tones fluid and melodious and strangely modulated for one of his power and size.

Pietro was speaking now, al Said's friend and his highest ranking officer. A girl, such as herself, could do far worse than Pietro, even if he was a Christian. He was a hairy beast of a man with big hands and a barrel chest. His voice was deep and gruff, but clearly understood. And Tanige gasped when she realized the importance of his words.

"I would not like to be in your boots, Ruy. How in the devil are you going to handle this?" Not waiting for a reply, his deep tones rumbled on, "If Yusuf no longer wants her because he believes she is defiled, deflowered, and her own father Mútadid disclaims her, it means only one thing. You, the infamous Cid Compeador, are saddled with her. A woman! A royal *princesa*. Thanks to your wild philanderings with the fairer sex, no one will believe you've left her untouched."

"There must be an answer!" Don Ruy exploded. "Not only does decency tell me I am saddled with her, we have lost the double ransom. I had plans for that booty. There must be a price someone will pay for her. She's a royal *princesa,* for God's sake! And a comely one at that!"

"Who? Just name the man who would take your word you've left her untouched and would take her off your hands. You live in a fool's world if you believe it possible," Pietro said in disgust.

El Cid's voice echoed Pietro's disgust when he replied. "Are you telling me in this whole land there is none who will take her? She does have certain beauty; she has brains in her head, and she definitely smells pleasant. I understand these traits are most desirable in a woman."

"As if you didn't know from firsthand knowledge," Pietro chided. "If I were you, when you list her sterling qualities I would omit the part about her having a brain. You will never be rid of her if you stick with that plan. How much would you hope to receive for her?" he asked craftily.

"Not a tenth of what I hoped to get from Yusuf and Mútadid. Defiled! In a pig's eye!" There was a pause in his tirade. Suddenly, he exploded again, this time speaking to his confessor. "Padre Tomas! *You* can attest to the fact that she has never been touched by one of my men or myself! You are a priest, member of the clergy. You will be believed!"

"No, my son," the confessor disagreed. "Anything I might swear to Yusuf will only be heard as the prejudiced oath of a Christian. Remember, Yusuf is a Muslim and will only believe the word of an Islamic prefect. I cannot help you there."

Eavesdropping, Tanige heard the smack of one fist into the palm of another. "This cannot be!" Don Ruy protested heatedly. "She is Mútadid's daughter! What father can turn his back on his own child? Yusuf, I can understand. Virginity in his wife is of the utmost importance to preserve the guaranteed lineage of his royal blood. Were I in his place I, too, would be most suspicious. But a father?"

"Ah, my son. Is it the father? Have you not received word that Emir Mútadid is ill and his scoundrel son, Hassan, has been seeing to his affairs? Only God can tell us if Mútadid truly knows of his daughters predicament. Also, there is another question to ponder. Perhaps Yusuf and Mútadid are quite happy with the exchange of properties that this forthcoming marriage has brought about. If Mútadid were to accept the *princesa* back, he would be called upon to return all of the gifts and properties he received from Yusuf. Yusuf, on the other hand, would be disgraced to accept her under these conditions. I have told you before this, Ruy: You cannot force the hand of kings!"

"There must be a way to change Mútadid's mind. Or Hassan's, if that be the true case!"

"Like a knife to his throat?" Pietro offered. "It can be arranged for a price."

"You have it all wrong, Pietro. I will not pay out money to get rid of her; I want money *for* her. That was the original plan," Ruy said bitterly.

"Then I don't believe you are so anxious to be rid of her at all," Pietro challenged. "She does make a comely picture as she walks through the fields, gathering flowers and herbs. You, particularly, seem to find the teas she makes for you quite agreeable. Face it, Ruy, you must make a decision, and soon. We are scheduled to break camp within the next few days. It is unsafe to linger so long in territories where we are not welcome. As a last resort, you can turn her loose and allow her to find her own way back to Seville. Better, you can even arrange an escort for her, if you insist on being chivalrous. Just send her back. You will still have the caravan meant for Yusuf, so you will not have lost entirely."

Padre Tomas spoke out quickly. "No, Ruy, you cannot just take her back to Seville. Think on it! If Hassan is acting for Mútadid, he will never allow her to live. You, yourself, have heard about his contrived brand of justice. If he accepts her back, he must return all Seville has gained from Yusuf. And you cannot send her to Yusuf, who does not want her and will not have her! He will make a claim against Mútadid saying she was not delivered safely. This has the stink of the beginnings of civil war between Granada and Seville, two taifa kingdoms who pay heavily into King Sancho's treasuries. Sancho will not like any interruption of these payments, especially when his lord champion and loyal vassal brought it about! Consider *yourself,* Ruy."

Pietro disagreed. "She is only a woman, Ruy! You can have thousands of women with the treasures in that caravan," he said with sarcasm.

"I cannot bring myself to betray her yet a second time. If I had contented myself with the caravan and returned her immediately to Seville, it would have gone differently for her. She would have been welcomed. Now that I have overplayed my hand, it would be a loss of face to escort her back to Seville and go limping off into the night with neither the *princesa* nor the ransom. And if I were to just turn them loose to find their own way and they are besieged by bandits, how do you think I would feel then?" Ruy demanded angrily.

"Like a fool because you failed to deflower her yourself. Don't ask me to solve your quandaries, Ruy. I am only your friend and no part of your second-in-command. I want no part of your *princesa* or that scrawny servant of hers. *Mi Dios,* I have seen more comely camels!"

"Just be careful she doesn't bewitch you with one of her curses. Half the men in this damnable camp are afraid to look at her. Another of her curses and I'll be forced to confine her to the tent," Ruy said in an amused tone.

They were talking about her, jesting and making a mockery of her curses. Tanige's too-small eyes narrowed and then widened to half-moon slits. She would put a good curse on Pietro and see what came of it. There were times she could be most charitable. Right this minute Pietro and the soldiers were the least of her problem. Should she repeat to Mirjana what she had heard here today? Some part of herself would take satisfaction in seeing the beautiful princess weep and wail to know she had been forsaken by both father and intended husband, to know the rejection that her handmaiden lived with day after day. But another part of Tanige wanted to protect Mirjana. Why, she demanded, beating at her rack-ribbed chest, did these decisions always befall her? Why was she made to live under a double-edged sword? Luck and her curses on one side and life on the other, waiting with its vengeful fangs to get her. She had lived by her wits before and always to her betterment.

Patience, never one of her better virtues, would be what she needed now to make her decision. She would wait, regardless of how difficult it would be. Besides, hadn't her mother always warned her against being the bearer of bad news? Somehow, someway, she and Mirjana would find their way out of this.

The hot, midday sun beat down on Tanige's bony shoulders, making her wince with the heat. Already the wild flowers clenched in her hand were wilted, drooping and as forlorn as she felt. She was about to toss them away when she thought better of it. How else, if confronted, would she account for being so near al Said's tent? She shrugged and a small smile tugged at her mouth.

Pietro stood outside his commander's tent and saw her pass. There was a speculative look in his eyes as he watched her trek back to the *princesa*'s tent. She looked worse when she smiled, he decided. A shudder of apprehension wizzed up his spine as he recalled Ruy's warnings about Tanige's curses. What if she decided he was to be one of her victims? What if she cursed his manhood? Another violent shudder raced through him. Death would be preferable.

Inside the relative coolness and dimness of his tent, Don Ruy Diaz slouched against the center pole, rubbing at his aching temples. He did not need this problem now, especially problems which concerned a woman. He was a fair and honest man when those qualities were called upon. He could not bring himself to cast the *princesa* aside like a sack of spoiled wheat. He had made a bargain with her, and he should have been content with the booty of the caravan. Yusuf had little need for the rich wedding tributes sent to him from Mútadid and besides deserved nothing for wedding himself to such a beauty as Mirjana of Seville.

Personally acquainted with Yusuf, Ruy winced at the thought of Mirjana bedding down with that obese pig. The very idea of it made Ruy's guts churn. How was he to anticipate the turn of politics that would leave the *princesa* abandoned with nowhere to turn?

There was only one person who could honorably see to the *princesa*'s protection: himself.

He didn't want her, did not need her. She would be a constant reminder of his own stupidity. Yet, in spite of his chagrin, Ruy liked her. She was entertaining, smart, and beautiful. Contrary to the image he perpetuated, he was not a beast. He had feelings and emotions, and could pity Mirjana's abandonment by her own people. He felt he could never bring himself to tell her about the predicament his betrayal had put her in. Padre Tomas must be the man to tell her. She was an intelligent woman, perhaps she could think of something to win her back into Seville. Who would know her father and brother better than she?

A wry smile played about his mouth when he recalled how she had accounted to him every last treasure in the caravan. She wasn't to be cheated, she had told him, and then had the audacity to demand the return of the caravan to herself, claiming he had defaulted on the bargain between them! Bad bargain! Women! Did she actually believe he would accede to the demands of a woman? Not El Cid, Compeador!

A vision of her appeared before him. She had appeared so tired and weary on the day they had made this new camp nearly twenty miles from where he had first accosted her escort. His conscience smote him for the barest second. Women were naught but trouble.

They gave a man pangs in his loins, headaches in heads, and pains in necks. He ignored the fact that she could make his pulse pound and his heart beat to a faster rhythm. He also refused to admit he liked the sound of her voice and the way she always smelled of fresh flowers and exotic spices. Her intelligence astounded him and left him at a loss as to how he should deal with her. It seemed she considered herself his equal, and was as well or better versed on any subject he chose to introduce into their conversation. Padre Tomas seemed doubly impressed with Princesa Mirjana and had privately confided to Ruy that he would like to convert her to Christianity.

Her eyes were a color he had never seen before, crystal gray when laughing and becoming dark as ashes when troubled. And she brazened to stare deeply, knowingly at him, as if she were searching his soul through his eyes. But it was her apparent verdict that displeased him. He measured up short in her opinion. It annoyed him, angered him. That any woman would find him lacking was a blow to his self-image.

God spare him, what should he do with her? There was only one choice, and he knew it even when he had spoken with Pietro and Padre Tomas. He would have to take her home with him.

His decision made, he felt an overwhelming weight drop from his shoulders. He smiled. It was a good sign for him, he thought. A man must know how to smile at himself, for perspective — which leads to balance, which leads to solid foundations to walk on, to soar from, to grow.

If Yusuf and Mútadid or Hassan had half a brain between them they would be on the march to retrieve the caravan. They might not want the *princesa*, but they would want the treasures packed upon the horses and the mules, and stashed in the wagons. His agile mind quickly figured the hours since they had received the two missives, the first from Yusuf and the second from Hassan. If he broke camp now, there would be several hours to put greater distance between himself and his enemies. He anticipated the *princesa*'s distress at his order to break camp. She wanted nothing more than to return to Seville. The question was why she would want to return to an ailing father and a brother who wanted nothing to do with her. Perhaps — he let his mind wander to his alternatives — he could induce Pietro to wheedle the information out of Mirjana's skinny servant. Suddenly, it was important for him to know why the beautiful *princesa* wanted to return to Seville. Not only was it important, he felt it was imperative.

Shouting the order to break camp, Ruy strode over to Mirjana's tent and entered without announcing himself. "Get ready to break camp," he barked to Tanige.

The *princesa* was astonished by his intrusion, and she quickly wiped at a tear in her eye. Ruy thought her beautiful with her dove-gray eyes and ivory skin. "How dare you enter my tent in such a manner!" she scolded him. "How dare you!"

"Do you always repeat yourself?" Disinterested in her answer, he continued to bark orders. "Do not allow yourself for one instant to believe it has gone unnoticed that your crow of a servant has been pilfering from the caravan supplies — pillows, sweetmeats, perfumes!" he said in disgust.

"You have not seen to my comfort," Mirjana accused. "Someone had to do it. And do not dare refer to Tanige as a crow again in my presence. Keep your derisive tongue and your barbarous habits to yourself. Leave this tent and never darken it again unless I have invited you."

Blood rushed to Ruy's head. Did this wisp of a woman forget she was speaking to El Cid, Compeador? By God, he *should* tell her that without him she would perish. "There is something you must understand, Princesa. This tent is my tent. Those luxuries which you use are also mine. I will not tolerate your weeping and wailing, or your offensive manner. Never forget who protects you. I could turn you over to the men for a little sport. It's been many months since they have been with a woman."

"Princess," Tanige gasped, running to her mistress's side, "what he says is true. Tell him we are grateful for his protection. Tell him we are well and comfortable. Please, Mirjana, please listen to him!" Once confronted with the possibility of being thrown to the men, Tanige panicked. That was not quite the condition she had entertained in learning what it was like to be with a man.

Mirjana stiffened under this double assault. "You call eating greasy wild game, still dripping with blood, being well treated? You call not having had a bath, a real bath, in ten days being well treated? You call this tent a luxury? You call yourself a Christian, a man who knows his God, but in truth you are a heathen, a pagan, a godless barbarian! Even your confessor tells me tales about you that make my blood run cold."

"At least it still runs. Try my patience and your blood will cease to flow through those icy veins."

"You sicken me," Mirjana continued her tirade. "All that is important to you are riches.

There is more to life than gold and jewels and the power to torment women."

Ruy drew a deep breath. "Name what is more important."

"You would never understand. Love," she blurted. "A meeting of the mind and the body. A spiritual communion. The love of a parent for his child. The love between brothers. Art, music, beautiful words and beautiful books. Knowledge . . . bah! There is no sense wearying myself in telling you what you will never accept."

Ruy threw back his head and laughed. The sound was deep and wonderful to Tanige's ears. This was a man! The princess must be a lunatic not to notice. "My men cannot eat pretty words," he said. "Nor can they read from beautiful books. Poetry and music do not fill their bellies. That, milady, is most important to a soldier. Now, clear this camp and be outside ready to leave within the hour."

Mirjana stood and moved toward him, lifting her head to look directly into his eyes. Her tone was softer, somehow more threatening. "You are a savage," she told him, sparks shooting from her eyes. "You are a man without honor. You take my wedding tribute, trick me into believing you will help me, and then you hold me your prisoner. You are not a man of your word."

Ruy's hands balled into fists. "For someone who is only concerned with aesthetics, you appear to be quite interested in money. Here," he said tossing her a small pouch fastened at his belt, "this is what you are worth to me. I rescind our bargain and will decide later what is to be done with you. One last thing, Princesa," he snarled "You will not refer to me as a savage, for if you do, you will never again open your lovely mouth."

"Are your threats as good as your promises?" Mirjana's voice had turned to silk. "You are a barbarian."

Ruy took a second deep breath. If he let her know he knew a barbarian was the same as a savage, he would have to make good on his threat. It would be best to ignore her for the moment, even though it was an almost impossible feat.

Tanige swooned and caught herself. Such a man! Such power! The princess was a fool. Or was she? She certainly knew how to gain this man's attention.

"One hour," Ruy thundered as he stalked from the tent. "Women," he muttered to himself. For one brief moment when he had first approached her, he had wanted to gather her into his arms and assure her he would find a way to undo the wrong he had done. The sight of her wiping away a tear had filled him with pity, making him want to protect her. She was afraid with no one to whom she could turn. She felt alone and betrayed. What would become of her when she learned how she had also been betrayed by her brother and Yusuf? Seeing himself as her captor, it was expected she would make him the brunt of her anger and disappointment, what he had not expected was the effect she was having upon him. He looked back over his shoulder at her brilliantly striped tent billowing in the gentle breezes and knew that from this day on his life would never be the same.

"You heard our master and slaver. Pack our belongings, Tanige," Mirjana said bitterly. She felt the tears welling again. "I feel so desolate, so alone. Why is my father taking so long in answering the ransom demand?"

"We have one another," Tanige said fiercely. There were times, like now, when she would almost lay down her life for her mistress. The moments were rare and far between, but she always felt cleansed by the experience, as if to make up for her past disloyalties. Of one thing she was glad: that she hadn't come running to Mirjana to tell her what she had overheard outside Don Ruy's tent. That would be a blow from which the princess would never recover, and although it was inevitable that she learn it in time, for now it was best to delay it. Tanige had never seen Mirjana so depressed and forlorn, and it worried her. She knew all too well what could come of the princess's desperations. Wasn't that what had brought them into this situation in the first place?

"Come, we'll wait outside, Tanige. Can't you find something to carry those pillows?"

Tanige rolled her eyes. There were times when the princess was ignorantly unaware of what energy and forethought it took to see to her needs. "No, Princess, there is nothing here save our own arms to carry your personal belongings. I will bear under the inconvenience to myself." Defiantly, she stared a moment at Mirjana. "Of course, you could carry two of these pillows and it would be easier on me. I would not like to drop them on the ground if you are to sleep on them when we make camp this evening."

"Of course, I'll help you," Mirjana answered distractedly, "but please keep your eye out for something to carry these in."

"If Allah lets something fall from the sky, I will certainly reach out for it. Until then, we must make the best of it," Tanige said tartly, shifting her eyes away from her mistress who looked at her questioningly.

"You seem to be in a quandary, child," Padre Tomas Martinez said quietly as he came to stand beside Mirjana. He was Ruy's confessor and priest, but his youthful, brawny appearance made him look more like a warrior than a member of the clergy.

"I am, Padre." Helplessly, Mirjana gestured to the men who were busily breaking camp. "First, I know Don Ruy is waiting for my father and Yusuf to comply with his demands, and next, he is breaking camp and moving. And I have no choice but to tender myself into his hands. Do you know what he is planning, Padre? Has he told you why we are suddenly leaving?"

"No, child, he has not," Padre Tomas answered truthfully. "Ruy is a man of many complexities, but of this I am certain: He will do the right and honorable thing where you are concerned."

"You are fond of him," Mirjana said softly. The Padre's words brought comfort. She liked this man with his gentle manner and warm, brown eyes.

"I am. However, I am not blind to his faults," Padre Tomas laughed, wagging a stubby finger for emphasis. "Ruy drinks to excess at times, and he is not immune to the temptations of wicked women. It is true he has little regard for the church and its laws, and for the most part he is a lonely man. There are few who ever win his confidence. He's clever, intelligent, and instinctive in battle. But listen to me prattle. You certainly know all of this, Princesa. I am certain you've heard the tales which circulate about our Compeador. A legend in his own time. But," he wagged a blunt finger again, "he is a fair man. I caution you not to cross him. Trust to his fairness and his sense of justice, and he will be your avowed protector."

Something in the padre's manner made Mirjana feel he was warning her. What did the man know that she did not? Whatever it was, she was certain it was of vital importance. "Are you trying to tell me something, Padre? Do you know where we are going?"

"Child, I never know till we arrive. Each day I say Mass and administer last rites to the wounded and dying."

Tanige was listening carefully. Padre Tomas had been in Don Ruy's tent with Pietro and knew full well that neither ransom for Mirjana was to be met. She also knew Mirjana suspected the padre of evading the truth. Regardless of how envious Tanige was of Mirjana's beauty and position, she nevertheless could not bear to witness her grief when she discovered that she was now a homeless waif, wanted by no one, belonging nowhere. Where, then, was Don Ruy taking them? She had her suspicions, but kept them to herself.

The padre was also moved to pity. "We will speak again, Princesa. Perhaps Ruy will allow you your books and poetry. I would impose on you to share them with me some evening."

"I would enjoy that, Padre Tomas. Do you believe El Cid would indulge me? He has been more than emphatic that whatever is in the caravan now belongs to him alone." Of late, Mirjana found herself using the Castilian pronunciation of Ruy's title, so used to speaking in Spanish was she becoming.

"Ruy is a generous man," he told her, patting her hand comfortingly. "I will speak to him myself. Until then, a safe and comfortable journey, Princesa. I must leave now and bless the men as soon as they are ready to march."

When the padre left, Mirjana happened to glance at Tanige. Was she mistaken, or was the same sadness she had seen in the padre's eyes reflected in those of her servant? It made her uneasy that they could possibly share a secret concerning herself while she remained ignorant of what they knew and of what was to become of herself.

CHAPTER 4

On the second day since leaving their former camp where they had awaited word from Mútadid and Yusuf, Mirjana walked along beside her carriage. She had become so restless within its confines, and she ached for exercise. Tanige was fast asleep in its comfortable interior, and her peaceful snores were irritating to Mirjana who felt as though she had not slept since leaving Seville.

El Cid was leading them northward toward his home in Bivar, a tiny province in Castile. The long, seemingly endless column of his army that headed the caravan kept the fast pace of soldiers on the march. The contingent of men was like a great, crawling caterpillar. The sun, glinting off their helmets and shields, made them appear to be a bright necklace of jewels in the distance as they rounded through the shallow hills and gullies. As they progressed northward the land was losing its flat terrain. Don Ruy had told Mirjana that Bivar was in the foothills of the Pyrenees Mountains where, although it was now early spring, snow still capped the mountaintops.

Mirjana had hardly seen Ruy since they had broken their last camp. He had spent his time riding his great destrier at the head of his column, the beginning of which was over a mile ahead of the caravan. She knew he had come to her tent late the night before, but she had pretended to be asleep, not wishing to join in still another argument with him.

She had wondered why, when they had begun this day's march, he had ridden beside her carriage and told her about Bivar, and that it was to be their final destination. He and his men had been in the field for more than a year, he had said, guarding the borders of Badajoz to keep Alphonso from riding in yet another attack on his liege, Sancho. He had been mildly surprised when she was able to discuss this last with him, and she knew he thought she had lived her life in an ivory tower in Seville, completely unaware of the state of the world and political events.

Their conversation had been pleasant and informative, and had been conducted most civilly. And it was not the first time she had realized that because of her terror and uncertain future she had behaved like a spoiled child, losing the poise and maturity to which she had been bred. If nothing else, sending Ruy her letter, proposing his intervention of the caravan, had been a childish caper. Leaving Omar and what she felt for him had sent her into a panic, quite the opposite from what she considered her normal behavior. Her own impetuosity had thrown her into this predicament, and now she found herself a victim of El Cid's greed and ambition, as well as his prisoner. Oftentimes, like this morning, she would catch him looking at her in a certain way, as though he wasn't quite certain what plans he had for her. It puzzled her, but then he rode away abruptly, apparently thinking of other things and duties, without giving her a second thought.

Ruy was more aware of her than she knew, but because of his quandary about what to do with her, he found it difficult to face her. He wasn't sure what he *should* do with her, and he was even less certain of what he *wanted* to do with her. In spite of his reservations, he was discovering that he liked her. She was entertaining, intelligent, and most certainly beautiful with her red-gold hair and slightly haughty manner. He was not a beast, he continually reminded himself, contrary to the image he liked to project when on a campaign. Ruy was feeling pangs of distress for Mirjana, pitying her and sensing her feelings of abandonment. It was difficult to stand under the frequent bouts of her sarcasm and blame, and even when she abused his chivalry, some shred of nobility even he had not known he possessed halted him from telling her that neither Mútadid nor Yusuf wanted her back. He had witnessed her sad expression as she gazed off into the distance toward Seville, and he shared that sadness. He would have liked to have sent her back to Seville, saving his own honor and face be damned. However, Mútadid or Hassan, whoever was actually sitting on the throne at this moment, would be forced to publicly disown Mirjana to protect Seville's new alliance with Granada. Even though Mútadid would care privately for his daughter, she would be without station or dignity. And if Hassan sat on the throne, from what Mirjana had told him, he would be without mercy. Yusuf was already claiming she had been defiled, and there was no sanctuary for her in Granada.

Defiled! Ruy could spit whenever he thought of it, which was often. Day by day he was becoming more attracted to her, but liking her and caring for her welfare, he had never acted upon his instincts. The last thing he wanted to do was ruin her and spoil her chances of ever being reaccepted into her own world and her chances for a royal wedding.

Never, considering his own homage to the royalty of his own country, could he forget she was a *princesa.*

All this thinking and he was no closer to coming to an answer than before. It was almost time for the midday meal, and on sudden impulse, Ruy turned his steed about and rode back down the column of men toward Mirjana's carriage. Perhaps with a bit of persuading, she would agree to share his table. He was well aware of the fact she considered him a barbarian, both due to his reputation and because, he knew, of his present appearance. A slow smile formed on his lips. Princesa Mirjana would be surprised when they arrived at his castle in Bivar.

When Ruy rode up beside Mirjana, he was carrying a bundle under his arm. "We are stopping now for the midday meal. I hoped you would join me. We could go off into that glade of trees over there." He gestured with his arm. "It will be free of the dust thrown up by the wagons and mules."

Her first instinct was to refuse, but the protest died unspoken because she feared he would guess she did not want to be alone with him.

"I've brought bread and cheese, and some kind of delicacy that was stashed in one of the wagons. Say you'll come with me."

His smile was so genuine, so persuasive, she agreed.

"All right then, come here so I can lift you up beside me." It was said so casually, so expectantly, she found herself halfway to his destrier before she remembered that first ride she had taken with him when he had carried her naked, wrapped only in his cloak, from the stream back to the camp.

As though reading her mind, he sobered. "I promise you your treatment will be considerably more dignified than the first time." His sincerity moved her, and she once again thought his Visigothic appearance incongruous with his manners.

"Put your foot in the stirrup," he told her, "and grab hold of my arm. I'll do the rest." In the space of a breath she was up on the destrier's back, sitting in front of Ruy, his arms holding her securely. From her position atop the animal's back the ground seemed miles away, and she was frightened. She had never ridden horseback in Seville, and she quickly became exhilarated with the ease of motion and the distance so quickly covered. If she could ride a horse, she could go anywhere in the world!

Into the copse of trees they rode, quickly eyeing a narrow brook trickling through the wilderness, deciding this was the perfect spot for their picnic. After he lifted her down from the saddle as though she were as light as a child, Mirjana watched him dismount and asked, "What do you call him?"

"Hmmn? Who?"

"Your steed. What do you call him?"

"Horse, I expect." He led her to a knoll overlooking the brook and which was shadowed by trees.

"Has he no name? He is a wonderful horse, a magnificent animal! Even the lowest of the low deserves a name."

Ruy glanced up from where he was laying the cloth and putting out their meal, and saw the distress in her eyes. "Milady, I am a knight, vassal to the throne of Castile. Soldiers and warriors do not name their steeds. If they do, I myself have never heard of it."

"Oh," she said meekly, looking to where his destrier grazed. "Pity the poor beast who serves his master and earns no name."

"You jest," he told her testily, feeling her recriminations and thinking she considered his nameless horse farther proof of his savagery. "What would *you* consider a fitting name, milady?" He almost winced thinking she would follow her femininity and decide a name like "Pansy," or "Nubbins," would fit the war horse.

"That is not for me to decide, sir. You know

him far better than I." She bent to help smooth the cloth, and sat down beside it. Hungrily, she accepted the wedge of sharp, hard cheese he offered, and tore off a fistful of the dark bread that traveled so well without becoming moldy. She watched him struggle with the cork on a flask of wine, and laughed when he grimaced over the stubborn stopper. At last he placed the cork between his strong teeth and easily popped the opening to the flask. He offered the wine first to her.

"I am a Muslim; wine is forbidden to me. I'll drink from the brook after my meal."

He bit into his cheese and bread, and took a healthy swallow of wine before he asked, "What would you suggest — a name for my horse? Perhaps if I tell you about him you can think of something fitting." As he spoke she watched his face illuminate with pride in his steed. He used words like valiant, courageous, obedient, and stalwart, fighting for the good of the realm to keep the lands free to serve Sancho, the king.

Mirjana's eyes darkened to the color of smoke, her golden-tipped, sooty lashes dipping to make shadows on her cheeks. "What of the Latin name 'Liberte?' It is certainly something as valuable as your steed is to you."

For a long, long moment Ruy watched her, something going dead within him. Was she speaking of his steed, or of herself — she, who was without freedom?

To avoid his gaze, Mirjana stood and went to the brook, kneeling down beside it. Cupping her palm, she dipped into the clear, sweet water and sipped. The sun glistened through the droplets and dribbled down the front of her gown. Her hair was the color of burnished gold in this light, and her skin was more fair than a babe's. He knew her hair would curl about his fingers and her skin would be silk to his touch. The deep stirring in his loins told him he had been without a woman for too long, and yet he was apprehensively aware of the fact that if he had bedded *three* women just an hour ago he would remain hungry for this one with her glib tongue and quick mind. All cats are gray in the dark, he admonished himself when he suspected that Mirjana's skin would be softer than any other he had ever touched, and that her lips would yield under his in a surprising return of passion.

She had returned to the spread cloth, poking through the bread wrappings and cheese. "Where have you hidden it, the delicacy you brought from the wagons? I confess to a compelling sweet tooth. Where is it?"

Reaching inside his tunic, Ruy brought out a little parcel wrapped in a spotless white cloth and handed it to her. "I've no idea what it is, but it looked tempting."

Curiously, Mirjana opened the parcel, and seeing its contents, burst into laughter, the sound filling the air about his head like the sweetest of birdcalls "You cannot eat this!" she told him, still rollicking with laughter.

"I am a soldier, I can eat anything! Boiled owl, pig's hooves, mule bellies . . . anything!" He felt ridiculous defending himself like a small boy parading his bravery.

"No, no, not this!" Mirjana cautioned as he reached for a handful of the pearl-sized, nutlike substance. "This, Ruy, is more potent than any owl you have ever boiled! It is a medicine for the stomach! Eat only a few and you cannot leave your chamber pot for an entire day!"

Looking at her with wide-eyed astonishment, he suddenly joined in her laughter, throwing back his head in that familiar way, his voice booming with glee. "You are unaware of what I have done, Princesa!" He laughed again, his eyes crinkling with a mischief that made him seem far younger than he appeared. "That damn Pietro was curious about what I was taking from the wagon and insisted he share in this delicacy. I myself saw him eat a handful! He thought them highly overrated for a treat and declined a second helping, praise God! If what you say is true, the poor man will have a restless afternoon's march!"

The vision of El Cid's second-in-command continually leaving the line with utmost urgency to run into the side brush sent new waves of excitement through Mirjana. Ruy was delighted with her amusement and lightheartedness even if it was at Pietro's expense.

After packing the leftover bread and cheese, he led her back to the destrier who was lazing in the shade, nibbling the grass. "We've lingered too long," Ruy said mildly, "and Liberte awaits. You are absolutely correct, Princesa. Freedom is more precious than gold, just as is my steed. I am only aggrieved that at this moment it is something which I must deny you."

Mirjana was so astonished by the sudden tenderness in his voice she turned to look up at him. He still held her hand, and she felt it grow warm within his. The air was suddenly still, the only sound the far distant cry of a bird.

Together atop Liberte's back they rode back to the caravan, and Mirjana was filled with half-formed questions. What had he meant when he said he must deny her her freedom? Why? Certainly it was within his power to send her back to Seville! Was it not?

Just as she was about to put her thoughts

to him, they came abreast of the caravan. She must save her questions for another time. She wanted to understand what he meant, but mostly she needed to know if she had only imagined that shadow of pity which had appeared in his eyes.

Firelight flickered bravely against the surrounding darkness. Weary from the day's march, the men had gratefully settled down, contenting themselves with murmured conversations and the pleasant sensation of their full bellies. Somewhere in the distance someone was playing a flute, its vibrant chords rising and falling in melodious echoes. Mirjana sat near the campfire outside her tent, her long, tapered fingers lovingly smoothing the covers of the book Padre Tomas had brought her.

"How did you know this was one of my favorite poems?" she asked him, already opening the pages to her best loved passages.

"I did not know, Princesa; I merely chose it because it appeared more handled than the rest. I am unfamiliar with Arabic script. Won't you read to me?" Padre Tomas settled his bulk near the fire, warming his hands and feet. It would be pleasant to listen to the *princesa* read to him from her book. Her voice was kind to the ears, unlike many women whose shrill tones could make a man wish himself deaf.

A long shadow fell over them and they looked up to see Don Ruy standing there. "Do you mind if I join you?" he asked, watching Mirjana, waiting for her answer.

Instead, Padre Tomas spoke for her. "Yes, Ruy, join us. You could do with some culture. Could he not, Princesa?"

"Only if it is what he wishes." Mirjana pretended disinterest. "However, my concern is for you, Padre. What you have brought me is a love poem."

"Before I became a priest, I was a man, eh Ruy?" Padre Tomas laughed, giving her his assurance he would not be offended by the content of the poem.

"Trust him, Princesa," Ruy told her. "Before he took up the banner of Christ, he toted the banner of King Ferdinando, and the ways of the flesh are not unknown to him. *Por favor,* Princesa, honor us with your reading."

Mirjana's eyes flicked over Don Ruy. At times like these, she almost felt as though she could close her eyes and hear culture and refinement coming from this man. His manners could be surprisingly genteel and respectful. It was only when she looked at him that she was reminded he was little more than a barbarian on the hunt for plunder and war.

"This is the story of Salámán and Absál," she told them, "and it was written by a Persian poet named Jámí who wrote these quatrains more than a hundred years ago." A slow smile appeared on Mirjana's firelit face as she saw Tangie creep closer to the fire to hear the love poem.

"It begins with the Shah of Yunan and his counsellor who was the keeper of the Tower of Wisdom. However, the Shah's counsellor was also a cynic. One day the Shah expressed his desire for a son, and his wish was fulfilled by magic! The fond father named his son Salámán and chose Absál for his nurse.

"Absál was a young woman when she took charge of the young babe, and 'as soon as she had opened eyes on him she closed her eyes to all the world beside.' Absál was devoted to the little prince, and because he was a magic babe, she called for a spell to be cast over her to keep her young and lovely until the babe became a man when she could then grow old with him."

Mirjana glanced up and saw that several other men had joined her near the fire, listening to her in rapt attention. Ruy also seemed to be leaning nearer, waiting for her story. "When the young prince came of age, Absál was no older than he, and the two became devoted lovers.

"Together they had spent a joyous year when the knowledge of their attachment came to the ears of the Shah, who admonished his son and suggested hunting in preference to 'dalliance unwise.' The cynical counsellor added his profound wisdom, but these admonitions only prompted the lovers to flee the city. Across desert and sea they went until they came to a most wonderful island, the island of all earthly delights." Satisfied and sympathetic sighs sounded for the young lovers, and Mirjana smiled that these harsh, fighting men could express such gentleness and concern for two young lovers.

"Ah, but that is not the end of the story," Mirjana cautioned, the result of which was to see them leaning in ever closer, the better to hear her every word. "The Shah was aware of his son's 'soul wasting' absence, and he peered into a magic mirror which reflected all the world and saw the lovers on their beautiful island." She dipped her head to the page and read: " 'Looking only into each other's eyes and never finding sorrow there.' "

Padre Tomas was nodding sagely, "*Si, si,* that is the way of love. Pardon, Princesa, please continue."

"Jámí writes about the beautiful Absál:

'Now from her Hair would twine a musky
  Chain,
To bind his Heart — now twist it into
  Curls

Nestling innumerable Temptations;
Doubled the Darkness of her Eyes with
  Surma
To make him lose his way, and over them
Adorn'd the Bows that were to shoot him
  then;
Now to the Rose-leaf of her Cheek would
  add,
Now with a Laugh would break the Ruby
  seal . . .
She solicited his Eyes,
Which she would scarce let lose her for
  a Moment;
For well she knew that mainly by THE
  EYE
Love makes his Sign, and by no other
  Road
Enters and takes possession of the
  Heart.' "

Glancing at Tanige, Mirjana saw she was weeping openly. She had heard this poem before, and she knew the fate of the beautiful lovers. "The Shah was an angry and jealous man," Mirjana told her listeners, "and he placed a wicked spell on them. Salámán and Absál feared their love would be destroyed by the Shah, and they became so melancholy they ventured out into the desert again, this time to cut down branches to make a pyre.

After a last kiss, a last swearing of faithfulness, together they sprang into the fire. They preferred death to losing their love to the demands and jealousies of the world."

Tanige gave an audible sob, and Mirjana herself was blinking back a tear. The men were all silent. Only an uneasy shifting of feet was heard. Ruy was looking at her with his piercing, dark eyes, seeming to read the emotions she was feeling that were stirred by the poem.

Looking up into the night sky, Mirjana pointed out two stars laying so close to one another they might have been one. "There are our lovers, Salámán and Absál. It is said they look down upon all who truly love to protect them from the cynicism of the world. Each night they rise into the sky, burning brightly with their unspoiled love and always within touching distance, one from the other."

Even the burliest of warriors was focusing on the stars overhead, and for a long, long moment all was silent. It was Don Ruy who broke the silence. "Princesa, we are grateful you've shared this poem with us. It is my wish you find all your books available for your use."

As she read, he had felt it was for his ears alone. He had sat by her side, his shoulder intimately touching hers. He had been aware of the sweet, clean scent of her and the way the firelight danced in her strange, translucent eyes. The tumble of her hair, red and gold, yet not truly either, curled around her face in the most fragile wisps and touched her ivory cheeks. He had watched her hands turn the pages of her book, had remembered their softness and gentleness when she had placed her hand in his earlier that afternoon when he pulled her up beside him atop the destrier.

Ruy found himself comparing Mirjana's beauty to the woman in the poem she had just read. A smile formed on his lips as he walked back to his own camp. If the poet had ever laid eyes on the *princesa,* he would have named the girl in his poem Mirjana.

On the sixth day of the seemingly endless journey to Bivar, Ruy announced to the camp that Pietro and he planned to ride through the evening to a nearby convent where he would join his mother and brother who had been attending the sick and infirm. "We will return in the morning to rejoin you," he called to Padre Tomas in a ringing voice. From the sidelong glance he bestowed her, Mirjana knew this was his way of explaining his absence to her.

Strangely, she knew she would miss his presence this evening at the campfire outside her tent, where she had come to the habit of reading from her books to all and any who cared to listen. Ruy was always among the first to appear, and she was always aware of the way he looked at her as she entertained the group. Each night the gathering had become larger, and finally, Ruy had suggested she sit on one of the wagons, the better to be seen and heard by all. But it was he who stood at her feet, looking up into her face, hardly seeming to hear her words at all, but making a study of her face.

Each day at the midday meal, Ruy would come, atop Liberte, and carry her off into a pleasant glade where they would share his rations. She found herself looking forward with anticipation to these private moments, and she was beginning to realize what a remarkable man the infamous El Cid really was. Quick of mind, sharp of wit, and curiously gentle, considering his reputation and appearance. Oftentimes, she would find herself trying to peer beneath his rough exterior and attempting to imagine what he would look like beneath his shaggy, black beard and wolfskin tunic that seemed to double his size.

Only yesterday when she had protested about the rawhide headband he wore with its singular center stud that gave him the look of a Cyclops, he had laughed and removed it. Later, when she saw him again, she noticed he had replaced it.

"Ruy made me promise I would not read a new story tonight," she said to Tanige who was standing nearby and had heard El Cid's call to Padre Tomas about riding out to meet his mother. "I promised I would repeat something I've already read."

Tanige smiled sagely. Of late, Mirjana had taken to referring to him as Ruy instead of "that savage," or "that barbarian!" What had begun as "Don Ruy" was now simply "Ruy" — and it was spoken with an oddly fond note.

"Just what we need," Tanige told her mistress, "a barbarian's mother and his troublesome brother!"

"Hush, Tanige," Mirjana rebuked. "Padre Tomas told me Señora Diaz is a noble woman, and we will have female companionship for the balance of our trip. You must learn to curb that viperous tongue of yours before you cause trouble."

"That is not what I overheard Padre Tomas tell you," Tanige inadvertently confessed to eavesdropping — again. "The priest said the Diaz woman was a devout Christian, that she was powerful and an overprotective mother to her younger son. That does not add up to your expectations, Princess. I believe the Padre was trying to warn you."

Wearily, Mirjana admonished her servant. "Firstly, I do not approve of your eavesdropping. Secondly, I find you too suspicious for your own welfare, Tanige."

"Hrmph! If you had paid more attention to my suspicions in the first place, you never would have sent that letter to El Cid! We would not be in the predicament we are now in, would we?" she challenged the princess to defy the correctness of her statement.

"And just what do you know of our predicament?" Mirjana asked, peering intently at her servant. "For some time now you have given me the impression you know something I do not. What is it? Tell me!"

Tanige gulped and quickly turned away, intent on stirring the contents of her cookpot that sizzled over the low-burning fire. "I know nothing," she answered absently, praying to Allah that the princess would believe her. Not for anything did she want to repeat what she had overheard in Don Ruy's tent.

Mirjana bit her lip. "I hope you're being truthful with me, Tanige. Every time I ask Ruy when he expects to hear from my father, he tells me he does not know and quickly changes the subject. I fear making him angry, so I don't press, but I tell you that each day that passes I become more and more uneasy."

And so you should, Mirjana, Tanige thought

to herself, so you should. Aloud, she asked, "Have you asked Padre Tomas? Surely, he knows something."

"I have also tried to press the good priest, with the same results. I don't believe he is lying, but I think perhaps he is evading the truth."

Tanige bent over her cookfire, refusing to look Mirjana in the eye.

That evening after the meal, Mirjana sat atop the wagon and read again the poem of Salámán and Absál. Again, the men seemed quite moved and thanked her. Padre Tomas walked Mirjana to her tent and bade her a good night.

"Padre, I would like a moment of your time," she told him, a revealing urgency in her voice. "I am most concerned that I have heard nothing from my father. When I left Seville, he was not in the best of health, and I fear something has happened to him."

Padre Tomas gently patted her hand, "Now, now, child. What could have happened that we did not hear? Ruy left runners behind at our first camp, and also we have several men in Seville. Also, the priest that relayed your letter to Ruy has been cautioned to remain on the alert for news. Go into your tent, sleep well, Princesa. Tomorrow will be a long day."

Before she fell asleep, Mirjana reflected on

Padre Tomas's assurances, and was certain Tanige was correct. The priest did know something concerning when Mútadid would pay the ransom for her. Why was everyone keeping it a secret? Why? Not for the first time Mirjana realized she was a prisoner. Regardless of the courtesy and consideration shown her, she was without her freedom, and Don Ruy Diaz, El Cid, had stolen it from her.

Burying her face into her pillow, a mournful groan escaped her. She was so homesick for Seville, aching for the sight of what was familiar. Worse, she felt helpless, nothing more, than a pawn of one man's ambitions. Sleep was a long time coming, and just before her eyes closed, she realized that in the past few days she had hardly given Omar a second thought.

Morning was creeping into the tent, brilliant and warm, waking Mirjana. She glanced at Tanige who lay curled into a ball, oblivious to the hour. It must be well past dawn, Mirjana thought. There seemed to be some commotion outside, and she sat up, thinking that Ruy must have returned with his mother and brother. Was the order given to break camp? If so, she would have to awaken Tanige and prepare for the day's march. She brightened when she thought of meeting Ruy's mother and sharing her company when they camped for the evening.

Cautiously, so as not to draw attention to herself, Mirjana drew back the tent flap. Riding on a rough, open wagon, such as they used for supplies, was one of the most impressive-looking women she had ever seen. Beside her sat a young boy of about ten who was dressed in scarlet velvets and white lace. This could not be Ruy's mother and brother, Mirjana thought incredulously as she peered through the opening. Firstly, the woman appeared too young to have a son as old as Don Ruy. Secondly, in her elegant mourning clothes she appeared too finely bred, too regal. How could she have a son who dresses in wolf-skins and Gothic armor, and possess such fine breeding herself? The two did not add.

Don Ruy stepped into Mirjana's line of vision, and reached up to help the woman from her perch on the wagon. A frown drew Mirjana's brows together as she watched Ruy help his mother. There was no trace of gentleness as the woman slid from the wagon seat into his arms. Even at this distance she could see that his grip was iron hard as he made certain the woman was secure on the ground, and there was no affection in his face when he yanked the young boy down beside her.

The boy shook himself free of his older brother's grasp and marched off in the direction of the bushes.

Tanige scrambled to her feet, wide awake. "Let me see, let me see!" she hissed to Mirjana as she forced her way to the tent flap. In her excitement and curiosity, she lost her balance, and clinging to Mirjana, both of them toppled to the ground. Mirjana was instantly aware of the spectacle they made and of the haughty stare of Doña Ysabel. Her words, while not loudly spoken, carried to Mirjana.

"So, Ruy, these are two heathens you spoke of. Keep them from my sight! I will have nothing to do with savages." With a wide flourish, Doña Ysabel whipped her riding cape about her and walked toward her son's tent.

"Heathens! Did you hear, Princess? She called *us* heathens! So much for your female companionship, Mirjana!" Tanige sputtered. "Are you not going to do something? Are you going to allow her to speak of us in such a manner?"

"What would you have me do, you silly girl? Can you blame her for thinking us savages the way we tumbled out of the tent? We must have appeared like two she-cats, scratching and spitting," Mirjana accused. "Also, we are her son's prisoners and hardly in a position to protest the doings of his mother."

Tanige bristled, her sharp, narrow eyes flaming. "If you will do nothing, then it is up to me to tell that goodly lady of whom she speaks!" Tanige made a move to leave the tent in search of her target.

"No!" Mirjana protested, seizing Tanige by the back of her gown. "Under no circumstances will we lower ourselves to beg courtesy from one who will not give it!" Her tone was harsh; she shook Tanige soundly.

"Speak for yourself, Princess. Look at us, we cannot be lower than we are already! We've begged, pleaded, and almost sold our bodies. What else can we do? I no longer have any pride, and I will do anything I must to survive. And if it helps us to go back to Seville, so much the better!"

Mirjana gasped. "What do you mean, *we* almost sold *our* bodies? Answer me, you stupid girl! Tell me you did not offer us to one of Ruy's men! Tell me!" she cried angrily.

Tanige almost crawled away as she read the intent in Mirjana's eyes to choke the breath from her body. "I will tell you, if it will make you happy. I did try to sell myself, but I could find no buyer. They laughed at me. It was only when I offered you that they showed interest."

Mirjana's hands shook. Color flamed her face, and if ever she wanted to kill, this was the moment. "How could you? Damn your eyes, Tanige! How could you?"

"It was all I could think of to make our escape," Tanige cowered. "Do you want to remain a prisoner the rest of your life? Besides, there was no harm done as there were no bidders," Tanige tried to assure her mistress. "Bah! All of them cowards, saying you belonged to El Cid, and comely as you are, you would be no use to a dead man!"

Heat forged through Mirjana. Her inclination to strike her handmaiden was hard to quell as her arm lifted to aim the blow. "If you ever —"

"Never! Princess Mirjana! Never! I am but a wretched servant and my life rests in your hands. I swear," Tanige whimpered.

"I wish I did own your life because then I would punish you severely. Our lives belong only to Allah. He will decide your fate as well as my own. Go see about breaking our fast. I will think about forgiving you later."

It was an endless day, the first of many. And as each day passed, Mirjana knew that her chances of returning to Seville were becoming dimmer and dimmer.

"This is a damnable outrage!" Tanige exclaimed as the wagon wheel hit yet another rut, bouncing her almost weightless body on the hard wooden bench that served as its seat. The sun beat down upon her unmercifully, and she was wretched with the heat. But most of all, she was frustrated and exasperated with Mirjana's silent acceptance of this insult.

Earlier that day, just when they were breaking camp, Doña Ysabel had spied the comfortable, well-sprung and upholstered carriage, belonging to Princess Mirjana. Never having seen anything as luxurious as this vehicle, the lady had inspected it with a calculating eye. Immediately, she reached the decision that the heathenish princess and her ugly servant should be given her own spartan wagon while she and her youngest son availed themselves of the royal carriage. If this were not enough, she further added to the insult by having Padre Tomas come and annoint the vehicle with a prayer and a sprinkling of holy water to bless it and chase out the devils, which certainly haunted its interior. Then, with a final adjustment of the wimple she wore over her gleaming, dark hair and smoothing the heavy, unrelieved black gown she wore, Doña Ysabel claimed the carriage for her own.

It was Don Ruy who suggested to his mother that she meet the princess and share the wagon with her. Tanige glowered when she recalled the sight the woman had made by pretending to go into a deadly swoon at the thought of associating with a non-Christian. "And she not good enough to lick the dust from your shoes!" Tanige said aloud, only to be painfully elbowed by Mirjana.

She, too, was extremely miserable riding in a supply wagon, but there was a small gratification that Ruy had considered her comfort by suggesting she join his mother in the carriage. It was Mirjana who signaled to him with a shake of her head that he would be unwise to press Doña Ysabel's charity.

"The whole entire family is despicable!" Tanige continued to rant. "The son is a barbarian the youngest son a sniveling brat, and the mother is an imperious dragon! Allah only knows what manner of beast fathered El Cid. To have lain with that one who is his mother he must have had two heads and no heart!"

Again an elbow was painfully jabbed into her side, ordering her silence.

"You, at least, Mirjana, will find the opportunity to wash this dust from your throat when Don Ruy takes you to share his midday meal," she whined. "I will be forced to sit here and nibble on a crust of bread —"

"Will you be quiet!" Mirjana scolded, having heard enough of Tanige's complaints for one day. "You will accept what is given you, and you will please not make me suffer for your inconvenience when I am not the cause."

"And I suppose it was my idea to contact that barbarian in the first place and have him intercept the caravan!"

Mirjana shot her servant a warning glance, "One more word on that subject and you will walk rather than ride! Do you understand? I have noticed you forget yourself, Tanige, and whom you serve. I am still a member of a royal family and you will not forget it."

"You will forget it sooner than myself, Princess," Tanige told her. "Have you ever lived in a Christian household? What do you know of how they treat the people of Islam? We will be fortunate if they spare us from burning at the stake!"

Confused, Mirjana looked askance at Tanige. "What do you mean we will be living in a Christian household? It is only temporary at best. Right this moment there is a messenger who is trying to catch up with us to say the ransom has been paid and we are to be taken back to Seville."

Suddenly silent, Tanige refused to meet her mistress's eyes. She should tell Mirjana what she had overheard, she reasoned, and as she was about to spit out the truth, the trusting look in the princess's eyes quelled her words. Angry as she could be, she could not bear to break the princess's heart. And it surely would break once learning that she was unwanted by her own father who valued the additions made to his treasury more than he valued his own daughter.

When Mirjana jumped down from the wagon, she found her legs and backside stiff and sore. She grimaced in her discomfort, and gingerly rubbed her haunches. "Allah be blessed!" she complained, "I am aching in places I didn't know could ache!"

"At least you have some flesh to cushion you where you sit; pity me!" Tanige joined, likewise rubbing her curveless hips and looking longingly at Mirjana's carriage which was far to the front of their own wagon. "And whose idea was it, do you suppose, to put us back here where the dust is the worst?"

Refusing to join Tanige in her complaints, Mirjana searched the line looking for Ruy to come and ask her to share his midday meal as he had done almost every day since the first. In a moment she saw him atop Liberte, but instead of continuing down the line of wagons, he stopped alongside the carriage where his mother and brother rode. Suddenly, he headed in her direction, riding on Liberte's back as though the legendary hounds of hell were on his trail. As he approached, she could see the hard, angry set of his mouth and the narrowing of his brows over the bridge of his nose. Something had caused him to become angry. Very angry.

Coming abreast of her, he skidded to a stop. "Are you ready, Princesa?" There was a trace of sarcasm in his voice and a hint of mockery in the depths of his mahogany eyes. For her?

"If you would care to forgo our midday meal . . ."

"I asked you if you were ready," he said angrily. "If I had wanted to forgo the meal, I would not have asked, would I?" He reached out his arm for her to grasp and heaved her up into his lap. High off the ground, sitting atop Liberte's strong, equine back, Mirjana almost forgot Ruy's unexplained anger. She loved being up here; she was thrilled that Liberte no longer turned his head back, showing her the whites of his eyes and issuing a warning snort. The destrier had come to expect the added burden of her weight, and without prodding he would prance through the tall grasses, obedient to Ruy's commands.

"He knows he carries a lovely lady on his back," Ruy told her, "and the old devil seems to like it. You've made a friend, Mirjana, and I must keep a vigilance that you don't take his loyalty from me."

"Liberte is too great an animal to be content with a woman for his master, Ruy. He has too much spirit to resign himself to pulling a carriage. He will leave that duty to some others who are not brave enough to carry their masters into battle."

Ruy laughed, the sound very close to her ear and sending little thrills down her spine. This man, she was learning, was a total contradiction in every way. He dressed like a Hun, a barbarian, his grooming appeared to be sadly lacking, and his black eyes burned with a fervor. Yet, when he spoke, there was a refinement in his speech, a certain gallantry that was paradoxical to his appearance. "Do you hear that, Liberte?" Ruy was saying. "The *princesa* has far kinder thoughts about you than she does of your master. How do you do it, old devil? You've won her heart in so short a time!"

"That is because Liberte is a gentleman," Mirjana teased, grateful that Ruy's mood had lightened, feeling some small sense of power that it had been she who had brought about the transformation. She had not liked that dark, glowering expression in his eyes, nor the firm, stubborn set of his mouth behind his thick beard.

"And I am not a gentleman?" he challenged.

"You, sir, are a nobleman. There is a difference, I fear. And it is the highest compliment you will receive from me this day. Content yourself with it and tell me what you've brought for our meal."

Laughing, he told her he had saved a portion of fresh meat from last night's supper and some honeyed figs he had found in one of the caravan supply wagons. Mirjana sighed with contentment. Everyday Ruy had brought her some sweetmeat from the caravan, remembering what she had told him about her sweet tooth.

While they ate, Mirjana watched him carefully, waiting for the right moment to broach the questions that had been haunting her. Finding no way to approach it delicately, she simply blurted, "What do you think is taking my father or Yusuf so long in answering your ransom demands?"

He had been about to bring the wine flask to his lips and nearly spilled the burnished liquid with the suddenness of her question. Recovering himself, he said evasively, "No word had come to me that I was not already aware of when we left our first camp on the March between Seville and Badajoz. Be assured, Mirjana, if circumstances change, you will be the first to know as soon as word comes to me." Of this, Ruy was sincere. He had come to dislike his role as captor. Even more, he disliked the fact that Mirjana believed he was standing between her and her freedom to return to Seville. Yet, those same shreds of nobility prevented him from telling her the truth. She seemed so vulnerable, quite unlike the image he had of her when he received her message imploring him to intercept the passage of her bridal caravan to Granada. Whatever had prompted that move on her part must have been something very close to desperation. While she was smart and clever, he did not see her as calculating and devious. He told himself this strange emotion that flailed delicate wings beneath his breast was nothing more than stirrings of pity for this homeless creature who could look at him with clear, gray eyes which were shadowed by thick, almost sinful, lashes that cast fragile feathery smudges beneath her eyes. He could not even tell her that he had left behind Alfredo, a man of powerful negotiating techniques, to plead her cause with Mútadid. Ransom be damned, he would send her back for a single gold talon if he could but know that her heart would be eased and those doubting shadows in her eyes would be erased.

For a long moment Mirjana stared at him, trying to read the expression it seemed he was taking great pains to hide from her. There was something obtuse in his statements, something she couldn't quite grasp. Brushing crumbs from the front of her gown, she heard the sharp, strident tones of Doña Ysabel from behind the glade of trees screening them from the body of the caravan.

"I will see my son!" she was saying to someone who was protesting her advance. "Save your simpering, Pietro, I demand to see my son, and I command you not to stand in my path! Teodoro, take my arm!" she instructed her youngest son.

Doña Ysabel burst through the trees, her face set in disapproving lines, her flat, dark eyes summing up the situation and conveying disgust. "So, this is how you spend your midday meals, Ruy. You, the Compeador, feeding sweetmeats to this harlot . . . this infidel! Leaving your mother to care for your baby brother and eat soldiers' rations of dry bread and spoiled wine!"

Ruy flashed a glance at Mirjana and then at his mother, who was standing before him, hands braced on her ample hips that even the rusty, black dress she wore could not hide. The filmy, black widow's veil she wore over her head quivered with each word she spoke. Her handsome features were twisted with scorn.

"I assure you, Madre, the wine you were served is not spoiled. However, if you wish to join the *princesa* and me, I am certain there are enough sweetmeats to please you." He extended his arm, gesturing to a place beside Mirjana.

Doña Ysabel was clearly shocked. "You expect me to sit beside that she-devil and eat from the same cloth? You are madder than I imagined! Come with me this instant! You forget this woman is your prisoner, and you spend far too much time with her. God help your soul, Ruy. I pray for you nightly and it does little good. Come! Now!"

Pietro, who had chased after Doña Ysabel, stood helplessly by, his eyes unable to meet Ruy's. "I suggest you return to the caravan with Pietro, Madre," Ruy told her evenly, only his eyes betraying the hostility and insult. "I am not a baby, as you refer to Teodoro," he told her, swinging his glance toward his younger brother who was standing beside their mother with a barely concealed sneer on his face. "And Teodoro would not be considered a baby if he were sent into service as is befitting a boy of his age. Content yourself with keeping one of your sons tied to your corset strings, Madre. Even God must have told you by this time that I am not a man to be ruled and dictated to by his mother."

Mirjana fastened her eyes on the honeyed figs, unable to face Doña Ysabel's scorn and insults. When Ruy spoke of Teodoro going into service, she knew he was referring to the custom of boys being sent to neighboring noblemen who would train them first as pages, then squires, and finally as knights of the realm. During one of their midday meals, Ruy had told her that he himself had been sent away from home at the age of eight to Don Michel Torreto's home in Tarranga, where he received his training. Doña Ysabel was determined not to part with Teodoro, refusing to have arrangements made to send him away for training. She preferred to keep him at her side, spoiling him obsessively, twisting his natural inclinations of boyhood into something recognizable only as unbecoming feminine traits. Mirjana was embarrassed by this confrontation between mother and son, and she could feel her cheeks flaming. It was perfectly clear to any and all that Ruy had little liking for either his young brother or his mother.

After a painfully long moment, Ruy got to his feet and stalked away, leaving her alone with Doña Ysabel and Teodoro. Pietro had slipped back into the shadows of the trees. She could feel the woman's piercing, dark eyes on her, and Mirjana's own were drawn upward, meeting the silent challenge. Still a handsome woman, it was evident that Doña Ysabel had been quite beautiful in her youth. Even now, there was a regality in her bearing. Black hair so much like Ruy's, holding the same blue highlights and gleaming like satin, was pulled back into a severe bun at the back of her head. Gleaming like oiled silk, its only relief was two startling streaks of white winging back from her temples, seeming to emphasize the straight, finely drawn brows and flashing dark eyes. Skin still smooth with only the faintest traces of expression lines, neck long and graceful, despite the softening along the jowls, the señora evidently took pains in preserving her beauty. A vain woman, and one obviously used to having her demands met, Doña Ysabel glared at Mirjana with unconcealed hatred. Without a word, she grasped Teodoro's arm and pulled him toward her, directing him to escort her through the glade back to the carriage she had confiscated from Mirjana. Issuing an order to the waiting Pietro to drive her back to the caravan, she left Mirjana alone with the unfinished meal and a heavy, ominous sensation in the pit of her stomach.

Resolutely, Mirjana got to her feet and began gathering up the cloth and the uneaten food. It would be a long walk back to the caravan. Instantly, the thought crossed her mind that if she had a mind to, she could run off in the opposite direction. She could run and run until the breath left her body, and when it returned, she could run again, away from Doña Ysabel, away from El Cid, Compeador, back to Seville and her father. Her eyes stretched to the far southern horizon and she knew the futility of the idea. They were miles from civilization, and the wilderness would not be kind to a woman alone. Inexplicably, she was loath to leave the security Ruy offered. What Doña Ysabel had said about her being his prisoner was true, but even being a captive was preferable to dying alone on the Marches between wherever she was now and the city of Seville. Also, she knew that even under the best of circumstances she could never make an escape from Ruy. He would scour the countryside until he found her. And remembering the power of his rage, she trembled. He was not a man she wished to anger.

Folding the cloth on which they had placed their food, Mirjana suddenly hesitated, realizing she was the one who should be angry! What right had he to bring her out so far from the caravan and then leave her to the mercies of his mother? He had merely gotten to his feet and stalked off, leaving her, uncaring of the long walk she was now forced to make! Bending over and grasping his wine flask, she tightened her grip around the slim, polished metal. And to think she had actually found herself admiring the way he had stood up to

Doña Ysabel, refusing to allow her to incite his rage, refusing to accede to her demands. But he had after all, hadn't he? Just as his mother had commanded, he had left her to return to the caravan, paying his obedience to the Doña Ysabel! He was cowed by his mother after her lip in distaste, especially in a man who is claimed to be a legend among the warriors. Warrior! Bah! These all! An ugly trait in a man, Mirjana told herself, curling afternoons she had thought they had formed a truce, a friendship even. She had believed she meant something to him, that he liked her. Obviously, this was not so. If he cared for her at all, he never would have left her to get back to the caravan on her own, abandoning her. Mirjana gulped back her confusion. Abandonment was something she was becoming quite familiar with of late. Filled with frustration, she raised her arm, hand clutching his wine flask, intending to hurl it into the brush.

"If you are determined to bounce that flask off my head, you should take better aim. I am over here." Ruy stepped out from the cover of trees to stand in full sunshine. The suddenness of his unexpected appearance brought a startled cry from Mirjana.

"I thought you had returned to the caravan . . ."

"You must think me a barbarian, Princesa,

to think I would allow you to walk such a distance unassisted." He flashed a smile to soften his teasing, his teeth very white against his black, cropped beard.

Mirjana lowered her arm, standing with a contrite expression on her face. "I did consider myself abandoned," she said softly.

"Never by me," he told her, realizing the impact of his words and the truth they held for him. "You have yet to learn that I never comply with a woman's shrill demands, even if that woman be my own mother." He was laughing, the sun bringing out the brilliance of his hair, the sparkle in his eyes, making him appear much younger than she gauged him. "Here, look, I've brought you something. I only left you long enough to return to Liberte's saddlebag to retrieve it."

He was standing very close to her, towering over her, and to look at him she had to throw back her head. He was holding a small, inlaid, camphorwood box which held her favorite trinkets saved from childhood. Eagerly, she took it into her hands, holding it close to her. "How did you know? How did you find it?" she asked him. "It was given to me when I was very young. It was my mother's." Gray eyes, the color of a dove's underwing, glistened with unshed tears.

"I thought it would make you happy, Mirjana. If I had thought it would make you cry, I never would have brought it to you." His face had fallen into concerned lines, his thick brows drawing together over the bridge of his nose.

"I am happy you've given it to me. It is just . . . that . . ."

"That you are a woman and very sentimental, yes?"

"Yes." Her fingers traced the familiar pattern of the Oriental rooster on the top of the hinged lid.

"I hear it rattling. Aren't you going to show me the secrets a young girl collects?" He was leading her back toward the shade of the trees, sitting down beside her, leaning against the gnarled trunk of a witch hazel tree.

Carefully, Mirjana opened her box, smelling the familiar and loved scent of the camphorwood from which it was made. Inside there were various bits of ribbon and stray beads and even a small vial containing the dried petals of a flower.

The next hour was spent describing the mementos she had saved and the events they commemorated. It was such an easy time, a happy time. There were moments when she would suddenly glance up and see Ruy looking down at her with amusement in his eyes. When she held up a tiny bell from the collar of her first kitten and she described her sorrow when it had died, she imagined she saw her grief reflected in those same eyes.

Before long, Ruy was telling her about his first pony, and how he remembered his own father sitting atop the finest stallion he had ever seen, finer even than Liberte. Then he told her of his father, Rodrigo Diaz, for whom he was named, and how he had acquired the nickname of Ruy. But came the time when he announced they must return to the caravan. They would arrive in Bivar by late afternoon of the following day, he told her offhandedly, expecting that she would be relieved that the long journey was almost over.

Riding across Ruy's knees, atop Liberte's strong back, Mirjana was filled with apprehension at arriving at Bivar. It was so far away from Seville, she told herself. And she was not looking forward to living in contact with Doña Ysabel. The look of contempt in that woman's eyes still haunted her, and Mirjana knew with certainty the Doña would be — and was — a formidable enemy.

Later, Mirjana would take consolation through the long, uncertain night from the small camphorwood box Ruy had been thoughtful enough to bring to her. He had known it was much loved by her, he had told her, by the wear the brass clasp displayed and also by the girlish souvenirs contained within. Mirjana was pleased and surprised that one as important and powerful as the infamous El Cid, Compeador, would concern himself with the things that were most important to her — his prisoner.

CHAPTER 5

Mirjana's bridal caravan out of Seville, driven by soldiers of El Cid, followed closely behind the marching infantrymen. Progress had slowed because the rounded foothills were becoming steeper and were more difficult for the carriages and wagons to transverse as they approached Bivar. Mirjana and Tanige clung to the sides of the supply wagon to brace themselves against the worst of the bone-jarring shaking the springless vehicle was affording.

Tanige stared at the familiar camphorwood box Mirjana was showing her. Her astringent, small brown eyes then peered up into her mistress's face. "It surprises me that you can be so pleased that El Cid pirates your own personal possessions and you accept them as gifts!" she told Mirjana acidly. "They are yours to begin with and cost him nothing! He should only match what his dear mother, Doña Ysabel, has taken for herself, then perhaps you would have something."

Mirjana looked at her servant open-mouthed. She had never considered that she had displayed foolish gratitude over Ruy's so-called generosity.

"Even that boy, Teodoro, has taken some valuable items for himself. This minute he is wearing the silver bracelets with the tiny bells you received on your thirteenth birthday. Doña Ysabel has taught her sons the art of thievery, and they've learned it quite well. That is where El Cid has learned to plunder for his own gains. Right there, at his own mother's knee!"

"Has it occurred to you, Tanige, that the arrangement between El Cid and myself called for him to take possession of the caravan?" Mirjana defended, not caring for the challenge her servant hinted at that she should protest the confiscation of the goods.

"And has it occurred to you, Princess, that although the bargain was struck it was never carried out? Here you are, along with me, riding north into Bivar instead of back to Seville. Correct me, but that was the bargain, was it not?" Immediately, Tanige was sorry she had spoken. Mirjana was looking at her again in that questioning way, suspecting that her servant knew more about why they had not been returned to Seville than she would admit. However tempted she was at times to burst the princess's optimistic bubble, this was a pain she could not bring herself to inflict. Not yet. Eager to draw Mirjana's thoughts away from the terms of the bargain, Tanige complained, "Have you noticed the hateful way Doña Ysabel stares at us?"

"Have I noticed?" the question was almost a cry.

"Learn to accept it, Princess. You'll find no comfort from that quarter, believe me. She sees you as a threat to her infamous son. Me, she discounts as a servant of little importance. Little does she know that I am your only living confidante," Tanige said smugly. "When we arrive in Bivar you will be reduced to a servile position. We will be equals, and both of us turned to the señora's service."

Tanige was rewarded when Mirjana gasped, "What? Where did you ever hear such a thing? Bite your tongue, Tanige! We will be returning to Seville! Who told you such lies?"

"From the boy, Teodoro — Teddy, as his mother sometimes calls him."

Mirjana was relieved. "He's only a child. What does he know? Must you believe everyone and everything you hear? For a moment you had me believing our fate would be in Doña Ysabel's merciless hands."

"Wait. See if I am not right. The boy knows, Mirjana. He delighted in telling me how he torments the servants —"

"Tell me no more. You forget, Tanige, we will be returning to Seville! You talk as though we are to live out a life's sentence as prisoners and servants in Bivar. You forget I am much more valuable as a hostage than as a servant, and El Cid is well aware of this fact! And so should you be!"

"You are far too innocent, Mirjana!" Tanige spit out angrily. After all, it wasn't her own foolish tricks that had brought them to their present situation. "Do not be so certain you have all the facts in hand! Have you wondered why El Cid's ransom is so tardy in being met? Even a princess must question her own worth from time to time . . ." Tanige swallowed back her words. She had already said too much, and the white-faced shock of Mirjana quickly brought her to her senses. Regardless of all else, she had decided she would not be the one to break the news to her mistress.

"Continue!" Mirjana ordered, knowing there was something of vital importance Tanige was withholding. "You were about to say something, Tanige, and I want to know what it was."

Lowering her head, refusing to face the one with whom she had spent the better part of her life and knew better than she knew another living soul, Tanige muttered, "I beg your forgiveness. My tongue does me disservice oftentimes, as you well know. It is only that I fear what lays before us." Curling herself into a ball, she lowered herself to the floor of the wagon and pretended to seek sleep, leaving Mirjana filled with unanswered questions.

Looking ahead to the front of the long column of men, Mirjana picked out Liberte's strong, powerful body and his dark-haired rider. Worms of apprehension crawled in her belly. There was something she was not aware of, something that Tanige and Ruy and even Padre Tomas were keeping from her. But what? Tonight, she vowed, she would approach Ruy and demand answers from him. She would beg him to release her and Tanige, allow them to return to Seville. Desperation, an emotion with which she was becoming all too familiar, roiled within her. Freedom was a precious commodity, she was quickly learning, and well worth fighting for. Desperate straits called for desperate moves, and she would prepare herself to make them.

Ruy rode at the head of the procession of infantry, allowing Liberte to choose his own route. His head was filled with contradictions and confusion, an unallowable state of affairs for one who prided himself on his quick decisions and actions. And Mirjana was the center of his confusion.

Only moments before a courier had reached him with the news that Mútadid was dead and Hassan had ascended the throne. He had held hope that Mútadid's paternal sympathies for Mirjana could be stirred. Hassan was a reprobate and had no sympathies. Hope was dead. Pietro, who knew him better perhaps than any other living man, looked askance at his leader's behavior since capturing the *princesa*. The midday breaks when he would take his meal with Mirjana were too lengthy, he knew. He ordered the end to the day's march too quickly, setting up camp when there were still hours of daylight left. Ordinarily, they would have reached Bivar two days ago, but what Ruy liked to think of as his deference to the women had cost them precious time. The men were eager to be home. Some of them would still have long distances to travel beyond Bivar to reach their destinations, and they were becoming disgruntled with the delays.

Stiffening his shoulders and straightening in the saddle, Ruy clamped his knees into Liberte's flanks. Let the men be disgruntled, he told himself. He was their leader, their general, and they were under his command. With rank came privilege, and it was at his own discretion to avail himself of it. Ever since receiving the missive from the *princesa*, his life had turned over. He had, at first, admired the spirit the girl had displayed in finding a way to control her own destinies. She was repulsed by the idea of traveling to Granada to become one of Yusuf's wives and had done something about it. If only he hadn't tried to turn the situation to his better advantage. He should have contented himself with the original bargain — taken the caravan, and allowed her to return to Seville. Now, all had changed and he was responsible for her. The unbidden image of Mirjana stepping out of the stream where he had first found her bathing flashed before him. He had thought her beautiful then, and more so now. Those long midday meals he took with her had become the highlight of his day, second only to listening to her read her books of poetry before the campfire each night. At midday, he had her all to himself. The sun shone down on her hair, illuminating the tousle of burnished curls that feathered around her cheeks and at the soft nape of her neck. Her skin was the color of honeyed milk, smooth and tempting to the touch. How often he had found himself wanting to place his lips on the sweet curve of her throat and taste the nectar of her lips. She was by far the most desirable woman he had ever met. And desire her, he did. Even now, thinking about her, there was a stirring in his loins and a tightening in the muscles of his thighs. That he had come to admire her only added to his desires. At night he had found himself dreaming about her, welcoming her into his visions, fantasizing that during their solitary midday meal she would entice him into seducing her, yielding herself to his lips, to his hands. . . .

Ruy jabbed his heels into Liberte's flanks, spurring the beast onward, needing the rush of air to sing past his head to cool his thoughts. Dreams were forbidden desires, he had once heard, and he knew it would be true. He was quite unused to denying himself the pleasure of a woman once he decided upon it, but in Mirjana's case it would only complicate matters. Yusuf was already claiming she had been defiled and using it as his excuse to reject her. To fulfill his own desires Ruy knew would only make the old bastard's words true and spoil any chance of Mirjana being reaccepted into her own society. It would undo any chance she might have for a fitting marriage.

Slapping the palm of his hand across Liberte's rump, he drove the animal forward, trying to escape his confusion, running away from his desires and wondering when, if ever, he had ever concerned himself with a woman's future once he had used and discarded her.

By the onset of evening, when the day's march had ended to make camp, Mirjana was half sick from the beating sun and the bone-wrenching ride in the wagon, whose wheels, it seemed, never failed to find the ruts and depressions in the grassy plains they crossed. Departing from his usual routine, Ruy had pushed his column of men unmercifully late into the afternoon, leaving barely enough time to start fires and cook suppers. Mirjana assumed it was because, as he had told her, they would arrive in Bivar the next day, and he was eager to be home and relieved of his duties at the head of his army. She could not know that it was the confusion she caused him and his own unwillingness to admit that he had eased the number of miles covered daily out of deference to her and also his own desire to spend a large part of each day in her company.

Gratefully, she had accepted a large ewer of fresh water shyly offered by a foot soldier whom she recognized as being a frequent listener around her campfire when she read from her books. Weary to the point of exhaustion, she only wanted to bathe with the cool water and change into fresh clothing, eat, and then sleep. Tonight it would be impossible. Tonight, after supping, she was determined to find Ruy and beg him to set Tanige and herself free to return to Seville. Something had gone amiss, she knew it; she could feel it in her bones. And Tanige, since their conversation earlier that afternoon, still refused to meet her eyes, busying herself with unnecessary chores, or pretending to sleep. Whatever it was, Tanige knew. And Ruy knew. And after tonight, she would know.

While Mirjana performed her toilette, Ruy was at the far end of the camp, barking to several of his drivers, ordering repairs of damages suffered to the wagons by the hard day's ride. The objects of his vented fury glanced at one another quizzically. Since when did El Cid ever concern himself with the details of the wheelwrights, or any of the other craftsmen who accompanied his infantry? El Cid occupied himself with decisions, the methods of winning battles, not with the greasing of axles and the forging of new iron rims for wagon wheels. The glances also spoke of their leader's strange behavior of late and of his wide swings of mood from benign benefactor to raging taskmaster.

Pietro, huge arms folded across his massive chest, stood in the background, watching his friend and leader. Rubbing his fingers through his wild, black beard, his eyes twinkled with speculation. Without a doubt, Princesa Mirjana was responsible for Ruy's mercurial behavior. Strange and unpredictable occurrences could be attributed to his friend since his plans to ransom the *princesa* had fallen through. Not the least of them was Ruy's sudden concern for trimming his beard and brushing his tangle of dark hair and rubbing his teeth several times a day with salt grains, not to mention his preoccupation for immersing himself in the cold streams that randomly wove their lazy paths across the plains.

"What are you looking at, Pietro?" Ruy demanded, refiring his anger when he realized he was the target of his friend's amused speculation. "Have you little else to do besides stand there gawking while I attend to your duties? Have these wagons ready before morning, or I hold you responsible!" Not waiting for an answer, Ruy stalked back towards his tent, stopping occasionally to scold one or another of his men before continuing to his destination.

Passing over a hillock behind Mirjana's tent, Ruy's eyes went unwillingly to the structure, seeing the fabric of the walls billowing gently in the breeze. A lamp was lit within, and he could see the shadowy image of a slender figure with arms raised over her head against the quickly descending twilight. Mirjana. His step faltered and his gaze fastened on the silhouette, imagining her as she brushed that riot of golden curls that defiantly framed her lovely face and enhanced the graceful length of her tender, curving neck. It was as though he could see through the obstructing tent, her image coming to him with the force of a blow: smoky gray eyes, like cinders in their intensity, fringed by thick, golden-tipped lashes; smooth, sloping shoulders; and round, feminine limbs, long of bone and smooth of flesh that lent to her grace and delicacy. The silhouette against the tent fabric trembled with the uncertainty of a candle flame, and that trembling was echoed within him — a quivering awareness of her, a shivering down the length of his spine, and an aching longing to take her in his arms and feel the fragility of her against him while he delighted in the fragrance of her skin and the softness of her hair. . . .

This desire for her was becoming maddening! Hours that would be better spent thinking of other things were filled with thoughts of her! If he didn't take control of himself soon, he would be useless as a warrior and fit only for chasing butterflies across the fields.

Leaving the hillock quickly, almost at a run, Ruy tore himself away from the wavering silhouette on Mirjana's tent wall, and covered the distance around the perimeter of tents until at last reaching the solitude of his own. He needed to think, dispassionately, coldly, to make a decision as to what he would do with this Islamic princess who was unwanted by her family and her intended husband. Solitude was not to be his. Waiting within his tent was Doña Ysabel who was sitting with her youngest son, Teodoro, popping honeyed figs into the boy's already too plump cheeks. Upon seeing Ruy enter, she jumped to her feet, meeting him head on.

"What are your intentions concerning that — that unholy devil you've brought among us?" she demanded, that strident, commanding note in her voice that he had come to hate.

"That depends upon what you mean by 'intentions,' Madre," he told her mockingly, insolently, purposely pretending to be obtuse in order to frustrate her.

"Intentions!" she told him. "Don't pretend not to understand me, Ruy. I want to know what you plan to do with her and her servant. I warn you, my house has been blessed, and only Christians are welcome there. In my day, those heathens were burned at the stake. And so they still should be. Were it not for these new tenderhearted politics King Sancho has adopted concerning these Muslims, the Way of the Cross and religion would not suffer these infidels among us."

"I hadn't realized you were conversant in politics, Madre," Ruy added to her frustration, sending a stern eye in Teodoro's direction that made the boy hesitate for an instant before popping another fig into his sticky mouth. "And in trust, Madre, you must admit that you have no house. The *castillo* in Bivar is mine alone, left to me by my father."

"As is the responsibility of a nobleman to behave as an example for the people of Bivar. If you continue to consort with infidels, your people will lose all respect for you."

"I must admire you, Señora, for your concern. However, I am certain you are only concerned for yourself and your pet, Teodoro. As I have told you, until circumstances change, the *princesa* and her servant will abide with me at the *castillo.* Would you have it said that in the midst of all our Christianity she was sent to live in the stables?"

Doña Ysabel's complexion darkened. Her piercing dark eyes were shot with fury, giving her a startling resemblance to her eldest son when his own ire was raised. "So, are we all to pay for your schemes that have misfired? Don't look so shocked, Ruy. How long did you expect your secret kept? I have known since the first day I joined you that the girl's brother as well as her intended husband in Granada refuse to acknowledge her."

"And who, may I ask, told you such?" Ruy pretended indifference, but all the while there was a ceaseless pounding in his brain and a heaviness in his chest. If Doña Ysabel knew the circumstances, it would only be a matter of time before Mirjana knew. For reasons unrevealed to himself, Ruy wanted to be the one to break the news to her. He would try to do it gently, all the while reassuring her that he would take an interest in her future and continue discussions on her behalf with Mútadid and Yusuf.

Doña Ysabel's eyes quickly flickered to Teodoro and back to Ruy. "I have my sources," she told him uncertainly, ready to place herself between Teodoro and Ruy's hostility.

"And are these sources content to stuff themselves with honeyed figs?" he asked solemnly, his tone deceivingly indolent. Lightning-quick reflexes charged Ruy, and within the space of a breath his grip tightened on Teodoro's tunic and he hauled the astonished boy to his feet. Doña Ysabel gasped, her hands flying to her mouth, and then outstretched, reaching for her baby, making a vain attempt to protect him from his older brother.

"How often have I warned you, Teodoro, about listening to conversations which are not meant for your ears?" The fury of Ruy's voice reverberated through the tent as he hoisted the boy off the ground and shook him soundly.

"Put him down! Put him down!" Doña

Ysabel screamed, rushing forward to pound on Ruy's back. Teodoro, seeing he had his mother's support, began to wail at the top of his lungs, his too plump face screwed into a mask of terror.

"See what you do to him!" the señora cried. "Give him to me, he meant no harm!"

Ruy dropped Teodoro suddenly, the boy's short, fat legs crumbling beneath him, sending him sprawling on his back. "*Beastia!* Beast! He is only a baby! Leave him be!"

"Were my father alive this day he would be sickened by what you have made of his youngest son!" Ruy said with disgust. "He will never become a man as long as he is sheltered beneath your wing," he told his mother.

"You hate him!" she cried, pressing Teodoro's head against her bosom, cradling him in her arms, protecting him from Ruy's further advances.

"No! I could never hate my own brother. Hate is too strong a word. He sickens me; he is a stain on the family name of Diaz. And he has only you, Madre, to thank for it. There will come a day, I warn you, when he will turn on you and despise you for making him a weakling."

"You promised, Ruy, over your father's deathbed. You promised you would never take

Teodoro away from me. It was already too late to save you, my eldest, from the dangers of war. You swore you would never take my baby. He is all I have left in this world." There was a desperate note in the señora's voice. Her eyes challenged Ruy to deny the promise he had made her.

"Teodoro was a babe in arms when our father died. You were a widow and I took pity on you. I would have promised you anything. I never thought you would keep Teodoro at your side like the daughter God saw fit to deny you. I never thought it would become a question of taking the boy from you. I merely assumed when the time for his training came you would send him yourself."

"Ruy, please, your mother begs you . . ."

Looking down at his mother, Ruy was filled with pity, both for her and for Teodoro. Her obsessive love for the child was destructive; if only she could see it. He didn't like to see Doña Ysabel this way, stripped of her authority, naked without her regal, haughty bearing, begging. Retreating to the back of the tent, turning his back on both of them, he said, "Leave me. Take the boy with you."

Rising to her feet, Doña Ysabel tugged Teodoro's arm, pulling him up with her. The boy sobbed pitifully, starting to follow her, but not until he had reached for another honeyed fig from the dish near Ruy's foot.

Glancing down, Ruy saw the boy greedily fill his mouth and look up to meet his brother's eyes with a self-satisfied smirk twisting his too pretty features. Pushed beyond disgust, Ruy reached down and seized the boy by the scruff of his neck, and lifted him off the ground for the second time. A bellow of rage erupted as Ruy carried the squirming, wailing child to the flap of his tent and tossed him out like so much rubbish. Aghast at this sudden turn of events, Doña Ysabel ran after them, intent on rescuing her baby from Ruy's clutches.

This was the scene Mirjana happened upon as she approached El Cid's tent. She had heard his bellow of rage and then witnessed the young boy, Teodoro, making a swift and hasty exit on the tip of Ruy's boot. She saw Doña Ysabel run to her youngest son beneath the onslaught of Ruy's loudly voiced epithets and heard Teodoro's open-mouthed, high-pitched wails of terror as he clung to his mother.

"Allah be merciful!" Mirjana whispered, stepping back into the shadows, shocked by this outburst of emotions. In her own culture tirades and uncontrolled emotions were frowned upon. Never, until she had been thrust among these hot-blooded Castilians, had she ever witnessed such a shocking display of passions.

As Doña Ysabel spirited Teodoro away under her comforting ministrations, Ruy continued his fury, kicking at a stockpile of supplies and armor stacked outside his tent, scattering the objects far and wide and into the shadows where Mirjana stood. An iron cookpot rolled to her feet, and she waited with trepidation as Ruy's eyes followed it. She wanted to run, to pretend she had never observed this chaotic family squabble. This was certainly not the time, she told herself, to plead for El Cid's mercy to send her back to Seville. Inwardly, she was trembling with the realization of his power and temper. She had come tonight prepared to say anything, do anything, that would gain her freedom; to beg, to plead, and to promise anything to secure her release. Now, all her hopes were dashed. Certainly, in his black mood, the infamous El Cid could not be persuaded.

He stood with his back to the fire, arms akimbo, staring at her. She could feel the heat of his gaze, could see the breadth of his shoulders and the firm stance of his powerful thighs outlined by the light. The wolfskins he wore over his leather jerkin added to his girth, and he seemed to her to be a monster of a man, more ready to do battle than to hear the pitiful pleas of a woman in distress.

"And to what do I owe this unexpected pleasure, Princesa?" he said gruffly, mockingly, his lamp-black eyes fixed upon her, filling her with freezing terror. Once before she had heard him use that tone with her, and she knew from experience it did not bode well for her.

Ruy was taken aback at seeing Mirjana outside his tent. How much had she heard? In spite of all his precautions, did she now know of her predicament with Hassan and Yusuf? How could she help but blame him for his interference that had reduced her to the status of a pariah, an outcast? And then to have her catch him having a tantrum that was only worthy of a child like Teodoro, not the great warrior who had earned the title of Cid! He watched through narrowed eyes as Mirjana cautiously stepped out of the shadows. Her form was a silhouette, and he was again reminded of the intimate scene he had witnessed against the backdrop of light on the wall of her tent as she was performing her toilet. He saw her step falter once, and noticed her hands were clenched at her sides. A wry smile tugged at the corners of his mouth. She was going to ask for a favor. Woefully, he realized what it must be.

There was a pride in her bearing that stirred

his admiration. She had begged no special favors; the treats and gifts he had brought her from the caravan were of his own design. She was not a woman to whine and cry. Even when Doña Ysabel had confiscated Mirjana's luxurious carriage for her own use she had not come complaining. If only all women were like Mirjana, his mother included. A fresh wave of anger seethed through him as he thought of his mother's complaints and directives, and of Teodoro's unending pranks, and how the boy insisted upon making a general nuisance of himself. Just as soon as matters were settled in Bivar and his household returned to normal after his long absence, he would take the boy in hand and make a man of him. Returning his attention to Mirjana, he saw that she had stepped close enough to the fire for the light to reveal her features, but not quite close enough should he reach out a hand to touch her.

She was elusive, like a cat in the dark, he told himself. Gentle, intelligent, yet a woman of spirit and fight. Her hair was a brighter shade of gold in this light, and her smooth complexion, many shades lighter than his own, took on the look of polished ivory. She was beautiful and unattainable — two qualities that never failed to challenge him.

A small curl of heat circled his belly, making

him aware again that it had been a long time since he had lain with a woman. Too long! And yet he knew he would have waited for a hundred years if he was promised the delightful charms this woman could offer at the end of that time.

"If you have a moment for me," Mirjana began tentatively. Then, becoming bolder, "I would like a word with you," she added firmly.

"You're tardy, Princesa. I expected you days ago." His tone was smug, almost insolent, and it grated on Mirjana's nerves. She would not allow him to undo her resolve. She must remember she was her father's daughter, daughter of a king! She would stand her ground, even in the face of his power.

"Did you?" How cool her voice was. A pity that composure was a mask and that inwardly she was trembling, shaking, fearing to face this man who held the rest of her life in his hands. Silently, he gestured to the opening of his tent, beckoning her within. She knew he was aware of her gravity, and yet he motioned her to sit beside him atop his pallet of blankets and furs. She was quick to notice that several satin covered pillows from the caravan had found their way to his bed.

"I will always have a moment for you, Mirjana," he told her quietly, making it difficult for her to believe this was the same man who had thrown his little brother and mother out of his tent in a torrent of anger. His eyes perused her, taking in the tousle of curls swirling about her shoulder and the soft amber dress with its wide flaring sleeves that revealed a finely stitched kirtle with long, wrist-hugging sleeves and high, laced neckline.

Mirjana stiffened her shoulders. "I want to know what is to become of Tanige and myself. I feel that by this time you must have had word from Seville. You told me we will reach Bivar tomorrow. It is your home, Ruy, not mine. I want to return to Seville. You have it in your power to grant my wish. The ransom will be met, I assure you. Return me to my father's house."

The curl of heat in his belly was like a snake, writhing and twisting and creeping through his loins. He stared at her for a long moment. How proud she was, sitting quietly beside him, making her request. And he recognized it was a request. She was making no demands. She was not pleading or begging as he had thought she might. How was he to tell her the truth — that no one, save himself, seemed to want her? What would happen to that proud woman? Would she weep inconsolably? Would her straight, slim shoulders slump, and her beautiful gray eyes become lusterless when all hope was gone? And the beautiful voice — would it become dreary and dead, or even strident and whining? He could bear her anger and belligerence, even her fury and sarcasm, but he knew that her defeat would in some way be his own. He had to light a spark in her and keep it smoldering until he could make amends with her brother. Bait her, make her angry, hold out hope.

When he spoke, his voice rumbled from deep within his chest, harshly, coldly. "You are my prisoner, Mirjana. You have nothing that is not mine already. You have nothing to barter for your freedom."

Mirjana bristled at this tone. How had she thought they were becoming friends during those midday hours when they would talk and laugh and forget they came from worlds apart? She peered at him through slitted eyes. "What price did you demand of my father for my return?" she demanded.

"I asked for the Taifa of Seville. Is a kingdom too great a price for Mútadid's daughter? Is he fool enough to part with a kingdom for a woman?" Ruy said churlishly.

"Only a fool would ask such a price!" Mirjana snapped. "I come to you for straight answers."

"I have given you the answer, Princesa. You are my prisoner, my hostage. Consider it the beginning and end of your inquiry." Inwardly, Ruy was wincing for the coward he was. He should tell her now, break the news, and the devil take the hindmost. He sympathized with Mirjana for the uncertainty of her future, yet the words would not come to his lips. The courage to witness her pain escaped him.

Although his attitude was churlish and even taunting, Mirjana suspected this was a guise. Ruy wanted her to believe his ransom demands were outrageous, but she knew him to be too clever to overplay his hand. No, there was something besides a handsome ransom that interested him. And his remark that she had nothing to barter for her freedom seemed to be baiting. This puzzled her. If he knew she was in possession of something that would buy her freedom, why did he not tell her outright? Lifting her chin, she found herself gazing into his eyes, recognizing the glow of desire there. So, this then was his price. Mirjana swallowed hard, random fears penetrating her sensibilities. How badly did she want her freedom? What price would she willingly pay?

Breaking away from her speculative stare, Ruy busied himself by pouring two goblets of the strong, raw wine he favored while campaigning. Offering one of the wooden goblets to Mirjana, he dared her to accept it, remembering she had told him it was against her religion to imbibe. Soft gray eyes stared into his, and he felt her cool, slim fingers touch his as she took the goblet. The wine was deep red, spilling onto her hand, staining her fingers.

"You will find it a strong drink, Princesa, heady and raw. The kind we soldiers prefer while campaigning. Hardly boiled forty times as are the ceremonial wines of your people." He was becoming uncomfortably aware of the stirrings within him. Christ be praised! She was beautiful. Even now, sitting here alone with him, when he could almost smell her fear, she kept herself poised and serene. An unsettling trait in a woman, he told himself, used as he was to quick-tempered women of his own race.

"It surprises me, my lord, that you have such knowledge of my culture. However, if it will please you that I drink with you, then I shall." She brought the goblet to her lips and drank deeply, feeling the liquid burn her throat and heat her innards. The sensation was shocking but not unpleasant, and she was satisfied to see the speculative gleam in his eyes. She knew he was thinking that if she would go against her principles to drink the forbidden wine, what other transgression might she commit against the laws of Muhammad?

Mirjana held the goblet carefully so as not to spill its contents. Sitting, she braced her arm on her lap in an effort to keep it from trembling. This man frightened her. She knew his temper, his power. Before she lost her courage, she persisted on her original line of reasoning. "Allow me to return to Seville. Tanige and I can fend for ourselves. Have you no compassion, Ruy? These past days I thought I had come to know you. I see now I was wrong. You will be rewarded, I promise you this, as long as you are realistic in your demands."

Ruy drank deeply of his wine, almost as though he were postponing his answer. "I have my Christian duty to see to your safety. At the moment, I am solely responsible for you."

"Do not speak to me of your Christian duty," Mirjana railed. "I have heard from Padre Tomas how you ignore the precepts of your church and its laws. You flaunt your wicked ways and seek the blessings of a priest. Spare me, Ruy, keep to your habits and ignore your 'Christian duty,' as you call it." Fearing her anger would overcome her better sense and she would say too much, she gulped her wine.

"The gravity of the situation still escapes you, Princesa. You are a prize and I am your keeper. Until your future is settled, you will remain in my keeping, and you will not continue to annoy me with pleas for your freedom."

"I am a woman, not a prize. I am a human being with needs and emotions, unlike you who care for nothing but lining your pockets with my father's gold. You are a mockery of all I believe in. You are less than a man. Look at you! Wearing wolfskins and armor, looking and smelling like a two-legged goat! You show no respect for anyone or anything. You are coarse and crude, a true descendant of the Huns, and you are everything I detest in a man!" Mirjana spat her loathing.

Ruy grinned. "Yet you sit here in my tent, drinking my wine, affording yourself of my protection, and offending yourself with my bad odor while you consider your next move to gain your freedom. If you could, at this moment, you would cheerfully kill me! Admit it!" Although his tone was amused, there was danger in his eyes. He noticed she had drained her goblet, and he refilled it.

Mirjana sat sipping her wine. She didn't care for the taste of it, and her nose wrinkled in objection. But she continued to bring the goblet to her lips, liking the after effects. It warmed her insides and was beginning to send a light buzzing through her brain.

Ruy remarked that if she found his wolfskin jerkin and armor objectionable, he would remove it. Mirjana barely heard. She had to think, to find some way to convince him to release her. She knew of his appetite for women; even Padre Tomas had told her. And she had noticed the way he had looked at her and his attentiveness during their midday meals, so she knew she was not unattractive to him. Even now, she realized fuzzily, there was a smoldering heat in his eyes, much the look she had seen in Omar's eyes when she had disrobed and offered herself to him. The sudden remembrance of those minutes in Omar's study brought a flush of color to her cheeks. Omar. How quickly she had forgotten! Her present predicament was because she had believed it was impossible to leave her tutor and romantic scholar, yet it seemed centuries since she had actively thought about him and yearned for him. The memory of the touch of his hands upon her skin flooded back to her, leaving her giddy and warm. Or was it the wine, or Allah forbid, the sight of Ruy's solidly masculine chest with its soft furring of dark hair that was now clearly visible between his wide open shirt front, now that his jerkin and breastplate armor were removed? Ridiculously, her fingers itched to touch it, to feel it curl beneath her palm, and to know the softness of it as it curled upward toward the base of his throat.

It came to her again that indeed she did possess something to barter: herself. She nearly choked on the wine as the thought struck her. She must be mad! Insane! To lay with this barbarian, this Hun! Yet, it was not so foolish as one would imagine, she calculated. With her body she could buy her passage back to Seville. She would have lost her virginity — not something to be taken lightly — and in losing it she would no longer be fit for a royal marriage. As if she cared! She would be free of obligation to her father. And Omar was the man she wanted. Didn't she? Yes, she told herself firmly. She wanted to return to Seville to be with Omar. Was that not her original plan? And Omar would forgive her. He would realize the sacrifice she had made for him and it would never stand between them. To him, the flesh was nothing. He lived on a higher plane where the heart and soul were everything. If she were despoiled, she could predict being given in marriage to the scholar, the man of her choice. Losing her virginity would erase the last hurdle standing between herself and that beloved man. He would no longer be concerned with her position and keeping her worthy for a royal marriage, and he would take her in his arms and keep her for his own.

Ruy was looking at her, a wry smile playing in the corners of his mouth. He was sitting very close to her; she could feel the warmth of his wine-scented breath on her cheek. Her heart tapped a wild rhythm. Could he read her thoughts? Did he know she was about to seduce him in order to secure her release? The wine buzzed pleasantly through her head, and despite the turmoil and indecision she was facing, it all seemed so far away, as though she were viewing it through a haze that obscured the harsh and sharp edges of her deliberateness.

Purposefully, before she could think better of it, she stretched out her hand, touching the warmth of his chest, surprised that the thick furring of hair was softer to the touch than she could have imagined. She heard his sudden intake of breath and averted her eyes against his questioning gaze.

Ruy looked askance at Mirjana's sudden move which broached the borders of intimacy, but she refused to meet his eyes. Her hand grazed the expanse of his chest, kindling new fires within him. He had expected she would immediately withdraw her hand, but she allowed it to linger, tracing a downward path from the base of his throat to his hard, flat belly.

Quickly, he captured her hand, fearing her explorations would drive him beyond the line of reason. He wanted nothing more than to take her into his arms, know the yielding length of her pressed against him, feel the sweet capture of her arms winding around him. She would not allow her hand to be stayed. Softly, it escaped his grasp, finding new patterns to wander, moving upward across the rolling muscles covering his ribs to the smoother, hairless skin of his shoulders.

"You removed your wolfskins and armor because I objected to them," she murmured, her voice softer than a summer's breeze. "I also object to this," she said, unlacing his shirt and pulling it away from his shoulders, touching the newly exposed flesh, smoothing the palm of her hand over the broadness of his back and trailing once again downward where his belt cinched his middle. "And this." Her fingers fumbled with the clasp at his waist.

Ruy realized what she was about: She had decided she possessed something to barter after all. The headiness of the strong wine and her own desperation had led her to this. He pitied her and would have called an end to it. But the question he posed was, How far was she willing to go? His curiosity, instead of diminishing his arousal, heightened it, and he offered no objection when she clumsily went about removing his boots. Stifling a laugh when Mirjana seemed at a loss as to what should be her next move in his seduction, Ruy suggested she make herself more comfortable by removing her own slippers. This she did, going one step further by standing on wine-wobbling legs and removing her gown, pulling it impatiently over her head, leaving herself with little else to protect her from his searching gaze than her thin, long-sleeved kirtle.

Mirjana faced him defiantly, no hint of her inward trembling and apprehensions visible on her beautiful, lamp-lit features. Her vibrant hair was tumbled about her face, hanging below her shoulders like liquid gold. The outline of her figure was revealed beneath the finely loomed fabric, delineating the swell of her breasts, the length of her torso, and the slim curve of her hips. He remembered the sight of her when she had bathed in the stream the first time he had seen her: beads of water laying on her skin like hundreds of jewels, the sweet turn of her limbs, the remarkable length of her legs ending in the twin, firm hillocks of her buttocks.

He should stop her, he knew, now, this minute, before she compromised herself any further. She was bartering herself in return for freedom, a freedom he could not give her. The protests would not come to his lips. He was helpless in the face of her sacrifice, of her sensual advances which sent a singing through his blood and a hungry need rising in his loins.

Still locking his gaze with her own, Mirjana stood on tiptoe to extinguish the lamp hanging from the tent struts. The interior was cast into sudden darkness, only the feeblest of light penetrating the side walls from the numerous campfires burning outside.

His awareness of her suddenly became more sensory rather than visible. He heard her take a step, felt her lower herself to his pallet beside him, felt her cool, delicate touch on the heated flesh of his midsection. Her provocative, elusive perfume assailed his nostrils, and when he answered her caress by taking her into his arms, he reveled in the feel of her — soft, yielding, permitting this intimacy, surrendering herself to it.

She touched the fullness of his beard on his face, trailing to the skin of his neck and the expanse of his chest. Then a lighter, moister touch, which he realized was her mouth, followed her fingers, nipping tenderly where her fingers had plotted their course. She pressed closer, pushing him back onto the pillows, following, leaning over him, the wealth of her hair falling onto his chest, his face, filling him with her scent and drugging him with her caresses.

The effects of the wine buzzed in Mirjana's head, but it was the deliberate boldness of her actions which intoxicated her. She had not been surprised when Ruy did not protest her setting about this shameful seduction. What astonished her was the warmth and the softness in the contact between them. Strong, powerful, she had not guessed that his corded muscles could be so pleasant to her touch, or that his skin, so different from her own in that it was coarser and more tightly molded to him, could respond so delicately to her caress. As her mouth followed her hand across his chest, the fine furring feathered over her lips, her nose, making her aware of his clean, manly scent, and she recognized the familiar spicy aroma of a particular soap which she had brought with her from Seville. Ruy's perusings through the caravan were not limited to sweetmeats and honeyed figs; he had discovered other, more sensory luxuries.

Her explorations found the velvety underside of his upper arms and the path of crisp, dark hairs that seemed to crackle under her fingers. She traced inquisitive patterns over his back, following the progression of his muscles up to his wide, broad shoulders and down again to where his chausses covered his legs and haunches, leading around to the flat hardness of his belly and the concave delineation of his ribs. She heard the intake of his breath as her fingers grazed his nipples, and she lingered there, bringing the responsive flesh to hard, circular nubbins which enticed her lips and tempted her tongue.

Ruy's hands were in her hair, twining it through his fingers, strands of silk beneath his palms. He sailed the golden river down her back, feeling her incredible warmth penetrating the thinly woven fabric of her kirtle, knowing the fragility of her bones and the delights of her flesh. He brought her face to his, finding her mouth with his own. Her lips parted beneath his own, soft, so unbelievably soft, pliant yet firm, returning his pressure, tasting faintly of the wine she had drunk. Leaving her mouth, he kissed her cheeks, her brow, the tip of her nose, and with each kiss he was aware that she molded herself more closely to his body, allowing the intrusion of his thigh between her own. She was still, so still, giving herself up to the caress of his hands and the inquiries of his searching lips. He was filled with a rush of tenderness for her, regardless that he knew this offering of herself was a deliberate blandishment to gain her freedom. Despite the fact she considered herself his prisoner, she had placed her trust in him to use her gently.

Mirjana's breath seemed to leave her body

as he captured her lips with his own. She was struck into a motionless awe, anticipating the next touch of his lips. His mouth was tender yet boldly defined against her own. His beard, lush and full, pleasantly prickled her cheeks, making his kiss seem softer and more gentle by comparison. His lips left her mouth, finding the hollow beneath her chin, the pleasure point under her ear, the curve of her throat where her pulse beat. She threw back her head, relishing this contact between them, anticipating the feel of his mouth on the fragile skin where he had pulled her kirtle away from her shoulder, exposing the top of her breast beneath which pounded the tremulous beats of her heart.

She had known a man's touch and a man's lips once before in her life. She had thought that night with Omar was engraved into her memory, there to be called upon at will, to be reexperienced time and again when her longing for him erupted into a physical need. Here, with Ruy, in his arms, she could not think of Omar, could not summon his face to her memory. There had been passion with Omar, but it had lacked this head-swimming sense of discovery, this total, vital need to offer herself to another's touch and surrender herself to his desires. What began as her seduction of this man had somehow become her submission instead.

He became impatient with the kirtle that prevented him from enjoying the full offering of her body, that stayed his hand when he sought the slender curve of her hips, and restricted the explorations of his mouth on her breasts. He wanted to tear it from her body, to rend the fabric into shreds giving himself full access to her beauty. How easily it would rip beneath his hand, from neck to hem, freeing her from it, exposing her to his passions.

As though sensing his needs, reading his impatience, and knowing his desires, Mirjana pulled away from him. For an instant he was fearful that his demands had frightened her, that she wanted to escape his searching hands and seeking kisses. Instead, he realized with uncompromising relief that she was divesting herself of the obstructing garment, shyly keeping her back turned to him. He could hear the rustle of the fabric as it slid over her skin, could feel the slight breeze her movements created and which brought the elusive scent of her perfume to him. He was eager to experience her nakedness against his own, wanted to know the warmth and softness of her totally. With a quick, smooth action he freed himself of his clinging chausses, realizing the brush of cool air on his heated flesh. And when she again came into his arms, the sensation of her nearly took his breath away. She slipped into his embrace with the lightness of a kitten, curling herself against him, imprisoning one of his thighs between her own. Her wealth of hair, rippling down to her shoulders, captured the feeble light penetrating the tent walls, creating curtains of dawn that beckoned him into its warmth, promising him an end to the night and revealing to him a glimpse of paradise.

Turning her in his embrace, he lay her back against the pillows, following her as she stretched beneath him. He nuzzled her throat, returned to the pleasure point he had found beneath her ear, feeling the echo of that sensation mirrored in her loins. He inhaled the fragrance of her perfume, learning that beneath its exotic scent was one of Mirjana herself, sweet and enticing, totally her own. His lips found her breast, circling yet not touching those appealing crests, returning to rediscover her mouth which answered his kisses and provoked his desires. His hands stroked the softness of her belly and thighs but never trespassed beyond.

Mirjana wanted to cry out, to beseech him to put an end to this exquisite torture, to have her and be done with it. She responded to every touch, returned every kiss, opened her mouth to his teasingly probing tongue without realizing she did. Every caress was echoed somewhere in the depths of her body and created a hunger for him that was beyond anything she had ever known. Wherever he touched her he left a delicate flame that ignited her perceptions and extinguished all caution. Her sensibilities were drowning in a sea of tactile sensation. She could not have said what had brought her here, or why. She only knew that the feverish heat of his skin seemed to singe her fingers and that the tracings of his lips circling her breasts would drive her mad.

Her hands found the smoothness of his torso, descending to the hollows of his groin, stroking, caressing. And she knew the strange sensation that the feel of him and the knowledge of his body was familiar to her, not something recently discovered, but with the comforting impression of returning to a place much loved and cherished. Somehow, in this small space of time, he had become a part of her, and she welcomed him, certain beyond reason of his gentleness, knowing he would not ruthlessly invade her.

He experienced the rounded swell of her bottom and the curve of her hips, and it filled him with a throbbing urgency that was unlike any he had ever known. He felt her tremble uncontrollably as his mouth moved down over her belly, and he anticipated her sudden withdrawal. But her legs offered no resistance as he opened them, and her body caught fire from this most intimate of kisses.

Mirjana bit her lips to keep from crying out with ecstasy. This was a sensation she had never experienced, had not known of its existence, had never guessed this sense of power and rushing of sensuality radiating from her in ever-widening circles pulsing from her center. She had called him a Hun, and he was the most gentle of lovers. She had called him a barbarian, ignorant of culture and beauty. Yet he was beautiful, perceptive of her every response, giving of his own passions to awaken hers.

A yearning ache sped through her, demanding satisfaction, wanting to satisfy. Her fingers wound through his hair, pulling him upwards on top of her, bearing his weight gladly as his chest flattened her breasts and stomach against his. Hungrily, her mouth found his, instigating new paths for the meeting of their lips and tongues. She captured him in her arms, feeling a thunderous need in her loins which sought relief by the involuntary roll of her hips against his hard masculinity. She whimpered, unable to find any release for these sensations that were erupting within her. Small, kittenish mewlings sounded in her throat as he hunched over her, covering her body with his own, protecting her from the night, creating a new world for her that was whirling, spinning, drawing her into the vortex of their mutual need.

He drew away from her and she cried for her loss, bereft for his embrace, though the distance that separated them was less than the width of her hand. He was clouded in darkness, yet she knew his eyes burned into hers. And when he spoke his voice was husky, heavy with desire, yet less than a whisper.

"I creep into the Mansion of her Moon and satiate her soul upon my Lips . . ." he murmured, quoting a phrase from the love poem of Absál and Salámán which she had read to him by her campfire an eternity of nights ago. Suddenly the words she knew so well held new meaning. "Tell me you want me, Mirjana. Tell me you must have me, above all else," he commanded. "I will not take you otherwise. Say it!" There was a thick note of desperation in his voice, yet he clung to the perimeters of his control.

A hard, driving need seized her as she tried to draw him back into her embrace. Her lips sought his, offering herself, needing to give herself. Ruy returned a steely resistance, though he believed he would shatter into fragments if she did not say what he craved to hear. Mirjana's eyes widened in the darkness.

She understood. This was not to be a barter. There would be no exchange of her body for her freedom; she could not give what he would not take. Her surrender must be because she wanted it, never because he demanded it. She should throw him off, kick him and cry, run out into the night where she could hide her defeat. But the hollow yearning that demanded to be filled could only be satisfied in him. Cursing her weakness, wishing to die with a failure she could not live without, she cried, "I want! I do want you! Must have you!"

His fingers bit into her shoulders, hard, commanding, shaking the last of her resolve, needing, wanting to hear her say it as much as she needed to have it said. "I must have you, Ruy," she whispered, finding victory in her defeat, her blood singing with the joy of it, knowing it to be the only truth she had ever known.

His mouth covered hers, putting an end to her cries. Her body opened to him, wanting him above all else, yielding to his manhood, knowing only a brief, sharp pain that was instantly quenched in these new fires he stoked within her. Fires that consumed yet restored, that destroyed yet cleansed. She was the sheath and he the scabbard, made for each other, two parts of the same whole.

And when she heard him cry her name from

the far side of his passion, it reverberated in her being and quickened her heartbeat. Rolling waves of exquisite sensations carried her upward, and together they sailed upon a crystal starship into the black depths of infinity where the moon shone a path to passion's way. It was without knowing that she answered him with the sound of his name upon her lips, "Ruy! Ruy!"

CHAPTER 6

Ruy lay with his eyes closed against the morning light filtering through his tent flap. He lay alone. Hours ago he had taken Mirjana back to her own tent. Hours ago, and yet he could still feel the touch of her hands upon his skin and was aware of the light, elusive scent of her perfume where she had lain amidst his pillows. Hours since he had sought sleep, wishing for it, knowing it would not be his. His thoughts were filled with her, remembering not only the intimate moments of last night but each and every moment since he had first put eyes on her — every detail of those quiet midday sojourns; the way the fire was captured in her hair as she sat before the campfire reading to her audience of rough soldiers who had taken a sudden and intense interest in Persian love poems. It seemed to him that all who crossed Mirjana's path were changed somehow for the better, himself included.

He had never been a man to give much

thought to women. War was his career, and he lived it each and every day. Since meeting her, knowing her, battles and sieges had been far from his thoughts. Instead, his interests were focused on butterflies and rainbows and the way the brilliant Castilian sun lit the grassy plains and sparkled like jewels in the wayward brooks and streams. His head was filled with thoughts of warm, velvet skin and hair that was neither red nor gold but an astounding shade somewhere between. Supple limbs, sweet fragrance, all of these Mirjana.

He had helped her dress last night, actually this morning when the sky was still dark. If he had expected a shy withdrawal or an embarrassed bumbling, he would have been wrong. She had been gracious in allowing him this intimacy, smiling softly as he kissed her breast and then her shoulder before covering them with her garments. Nor had there been any accusations in her eyes as he bent to help her with her slippers. She had set about seducing him in an attempt to barter herself for her freedom. From any other woman he would have accepted the bargain, but never from Mirjana. He had wanted to possess her through her willingness, through the demands of her own passions. He had demanded it and she had not refused him. Her cry of his name still rang in his ears and set his blood pounding.

Later, outside her tent, he had expected her to claim he had tricked her, used her, but she had merely smiled that strange, tender smile of hers and caressed his cheek before slipping into her tent. He smiled, remembering the sweetness of her gesture, then frowned for the quandary in which he had placed himself. Nothing had changed. Mirjana was still abandoned by both father and betrothed, and he, Ruy, was still burdened with her future. A renewed hunger for her made him hope that her predicament would not change; saner reasoning made him wish word would reach him this day that Hassan had reconsidered. There was no room in his life for a woman, he told himself, not even one as beautiful and desirable as Mirjana. He had a duty to his career; he had pledged himself as vassal to his king, and there were his duties as lord of Bivar. No room for a woman! Especially not a woman whose every waking hour was devoted to gaining her freedom to return to a father who no longer wanted her!

Tanige lay on her pallet across from Mirjana's, watching her mistress sleep and hearing her softly murmuring indistinguishable words. The princess had been gone more than half the night, and there was no doubt as to where she had been. El Cid's voice, bidding Mirjana good night, had come to her through the tent.

And when Mirjana had slipped out of her dress and lain down on her pallet, she had heard the soft sighs, and soon after the deep, even breathing of sleep. This last, more than anything, puzzled Tanige. When Mirjana had been absent for so many hours, Tanige had paced the confines of the tent tormenting herself that she had not confided to the princess what she knew of El Cid's ransom demands and how they refused. She realized that Mirjana was probably attempting to strike up some kind of bargain with El Cid, and having witnessed for herself the look in his eyes when he watched the princess read near the campfire, she had a very good idea what that bargain would involve. Poor Mirjana, Tanige mourned, she had paid with her body for a freedom El Cid was not able to give!

Determined that Mirjana would not read the pity in her eyes, Tanige crept from her pallet through the tent flap into the early morning light. She would heat water for washing and find something for their breakfast. If Mirjana must discover she had suffered El Cid's intimacies the night before to no avail, it would not be on an empty stomach.

Tanige was bending over the low-burning fire heating water for the herbal tea Mirjana preferred when her mistress stepped out of the tent into the sunlight. She was dressed and groomed for the day, wearing the slim-cut yellow caftan over her long-sleeved, high-necked kirtle. Her hair had been brushed to a high gleam and secured to the top of her head. Her cinder-like gray eyes held a secret of a smile, and she appeared refreshed and ready for the day ahead. So, she still did not know, Tanige surmised, narrowing her eyes and speculating on the events the night before which seemed to leave the princess's beauty enhanced and her mood decidedly tranquil.

Almost at the same moment that Mirjana stepped from the tent, Doña Ysabel approached with young Teodoro in tow. With a regal wave of her arm, Doña Ysabel motioned Tanige aside and confronted Mirjana. Her voice was cold and disdainful, her demeanor overbearing.

"I want it understood now, before we arrive in Bivar later today, that I wholeheartedly disapprove of you. I would have you left by the roadside, but my son, lord of Bivar, insists we will practice our Christian duty and give you shelter in our home." Doña Ysabel's lip curled in distaste, and her words were so forceful that Mirjana found herself stepping backward, retreating from the loathing in the woman's eyes. "There will be naught but trouble if you come with us, and for that reason and for the saving of my son's soul, I am prepared to help you make your escape. Ruy tells me you wish only to return to Seville. I don't understand your reasons since your brother, Hassan, who now sits on the throne, wants no part of you. I fail to see how a woman in your circumstances can hope to persuade as ambitious a man as Hassan to reconsider his decision to secure his alliance with Granada and disregard your personal circumstances."

Doña Ysabel was quick to see the shock on Mirjana's face, and she took pleasure in it, continuing in a more sympathetic tone which was clearly a facade for her true feelings. "Would it not be better to throw yourself upon Yusuf's mercy and beg him to give you shelter, regardless of your immorality last night?"

Mirjana gasped, the sound tearing from her throat.

"Oh, yes, Princesa," Doña Ysabel sneered, "do you think me so remiss a mother that I am not aware of my son's weaknesses?" Her hand went to the top of Teodoro's head and ruffled through his dark hair in a possessive gesture. Realizing the young boy's presence, Mirjana was doubly humiliated by the woman's accusations.

"Do not pretend with me, Princesa," the woman mocked. "I know a whore for a whore when I see one. As I see it, the best you can do is agree to beg Yusuf's mercy. Ruy will even intervene on your behalf." How self-righteous she sounded, how certain of herself and her son's thoughts.

The full impact of Doña Ysabel's words slapped Mirjana. It was impossible! She couldn't believe, would not believe it. What had happened to her father? Why was Hassan sitting on the throne of Seville? Even Hassan would not disown her . . . She knew Hassan would, knew he had. He was an ambitious man and had waited with great impatience to gain the throne. There was nothing more important to Hassan than filling the treasuries.

Mirjana straightened her shoulders and stared deeply into Doña Ysabel's eyes. "Thank you for your kind offer, Señora, but I neither want nor require your assistance. Excuse me, it is almost time for the caravan to depart and there is much to be done. *Buenos días,* Señora," she said in an emotionless tone before slipping back inside the tent. She wanted to disbelieve, to cry that all Doña Ysabel had told her was untrue, and yet she knew it for truth when she had glanced over the señora's shoulder and seen Tanige's stricken face. How long, she wondered, had Tanige known? So this was the secret then that Tanige had been keeping from her.

Doña Ysabel's efforts to wound Mirjana were frustrated by the *princesa*'s quiet poise and cool graciousness. Looking down, she saw her son's sly smile at the way his domineering mother's game had been called and so regally bandied. The smile was wiped from the boy's mischievous face by a resounding slap from her hand that produced a high-pitched whine of complaint — which she immediately soothed by clucking and popping a sweetmeat from her pocket into his mouth. The boy continued to tug at his mother's voluminous skirts as she led him away back to their quarters, from time to time finding another treat and feeding it to him.

Tanige found herself looking after them, disgusted by Doña Ysabel's display of treating the boy like a coddled infant without half a brain. Teodoro was quite intelligent, Tanige knew, and cunning like a fox. And there was a streak of evil that ran through him which was enhanced by his mother's pampering and lack of control over him. Someone should do something about him, Tanige thought. But right now, her attentions must be directed to Mirjana who was no doubt sitting inside the tent this moment crying her heart out.

When Tanige entered the tent with a steaming cup of tea, she found Mirjana perched on an empty water barrel, sitting as still as death itself, staring off into a corner. Yet she could sense a restlessness that frightened her, truly frightened her. She could have understood if the princess was screaming and crying, raging against the will of Allah himself. But this deadly calm was something she could neither understand nor dare to disrupt.

Tanige offered her mistress the tea, watching carefully for a break in her dreadful calm. Mirjana's hand was steady as she accepted the cup, her features lifeless as she sipped the scalding brew.

After a moment, Mirjana stood and carefully put the cup down on the barrel. Taking a moment to smooth her dress and square her shoulders, she stepped out of the tent and turned to the left. Tanige watched her, certain above all doubt that she was going to confront El Cid, knowing that the princess's last hopes would be dashed when he told her all she had heard was the truth.

Head high, ignoring the polite greetings from both Padre Tomas and Pietro, Mirjana walked toward her destination. Soldiers, busy with their chores to prepare for the day's march, silently cleared a path for her. Their eyes followed the bright hair and stiff shoulders, noting her regal bearing and sensing that something was troubling the laughing, smiling woman who had entertained them with her poetry.

Without thought for etiquette or decorum,

Mirjana entered Ruy's tent, leaving the flap open and allowing sunlight to stream into the dim interior. She found him lying upon his pallet, seeming to be asleep. She stared down at him, willing him to sense her presence.

He did. Opening his eyes, Ruy saw her standing over him, shadows staining her cheeks, the dove-gray eyes hollow and lifeless. A charged silence surrounded them and his voice, when he spoke, was rife with sympathy. He knew why she had returned to his tent, knew the reason for the gaunt shadows under her cheekbones and why the crystal, gray eyes held traces of ashes. "I wished to be the one to tell you, Mirjana."

As if at the sound of his voice the life flowed back into her, Mirjana felt herself respond to all that had happened. A seed of fear was flowering in her middle. It was true, Doña Ysabel had spoken the truth. And he was sorry. He sympathized. He pitied her!

"Why was I not told? Why did you leave me at the señora's mercy knowing she had none for me? Why?" It was the cry of a wounded bird, an animal trapped with no hope of escape. It ripped at Ruy's innards making him incapable of answering. He watched as her eyes moved in concert with her trembling hands and heaving breast. He wanted to reach out, to comfort her, to assure her he would always remain her protector. Instead, he said nothing, waiting for the tears that never came.

He was stunned into further silence when she again spoke. "I can forgive you, my lord, for last night. What a fool I was to think I could barter myself for something that was not yours to give — my return to Seville! I will even forgive your greed which placed me in these circumstances. What I can never forgive is your keeping the news of my father from me. I assume since Hassan has ascended to the throne, my father is dead." She waited for a moment and saw his solemn nod. "What you have done to me is unforgivable." Without another word, without another glance, she turned quietly and left him, her back ramrod straight.

Ruy sat in stunned silence. His masculine defenses provoked him to white-hot anger. Damnable woman! By what right did she forgive or not forgive? All he had done, tried to do, was shield her, protect her, save her dignity. And what thanks did he receive? She would not forgive him! Damn her!

Ruy was disturbed by his emotions, feeling as though he had kicked a sick dog. He didn't remember ever feeling this way. Reaching for the nearly empty wine flask, he took several deep swallows to dispel the bitter taste in his mouth. It was time to prepare for the day's march. By nightfall he would be in Bivar, settled once again into his own household. Home. It had been too long, and he was tired. He needed to be home, feel his belongings surrounding him, and most important of all, to go among his people.

A sudden rush of raw anger rode up in his chest, making him clench his fists and lash out to smash a water jug. Being among his own people and winning their praise over his exploits and feeling their respect would not soothe the loss of Mirjana's approval. His guilt was engulfing him, and he would find no peace, he knew, until he shed it like a snake sheds its skin. And in his heart he knew he was facing the most arduous and difficult battle he had ever fought.

Mirjana rode silently in the wagon beside Tanige. Heartsick, forlorn, she stared straight ahead into the distance. Bitter, scalding tears burned behind her eyes. Today was the day when she had learned the meaning of despair, what it meant to be lost and have all that was loved and familiar taken from her. Today, she had lost her identity, becoming a nameless person without heritage, her past and future obscured. Only yesterday she had thought she possessed all these and had taken them for granted. Yesterday, she had still possessed her self-respect. Now she was shamed, degraded, feeling without worth.

A pawn, that was all she was. To be used or discarded at men's whims. A pawn of their greedy ambitions. And a fool, with only herself to blame. She had tried to shirk her duties to become Yusuf's wife, and had taken the first step to her downfall by writing that letter. Ruy had been greedy in trying to ransom her, but the ultimate blame was her own. How could she have been so naive and so clumsy to think she could seduce her way to freedom? She had cheapened herself and might have worsened her situation. A bitter laugh of self-rebuke broke her unnatural silence. And to think it had all begun because of her infatuation with her teacher when for these past weeks she had barely given thought to Omar. Last night, in Ruy's arms, no other man had ever existed for her. The poet was forgotten; only Ruy's searing mouth and searching hands remembered.

Womanly defenses rose. She wanted to blame Ruy for using her, for lying to her and keeping the truth from her. But she knew now his reason for demanding she admit she wanted him to make love to her, demanded she say it aloud, leaving no doubt there was to be no barter of her body for her freedom.

And she had cried out her need for him, her wants. Could she fault him for wanting to protect her from defeat she now realized? Could she hate him for giving her shelter and burdening himself with her when he could have just cast her out onto the Marches and forgotten her existence? Slowly, Mirjana's sense of herself seeped back to her. Ruy had known he would not receive a dinar in payment for her return to either Seville or Granada, and yet he must have found her to have some value since he had not abandoned her and Tanige, or even murdered them as she knew he was quite capable of doing.

She must have been a trial to him these past weeks, she realized. He must have been quite uncertain as to what should be done with her, and yet, in the beginning he had withstood the onslaught of her anger and even the sharp edge of her insults until he had courted her into a friendship. Even the night before, when he could have used her, he had not. She had set about seducing him and was seduced in return, willingly, gladly, sharing her passions with him, realizing all the while no bargain would be struck. If he had been less than honest with her concerning her situation, at least he had not tricked her, used her, or discarded her as had Yusuf and Hassan.

Mirjana's chin lifted; her eyes lit from the

shadows of her despair. She was Mútadid's daughter, princess to the throne of Seville. She had been educated and bred to royalty, and trained to seek the truth and face it, however difficult. Stubborn, optimistic, and holding a faith in her god, new strength and determination were reborn. It was Allah's will that she leave Seville, and she was certain it would also be Allah's will that she return. Somehow, someday. For now, she must resign herself to this new life before her and live it the best way she could. It would be difficult, she knew, but she also knew that should her situation change and she be welcomed back into the bosom of her family, Rodrigo Ruy Diaz, El Cid, would help her.

The day wore on and the sun was slowly sinking when the caravan overtook a steep incline. They had left the open March, and for the better part of the day had followed a road leading through tall trees and cool, green grasses. Coming to the top of the rise, Mirjana looked down and saw the town of Bivar and the *castillo* of El Cid laid out before her. Stone buttresses caught the red-gold glow of sunset, and the moat that separated the high, thick walls of the city from the outlying fields and farms mirrored the brilliance of the sky. Twin, monolithic towers rose from the *castillo*, casting long, purple shadows over the town that nestled at its feet, and yet their gray, rough stone captured the tinge of bloody gold from the sky. Further on the horizon stood the Pyrenees, still deeply snowcapped, but their foothills were lush with new spring growth. Flags were flying atop the jagged battlements in celebration of El Cid's return, and within the walls of the city there appeared to be a gathering of people to welcome him.

In spite of herself, Mirjana was filled with a sense of adventure, she who had never been outside the city of Seville and had only heard and read of these feudal towns on the outreach of the Marches, which separated the opposing worlds of Islam and Christianity.

From the distance came the toll of church bells, chiming melodiously, welcoming home Bivar's lord and champion. As they approached the town following behind the long column of foot soldiers and mounted officers, a thunderous roar of cheering welled up in the crowd. Mirjana and Tanige sat in alert attention as they entered the horseshoe arch and the gates to the city. The townspeople were throwing garlands of pungent herbs and field flowers, and the shops were decorated with laurel leaves and banners. El Cid had returned home victorious from his siege of Badajoz, and the news of his valor had reached his people. Eager to see it all, Mirjana stretched her neck, viewing the numerous footbridges and thatch-roofed structures. The bells continued to toll, louder now, coming from a tall tower whose gabled roof was topped with the symbol of Christianity — a cross.

The soldiers began to disperse among the throng, accepting wine-filled skins with which to quench their thirst. Some were met by mothers and wives who clutched the men to themselves in anxious embraces, their faces lit with smiles and cheeks stained with tears of gratitude for their returning warriors. Others searched the crowd for loved ones, some of whom had been left dead on the Marches outside the city of Badajoz or some other place where they had met their fates. Some children cried and clung to women's skirts, frightened by all this commotion, while others curiously watched from the safety of their mother's arms.

The drawbridge to the castle was down, spanning the moat surrounding it. At this proximity, Mirjana could see the way moss and slime grew on the rough stone walls, and the filth floating in the moat. A curious brown color had washed out of the stone battlements and down the exterior walls like ancient blood stains. The streets they had traveled to achieve the castle were unpaved, muddied and trampled by thousands of footsteps. Mirjana's first impression of Bivar was suddenly altered. What had appeared to be a lovely city by the sun's setting glow was, in reality, more like an open cistern. A thick, malodorous stench came to her nostrils — sewage in the moat and in the streets creating streams of middens. The peasants, filthy and unkempt, were clothed in rags, and flies feasted upon the droppings from pigs and dogs and other barnyard animals which were allowed to roam the streets.

Seville, Seville, jewel of Andalusia, Mirjana's heart cried. She knew the Christian towns and cities were far below the standard of Islam but she had never quite expected this. In Seville all streets and main concourses were paved, and animals were restricted to back avenues on their way to market. All the buildings were washed white, unlike these hovels here in Bivar, and were scrupulously scrubbed and kept. Boulevards were lined with trees and flowers of the season, and the palace itself stood out like a pearl, white and sparkling, surrounded by flower-ringed patios and bubbling fountains. Here, all was of a color — dun. There were no tiles over the archways, no bas reliefs, no fretted doorways. It was as though the outward signs of civilization — art and beauty and cleanliness — had never reached the walls of Bivar.

"Already it disgusts me," Tanige whispered, shutting her squint eyes against the ugliness. "Allah has cursed us to send us to such a place."

Mirjana was silent, her thoughts echoing Tanige's. The wagon's wheels rolled hollowly over the drawbridge, and pulled them into the courtyard of the *castillo*. Doña Ysabel was issuing orders for the transference of her belongings to her quarters, and young Teodoro was busily chasing a slat-ribbed dog between the horses' legs and wagons. The stench from the moat had followed them into the courtyard, and Mirjana was eager to be away from it. It was doubly overpowering compared to the fresh, open outdoors in which she had spent these past weeks. It was a dismal trek from the courtyard through the heavy wooden gates protecting the great hall just behind. The same dull gray walls as the exterior, smudged with red-brown streaks, vaulted to a high ceiling stained with soot from decades of smoldering torches. Crossbows and armor were hung and displayed among racks of spears and shields which were held in readiness against attack from invaders. A long, roughhewn table surrounded by narrow benches was placed directly in front of an ancient, massively designed fireplace. To the right, stone steps led upwards, no doubt to the quarters above.

Mirjana was depressed by this windowless cave filled with arms and the lingering aroma left by thousands of meals prepared in the hearth. Underfoot was an earthen floor covered with trampled bulrushes and browning straw. Mirjana and Tanige, standing close together in shocked silence, were approached by an old woman servant dressed in drab shades of brown and a kerchief tied over her gray hair. "Doña Ysabel says you are to share a chamber in the tower."

Motioning for them to follow, they clutched the meager belongings they had managed to carry from the wagon, and climbed the wide stone staircase to the second level. The steps were worn into hollows from centuries of use and were treacherous to an uncautious ankle. On the second level there was no gallery, no long, open hallway as Mirjana had expected. Instead, it was a long, dimly lit corridor that was punctuated by stout, rough-timbered doors, no doubt opening into the family's private chambers.

The aged woman led them down the corridor, which swung sharply to the left around the perimeter of the great hall below until coming upon a narrow portal that opened with squeaking protest onto the circular stone steps immediately within. Grunting with the effort of the climb, the servant lit an occasional wall sconce as they climbed, lighting the interior of the tower into dim light and long, ominous shadows. It was obvious from the hanging cobwebs and thick dust that the tower had not been used in years. An occasional narrow, slotted opening allowed in daylight, and since they were not glazed or shuttered, they also allowed in insects in the summer and chill winds and snow in the winter. And from the puddles and damp stains on the walls, she knew they also permitted the entry of rain.

At the top of the stairs stood a wooden door, narrow and scarred and boasting a huge lock on its outer bolt. Tanige's eyes widened when she saw it, realizing that the chamber assigned to them had been used as a prison cell. And when they stepped into the circular room with only one high window, unglazed as were the ones on the staircase, they realized this to be exactly the case.

The proportions of the room, the cell, were narrow and confining, containing only a broken wooden cot and a filthy straw-filled mattress. Tanige dropped the belongings she was carrying and stood in the center of the cell, disbelief in her eyes.

"Mirjana! This is an insult! You cannot allow this! You are a princess, member of a royal family —"

"Hush!" Mirjana ordered, the old authority returning. Then turning to the servant, she spoke in the woman's native Spanish, "There is only one cot. Since there are two of us, another will be required, immediately. Can you see to it?"

The woman shrugged. "Doña Ysabel said nothing of another cot. Perhaps you can take one from the chambers below if it is not to be used." Obviously, the woman could not be responsible for making a decision or taking it upon herself to have another cot brought up. Seeing she would get nowhere by pressing her, Mirjana tried another tack.

"And the bedding," she said, plumping the filthy mattress, seeing the straw within had decayed and powdered and was of no use whatever.

Again the servant shrugged. "There is straw in the stable . . ." And then, remembering, "Doña Ysabel wishes you both to use the kitchen stairs. You will find them at the far end of the lower corridor." This was said firmly, the señora's words repeated faithfully. So, even in the confusion of homecoming, Doña Ysabel had given enough thought to Mirjana's stay at the *castillo* to remember to advise both Tanige and herself to use the servants' stairway.

Giving thought to their immediate needs,

Mirjana pressed. "There is no chamber pot, no container for water for washing . . . Tell me, are the rooms below unlocked? If so, we could obtain these things."

Again, the woman shrugged. "I do not know. It has been years since I have been above stairs. My work is in the kitchens." Dismissing them and any concern for their needs, the woman shuffled toward the door, pulling on her ear and wincing.

"Does your ear pain you?" Mirjana asked quietly.

The old woman's eyes widened at the question, and she nodded in the affirmative, obviously surprised that anyone should notice or inquire for her pain.

When the old woman had gone, Tanige allowed herself the luxury of her reaction to the quarters they had been assigned. Her mouth dropped open and a fine edge of hysteria pitched her voice. "There must be a mistake. Human beings do not live in these conditions!" Then, as if touched by a lit taper, she rushed to the door and struggled with the rusted padlock that swung from the bolt. "At least if we are to be locked into this dungeon, it will be from the inside!" she cried.

Mirjana's eyes dropped to the cracked stone floor. It was bare and filthy, and their footsteps had left prints in the dust. Experimentally, she rubbed her foot across the stones. Grit and grime screeched in her ears. Tanige was right; this was a dungeon, although it be high in the tower and not below ground level.

Curious as to what their location was in respect to the *castillo,* Mirjana tried to see out the knife-slim window, finding it was too high and she not tall enough. Indeed, a man as tall as El Cid would have difficulty seeing out. Dragging the wooden cot beneath the window, she stood on the top supporting rail and peered out. The sky was leaden gray now, the sun at last having slipped below the horizon, and darkness was falling quickly. Beneath her was the courtyard, and if she stretched her neck, she could just see the drawbridge and the town beyond.

Horses stood in the courtyard, waiting for the hostler to stable and feed them. The most outstanding was Liberte, black and sleek, his muscles still twitching from the long day's ride. Beyond the walls, in the town, revelry was continuing with the return of the men. Torches glowed, fighting the oncoming darkness, and from somewhere came the sound of a flute, played lightly and with a dance rhythm. So this was Bivar, she thought. This is where he came from. And from here he went out into the world and made himself a legend. Humble beginnings for such a man, she told herself. Humble and unworthy of him. He had seen, she knew, the splendors of Islamic palaces. He was a frequent visitor to Zaragoza, he had told her, and was familiar with the customs and life-style of her people. Yet, he had done nothing to improve his home, obviously contenting himself with it, sticking to his own culture and background. Or was it because he was a military man, a vassal of the throne of Castile, that he preferred these fortresslike surroundings? Or was it because Doña Ysabel's influence and her determination to keep her home austere and crude rather than to sin against her religion and adopt the luxuries of the Eastern world? This last, she suspected, was closer to truth than the first. "Let her have her austerity and her accumulated filth!" Mirjana exclaimed. "I will live the way I have been taught! Like a human, not an animal in a stable! Tanige!" She turned to the woebegone girl who sniffled back her tears and held shadows of defeat in her small, squinted eyes. "Tanige, we will not live like this! Like animals!"

Tanige brightened, rubbing the back of her hand under her nose. "Princess, you are going down to protest this — this insult? You will demand appropriate quarters? Remind them who you are."

"No. You know my circumstances. I have

no right to demand anything. Instead, we will make this chamber habitable by humans. I want you to go down to the kitchen. Remember to use the back stairs. Find a broom, some water, rags — whatever we need to make this fit to sleep in. Hurry, now. Meanwhile, I'll go below and find an unoccupied chamber and take what we need. Hurry! And then find out what has become of the remainder of our belongings and see if you can find someone to help you bring them up here."

Backbreaking hours later, Mirjana and Tanige were still hard at work. Together, they had swept down the walls, banishing the stubborn cobwebs. Among the items they had purloined from an unused chamber below were several lamps that when lit dispelled the gloom. While Mirjana got to her knees to scrub the floor, Tanige had gone to the stables to fill the mattresses with fresh straw. Another cot had been carried up the steep, winding staircase, leaving them sore and breathless. An old trunk with a broken lock also found its way upstairs, as well as a low table and spare blankets. Something must be done with the window, Mirjana realized, foreseeing the flurries of insects that would follow the glow from their lamps into the room. But that could wait until another day.

With the help of an unwilling stable boy,

Tanige had brought the remainder of their meager possessions up to the tower. And when the boy saw the restoration and housekeeping taking place, he blinked and smiled sourly. The scrawny one, who had ordered him to give her assistance with the *princesa*'s belongings, had tricked him. He had only agreed in the first place so he could tell the others he had seen a royal *princesa,* and whom should he find — a scullery maid, skirts tucked above her knees, back bent, scrubbing the floor!

When they had finished, they both collapsed onto their cots in weary satisfaction. The old trunk with the broken lock stood beneath the window, and by standing on it, they could look out. The yellow, fluttering light from the lamp gave the cell a cozy glow, and although the floor was still damp underfoot, at least it was clean and would not dirty the hems of their skirts. The straw hay stuffed into the mattress ticking gave off a sweet smell, and the blankets and pillows they had purloined promised a warm night, even though they were of crudely woven cloth and scratchy to the touch. And they were not excessively clean, Mirjana thought, but at least there was no evidence of fleas and other vermin. At best, the cell was clean; at worst, it was dismal compared to the suite she had left behind in Seville.

Tanige's stomach grumbled hungrily, reminding Mirjana that it had been hours since she, too, had eaten. Nothing had passed her lips since the hot tea Tanige had brewed for her early that morning. That morning. Had it only been less than a day since discovering the results of her foolish scheme to avoid going to Granada to marry Yusuf? Only hours, really, since Doña Ysabel had taken such delight in informing her that she was an abandoned non-person, forsaken by both family and betrothed? Less than a day, and yet an eternity.

Pity for Tanige prompted her to tell the girl to go down to the kitchens to see what she could find for them to eat. "Inspect it carefully, Tanige. If their housekeeping is any indication of their cooking, you would be wise to choose carefully!"

Hopefully, thinking of her empty stomach, Tanige told her there had been a great deal of activity in the kitchens, and that a haunch of lamb was being roasted in the hearth in the great hall. "I heard one of the cooks say supper was later than usual because of the lord's return. Doña Ysabel required a nap to refresh herself before eating. There should be much to chose from for our own meal," Tanige told her, smacking her lips in anticipation and hurrying out of the room.

Mirjana sat on her narrow cot and leaned

back against the wall, weary to the point of exhaustion. The drudgery of housework was as unfamiliar to her as flying. She looked at her hands, at the chapped, rough skin and the broken fingernails. Her gown was filthy, stained by dirty water and years of grime. The night was warm, for the first weeks of spring were upon them, but not warm enough to justify the dark rings of perspiration under her arms and the damp curls that hung about her face. Ordinarily, her clothing never came into such a state of shambles, and a tiny, stubborn stain on the bodice was reason enough to discard the garment. Now, there was no way of knowing when, if ever, she would have another to replace it. And the others in her wardrobe were so few she realized she must become thrifty in her use of them. This minute, there was nothing she wanted so much as a bath and a change of clothes.

Mirjana heard the slamming of the door at the bottom of the stairs leading to the tower. Quickly, thinking it was Tanige coming with their meal, she removed the lamp and her hair brush and hand mirror from the flat top of the trunk under the window. At least they would have a table of sorts.

"I've cleared a space, Tanige," she said over her shoulder, brushing back tendrils of hair from her face with the back of her hand. "Bring it over —"

Turning, her words choked off in her throat. He stood there before her, his tall, broad shoulders framed in the doorway. Were it not for his flashing smile and laughing, dark eyes she would have thought him a stranger. There was no other word that could describe this change in him except to say it was a transformation. Gone was the bristly black beard and shoulder length hair which had been held back with a studded headband. Gone were the breastplate armor and bulky wolfskin jerkin.

His face was clean-shaven except for a closely trimmed moustache on his upper lip, defining his mouth and softening the line. Dark hair, barbered short to graze the top of his ears, curled softly around his head, just touching the collar of his short, fitted, leather tunic worn over knitted chausses that ended in knee-high-boots of the softest leather. But it was to his face that her eyes returned, seeing the dimpled indentations in his cheeks that set off the squareness of his chin and jaw. She remembered those times when she had been with him, and his easy laugh and bright eyes had given her the impression of a far younger man than either his appearance or his reputation allowed. And she blushed to remember the night before when she had lain in his arms, her exploring fingers finding the hardness of his muscles and the flatness of his belly.

"Does the sight of me displease you, Mirjana?" he asked. "Would you prefer to see me in my wolfskins? No, I think not. As I remember, you told me you found them objectionable. And there were other items of my dress you also found objectionable. Let me see if I can recall . . ." His eyes challenged her to deny that the night before she had almost stripped him of his garments, making her remember how she herself had pulled off her shoes and gown before sinking down beside him and entering his arms.

Quick to dispel this line of conversation, Mirjana interrupted before he could continue. "I approve of both my lord's barber and tailor," she told him, suddenly aware of her own sad appearance.

"I will relay the compliment, milady." He performed a courtly bow. "I trust you find your chamber comfortable?" He glanced about the small cell approvingly, seeing the cleanly scrubbed floor and readied cots, complete with pillows and blankets. "I thought this rather confined and small, but I was assured it was to your liking."

Mirjana's eyes widened. Who had told him it was to her liking? Doña Ysabel? And yes, the cell did appear comfortable — now, after all of her and Tanige's scrubbing and carting furniture and other necessities! Mirjana silenced her erupting objections and desire to qualify just what she thought made a chamber comfortable. For the time being, it was enough to know that he himself had not assigned her to this lofty dungeon and had been unaware of its disrepair. She did not want him to think her spoiled for luxury. There was always the possibility that he would insist upon her occupying a chamber on the second level. And from what she had seen of them, she and Tange would have to begin their scrubbing all over again!

"The chamber suits me, my lord. Perhaps for the lack of a table on which to take meals," she told him shyly, realizing she did not want to make demands of him. As it was necessary for her to accept his hospitality and shelter, she had the few and resented privileges of an unwanted guest.

"Milady will not be taking meals in this room. You are expected to join the family in the great hall. This was my purpose in coming up here, to invite you to the table. Your handmaiden will be eating in the kitchens with the other servants."

Was he then differentiating between the position she was to maintain in his household and that of the servants by insisting she take her meals with the family? "If it is what my lord requires of me," she said softly, communicating her sense of obligation.

"By the devil's toenails, Mirjana! It is not what I require but rather what I wish!" he burst forth angrily.

Taken aback, Mirjana rose to her defense. "Since it is that I am in your debt for the shelter and protection you provide, I am well aware of my obligations to fulfill your wishes. However, I would plead my obligations begin tomorrow since, as you can see, I am hardly presentable to attend your table." Her hands smoothed the front of her gown, bringing his attention to her appearance.

Noticing the stains and soil, and her hair which was in a roiling disarray, Ruy laughed. "I've seen scullery maids in better attire. What have you done to yourself?" Not waiting for an answer, he told her, "Hurry and change your gown. The meal is waiting, as are Padre Tomas and Pietro. Were it not for my mother's insisting upon a nap, we would have eaten hours ago. I'm starved!" he complained.

Mirjana shrank backwards into the shadows. "Please, my lord, permit my absence from your table this night."

A dark scowl formed on Ruy's handsome features. She had become used to his glowering at her from behind his thick, black beard. Now, since his metamorphosis, it was like facing a stranger's anger, and she wasn't quite certain how to deal with it.

"Firstly," he told her, stepping further into the lamplight so she could see his seriousness and impatience, "I do not care for this sudden formality between us. When did I become 'my lord' instead of Ruy? Secondly, as I told you at the beginning, I rarely repeat an order twice!"

"Forgive me . . . I was merely showing respect for my protector . . . my guardian . . ." Her words were sticking in her throat.

Ruy hated to see her this way, hated to know he had caused her defeat and obeisance. Where was the woman who could speak her mind and rail against him? Where was the woman who had dared to upbraid him for his "Hun-like" appearance and his "barbaric" behavior, and who had spit her fury at him time and again? She was behaving like a whipped and beaten dog licking at its master's boots. He knew she considered herself in his debt, and he disliked the position in which she had placed him. Seeking to alleviate her fears, he said, "Mirjana, I want you to know that I will continue to intercede on your behalf with your brother, Hassan, and will do all I can to insure your return to Seville. Unfortunately, because of the distance between Seville and Bivar, negotiations may be lengthy."

"Am I to understand then that you have

dropped your ransom demands?" She watched him sharply.

"Of course! Dammit! We were both fools, Mirjana — you to try to trick your way out of a marriage to Yusuf, and me to think I could force my hand in demanding a double ransom. Had Mútadid lived, no doubt you would have been returned to Seville. But have you considered under what condition you would have returned?"

Mirjana hung her head. Certainly she had considered the conditions. Mútadid more than likely would have secured her release from the infamous Christian as a matter of pride, but her father's retributions would have been swift and merciless. He would have disowned her *publicly* in order to maintain his alliance with Yusuf. After all, she was but a worthless woman, regardless of the affection between Mútadid and herself. All the more reason, she realized, to be grateful for Ruy's intercession. A woman in this world could do nothing for herself. Her power was only as great as the influence of the man who championed her. And now, since Hassan sat on the throne, it was well that her champion was the powerful El Cid. Perhaps nothing more than family pride would prompt Hassan to accept her back into the bosom of the family.

Her dejection infuriated him, made him realize his guilt. If only he had not tried to ransom her . . . If only he had contented himself with the priceless booty of the caravan . . . If only . . . if only. The boiling emotions were cooled by his need to protect her, and he found it was a double-edged sword. Mirjana's needs were not merely physical, they were also emotional. She was a *princesa,* a member of royalty, and he would not allow her spirit and self-respect to be crushed. It was also the main reason he had come to her room to take her to the table. He intended to make her position in his household clear to one and all right from her first night here. This was especially imperative where Doña Ysabel was concerned, and he would not allow her to evade this chance to establish herself in the eyes of his mother, his friends, and to all of Bivar.

"Change your gown," he said authoritatively. "The meal awaits us."

"I need more than a change of gown. I need a bath! If you had used your head and your eyes, you would have known I could not have stayed the night in this room in the condition it was in. You say you have seen scullery maids in better attire? No doubt," she said sarcastically. "If this room was any indication of how your house is kept, your scullery maids' hands have never touched scrub water!"

Ruy smiled, the sparkle and deviltry returning to his eyes. This was the Mirjana he knew! Fighting, spitting, demanding justice for herself. "Get your change of garments," he said darkly. "I will see to your bath." There was a sudden hunger for her building in his loins. She had no idea how beautiful she looked — hair wild and tumbling, gown wet and clinging from the scrub water.

"It will do you no good, Ruy," she said warningly. "I am known for my lengthy and leisurely baths. It would be best not to wait supper on my account." She opened the trunk and removed a change of clothing, including long, finely knitted stockings and a fresh kirtle. "Now, if you will have the servants bring me a tub —"

Her words were cut off in midsentence as Ruy seized her as easily as he might pick up a child. With his free hand he gathered up her fresh clothes and carried her out of the room. Spitting and scratching, she fought him all the way down the tower stairs and along the corridor to the stairway leading to the great hall. He had her firmly tucked under his arm, her heels dragging on the stone floor. Just at the top of the main stairway, he released her, only to pick her up again with one powerful arm and sling her over his shoulder. Her fists beat against his back. Her voice was raised in a clamor as she cursed him in the tongue of Islam. Her hair broke free of its pins and tumbled down over her face as she continued her struggles. Only the harsh and imperious sound of Doña Ysabel's voice made her realize that he had carried her down to the great hall.

"Ruy! Ruy!" Doña Ysabel screamed. "What are you doing? Where are you going? I insist you stop this and come to the table immediately!"

Teodoro's young voice piped, repeating his words over and over. "Are you going to beat her, Ruy? Huh? Are you going to beat her? Can I watch? can I?"

Mirjana's struggles ended. She had never been so ashamed in her entire life. She lay limply over his shoulder, derriere high in the air, her head hanging down his back, her arms covering her face to hide her disgrace.

"I will come to the table, Madre, after the *princesa* has had her bath! You will await our return!"

"A bath!" Doña Ysabel screeched. "In my home? A home devoted to the teachings of the church? Never! *Mi Dios! Mi Dios!* Padre Tomas! Speak some sense to my son! A bath! Did I not tell you she was a devil! Did I not? Not from the day of her Christening does a woman bathe! Tell him, Padre!"

"There would be little use for it, Señora,

since the *princesa* is a Muslim and therefore has never been baptized." Padre Tomas rolled his eyes upward and shifted his bulk on the wooden bench where he sat. "Would that few good women were christened," he mourned, "no doubt the air around them would be more pleasant."

Doña Ysabel sputtered her disbelief while Teodoro whined, "I want to watch Ruy beat her! Madre, I want to watch Ruy beat her."

It was with enormous relief that Mirjana heard the door slam behind them, shutting out the din from the great hall.

CHAPTER 7

Immediately after he had kicked the door shut behind them, Mirjana continued her fast and frenzied struggles, beating on the broadness of his back, kicking her feet, aiming for his vulnerable regions.

"Oh, no you don't, Princesa! You requested a bath and a bath you shall have!" He carried her across the courtyard, gaining the attentions and speculations of the curious eyes of the stable hands, along the path to the right, skirting the *castillo*'s walls, beyond the stables to a low-roofed structure of the same stone as the castle. Ruy went to the door, kicking it furiously, shouting, "Come out of there! Now! Come out!"

Mirjana could hear the sounds of startled men from within, making protest at this invasion. The door opened suddenly. A naked man wielding a broad sword and ready to do action stood there, and when he realized the interloper was none other than the Cid himself, his mouth dropped open in astonishment, which was doubled when he realized Ruy hefted a female on his shoulder.

"Clear out!" Ruy ordered again, setting the man into action, repeating his leader's orders to all within. It was with red-faced embarrassment that Mirjana realized he had taken her to the bathhouse where warriors and guardsmen could steam away the pains of battle and their rigorous training. Vaporous steam hissed from within, blasting and swirling foggily into the sudden rush of cool air from the open doorway.

No less than eight men rushed the doorway, giving hasty salutes as they passed their leader, their eyes politely shifting from Mirjana's presence. A few of them were too surprised to do more than gape while others laughed outright in good humor at her predicament.

"Put me down!" she cried, eager to be away from these curious glances, and frightened at what Ruy planned to do with her now that he had her here. She had demanded a bath and he had said he would see to it himself. And he never repeated an order twice, as he was quick to remind her!

Stepping over the threshold, Ruy kicked the door shut behind him and dumped Mirjana unceremoniously onto a bench with such force her teeth rattled. The interior of the bathhouse was steamy and dimly lit. There were several chest-high square enclosures constructed of wooden planking with tarred seams that served as tubs. In the center of the low-ceilinged room was a glowing brazier of immense proportions around which stones were piled and glowed red. Beside this stood a pail of water and a dipper from which, when water was sprinkled over the rocks, steam would sizzle and fill the room.

"Undress," he told her, his eyes giving challenge.

"Surely, you do not expect me to — to bathe in your presence?" She heard her own voice tinged with fear, knowing full well that was exactly what he expected.

"I do. If I remember correctly, the first time I set eyes on you, you were bathing. You carried yourself quite well at that time, if I remember. I was astounded by your lack of modesty. Tell me, Mirjana, what has caused you to change your ways?" There was that slow smile she had come to know so well, that dark, amused mockery in his eyes.

"I did not know you then!" she answered inanely, crossing her arms over her breasts in an unconscious gesture of defense.

"Oh, am I to take it you only disrobe for strangers then?"

"Oh . . . oh, you are enjoying this, aren't you!" she spit angrily.

"Why would a woman of your seeming intelligence think I was enjoying this?" he laughed. "Do you think it is my pleasure to wait upon you like a humble servant? Do you think I enjoy attending you at your bath?"

"Yes, damn your eyes, I do!"

A wicked grin worked its way around Ruy's mouth. He winked insolently, bringing her temper to a flare. "You are quite astute, for a woman," he teased. "Now, will you undress, or will I do it for you?"

"You wouldn't!" she gasped, then trying to reassume her dignity, she said haughtily, "I am no slattern, my lord, and I am quite capable of seeing to my own needs."

"Ah! But what of my needs, Mirjana?" His eyes half-closed sleepily, insolently. "Besides, what have you that I have not already seen?" he asked, bringing her closer to him, working the back laces of her gown, pulling it down away from her shoulder. "What can you be hiding that my hands have not already caressed?" The gown slipped to the floor and her kirtle was being lifted over her legs, already exposing the soft white flesh of her thighs. "And have you some secret my lips have not already kissed?"

Mirjana was mesmerized by the slow deliberateness of his hands as they undressed her and by the husky intimacy of his voice. She wanted to run, or to stay and fight, to protest this casual use of her. But his hands were already plotting courses down her shoulders and back, and his lips were navigating the curve of her neck and the valley between her breasts. Breathless, her protests died in her throat. The existence of a world outside the span of his arms and the touch of his lips was lost to her. While her mind screamed complaints of these intimacies, her body was betraying her.

He stripped her — gown, kirtle, stockings, everything — leaving her naked and beautiful and within access of his hands, his eyes, his lips.

His hands were hard, rough on her skin, but his touch was gentle. His were the hands of a warrior, calloused and tough, used to wielding a sword and the reins of his mount, not given to the softness of a woman's skin and the silky strands of her hair. And she loved his touch, welcomed it, allowing it to stir the embers of the passions she had discovered only the night before into a blaring fire.

He found her lips with his own, felt them yield beneath his. The room was steamy, hot, making her body break out into beads of perspiration that slickened her skin and gave it a sheen, like a pearl from the sea.

He was impatient for her, wanting her, feeling as though he would never have enough of her. Her lovemaking from the night before had not satisfied him. He doubted he would ever be satisfied, always wanting more of her than she would give. She was a woman of profound depths, and he wanted to plunge himself into her, seeking out the farthest recesses of her, hungry to possess her completely, totally, body and mind.

Mirjana wedged her arms between herself and his chest. "Ruy," she reminded him breathlessly, "you brought me here for a bath."

His lips trailed lazily up her throat finding the hollow and pleasure point beneath her ear. "Hmmm. Yes, so I did." Reluctantly, he released her, allowing her to dart across to one of the tubs. She plunged in, settling herself in the hot water up to her shoulders.

Mirjana felt the heat from the water seep into her bones and aching muscles. Various pungent herbs hung from the rafters, releasing their fragrance in the steam from the rocks. A sigh of contentment escaped her and she lowered herself deeper into the tub.

The heat from the water was not as hot as the touch of his hands upon her skin as his fingers trailed over her shoulders and down to her breasts. Mirjana tipped her head back, allowing his lips access to the pulse point at the base of her throat. When he leaned over the rim of the tub to avail himself of her white, rosy-tipped breasts, she was surprised, but not alarmed, to find he was naked.

The coppery glow from the brazier lit the bathhouse in a rosy glow, giving deep bronze tones to his skin. The night before when her fingers had explored him greedily, the darkness in his tent had cloaked him from her view. Now her gaze covered him, searching, voyaging his body, and seeing the patterns of dark, soft hair covering his chest and narrowing down his belly as though to direct her eyes to the swell of his manhood and the power of his thighs. His hips were slim, punctuated by the high roundness of his haunches. He was beautiful, she thought, sleek and clean of line, like a panther she had once seen that was brought from the jungles of India. Dark, wavy hair tumbled over his forehead, lending him a boyish look, but the expression in his eyes was all man, hungry, wanting, demanding to have her.

She opened her arms to him, fulfilling a need he created within her, inviting him into her embrace. He slipped into the tub beside her, seizing her in his arms, sliding his length against her water-slick body, feeling each distinguishable curve of her breasts, her hips, her thighs. His gaze scorched her being, a dangerous look, compelling her to return his passions, to feed herself on them, and in turn, to satisfy him.

Her eyes had turned from crystal to an ashy, cinder-like gray. Her lids were partly closed, giving her a sleepy expression which belied the movement of her hands upon his flesh and the charge of passion that dwelled on her lips. She was all that was beautiful, womanly; her mouth was made for kissing, ripe and full and his for the taking.

Her responses to his lovemaking unleashed a driving need that set his pulse pounding and heightened his awareness. He wanted to take her immediately, believing he would shatter into thousands of fragments if he did not possess her at once. More generous sensibilities overrode his desires. Mirjana's body responded beneath a gentle touch, a slow progression of intimacies, and he was sensitive to her needs to be loved softly, slowly, allowing her hungers to build until they were as ravenous and voracious as his own. Making love to Mirjana was a seduction, and he knew that each time he would have her she would come into his arms willingly, happily, trusting him to fire her sexuality.

Her light, sensual touches found his buttocks, grazing the backs of his thighs, slipping between them. There was fluidity to her caresses, silkened by the water. The tub had become too confining for his liking. He wanted to stretch out beside her, wanted to see her in this coppery light that lit her red-gold hair to fire. In an easy, smooth motion he rose from the tub, gathering her into his arms, carrying her to a mat of toweling where he lay her down. Her wet skin glistened, sleek and polished, the light catching and emphasizing each vulnerable curve and swell of her body. Downy, golden hair below her stomach bloomed triumphantly on the swell of her sex, and he knew an unquenchable desire to kiss the smooth skin of her inner thighs and explore those regions that were so sensitive to his touch and were doubly so to his lips.

Mirjana's fingers slid through his tangle of dark chest hairs. She triumphed in the hardness of his body and his obvious desire for her. His hands moved over her gently, slowly, spending time to bring her to full arousal, and would not be satisfied with less. His hands spanned her waist, then slid down to her hips, raising them, lifting her for access to his lips. The world seemed to spin around her, leaving her frozen with anticipation at its vortex. She found the thick, curling hair at the back of his head, gripping it between her fingers, pulling it, while she followed his greedy mouth with her body, yielding her flesh to it.

And when his lips returned to her mouth she could taste herself there, her body molded to his, fitting her curves against the hard planes of his body. She shivered with expectation when his thighs parted her own and he lowered himself over her, taking her quickly, sensing her urgency that he make himself part of her.

There was a sunburst at her very center, searing, exploding, bringing her ever closer to that exquisite pleasure. She matched his rhythm, driving herself against his hardness, her legs wrapped around his hips, locking him within her. And when he heard the cry of his name upon her lips, he silenced them with his own, knowing she had found her release, driving himself ever deeper into her, searching for his own.

They lay in each other's arms, legs entwined, arms embracing. His lips traced along her hairline where the red-gold fury of hair met the whiteness of her brow. His hands cupped her breast in a lazy caress, rubbing his thumb over the coral tip more with a desire to soothe than to enflame.

Mirjana lay with her head upon his shoulder, listening to his quiet, deep breaths, finding this intimacy after lovemaking delicious and tranquil. She was learning this was something Ruy enjoyed almost as much as the exchange of passion. Even the night before while in his tent, he had held her this way after the loving. He was a passionate man, a sensual man, encouraging her to caress him, to hold him while he did the same for her. She realized, though inexperienced, that without this gentle and tender aftermath, she would have felt used, discarded, the abrupt end to her passion leaving her cold and unfulfilled. How did he instinctively know this part of lovemaking was essential to her?

Ruy placed his lips close to her ear, telling her how he had delighted in her, bringing blushes to her cheeks as he described to her in detail how wonderful she was and how she had made him feel. He told her she was like no other woman, listing those things he found intrinsically hers alone. Whispers fanned her cheek as he told her how he worshipped the return of his passion, the fullness of her breasts, the lovely, delicate skin between her thighs. But most of all, he liked to watch her eyes when she was about to realize the reward of her desires — half-open, looking into his, melting her being into him. And how the sound of his name, deep and vibrant in her need, was echoed in the wild thrusts of his haunches and in his total joy of her.

Mirjana nestled snugly into Ruy's arms,

rendering herself up to the glory of the moment.

When Ruy and Mirjana finally returned to the great hall within the *castillo* it was to face Doña Ysabel's stare, her eyes as small and hard as little black stones. While she voiced no recriminations, she was obviously offended at the behavior of her eldest son and this wicked woman he had inflicted upon her. The señora's eyes were quick to notice that Mirjana had changed her soiled gown in favor of a turquoise one of light wool, elaborately embroidered at the sleeves and hemline by skilled hands. The girl's kirtle was startlingly white against the blue, and her hair, still damp from the steam in the bathhouse, clung to her temples and the nape of her neck in shining ringlets. Yes, Doña Ysabel knew her son had carried this heathen off to the bathhouse, and it did not take much imagination on her part to know what his purposes were.

Torches smoked black against the stone walls of the hall, and the fire in the hearth had been recently replenished. Teodoro confronted them accusingly, still whining how hungry he was while he stuffed his mouth full with chunks of dark bread. Pietro, still in his newly tailored tunic of burgundy cloth, looked admiringly at Mirjana, successfully hiding his welcoming smile from the señora whose wrath he had met once too often. Only Padre Tomas stood to greet them, gesturing to Mirjana a place beside him while Ruy took his usual seat at the head of the table between Teodoro and Doña Ysabel.

Ruy offered no excuses as to why the meal had been delayed on his account. Instead, he lowered his head and asked Padre Tomas to bless the table. He had taken as his due his right as head of household that the meal should not commence until he was ready to break bread.

Mirjana could feel the señora's piercing gaze upon her while Padre Tomas said the prayer. She realized Ruy's insistence upon having her sit with his family was to make it clear to everyone, especially his mother, just what position she held. She was a guest, not a servant.

A sudden rush of color stained Mirjana's cheeks. There was no doubt in her mind as to what position she held in the Diaz household. In return for Ruy's protection and intervention with Hassan, she had become his whore!

The next morning, after a surprisingly peaceful night's sleep, Mirjana went down the back stairs to the kitchen area, deciding to avoid the great hall entirely. More than likely,

Doña Ysabel was there enjoying her breakfast and meeting with the servants to dispense their orders for the day ahead. Tanige had gone down earlier, carrying soiled garments and other items to be laundered.

The back stairs, while not dusty and grimy as had been the stairs leading to the tower, were nevertheless filthy. Bits of spilled food and crumbs littered the corners, inviting insects and other vermin. The total disregard for cleanliness surprised Mirjana who had always considered Doña Ysabel remarkably well-groomed and turned out. Apparently, the señora's interests were more to her person than to her household. She made a mental note to have the stairs swept and scrubbed, even if she must do it herself.

Passing through the kitchens where the hearth burned brightly and bread baked with its pleasant aroma, Mirjana was quick to see other affronts to her meticulous upbringing. The floor was littered with spilled food, and the covering of rushes was the perfect hiding place for vermin of all kinds while mangy dogs perused the corners looking for fallen scraps. Underfoot, the earthen floor was muddy from spilled liquids, and in other places footsteps had worn it into treacherous gullies. Did all Christians live this way? she wondered, remembering the sparkling freshness of the palace in Seville. In Islam, cleanliness and order were mandates of Allah and the prophet Muhammad.

Mirjana asked for Tanige and was told by the same aged servant who had shown them to their tower room the night before that she would find her handmaiden in the pantry just beyond the kitchen. She knew the old woman was correct when she heard Tanige's high-pitched screech of anger. It was a sound she dreaded and knew by heart, having heard it at least once a day since she was ten years old.

By putting her weight against the stout kitchen door that hung crookedly on its hinges, Mirjana managed to push it open. Tanige was in the pantry, the laundry scattered about her feet, scuffling with a youth, pushing him toward the entry to the kitchen yard.

"Tanige! What are you doing?" Mirjana shouted above the din.

"This — this insult to the eyes of Allah seems to believe he can issue me orders! He says he has other duties and cannot make a fire for the wash water. I told him I would do it myself and he said I could not. He seems to think I, attendant to Princess Mirjana, have no rights!"

Mirjana's soft gray eyes turned to lava as

she stared at the youth who was uneasily attempting to back out the door into the yard. "Is what Tanige tells me true?" She saw how frightened the youth was and softened her tone. "Perhaps you do not understand what is required. Firstly, water heated, with which to wash our garments. Secondly, and no less important, a tub. What is your name?" she asked him, forcing a smile. Allah be blessed, was everything to be so difficult here in Bivar?

"Alvar," the boy said shyly. Then braver, "I would like to help but it is forbidden. I will be whipped."

Mirjana frowned. "Who will whip you?"

"Doña Ysabel. She will have me whipped," he said, scuffing his feet together.

"Did Doña Ysabel tell you it was forbidden to help us heat water to wash our clothes?" Mirjana asked. He shook his head. "Then you will not be punished. I will see to it myself. Now, please Alvar, help Tanige with the water. First bring a tub."

After Alvar had left the pantry, Tanige sidled up to Mirjana and whispered, "Princess, you have no right to promise him anything, much less that he will not be beaten."

Turning on Tanige, sparks glinting in her eyes, Mirjana was quick to chastise. "You had that boy frightened half to death, do you realize this? With all your caterwauling I'm certain he's fled and will not return."

Mirjana was proved wrong when Alvar returned with a wide tub and helped Tanige bring hot water in from the fire in the kitchen. He was obviously still quite frightened because as soon as he filled the tub from the pails he ran out of the pantry. Mirjana looked after him, wondering if she had been too hasty in demanding that he assist them, wondering if she had been too quick to promise him he would not be punished. From the attitude of the kitchen help, it was plain that Doña Ysabel had ordered there was to be no fraternizing between the lord's houseguest and the staff.

The sun rode high in the sky when Tanige crept silently into their shared tower room. The soft smile on Mirjana's sleeping face did not go unnoticed. Although her mistress had not shared the fact that she was sleeping with El Cid, Tanige knew it to be true. Down in the kitchens and out in the courtyard the servants were buzzing with the news that their lord had brought himself an Islamic princess who warmed his bed and put lightness in his step.

"Mirjana, Mirjana." Tanige shook her shoulder, waking her. "Doña Ysabel demands you see her in the hall. Now. Please wake up, Doña Ysabel wants to see you."

"Mmm," Mirjana mumbled sleepily. The

stress of situating herself in this house and the labors with the laundry that morning had exhausted her. "Go away, leave me be." She contradicted her words by rubbing at her eyes and sitting up on the narrow cot. "What time is it, Tanige?"

"Past midday. I had not the heart to awaken you until Doña Ysabel caught me in the corridor and commanded you meet her in the great hall. Now!"

Regretfully pulling herself from the last vestiges of the dream she was having where she was lying in Ruy's arms and he was repeating the most wonderful things into her ear, Mirjana snapped to attention. She had been expecting to hear from Doña Ysabel sooner or later, and this was an audience she had decided to face head on.

Quickly bathing her face from the water in the ewer, Mirjana raked her brush through her hair and braided it, artfully arranging it at the back of her head.

"Hurry, Mirjana. Doña Ysabel was like a fire-eating dragon. She has the sting of a viper, and that little plotting devil sits beside her while he dreams up new ways to torment the servants." Tanige's upper lip curled in disgust.

"Perhaps if Teodoro were not shown such animosity, he would be more inclined to be kind to others," Mirjana defended. Little as she liked the boy herself, he was a child, and the blame for his behavior was more justly placed on the influence of those around him.

Doña Ysabel was waiting for Mirjana in a chair by the hearth in the great hall. The atmosphere was still smoky and stale from the night before and was in need of a good airing. Several of the dogs she had seen in the kitchen were rooting through the matted straw under the long, planked table searching for scraps in their never-ending hunger. The señora was dressed, as usual, in somber shades of gray and black, the only relief being the exquisite lace on her collar. Her gleaming dark hair was pulled severely back from her face, and a mantle of finely woven linen draped from her head to her narrow shoulders.

"Come here!" the señora commanded when she saw Mirjana come down the stairway. "I believe you were told to use the kitchen stairs, were you not?"

"Yes, I was." It was a statement and she would offer no excuse as to why she had not followed the order. "I was informed you wished to see me."

Disregarding Mirjana's insolence in disobeying the order concerning the correct staircase to use, Doña Ysabel launched on a hasty attack. "In my son's household we do not lay abed in the middle of the day. Everyone is expected to contribute his or her share to make the *castillo* of El Cid run smoothly and efficiently. My son is a military man" — the woman lifted her chin proudly — "and in the military, order, not chaos, is valued. Since you have no female guardian, as a favor to my son, I intend to take you in hand myself." The señora's words were clipped, authoritative, broaching no argument. "The girl you brought with you can be put to use in the kitchens while you will be in charge of the bed chambers. That would seem a likely place for your talents, would it not?" A wicked smirk twisted Doña Ysabel's mouth, and the smack of insult was not lost on Mirjana.

"What exactly do you mean?" Mirjana challenged.

"It means exactly what you take it to mean." Then, more innocently, "You will see to the chambers, laundering bed linens, and emptying chamber pots . . . among other things. Although I believe you take a special interest in laundry, is that so?"

"All things interest me, Doña Ysabel." Her tone was smooth, even respectful, but Mirjana's glinting eyes and imperious tilt of her chin infuriated the señora. "And if I refuse your generous offer, Señora?"

It was clear the idea of Mirjana refusing her

direct order never occurred to Doña Ysabel. "Then I will have to take it up with my son. I assured him I would take you under my charge."

Mirjana's eyes dropped to the stone floor where Teodoro sat curled at his mother's feet, playing with the straps of her shoes. He was industriously fastening the straps together.

"Then, Doña Ysabel, it would be wise of you to confer with your son again. You can tell him you suggested certain household chores for Tanige and myself, and Princess Mirjana refused your offer."

"You what?" Doña Ysabel sputtered.

"I refuse to become your servant." Her words were cool, smooth, despite the roiling anger that beat through her.

"I have told Ruy it was a mistake to bring you here. You are beyond salvation! I have already offered you my assistance in sending you back to where you came from. You also refused that! I warn you, Princesa whoever-you-are! My son will not be hampered by one such as you. He is a mighty military leader, strong and victorious. He has only begun his illustrious career. He is a Diaz, truly his father's son. He is consort to royalty; all of Castile looks to him for leadership. He is an honor to both his country and his family, and

I will not allow you to tamper with his future!" Her words were barely a hiss, her face pinched, red with hatred. Mirjana had found an enemy in Doña Ysabel who was clearly ambitious for her son's career and was determined that nothing and no one stand in his path to glory. Plainly, the señora had seen Mirjana at first as a temporary inconvenience. Now, since Ruy had placed her at the table among his family, Doña Ysabel saw her as a threat to his future.

"Also, this is a Christian household. I will not abide your flights of vanity. Nor will I treat lightly your countermanding my instructions to the servants. Oh, yes, I am well aware of your bathing last evening, as I am aware of your fetish to launder your gaudy dresses. You should know that the boy, Alvar, will be punished for assisting you."

"Madre, Madre, I want to do it! I want to punish him!" Teodoro whined.

"We will see," Doña Ysabel said fondly, running her hands through the boy's curly locks.

Mirjana's eyes dropped to the floor again to see Teodoro's eyes bright with anticipation. "Señora, you cannot mean to punish a boy for bringing a tub for laundry." Her voice was incredulous.

"I can and I do, Princesa," the señora said

dryly. "As mistress, I have a certain duty to my people. Among those duties is the keeping of their religion and their soul to God," she said piously. "Teddy, *caro,* when Alvar has completed his work for the day, you can give him five lashes with the whip." Doña Ysabel smirked as she stared straight into Mirjana's unbelieving eyes.

"Señora, you would not have a boy beaten. Certainly, Ruy would not allow it."

"My son does not concern himself with the household. He is a warrior, vassal to the realm, destined to become a part of Castile's ruling history. The duties of the *castillo* are women's work. You do not seem to understand, Princesa. The boy, Alvar, is a regrettable victim of your own vanity! Here in Castile, among Christians, women are taught to be more concerned for their souls and preparing the way to heaven than they are for vain habits that are of the devil's contrivance to turn a man's eyes away from his Savior and towards carnal temptations. Another consideration, Alvar must be made an example of so the others will know that I, their mistress, disapprove of disobeying orders. Vanity, Princesa, is a sin against God and will not be tolerated!"

Despite her show of bravado, Mirjana's knees were shaking. She had never faced such fanaticism, and it frightened her. She realized many sins against humanity could be condoned by claiming religious fervor. "Since the sin was mine, I will take Alvar's punishment."

Teodoro quickly looked up from his busy fingers, first at his mother and then at Mirjana. "You will *both* be whipped!" he piped in his child's voice, a malicious satisfaction evident on his too plump and pretty features.

Mirjana's movements were panther quick as she reached out to grasp Teodoro's arm. She pulled him to his feet and then bent over till she was on a level with his eyes. "Listen to me; I will say this but once. If you so much as touch Alvar, I will take a whip to you myself. This is not a threat but a promise!"

"Madre, Madre, help me!" he cried, struggling to escape Mirjana's grip. "She's hurting me, Madre!"

"Take your heathen hands off my son! Don't dare to touch him!" Doña Ysabel screeched. "Ruy will hear of this!"

Aghast at what she had done, Mirjana released her hold on the wiggling child. She backed off a step as Teodoro rushed past her, his eyes wide with fright. Doña Ysabel stood to rush to her son's defense. She staggered, cried out with surprise, and fell forward. Cries of, "You wicked, wretched child!" echoed in Mirjana's ears as she hastily left the room.

She ran headlong into Tanige who was eavesdropping at the top of the stairs. "What are you looking at, Tanige? Wipe that look of horror off your face! You should be proud of me; I have refused the señora our services as additions to her household staff."

"Very proud, Mirjana. But you volunteered for a whipping. It is at times like this I question your education and logic." A thought occurred to Tanige, and she narrowed her eyes and pinched her face into stubbornness. "Since you offered yourself to stand in for the boy Alvar, do not look to me to stand in your place."

Mirjana laughed, "Tanige, I better than anyone am well aware of how deep your allegiance to me runs."

"You let your mouth run away with your better senses, Princess. Now Doña Ysabel will find other methods of revenge."

"We must defend our rights, Tanige. We must never humble ourselves or forget our self-respect. There is a saying that if one lays with dogs he will rise with fleas! What Doña Ysabel calls vanity is merely self-respect."

Tanige, holding fast to her decision that Mirjana's offer to accept the boy's punishment was still foolish, said sourly, "And did you maintain your self-respect when you took hold of Teodoro and threatened him?"

Color rose in Mirjana's cheeks. "I must not

allow myself to forget he is but a boy and a product of his mother's spoiling. I was wrong to threaten him, but fair is fair. Alvar does not deserve a whipping. It is you and I who are to blame for forcing him to assist us against his orders."

Tanige regretted seeing the reasoning behind Mirjana's statements. Still, she told herself, Mirjana had best not attempt to place blame on her for Alvar's misfortune. Even though she was the princess's servant she still had rights, and she would not take the punishment for which Mirjana had volunteered herself. "Why was Doña Ysabel screaming at Teodoro?" she asked, wanting the last piece to the puzzle of the commotion she had overheard.

"Oh, that," Mirjana smiled. "Teodoro tied the señora's shoe-straps together and she toppled over like a great stone wall. I could hardly believe what I was seeing! You should have been there, Tanige."

"I should have," Tanige replied smugly.

It was later in the afternoon when Mirjana went out into the kitchen yard with Tanige, lifting her face to the warm sunshine, enjoying the fresh, pleasant smell of their laundry as Tanige took it down from the line. The pungent aroma of newly turned earth from where several men were spading for the planting of vegetables and herbs caused her to remember the lovely gardens surrounding the palace in Seville. Not for the first time, the thought occurred to her that this *castillo* could become quite lovely, if rustic, under the right hand.

Mirjana sighted the storerooms, two-storied stone structures erected behind the stables. Outside stood the empty wagons which had been filled to brimming with the gifts Mútadid had intended for Yusuf to celebrate the marriage. The thought of her personal belongings almost brought tears to her eyes. How comforting it would be to have her own precious possessions around her in this strange and alien place.

"Tanige," Mirjana called, "finish with our laundry later. For now, there is something more important we must do." Quickly, she related her intention to retrieve her personal belongings from the storehouses. "We will just take what we need for now. And only those things that belong to us. While I go see if I can find someone who will help us, try to find that Persian carpet that used to lay just inside my balcony doors. Its bright colors will serve well in our dingy tower."

An hour later Tanige was muttering in complaint as she helped ransack the trunks and barrels, searching for her own personal possessions as well as Mirjana's. They had gathered most of the furnishings from the suite in the palace as well as their clothing. "Princess, see what I have found!" she cried exultantly. "Look — spices, herbs, cooking oil. No doubt it was meant to supply the caravan all the way to Granada and back again. For the two of us, it will last many months!"

Earlier that day Tanige had complained to Mirjana about the unseasoned food — too salty and less than fresh. On the one hand she was glad to have found the rare spices and seasonings; on the other she regretted her statement that it would last them many months. It was a dismal thought to remember that their future was still in question, and they did not know when, if ever, they would return to Seville. Quickly, before Mirjana's thoughts ran along the same line as her own, she offered to prepare dinner for them. "Tell me, Princess, what do you fancy?"

Mirjana laughed, her mood considerably lightened by the knowledge that the tower room would be less bleak and austere now that she had reclaimed her things. "I care little, Tanige. Something simple. With a lot of paprika and yogurt sauce?"

Immediately, Tanige's face fell into a dissolute frown. "Yogurt? Where am I to get yogurt? Better to ask for sherbet, or strawberries, or honeyed lamb!"

"I understand clabbered milk is much like our yogurt. Tomorrow, early, we will see to it."

"And where did the princess acquire such knowledge about cooking?" Tanige squinted suspiciously. She did not believe for one moment that Mirjana was acquainted with food preparation. Never, in all the time she had known her, had Mirjana shown an interest in menial chores.

"From a book, of course," Mirjana told her blithely. "As I recall, it was an exploration of the differences and similarities between Islamic culture and Christian —"

Tanige rolled her eyes. "Enough, Princess. If it is clabbered milk you desire, you will have it. And you will be wanting the service plates and goblets as well as the table linens?"

"Certainly," Mirjana answered, thinking of how she disliked the stale bread trenchers the Castilians used in place of tableware.

A voice behind her suddenly spoke. "My lady, you may not remove these things from the storehouse." It was a burly, giant of a man dressed in peasant's clothing. He tugged at his forelock politely but his expression was forbidding, fearful.

"You are mistaken. They are already removed. As they belong to me, I mean to have them. They were only being stored here until

I could claim them." Mirjana spoke quietly, softly, immediately liking this big man. Did everyone in this house live in fear of punishment? First it was the old servant who pulled on her ear, then it was the youth, Alvar, and now this man.

"You possess many beautiful things, milady. If you are certain you have permission to take them, I offer myself to carry them for you."

Mirjana was touched. How well he spoke, how gentle he seemed. "What is your name?" she asked as he hoisted a barrel of table linens to his broad shoulder.

"Gormaz," he answered as he hoisted the barrel onto a two-wheeled cart.

"Have you always lived in Bivar? Do you have a family here?" Mirjana saw Tanige throw her a quizzical glance. Since when did the princess acquaint herself with servants? And when had she become so interested in the private lives of those who served her? But Mirjana was thinking of how Ruy had known the name of the captain of the guard who had escorted the caravan out of Seville, while she who had spoken to the man on several occasions had never thought to ask. She was remembering the shame she had felt as she stood there on the battlefield and saw the loss of lives of those who had only tried to protect her, never knowing it was her own treachery that had defeated them.

"I have lived in Bivar all my life, and took a wife last winter. My wife is with child, but she is ailing, and the old women say she will lose the child or die with it." The concern in his voice tore at Mirjana's heart.

"Has she seen a physician?" she asked ignorantly.

Gormaz halted his movements to look at her blankly. "My lady?" Clearly, he did not know the meaning of the word.

"Someone who tends to the sick and ailing?"

His face brightened with understanding. "Several midwives in Bivar care for the sick — and, of course, Doña Ysabel. But all efforts have been useless, and my wife is in great distress."

Prompted to do something for this kindly man, Mirjana rummaged furiously through a trunk of books and ordered Tanige to discover the whereabouts of a certain coffer of medicinal herbs and powders. "These books," she told Gormaz, "were written by learned physicians, healers. Leave these things for now and take me to your wife. Trust me, Gormaz, if I can help her, I will."

"But Don Ruy? What will he say if his . . . lady tends to his peasants?"

Mirjana heard the slight hesitation in Gormaz when he qualified her relationship with Ruy. So, all of Bivar knew by now that she was their lord's whore. Yet, Gormaz hadn't placed a judgment, and perhaps others would also be as kind. "Don Ruy will be happy if your wife recovers. He places value upon his people," she said confidently, knowing this to be true. It was Doña Ysabel who decided Ruy was not to be concerned with his home or people in Bivar, prodding him on to distinguish himself in service to the throne and not to those who depended upon him for their livelihood.

"My home is not far, milady, but we must walk. My wife will be most grateful. For months she has not been able to keep food in her stomach, and she becomes weaker as the child grows. I — I fear for losing her. I was not a young man when I married. Do you think you can help her?" There was such hope in his voice, and it was obvious he loved his wife dearly. Mirjana was filled with compassion for him.

"I cannot promise, Gormaz. I can only do my best."

Just outside the *castillo* walls and over the draw bridge was the home of Gormaz. It was a humble hut with an ancient, thatched roof, and outside in the yard the summer garden, obviously planted with great care, was already sprouting with tender green shoots. The front steps were swept clean, and inside, in the one room which served as both kitchen and bedroom, the earthen floors were scattered with sweet, freshly cut straw with occasional sprigs of thyme and sage that when crushed underfoot gave off a pleasing aroma. She could not help thinking of the disorder and careless tending in the *castillo*.

On the double-rope-strung bed between scrupulously clean bedding lay Gormaz's wife, Ilena, her cheeks white and deeply hollowed. Beside the bedstead was a basin placed conveniently for the girl's sudden, urgent need to empty her stomach.

"Don Ruy's lady has come to see you, Ilena," Gormaz said, shy before Mirjana. "Perhaps she can make you well."

Ilena looked trustingly at Mirjana and smiled weakly as she attempted to sit up. "Oh, my lady, it is unfitting you should find me this way. Gormaz, please, heat water for tea."

"Do not trouble yourself," Mirjana protested. It was obvious to her that these people had barely enough for themselves, and she did not want them to waste their precious herbs in brewing her tea. That was more than likely most of Ilena's problem, poor nutrition.

Quietly, Mirjana asked Ilena her symptoms, after which she pored through her physician's manuals. Finally, she opened her coffer of medicines and brought out a vial of seeds. "Make a brew of these and sweeten it with honey. Drink it often. Also, your meat must be cut lean and cooked well." She patted Ilena's hand comfortingly. "I will come to see you tomorrow," she promised, making a mental note to bring some delicacy to tempt the girl's appetite.

On the walk back to the *castillo,* Gormaz questioned the medicine Mirjana prescribed. "It's fennel. The books say it is soothing to the stomach and eases the digestion. I expect Ilena to improve, Gormaz, but she is near her time and should not work so hard. Keep her off her feet as much as possible, will you?"

The huge man smiled his gratefulness and promised he would do what he could.

"Come, we must return to the *castillo* and move my belongings up to the tower."

Mirjana and Tanige sailed through the great hall carrying baskets of oils and scents while Gormaz followed behind toting a massive load of furnishings that boasted his strength. Behind him trailed Tanige and two stable hands equally laden. Within the hour Mirjana sat on her cot surrounded by her treasures, telling Tanige about her introduction to Ilena and how clean her little hut was kept.

"So, not all Christians are pigs!" Tanige

glowered. "Princess, the kitchen in this *castillo* is overrun with mice and other unspeakable vermin. And the scullery maids itch and scratch and pinch at the fleas that torment them. Bah! So much for Christian holiness! I myself prefer the sins of vanity we Muslims commit each time we bathe and launder our clothes. The laundry!" Tanige screeched, remembering the abandoned garments hanging in the kitchen yard. Like two children, Mirjana and Tanige trampled down the stairs, laughing and squealing.

Using the main staircase down to the great hall, the two skidded to a stop when passing the stout double doors leading to the front courtyard. There was a congregation of people, most of whom they recognized as servants from the *castillo,* and their faces were drawn into silent lines of resignation. A woman, hands covering her face, was weeping, her shoulders shuddering pathetically.

Mirjana's momentary laughter was stilled. Apprehension tickled the hairs on the back of her neck. Forcing herself forward, her steps quickening with each thud of her heart, she pushed herself through the closely gathered throng. Tanige dragged behind, suspecting the reason for this spectacle and cringing from the thought of it.

Alvar, hands securely fastened to a hitching

post, head hanging between his arms, stood ready for his punishment. Teodoro, looking less than certain about whether he regretted obtaining his wish, stood several feet away, wielding a whip that was twice the length of him. Doña Ysabel, hands folded beneath her flowing sleeves, stood behind her son, a sly gleam lighting in her sternly narrowed eyes.

"Ah! Princesa, I find you a woman of your word." The señora's long, thin upper lip curled in a sneer. "Am I correct, did you not volunteer to stand in Alvar's place?"

A gasp went up from the *castillo*'s servants, and all eyes were turned on this strange manner of woman whom their lord had brought from the outer reaches of Castile. Mirjana was silent, frightened by the expression in the señora's eyes and her curious calm. Alvar turned his head, looking at Mirjana through a child's terror. Even Teodoro appeared terrified, confused, and remarkably, Mirjana felt more sympathy for him than even for Alvar. Looking back to the señora, Mirjana nodded. "I did volunteer to stand in Alvar's place. He acted upon my orders, and if any punishment is deserved, it is mine."

Another gasp from the servants, an undertone of chattering and speculation. Doña Ysabel shot a glance of consternation and they became silent. Her mouth curved into a smile.

"It is your privilege, Princesa."

Mirjana's innards were quivering with rage, heaving with trepidation. The señora was too satisfied, too glib to be trusted. Having committed herself to take Alvar's place, Mirjana moved mechanically to the hitching post and released the frightened youth. All the while she was telling herself that Teodoro was only a child, and his inaccurate expertise would be more punishing in the way of humiliation than in physical abuse.

She could feel the señora's eyes on her, watching her every move, satisfied and triumphant. Voluntarily, Mirjana's hands closed over the post. The rough, weathered timber bit into her hands. She glanced backward over her shoulder to Teodoro. "I am ready, Teodoro, and because you are only a child, I forgive you." She wished there were more confidence in her tone.

"*Denada,* Princesa. You have no reason to forgive Teddy. Since you have offered to take the place of a child, I have seen it fitting that you are not punished by a child." One slim, pale hand appeared from her sleeve, and she crooked her finger to signal someone standing behind the portico. From out of the shadows stepped a hulk of a man, his weight and the size of his boots crunching the earth beneath his steps. A thick, wide belt girthed his middle.

His shoulders were bulky and overdeveloped beneath the thin cambric of his shirt. And in his hand he carried a long, snaking whip wound into many coils.

Mirjana's knees buckled, and she clung to the post for support. She heard Tanige's cry of alarm. "Teddy, *cara,*" Doña Ysabel was saying smoothly, gently, in that voice she used only for her youngest son, "come over here to me. You will watch how an expert performs his art."

Teodoro ran to his mother, burying his face in her skirts, whimpering. Despite her circumstances, Mirjana felt pity for the boy. So young, so malleable, with a heart that was actually more inclined to good than the evil effects of his mother's spoiling. She knew instinctively that the child was not whimpering for an opportunity lost. His tears were a combination of relief and fear.

"Begin," the señora's reedy voice echoed through the hushed courtyard, and the first crack of the whip, expertly wielded, sounded.

The blow struck her right shoulder, snaking with exquisite shock across her back. The ensuing pain was paralyzing, and reflexes stiffened her spine as she arched away to press herself against the post. Rough timber bit into her palms. Her nails splintered the wood. With the second blow, aimed at her left shoulder, she heard her gown rip and shred under the biting leather.

When the whip cracked for the third time they came from three directions — Gormaz, with a belly-thundering roar from the stables, Tanige screeching, and Ruy from only Allah knew where.

Sweat poured into Gormaz's eyes as he shouldered Ruy out of his way and pried Mirjana's fingers from her death grip on the post, and she fell into his arms. Her face was white, her soft gray eyes glazed with pain. She only half heard Tanige shriek her name.

Another voice rang above the bedlam. "Who has dared this outrage?" The sudden silence was ominous, deadly, and accusing.

"No outrage, Ruy, rather justice!" Doña Ysabel stepped forward, compelling her eldest son to recognize her rights as chatelaine of his *castillo* and as his mother.

"You! Why?" he demanded, his features darkened with fury. "No, I care nothing for your reasons. No doubt this was all done in the name of Christianity! I have tolerated your bigotry, your overbearing dominance of my household, and I have even sacrificed my own brother to your selfish spoiling against all I know to be right and what my father would wish were he alive! No more of it, Madre. It is ended. I suggest you prepare to leave for a mercy tour of your convents. No doubt the nuns will welcome you to tend their sick. And prepare for an extended tour, Madre. I doubt I will find my tolerance for you renewed for some time to come."

Teodoro, hearing that his mother, his protector, was to be sent away, threw himself against Ruy, attacking with clenched fists and gritted teeth. Grappling with the child and hoisting him upward by his doublet, Ruy laughed. "There's hope for you after all, Teddy! We'll make a man of you yet. While your guardian angel is making her tour of the convents you will remain here and work in the stable with Gormaz."

"No! No! Madre!" he cried.

"Yes, yes, Teddy! You will work with the animals and clean after them and learn some humility." Teodoro spat into his brother's face and was rewarded by Ruy's resounding slap. "Give me the *princesa,* Gormaz. Take my brother back to the stables with you. Fix him a bed and give him work, hard work. Don't allow him out of your sight, and when next I see him, I expect him to display some manners."

Ruy tossed Teodoro away from him and watched with a frown as the boy once again buried his face in his mother's skirts. It saddened him to see the señora's pale and trembling hand reach out to comfort the dark, curly head. "This is *your* punishment, Madre," Ruy said coldly. "It is little wonder why Mirjana's people know us as savages and barbarians. Your actions are inexcusable, ruthless, and beyond my experience with cruelty. And I have been to war."

Gormaz lifted Mirjana into Ruy's arms. "Gentle with her, my lord. She is in pain."

"As I can see," Ruy said hoarsely, taking her into his arms. Tanige followed him into the *castillo,* bleating her distress for her mistress. Behind her, Doña Ysabel.

"The princess has an ointment," Tanige told him. "I'll see to her injuries."

"Then you will do it in my chamber. Find your ointment and be quick about it! There is barely room to turn around in that pigeon cote of a room."

"Ruy . . . Ruy . . . I beg of you, listen to me — your mother!" Doña Ysabel pleaded.

"I have listened to you, Madre, and I have seen the results. I should have taken Teddy in hand much before this. And as for what you have done to this woman, it is unforgivable! She will more than likely bear the scars of your doing for the rest of her life."

"What matter is that?" the señora argued. "She is a heathen, a devil! I am your mother! I gave you life and fed you at my breast. You cannot turn on me this way. Ruy, I implore you . . ."

Ruy looked down into Mirjana's face, saw the white pain there, and could have cried for what he had brought her. If only . . . The never ceasing condemnation for his ransom attempts welled within him. How innocent she was, how giving, how feather-light in his arms. Something rose in his throat and he could not swallow it. His desire to protect her was an actual pain in his middle, and yet he had failed her. Again.

CHAPTER 8

Mirjana made a small and vulnerable figure on the wide expanse of Ruy's bed. The late afternoon sun streaming through the high, unglazed windows seemed to emphasize her whiteness and the tumbling wealth of burnished gold hair. Ruy paced near the foot of the bed, eaten up with recriminations while Tanige attended her mistress.

"This is not the end of this, Tanige," he told her. "I've still to deal with my mother's henchman who wielded the lash!" He pounded one fist into the palm of the other.

"Don Ruy, come see," Tanige gestured to the exposed skin on Mirjana's back. "Look, the skin is not broken." Ruy rushed to her side, inspecting Mirjana's wounds. It was true. While welts rose on the creamy white flesh, it was not broken. Mirjana's pain was real, but she would not be marred for life.

"How is this possible?" Tanige asked. "I myself saw the size of the man and heard the crack of the whip."

"The man is an expert. No doubt he could slice the wings from a fly with his lash. At least we have this to thank him for; he obeyed the señora but did as little damage as possible. But it is not enough!" Again the smack of his fist into his palm.

Tanige's hands were gentle yet quick and efficient as she liberally spread greasy salve over her mistress's back and deftly sprinkled a white powder, careful to coat each welt evenly. A compress of soft cloth was applied. Mirjana lay still, sleeping with the effects of an opiate Tanige had found with the medicines.

"She should sleep for several hours," Tanige murmured. "If I have your permission to stay here, I'll tend her when she wakes."

"Yes, of course," Ruy said impatiently, "this chamber is ample for the lot of us. I want you to see she has every comfort, everything she needs." His eyes kept returning to Mirjana, seeing the soft, yielding flesh that was so tempting to his hands and lips.

"We retrieved our personal belongings from the storehouse earlier today," Tanige said with a hint of defiance in her tone.

"As I was informed. Go, get what you need and I will remain here until your return."

When the door closed behind Tanige, Ruy

sat beside Mirjana on the wide bed. How small she really was, he thought. She hardly disturbed the bedding or feather mattress with her weight. Her face was in profile to him, and he saw the slim, straight nose and full, almost petulant, mouth that seemed so ripe and ready for his kiss. He touched the defiant curls drifting over her cheek, saw a slight flutter of eyelash and quickly took his hand away. He wanted to pick her up and hold her in his arms until the pain subsided. But she appeared so delicate, so fragile, he feared she would break beneath his touch. It was strange to think of Mirjana as delicate, remembering the strength of her temper when she was fighting for justice. And she did not think of herself as fragile, else she would never have offered to stand in Alvar's place.

Tanige returned quickly, her arms full. "I have taken the liberty, earlier today, to prepare supper for the princess and myself. Even now, it is simmering slowly. There is more than enough for my lord."

"I have no appetite. I only want to sit near her for a time. Will I interfere with your duties?"

"Certainly, you'll interfere. You make me nervous under your too watchful eye. And I cannot bear to see your marked concern, although I am certain the princess would appreciate it. There is nothing you can do here."

"What would you have me do?" he asked, puzzled at Tanige's bluntness and his own indecision. He wanted to escape from the evidence of his guilt, and yet he could not bring himself to leave.

"How should a humble servant know?" she voiced her annoyance. Then she softened, pitying his torment. "Later, when the princess awakens, perhaps you can return and take supper with her."

Ruy nodded, glad to be given his opportunity to leave, happy to be invited back.

"Then, my lord, before you leave perhaps you would clear that table of your maps and parchments. I'll lay it in preparation for the princess's supper at my first chance."

Ruy quickly followed her instructions to the letter and quietly left the room, closing the door behind him. When she was certain he would not return, she rushed to Mirjana and removed the coarse coverlet and replaced it with a silken one that was sewn with rainbow bands. She added pillows, all bright and vibrant, some embroidered with scenes from the forest with young animals living together in harmony. Tanige grimaced at the wooden cross bearing the crucified figure of Christ hanging over the master's bed. In the Islamic religion, deity was never personified, and this figure with its represented agony was quite disturbing. She carefully avoided looking at it.

Tanige smoothed her hand over a pale yellow nightdress of sheer silk which was embellished at bodice and short puffed sleeves with the finest white lace loomed by the artisans of Seville. When the princess awakened, it would be there, ready for her use, and its cheerful, sunny color would relieve the gloomy austerity of Don Ruy's chambers.

Stepping back to admire her handiwork, she was satisfied with the results and proceeded to prepare the table for supper. A richly embroidered cream-colored cloth covered the table and was ready for the polished silver service plates on top of which she placed fragile ceramic bowls from the Orient. Rare amber glass goblets and wrought silver utensils flanked the plates. Tanige smiled, happy to be among signs of her own civilization. Now, all that was left to do was to find Don Ruy's favorite wine to accompany his dinner. Her smile broadened. Things could not be better, she thought romantically. Especially considering the circumstances. She and the princess would not be put into a servile capacity. As for herself, her duties would be, as always, to Mirjana, and she would not be made to attend Doña Ysabel as was her fear. Also, Don

Ruy had metamorphosed from a rough and bearded barbarian into a handsome courtier. Thirdly, and most importantly, she herself had witnessed that look of concern in his eyes as he carried the princess up to his chamber. Yes, most definitely — Tanige suppressed a giggle — the fates were much improved. And she could not remember the last time Mirjana had mentioned Omar's name!

Tanige sat near the sleeping Mirjana, watching over her, her eyes drooping wearily. It had been such a long day. So many things had happened. Her stomach heaved threateningly. There was more to come, she was certain of it. As long as Doña Ysabel was in the *castillo,* she was a threat. True, Don Ruy had said the señora was to be sent away from Bivar until he could take the training of Teodoro in hand, but there would still be several weeks before she actually departed, if what Tanige had heard in the kitchens was true. Havoc could be wreaked in much less than ten days. A chill raced up Tanige's too skinny body.

Mirjana should be waking soon. Did she dare to go to the kitchens to make the last preparations for supper? Her stomach rumbled ominously, making her realize how long it had been since she'd eaten. The thought of the seasoned lamb dish she had prepared and the flaky pastry topped with honey was tempting. She wondered how she would keep the food at the correct temperature for serving. The hearth in the chamber was filled with old ashes, and it seemed not to have been used in years. A brazier would be the answer. She would have one of the kitchen boys, perhaps Alvar, carry it up to place near the table. The food would keep warm until the princess awoke and Don Ruy returned.

Down in the kitchens, Tanige ate quickly, savoring each morsel, thinking it to be the most tasty meal she had ever consumed. Since leaving Seville, at any rate. The princess would be proud of her handmaiden's efforts.

Only the mention of Don Ruy's name was needed to gain the cooperation of a kitchen boy to carry the brazier up to the master's quarters. Tanige herself carried the stewed lamb and the plate of pastries, and a skin of Don Ruy's preferred wine, tucked under her arm. A small, grubby child, no older than seven, trailed behind Tanige with a loaf of warm bread and a crock of yellow butter.

Making hasty preparations, Tanige was satisfied the stew was warming nicely in its kettle on the brazier. Mirjana stirred restlessly and settled back into a half sleep. One of the lamps sputtered fitfully and glowed brightly, bathing the chamber in its ruddy glow. Don Ruy's chamber had taken on new life since the princess had been installed here. A touch of bright colors, a small amount of personal comforts, tantalizing aromas from the brazier. Would he find it to his tastes? Or would he consider these comforts unnecessary and heathenish, as would Doña Ysabel?

Mirjana opened her eyes, looking about her. Where was she? She realized a discomfort and cautiously moved on the silken coverlet. The memory of her lashing flooded through her. "Tanige," she called hoarsely, "what am I doing here?"

Perching herself on the edge of the bed, Tanige proceeded to enlighten her mistress. "You will be up and about tomorrow, Mirjana. I applied ointment to your wounds, and believe me when I tell you, the skin was not broken. It would seem Doña Ysabel's henchman had sympathy for you. Thank Allah, he is such an expert with the whip."

"I remember being so frightened, everything seemed to swim before my eyes . . ."

"Do you remember Gormaz? He is the one who rushed out and saved you. But it was Don Ruy who carried you here, insisting you be placed in his own chamber. The entire *castillo* knows his affection for you, and Doña Ysabel was almost foaming at the mouth, like a mad dog. The señora is being sent to tour the convents, and little Teodoro has been placed in Gormaz's care for his training."

Mirjana remembered the terror on Teodoro's face and winced with the memory. Such a small child, not responsible for the señora's influence over him. There was a great deal of goodness in him, she was certain of it. "What is that delicious aroma?" Mirjana questioned, her fingers smoothing the coverlet.

"Supper. Don Ruy is to sup with you. See, I have prepared everything! When he returns I will have him move the table closer to the bed. But now, you must change out of that gown and you will need your hair brushed."

Mirjana subjected herself to Tanige's ministrations, still too sore to accomplish much for herself. At last, resting lightly against the pillows, she asked, "Well, how do I look?"

"Never less than beautiful, Princess," Tanige lied. "Your eyes sparkle, your cheeks glow, and your lips are pink."

"In other words, I look feverish and quite deplorable. Why must you always lie to me, Tanige? You know I have only to look into your eyes to see the truth."

"If you look slightly less than beautiful, it is excusable, considering your experience. Don Ruy was quite protective of you. Do not rush your recovery, enjoy the circumstances and bask in his attention." Tanige's voice dropped to a whisper. "It would be best for your *slow* recovery. At least here, in the master's chamber, we have some protection from Doña Ysabel. Do you understand?"

"I am not an idiot, Tanige. It was my back, not my head that was wounded. What you're trying to say is I should deceive Don Ruy and allow him to think my suffering is greater than it is. You want me to play on his sympathies."

"Exactly," Tanige said excitedly.

Before Mirjana could tell Tanige exactly what she thought of the idea, there was a soft tapping on the door. When Tanige opened it, there stood Don Ruy.

Mirjana heard his deep voice murmuring inquiries about her. Almost shyly, he stepped into the chamber, filling the large proportions of the room with his bulk. He was freshly shaven, she noticed immediately, and the spicy scent of the soap he had taken from the caravan came to her. "Tanige tells me you have awakened."

He seemed so uncertain, so unsure of himself, that her heart suddenly went out to him. She rewarded him with a smile, her lower lip trembling a little that this all-powerful man could be so concerned about her that he was humbled to the shyness of a child. She wanted to reassure him, to tell him he need not worry, to banish the frown line that appeared between his thick, unruly brows.

Ruy's eyes drank in the sight of her. She had been so pale, so wounded as he had carried her up the stairs. He had come to treasure her, he had realized, and the injustice she had suffered burned into his soul. He and his own had brought her nothing but grief.

Stepping close to the bedside, he reached for her hand, taking it within his own, feeling the warmth of it. Her resiliency astounded him, and he again was reminded that he had always considered her remarkable. "How are you, Mirjana. I wish I could turn back time and you never would have suffered at my mother's hands."

"I will recover quickly, my lord," Mirjana reassured him, refusing to acknowledge the clatter of the kettle lid and Tanige's accusing glances. It was true, she would recover, and she could not bring herself to lie to him. She could not bear to see his guilt and self-recriminations continue. The sooner she was up and about, the sooner he would forget this incident.

Ruy looked down into her soft, gray eyes and felt a terrible rushing through his veins. Not a stupid man, he realized another woman might be tempted to have him at her mercy by playing on his sympathies and guilt. His hand reached out to brush a stray tendril of ruddy-gold hair from her cheek. His touch was familiar, and almost as a reflex, Mirjana turned her cheek into his palm. It was a familiar gesture, in some ways more intimate than if he had caressed her breast. Although she had lain with him and he knew every turn and curve of her body, he had never reached out quite this way to touch her so casually. And when he brought his hand away from her check it was to recapture her hand and hold it warmly in his.

Tanige entreated Ruy's help in moving the table close to the bed so Mirjana could join him in supper. One glance at the beautifully appointed table and Ruy praised the servant's preparations, enflaming the girl's cheeks with his flattery.

The stew was perfection, the pastry the flakiest, and Ruy ate with relish, serving both himself and Mirjana, seeing to her every need himself, lest he be asked to have Tanige return. He wanted Mirjana to himself, to be aware of her every need and comfort. The conversation between them never touched on the events of the afternoon; he did his best to keep it lighthearted and entertaining, telling her instead of Gormaz's astonishment to learn that the lord's destrier had somehow acquired a name, and more remarkable yet, answered to it.

"Liberte. A fine name for a fine steed," he told her, confiding how he had feared she'd select something innocuous like Pansy or Nubbins.

Mirjana joined in his teasing, pretending insult that he would think she would ever make a poor selection for El Cid's mount. Although the banter was light and Ruy was a charming host, Mirjana sensed something was troubling him and hated to think she had brought him this concern.

Through the evening they talked, enjoying this newfound ease between them, entertaining one another with stories from their childhood, and so engrossed in one another they hardly noticed when Tanige came to retrieve the remains of their supper, closing the door quietly behind her, leaving them for the night.

Ruy stood before the narrow window, goblet of wine in his hand, looking out. He had begun to fear Mirjana was growing weary of his company and exhausted from her wounds. He thought he might stay in the chamber, quietly, until she fell asleep.

As he stood near the window, looking down into the courtyard where glowing torches fought against the darkness of night, Mirjana watched him. Something was definitely troubling him. There was that tiny frown again between his brows. It was much the same expression, she realized, as those countless times when she would inquire about word from Seville and he had been unable to give her an answer. He had thought to be protecting her then and she could not find it in her heart to hold it against him, but now, unexpected fears rose in her again. Had his mood something to do with word from Hassan?

Unexpectedly, another fear rose in her. What if Hassan had finally recapitulated and had agreed to accept his sister back into the palace? Mirjana suddenly realized she was not yet prepared to leave. Not yet, she found she was telling herself. Not until he sends me away.

"Ruy," she said softly, at last finding her voice. "Come and sit here beside me and tell me what's troubling you. Perhaps it will help to talk about it." She patted the mattress, inviting him to stretch out beside her. He did not seem to notice her gesture.

It was a long moment before he spoke, but when he did, his words seemed to explode from within him. "It is my King. Sancho. He has been murdered! And the bastard who did it is his own brother, Alphonso!"

Mirjana was aghast. A king, murdered! By his own brother! This was something very close to her, she whose father was a king. Regicide was not unheard of; through the ages in every culture there were those who lusted for power. She allowed the words to tumble from Ruy, not interrupting, listening to his curses and grief. This had been a terrible day for him. First, learning that his king was murdered, and then the ordeal and consequences of the whipping. Poor Ruy.

"Ruy," she called again, "please sit down."

After a moment he accepted her offer, needing to be comforted in some way. His entire world was falling apart, his future hung in the balance. Settling beside her, goblet still in hand, he was aware of her warmth, and he tenderly and gently slipped his arm around her shoulders, careful of her injuries, and felt her slip into the crook of his arm. Her cheek was pressed against his chest, and she quietly waited for him to speak, unlike other women who would insist on prying the words from a man before he had even spoken them in his own brain.

As he spoke, Mirjana stretched her intelligence and memory, trying to recall all she knew about the volatile rulers of Spain. Alphonso, she knew, was the second son of Fernando, also known as Ferdinando I. As such, Alphonso had inherited the province of Leona, while Castile, the most important dynastic holding, had gone to the oldest son, Sancho. The lesser and most northern province, Galicia, had been bequeathed to the third son, Garcia. It was a foolish and irresponsible act on Fernando's part to divide his kingdom this way; as a politician, he should have known the grief and strife it would cause between the brothers. As had happened before and would more than likely happen in the future, the brothers began to fight immediately, each trying to gain the entire heritage. Ruy, under the prestigious title of El Cid, was field commander of Sancho's armies.

"I was a fool to think that my keeping Alphonso in banishment in Badajoz was protection enough for my king!" Ruy told her, his words more bitter than gall. "Garcia is a weakling and a fool, and is happy enough to be left to himself in Galicia. There was little enmity between Sancho and himself."

"Perhaps their relationship was sound because Sancho knew that any time he wanted he could take Galicia for himself, Garcia was too weak to afford much resistance," Mirjana offered.

Ruy looked down at her as she lay against his chest. His lips grazed the top of her head and he could smell her sultry perfume. "Beauty has been no price for your intelligence, *cara*. There is truth in what you say. Yes, Garcia is a weakling, overshadowed his entire life by the brilliance of his brothers.

Alphonso has always been the thorn. Twice, I have defeated his armies, and each time he has sought political refuge in Badajoz and Toledo. Sancho and I both lived in a fool's dream to think he could be suppressed! And all the while Urraca was doing her worst against Sancho."

Ruy explained to Mirjana that the Infanta Urraca was actually the eldest child of King Fernando, and she was more a man than a woman in her ambitions. "I have always suspected an unholy alliance between Urraca and Alphonso, and now I know it to be true. It was she who put Alphonso's plans into action. And if Alphonso is guilty of murdering his brother and killing my king, Urraca shares the sin."

Mirjana slipped her arm around his middle, hoping to give comfort to the pain she heard in his voice. There was much he was not saying, she knew, from past conversations during the journey across the Marches. He had told her how Sancho and he had been boyhood friends and that there was a distant family relationship through Doña Ysabel. He grieved for his friend and sorrowed for his king.

Draining the last of the wine from his goblet, Ruy laughed bitterly. "All the while I thought to be holding Alphonso in Badajoz, keeping him from gathering his armies to ride out once again against Castile, Urraca was carrying out a plot."

"How do you know this?"

"I knew Sancho. He had often voiced his suspicions of Urraca to me. It is proof enough to me that while I was far to the south laying siege to Badajoz, Sancho led his army to Zamora, which is a property of Urraca's. He must have learned of her collusion with Alphonso. What he never suspected was to be murdered in his tent. The report I received this day tells there was evidence of poisoning, clearly a woman's weapon. And if that were not enough, when Sancho was too weak to protect himself, he was felled by a broadsword. Sancho was a warrior, unafraid of death when honorably dealt. He should have met his end atop his charger, leading his army into battle, the fallen enemy in his sight, and the sound of the bugle in his ears."

For a long time afterward, Ruy was silent, refilling his goblet and draining it time and again. Mirjana sat with him, in silent tribute, with him in the death of his friend.

He was so silent, so still, Mirjana thought him to be asleep. She moved to remove the goblet from his hand when he spoke. "And now, to add insult to injury, Alphonso is seeking twelve men, good and true, to swear his oath to ascend the throne. He has seen it to his advantage to select me as one of these men, and it is I whom he expects to administer this oath."

Her heart would break for him. Without his explanation, she realized the strategy of Alphonso's move. Ruy, El Cid, was military chief, Sancho's staunchest supporter. If he were to administer the oath that would absolve Alphonso of any implication in his brother's death, it would still wayward tongues and satisfy even the most suspicious.

"I hate the man!" Ruy's voice thundered in his chest, his heart beating like a captured bird beneath her cheek. "He is domineering, intolerant of his inferiors, and prejudiced against his betters. Have you heard the tale of his betrayal of the Mozarabs only last year?" The Mozarabs were those Christians who kept their faith even while living and working in Islamic states.

Ruy repeated the story for her. There was a move by church and state against the keeping of the Mozarabic liturgy, which was so dear to all Spanish Christians to whom it represented centuries of a faith upheld even in the heart of Islam. Conformity with the rest of the Catholic world was urged by Pope Gregory VII and the monks of the Cluny Order. The argument became heated when the Pope deprecated the work of St. Isidore and other venerated Spanish clerics, classing the Goths, from whom the aristocracy claimed descent, with the Moors. A decisive trial of arms was decreed to be held in Burgos and the champion for the Mozarabic rite was a Castilian named Lope Martinez. When Martinez won the duel, the Catholics were dissatisfied and another trial, this time by fire, was ordered. Both liturgies were thrown into the bonfire but, miraculously, the Mozarabic one sprang out of the flames. Never a man to be thwarted, Alphonso kicked it back into the inferno. His voice rang above the roaring fire, above the din of onlookers, "Laws go the way kings want!" Because of his daring and betrayal of the Mozarabs, Alphonso won Pope Gregory's alliance and the Cluny Order's gratefulness. Two powerful clubs against his enemies.

Listening to Ruy's account of Alphonso's betrayal of his people, Mirjana agreed with his conclusions. "And now he is king," she whispered, hardly daring to break the ensuing silence.

"Yes, my little bird, he is king. And there is nothing to be done for it unless I decide to take up my sword against him." Ruy's voice rang strong, clear, rising to the high-vaulted ceiling.

"And should you take up your sword, all

of Spain will engage in civil war. Brother will fight brother and peace will be forgotten." Her words quelled his outcry.

"Are you saying, little one, that for the good of all Spain and to save Castile, I should forget my disgust of the man and swear the oath to Alphonso?"

"Only you can decide, my lord. Only you." She raised her face from his chest, looking up into his eyes, her thick lashes creating those feathery shadows on her cheeks, fluttering in the quivering light of the sputtering candles.

His hands came to her hair, twining the silken strands between his fingers, a sad and haunted smile coming to his lips. She offered him her mouth and he took it with his own, finding solace there for his sorrow. Sweet arms clung to his neck, fragile curves and slender waist availed themselves to his caress. In her arms he found his ease; she was a vessel into which he emptied his misery and uncertainty. And when she took him into her, she was a miracle, restoring his power and confidence, reminding him he was a man.

And all this he told her in the quiet solitude following their lovemaking. He called her his little bird, beating her wings to chase away his sorrows. He named her his miracle, the words breathed softly into her ear. And in the darkness, she soothed him into sleep, feeling her contentment cover them like a blanket against the demons of the night. Her heart was filled with this man, and she realized a meeting, a partnership, between them, a marriage of kind, in the joining of their bodies and their minds. Clinging to him in sleep, nuzzling her face against the thicket of hairs grazing his chest, she knew contentment, and in the dark days to come, she would think often of this moment when she lay in his arms, a woman fulfilled.

CHAPTER 9

Muted lavender shades of early dawn were fast melting into the ripe golden colors of a new day. Doña Ysabel tore at her hair, the shadows of sleeplessness's dark stains beneath her eyes. The nightmare of yesterday was still with her. Her own son was literally banishing her from his household, taking Teddy from her maternal arms and depriving him of the mother the child so desperately needed. The separation of a mother from her son was a sin she would not easily forgive Ruy. Her own flesh and blood was causing her this suffering, and the Blessed Virgin, mother of Christ, would see to his punishment.

It was true — Teodoro was a spoiled child, but he was her own and she loved him. What did Ruy know of a mother's love? He had been sent away before the age of eight to a comrade of his father to train for the military. Ruy had been torn from her arms in much the same way Teddy would be taken from her. Poor, poor Teddy. What would become of him? He was not made for the military. Her dreams to have him become a member of the clergy seemed so distant now.

Anguished tears rolled down her cheeks as she stared at the suit of clothes the boy had worn only yesterday. Now he would be dressed in rags, tending the horses and cleaning the stables. Ruy, how could you do this to your mother? she thought. Teddy had been a gift from heaven itself, a seed planted in her belly when she had thought the comfort of children was lost to her forever. He was a child of her middle years and more precious because of it. Teddy was the last legacy left her by his father who was killed in battle before the babe had cut his first tooth.

A fresh onslaught of self-pity and fear for her child shuddered through her. She must do something. She was a powerful woman, strong and willful. There was still time before being sent away. Much could be accomplished. There was no telling how long she was to be in exile; Ruy's heart was cold and hard, unlike his younger brother's.

This was all that woman's fault, Doña Ysabel comforted herself. She was a heathen, a devil with soft, white skin and hair the color of hell's fires to tempt Ruy. He should have been married years ago; a wife and children would have lessened his vulnerability to the princess. And he never would have been free to bring her here to Bivar, to reside in the *castillo!*

Doña Ysabel knew the ways of beautiful women; she had once been very beautiful herself. Now she was a dowager, a widow, left without the comfort of a man and now without the comfort of her sons. Ruy was a fool, he had always been a fool! While he was already a legendary military figure, he was an innocent when it came to women. Mirjana had wormed her way to Ruy's protective nature, filling him with desire for her. Doña Ysabel felt the heat of a flush rising to her cheeks. Ah, yes, she too knew the ways of the flesh, and not so many years had passed that she cried out in the night for her loneliness following Don Diaz's death. Her one comfort had been Teddy, and Ruy had promised never to take him from her. Why, oh why, had the child been born a male. A daughter could comfort her mother's old age. A daughter remained so all of her life! When her belly was growing with Teddy, she had made novenas, prayed day and night the child would be a girl. And the Lord had not seen fit to answer her prayers. He answered them little of late. She blessed herself and sighed deeply. Perhaps she asked too much of God. It occurred to her that she should seek Ruy's confessor to intercede for her, to discourage this unholy alliance between her son and this heathen princess. Perhaps Padre Tomas could talk some sense to him.

Doña Ysabel sank back on her chair, shoulders slumping, fingers playing idly with her rosary beads. It was not likely Padre Tomas would assist her. Once Ruy made up his mind, the Almighty could not change it. If anything was to be done, it must be by her own hand.

Daintily, the señora dabbed at her nose with her handkerchief. At least, until the time came to leave, she was still chatelaine of the *castillo,* Ruy would not dare to take that from her. She knew Mirjana had been taken to Ruy's chamber the evening before, and this adultery under her roof filled her with rancor. Ruy had lost all respect for his reputation and his home. The first thing she would do would be to move the girl back to the tower room. As long as *she* was mistress she would ensure the dictates of her religion were followed in her own home! Enough gossip surrounded the doings of her son. The question remaining was what method she would use. She had no desire to face the *princesa*'s brazen-tongued, homely serving girl, nor did she wish a confrontation with the *princesa* herself.

Doña Ysabel clapped her hands loudly, bringing a timid serving girl into the room. She waited respectfully until her mistress acknowledged her presence. "You will go to my son's quarters, Dulcimea, and assist the Princesa Mirjana in returning to her own quarters. Whatever belongings you find in the lord's chamber are to be removed by you. As my son is an early riser, you are certain to find the *princesa* alone. You will see to this immediately and convey to the *princesa* that you act upon my orders."

Out in the dark, shadowy corridor, Dulcimea took a deep breath. Everyone in the *castillo* knew that Don Ruy himself had carried the *princesa* to his chambers. Everyone knew he had spent the night with her. And now Doña Ysabel was ordering her to force the *princesa* to return to the tower. The girl's eyes were bitter as she trudged down the corridor. What was she to do if the *princesa* refused to obey? What if she was in pain and could not leave? Would a punishment be in order because she had failed to carry out Doña Ysabel's orders? Dulcimea shivered in the early morning damp.

Hesitantly, Dulcimea rapped on the stout wooden door leading to Don Ruy's chamber. When she received no reply, she knocked again, louder.

Tanige opened the door, expecting to find Don Ruy.

"*Por favor,* you must understand, Doña Ysabel has sent me to assist the *princesa* back to the tower room," Dulcimea said in a quivering voice.

"Move?" Tanige demanded.

"Yes, back to the tower room. Doña Ysabel," she reemphasized, "wishes the *princesa* to return to her assigned chamber."

"What is it?" Mirjana called.

"Wait here," Tanige commanded as she closed the door.

"It is one of Doña Ysabel's serving girls. She is here to help us move back to the tower. What should I tell her?"

"You will ask her to please convey to the señora our regrets. Don Ruy has placed me here and only under his wishes do I leave. Be kindly, Tanige, pity the poor girl who must return to Doña Ysabel with my refusal of her orders. I am certain the señora is also interested to know where her son slept last night."

"Just as I am certain she is already aware or she would not have sent the servant to move us back to the tower."

"I know exactly what you mean, Tanige. Go, do not keep the girl waiting. And Tanige, perhaps it will be necessary for you to go to Doña Ysabel yourself. Everything concerning the señora seems to become muddled and misunderstood."

Tanige muttered sourly as she stalked from the room. The last thing she needed this morning was to confront Doña Ysabel.

When next Tanige appeared in Don Ruy's chamber, Mirjana saw her face was a mottled purple. She could barely gasp out the words, she was so angry.

"Calm yourself, Tanige. Just please tell me that you were at least respectful."

"Certainly, I was respectful! I kept repeating over and over that it was Don Ruy's wishes that you remain here until you are fully recovered. It was terrible how she kept blaming you for having Teodoro taken away from her and how you were corrupting her son and stealing his soul from heaven. She said she would see to it you regretted this interference in her family for the rest of your life."

Mirjana remained quiet, seemingly unmoved. But within, she was bitten with the accusation and felt an empathy for the señora. Tanige continued her report. "The señora said that if it was your intention to make permanent your stay in her son's chambers you are sadly mistaken. She told me to tell you that you are merely another in a long line of whores who presented momentary fascination for her son, and like the others, he would soon cast you aside. The señora said to tell you she was trying to spare you further heartache."

"One day I must thank her for her consideration," Mirjana said, the wounds from Tanige's message ravaging her face. Tanige was alarmed at how pale Mirjana had become. Surely, Don Ruy did not think of Mirjana as another of his whores. Not the princess. Never the princess.

"What are we to do, Mirjana?"

"Nothing, Tanige. At this moment we are guests of Don Ruy and we must follow his wishes. In his hands he holds the hope of our return to Seville." Even as she said this, she was stung again that she could not comprehend leaving here, leaving Ruy. Then, in a brighter, more determined tone, "You have taken great efforts to make me comfortable and I truly appreciate it. Don Ruy, himself, commented last evening how delighted he was with the pains you took for his supper. He even admitted he liked the small comforts of the coverlet and pillows. Of course, I realize, as must you, that this is a temporary arrangement, and soon he will want the peace and solitude of his chambers returned to him. We must be certain not to take advantage of his hospitality. He is a most remarkable man, in many ways. At first, I believed there was no compassion in him, but I was wrong."

Mirjana's eyes had become dreamy and soft as she remembered the night before.

"I thought you detested the man," Tanige argued slyly. "Have you contracted a fever? What has made you reconsider? Can it be that beneath all those wolf-skins and armor you had no idea such a handsome and exciting man lurked? Ah, I see I am right. Do you know what I think?"

"Do not think, Tanige!" Mirjana said wearily.

"Very well, I will keep my opinions to myself and so much for your loss," Tanige told her tartly. "What would you like me to do for you today?"

"While you were with the señora, I have planned the day. Firstly, go to the stable and see how Teodoro fares. No doubt, he is quite frightened, being away from his mother for the first time in his life. Secondly, speak to Gormaz and find the way to his hut. I want you to visit his wife, Ilena, and prepare more fennel tea. Also, before you go, go to the kitchens and find a cut of the leanest meat, fresh vegetables, and honey. And yes, a confection to tempt her appetite. While you visit with her, prepare the meat and the tea, urge her to drink it, and report to me if she is faring better than when I saw her. Assure her, that as soon as I am able, I will come to see her."

"I will see to it, Mirjana. Now, for your own supper? Will Don Ruy be joining you again this evening?"

"Yes, I believe so, but not until quite late. Prepare something tasty, Tanige. He was astounded at your stew. And would it be possible to locate my chess game? I believe we brought it from Seville, the one with the white jade figures. Don Ruy said he would like to challenge me."

Tanige snorted. The princess was an excellent player and could even trounce Emir Mútadid soundly whenever they would play. "Will you allow Don Ruy to win?" she asked.

"That is ridiculous. Of course not! Whoever deserves to win will win!"

"I think you should allow Don Ruy to win, he will find himself more susceptible to your charms."

"I do not need any help from a chess board," Mirjana sniffed.

Tanige was glad to be outside the *castillo* on such a lovely spring day. She looked forward to the walk to Gormaz and Ilena's hut. Mirjana seemed to think highly of Gormaz's wife, and perhaps she and Tanige could become friends also.

Doña Ysabel paced before her windows. A

black scowl crossed her features as she noticed Tanige walk across the courtyard. She watched her progress to the stables with menacing eyes. Her plan to remove the *princesa* back to her tower room had been brazenly thwarted and no doubt Ruy would hear about it. She did not worry about him, he had already done his worst. Nothing could be worse than exile from Bivar. Desperate, she realized she must use her cunning to have Teddy returned to her. She would pray and connive to that end. Nothing and no one would interfere with her plans.

In the early evening, Mirjana gave herself up to Tanige's gentle ministrations. She was bathed, and the bandages were removed from her back. The welts were still present, but they had lost their heat, thanks to the ointment, and they appeared to be healing quickly.

Mirjana brushed her hair, bending from the waist, the riot of red gold catching the last rays of late afternoon sun that streamed through the slotted windows. After Tanige performed her handiwork, arranging Mirjana's hair into a lovely design that swept it back from her temples and brow, yet allowed it to drape freely around her shoulders, the handmaiden stepped back and nodded her approval.

"Princess, you have not looked so lovely since before leaving Seville. Don Ruy will be most impressed with you this evening. And see what I have brought for you to wear!" Tanige quickly held up a white silk gown, designed with the oriental flavor. The bodice was cut low, daringly, made to hug the body down to the waist where, because it was cut on the bias, it swirled out in fullness over the thighs down to the floor. The sleeves were cut narrow at the top and widened to graceful points at the wrist. A light coat of the same material accompanied the nightdress, and both were completely free of any ornamentation. In this gown, the woman was the decoration.

Ruy arrived late. Mirjana had about given up hope that he would arrive at all. He strode into the chamber, his eyes immediately going to the bed, lighting with relief when he noticed her sitting near the glowing, welcoming hearth. She had no idea where he was performing his ablutions, but he was freshly shaved, and there was the fragrance of the spicy scented soap she believed could not smell so pleasant or exciting on any other man but he.

Mirjana noticed a certain weariness around his eyes and guessed he still pondered what his reaction to Sancho's death should be. "If you are ready to sup," she said lightly, "Tanige has performed another of her miracles."

At the sound of the word "miracle," that wondrous name he had called her last night, he swung around to look at her, the fires of intimacy burning in his eyes, as though by the mention of the word she had ignited a fuse. Taking her hand, he kissed it, never taking his eyes from hers. "You have brought many miracles to my life, Mirjana." His tone was husky, sending her pulses racing. Then, remembering Tanige's presence, he became more formal, leading Mirjana to the table and seating her.

Pouring a goblet of wine for himself, water for Mirjana, he inquired after her health.

"I am quite well, Ruy. With Tanige's excellent care, I believe I can be up and about tomorrow. We will then move back to the tower room. I cannot allow you to be inconvenienced longer than necessary."

"Only your leaving can inconvenience me, Mirjana. I would like it if you would stay." He had said the words that changed her universe. He wanted her there, available for his touch, for his kiss, for the magic they shared, and Mirjana's heart knew music.

Ruy thought her extraordinary that she was concerned for his convenience. Did she not know how long his nights would be without her? How empty his bed, though she had shared it but one night?

Tanige served their supper, a delectable dish of fresh spring lamb and jelly made from the mint leaf. The bread was warm and thickly buttered, and while Ruy enjoyed his wine, Mirjana drank a tea made from pungent herbs and orange skins.

After they had eaten, she allowed him to win at chess. If it amused her to allow him to win, Ruy thought, he could not be less than gracious in winning. But in their second game she could not help trouncing him badly. Mirjana looked aghast and apologized for her good fortune. Honeyed figs were brought to the table, after the board was cleared away, and Ruy made a joke of feeding them to the victorious Mirjana, kissing away the sweet stickiness he left on her lips. Although his spirits seemed high, she knew that at his core he was deeply troubled.

"Why don't you tell me about it, Ruy?" she asked only once before his indecisions concerning Alphonso's coronation came tumbling out. Even as he repeated what he had told her the night before, he considered what a remarkable woman she was. He had thought of her almost continually all through the day, and here, now, he was forced to admit that he was ready to take her advice in the interests of all Castile, to administer the oath to Alphonso and thus save his people from civil strife. His only regret was that he would be made to leave her for God knew how long to attend the coronation, and this was something he would almost rather gamble a civil war than do.

"I have decided to accept Alphonso as king," he told her simply. "You were correct. To do otherwise would mean civil war, and I have no liking to see men killed for my uncertain principle. While Sancho was my king and my friend, I believe he would tell me not to strike out against Alphonso for what cannot be changed. Sancho loved Spain and would have gladly sacrificed his life for his country."

She listened, patient and without prompting. Ruy must come to his own decisions, and it was one he would have arrived at without her. He was a leader of men, a man of power and confidence. He would do what was right.

"When will you be leaving?" Mirjana asked, already mourning his departure.

"Not until I am called. By Visigothic and old Roman rite, twelve good men of truth are necessary to absolve Alphonso of his guilt. I intend to be the last to arrive. I would like to see him sweat a little. All of Spain knows of the friendship between Sancho and myself; no doubt as far as Alphonso is concerned my witness at the coronation is the most valuable. Certainly if I, Sancho's vassal, cannot find fault with Alphonso, neither will Spain."

"I see," Mirjana teased. "As Cid goes, so goes Spain!"

"Exactly! And what of you, Princesa Mirjana? As Cid goes, so goes you?"

"At your bidding, my lord."

"Cid goes to bed," he told her, laughing, standing to reach down and lift her from her chair and carry her to his bed. She squealed in delight, loving the moist kisses he trailed down her throat where her pulses beat like the wings of a hummingbird.

They loved each other with slow vigilance, finding each time they came together this way was better than the last. They purposely strung out the minutes into hours, prolonging their pleasure in one another. His caresses were eloquent, echoing the words of pleasure from his lips. He told her how he loved her hair and the way it hung in curtains filled with sunshine over his face when she was atop him, her breasts pressed against his chest, their coral tips excited and stimulated by their contact with his chest hairs.

Mirjana laughed her pleasure, yielding herself to his hand and lips, playfully biting the flesh of his shoulder, her husky, joyous sounds evolving into a contented cat's purr of pleasure as he entered her and held himself there, still and deep. And when he began to move within her, she chorused his cry of passion and spoke his name as he loved to hear it.

In the soft glow of the candles and the dying embers in the hearth, Ruy's little miracle lay across the bed on her stomach, haunches bare and lifted for his touch. He smoothed his hand over the small of her back and followed the white curve over her buttocks, stopping to stray in the mysterious shadows between her thighs.

She lay across his lap, her fingers tenderly playing with the dark, downy hair on his naked thighs. They had made love, finding it wonderful and joyous, claiming one another for themselves.

"You liked it, didn't you?" he asked, certain of her answer but wanting to hear it all the same.

"Liked what?" she teased, and was rewarded with a sound slap across her bottom. "Ouch! Unhand me, you barbarian!" Her teeth playfully nipped at his thigh.

"She bites like a bitch in heat and has the gall to name *me* the barbarian!"

Mirjana sat up, tickling his ribs in a surprise attack, setting him reeling with laughter. "Stop, unhand me, else I'll be forced to call for my mother like little Teddy!"

At the mention of Doña Ysabel, Mirjana instantly sobered. She crawled up to the pillows where Ruy rested his back, fitting herself comfortably into the crook of his arm.

"Ruy, there is a matter I wish to discuss with you. It concerns young Teodoro and your mother." She lifted her face to him, watching the hostility creep into his eyes. "Please, listen to what I have to say," she pleaded quickly. "Teddy is so young. More an infant than most boys his age. He has much to learn, yes, but it should be gradual, and you should take an active hand with him, not leave it to some other whose interests are less than your own. Teodoro can become a man you would be proud to call your brother, but only under your own hand. I have also heard Doña Ysabel is to be sent to the outer provinces to take an extended tour of the convents. Will you reconsider?"

"No!" It was such an explosive reply, Mirjana cringed. Ruy jumped up from the bed, reaching for his dressing gown, tying the belt firmly around his waist. "It is time my brother grows and learns that manhood must be earned, both by heart and deed. And I am not punishing my mother, regardless of what you believe. She also needs to find a life without young Teddy, and this she would never do willingly and of her own accord. It is a painful separation, but I can no longer close my eyes to them, having them disease one another with their own selfishness until they are both destroyed!"

Ruy paced the room, stopping only to refill his goblet with the dregs of the wine. "The señora is a very strong and resourceful woman, Mirjana. Believe me, she will be happy visiting the convents where she can do as she pleases and visit old friends whose *castillos* are nearby. At the convents, she can play lady bountiful from morning to night and know the undying gratitude of the nuns and her beloved church. Perhaps she will strive for sainthood; one can never tell with my mother. Trust me, Mirjana. Do you?"

Mirjana met his gaze, saw the softness in his eyes, knew that his outburst had more to do with the pain of separating his family than because his authority and judgment were questioned. Should she trust him as he asked? She smiled, a vision of loveliness in his eyes, young and fragile, and becoming so dear to him. Of course she would trust him, with her heart, with her very soul.

These were idyllic days for Mirjana — yellow, golden days, days with Ruy. And the nights were blue, silver nights. Nights spent beside him, in his arms.

Mirjana never broached the subject of Doña Ysabel again, fearing to disrupt this new ease between herself and Ruy. But she did visit Teddy several times a day, ignoring the child's churlishness, taking a genuine interest in him as he learned under Gormaz's disciplining eye. The boy was learning to ride a chestnut brown filly and was learning to accept full responsibility for the animal. Gormaz and Mirjana believed, despite Doña Ysabel's overprotective love, that the child was basically lonely, frightened, and despite his spoiled tantrums, quite lacking self-confidence.

It was clear to Mirjana that Teddy idolized his older brother and felt he could never measure up to Ruy's achievements. If only Ruy would be more patient with the boy, more giving of his time, then instead of competing with Ruy in a negative sense, Teddy might try to emulate his sense of justice and generosity.

As her relationship with Ruy became deeper and more complex, she found herself involved more and more with everyone in the *castillo* and in the town of Bivar. Everyone seemed to be a part of a huge family, having lived in Bivar all of their lives as had their grandparents and great-grandparents and even further back. Their roots were in one another;

they cared about one another. And from their genuine smiles and out of respect for their lord, they were coming to care about her. The day she had offered to step in for Alvar, one of their own, she had earned their respect. Doña Ysabel was a tyrant with a mercurial nature, and had never seen the villagers or *castillo* servants beyond their services to her.

Tanige and herself were making friends here in Bivar, and until now, Mirjana had never known how isolated her life had been. In Seville she had spent her youth in the harem, living among her father's wives and their children. They were her family, but there was such hot rivalry between them for Mútadid's attentions, and being without a mother to watch over her, Mirjana was often the victim of their jealousies. Even when Mútadid had agreed to her having her own suite in the palace, her acquaintances were restricted to her half brothers and half sisters and, of course, Tanige. Perhaps, that was why she had become so enamored of Omar. He had been the only man outside of her family with whom she had had contact. True, he was wise, learned, and so gentle. But now she found herself questioning if he had had any real emotion for her. Fresh color washed her cheeks as she remembered how she had thrown herself at him. And he had sent her away, kindly, it was true, but nevertheless he had sent her away. No doubt, the position he enjoyed in Mútadid's palace was more important to him than a lonely girl's passion for him. Ruy, on the other hand, would never have allowed anything or anyone to stand between himself and the woman he wanted. He would have carried her off in the night, keeping her for himself, protective and passionate. A smug smile tugged at Mirjana's mouth. And that was exactly what he had done — swept her away, kept her for his own. True, their beginnings were less than romantic and for other reasons entirely, but it was always the ending that mattered, was it not?

The villagers of Bivar waved their greetings as she walked through the town. They approved of the beautiful young woman with the smile of a thousand candles. They saw her ready smile and the gentleness in her eyes, and heard the softness of her laugh. She loved their children, singing little songs for them and telling them tales about fairies and dragons and handsome princes. They saw her walking to Ilena's hut and the way Gormaz's young wife was blooming under Mirjana's care. Her eagerness to see and learn everything with joyous enthusiasm gave them a pride in their work they had never known. And all of them shared the hope that their lord, Don Ruy, would always be kind to her, keeping her as his own, and never causing her grief. There had been others, they knew; a man as vital and important as El Cid must have had many women. But he had never brought them to Bivar as he had Princesa Mirjana. And although she came from a world and a culture so very different from their own, she was becoming one of them. She was a Muslim and they were Christians, but these hardy peasants had little use for bigotry; that was a luxury of the idle rich.

Even their lord, Don Ruy, seemed changed to them. Often times he would accompany the *princesa* through the town to commission work for the *castillo*. He looked younger, happier, more content to stay here in Bivar than they had ever known him to be. Always, after only several days, Don Ruy was itching to find matters to concern him elsewhere, away from Bivar. And they saw the way Don Ruy's eyes followed Mirjana wherever she went, smiling at her with a surprising tenderness.

Mirjana was aware of the speculations of the villagers and servants, but did not allow them to concern her. She was much too happy making new friends and finding purpose to her life. The beauty and luxuries of Seville were nearly forgotten, disregarded. She much preferred the austerity of Bivar with the warm friendships she had found to the cold loneliness of her home city. Bivar was becoming home. Here were the roots of Ruy's beginnings; it was to here that his thoughts traveled home. If the pits of hell were home to him, there she would want to be.

Easter Sunday dawned with sunny perfection, a conspiracy of nature to insure the success of the festivities signaling the end of Lent. Doña Ysabel had already proclaimed she would abstain from this year's ceremonies, preferring to hear Mass privately in the *castillo* chapel. Also, she had no taste for the fiesta following Mass. Teddy seemed crestfallen at this news from his mother, and it was only with prodding from Gormaz that he resentfully accepted Mirjana's and Ruy's invitation to attend the fiesta with them.

After Mass in the village church where Padre Tomas had conducted the ritual, Gormaz and Ruy had come back to the *castillo* for Mirjana and Tanige. Everyone was gathering at the fresh water pond outside the village, bringing baskets of food and hot loaves of bread. Gormaz had already hitched up one of the wagons and handed Mirjana and Tanige up, placing himself as driver. Ruy, riding Liberte, had denied Teddy's request to ride his chestnut filly to the picnic. Mirjana saw the boy's face fall into disappointment, and she glanced at Ruy who, seeming to read her mind, hoisted the boy atop Liberte.

The profound joy on Teddy's face tugged at Mirjana's heart. The boy adored his brother and expected only negligence and disinterest in return. To ride atop Liberte this way to the fiesta was a great honor.

The grassy plains outside Bivar were brilliant with that shade of tender green appearing only at this time of year. The pond, still and blue, reflected the glory of the sky above, and the copse of trees brought relief from the sun. Children chased one another, playing their games while their mothers prepared the food and delicacies which were traditional for this holiday. In the wagon, Tanige and Mirjana had overseen the preparation of a whole lamb with jars of mint jelly and a special sauce made from preserved apricots and pears. Large jugs filled with their secret contents rattled and clinked; Mirjana had planned a surprise for later.

Several of the men were tuning musical instruments, plucking the strings in mindless melodies. When the food was laid out, mothers scolded and slapped at greedy hands. Not until Padre Tomas led them in prayer would a morsel of food pass their lips.

Watching Teddy, Mirjana held her breath

as one of the children invited him to join a game of tag, and she was relieved when the boy gleefully joined them. Her heart squeezed for the child who looked so much as Ruy must have looked when he was the same age — dark hair, softly curling about his ears and over his brow, dark eyes with the same sherry-colored glints, and stubbornly set jaw. It made her laugh to think of Ruy as a child, and at the same time it brought him closer to her.

Mirjana and Tanige were welcomed by Ilena whose profoundly pregnant belly made her sit awkwardly on the blanket Gormaz had placed beneath the trees closest to the pond. Ilena had bloomed under Mirjana's care. Tanige went daily to prepare tea and to visit, and Mirjana was especially vigilant about calling shortly after the noon hour to encourage her to rest and to bring her food prepared in the *castillo* kitchens. Mirjana was concerned for Ilena. She was a small girl with narrow hips, and the babe promised to be large and big-boned like its father.

The afternoon wore on, becoming warmer and warmer from the beating sun. Everyone had eaten gluttonously, licking their fingers and praising each housewife's efforts and special contribution to the fiesta. Ruy sat among the men playing a game with polished stones and telling jokes about his adventure while on campaign. He enjoyed an easy camaraderie with his people, and while they were respectful, always remembering he was their lord, they honestly enjoyed him.

The musicians played rousing melodies that encouraged dancing, and even the children joined their parents, awkwardly imitating their steps. Ruy pulled Mirjana to her feet, slipping his arm around her tiny waist and brought her out among the dancers. She was quick to learn the steps, laughing with the sheer joy of it, linking her arm through Ruy's as he swung her around. Even Teddy had found a little dark-haired girl to dance with, and once, as they changed partners, Mirjana found herself opposite him. There was no hostility in this child as he laughingly imitated his brother's motions, slipping his arm gravely around Mirjana and leading her into the dance.

"Gormaz tells me you have brought a special surprise for the fiesta," he told her. "He says it's a secret. I should have brought something too" — his little face fell into lines of worry — "but I did not know what."

"Would you like to share in my secret, Teddy?"

"Oh, yes! What is it? I love secrets. What did you bring, Princesa?"

"I will only tell if you promise to call me

Mirjana. Will you do that?" She watched him carefully, afraid that in this easy, happy situation she had pressed him too fast and too far. She realized that Teddy had reason to blame her for the separation between himself and his mother, and his banishment to the stables.

"I promise. Really, I do, Mirjana. Now will you tell me the secret?"

"I will do better. Come with me, I have something to show you." She led him back to the wagon that had six barrels packed in straw in its bed and was parked beneath the trees. Gormaz had followed her, believing she was ready to reveal her surprise.

Teddy watched as his new friend told Gormaz to open one of the barrels. Peeking inside, he saw it was filled with ice and snow, He looked at Mirjana questioningly.

"From the mountains, Teddy." She pointed to the not too distant snow-capped peaks of the Pyrenees. "Only yesterday it was brought down."

Frowning, Teddy looked at her questioningly. "It doesn't seem much of a surprise," he told her, disappointed. "Every winter it snows and no one seems happy for it."

"I'm certain," Mirjana said seriously. "But have you ever eaten it?"

"Once I put it on my tongue and it turned to water."

"But this is magic. Here, I will show you. Now, close your eyes and don't peek!"

Tanige, overwhelmed with this change in Teodoro, however temporary she believed it, handed Mirjana a grape leaf spindled into a cone. Gormaz, using a sharp, thin pick, chopped at the ice, scooping a handful of the glittery frozen substance into the coned leaf. Tanige deftly poured a syrup of crushed blackberries sweetened with honey over it, and Mirjana told Teddy to stick out his tongue. She touched the sweetened ice to it and watched laughing as he tasted it, his eyes opening in wide surprise. "More!" he giggled, taking the grape leaf from her, the sticky juice running down his chin.

"What do you think of our secret surprise now, Teddy?"

"Wait, I'll call my friends!" He scurried away, calling to the children.

Gormaz stood in the wagon, hands on hips, laughing with satisfaction. "There is hope for the boy," he said. "He is not the same child Don Ruy placed in my care."

Children came running to the wagon, followed by their curious parents, where this strange new delicacy was dispensed. Mirjana carried a portion of ice and syrup in a shallow wooden bowl over to Ilena who cooled her tongue with it and pronounced it delicious.

"I only hope we have enough for everyone," she said, licking the stickiness off her fingers. Ruy could not resist the sweet berry stain near her lips and boldly leaned down to kiss it. "Food for the gods," he told her, a wicked glint in his eye causing her to blush. They were lost in each other for the moment and were unaware of the nodding smiles of approval from the adults who witnessed this gentle intimacy.

After the holiday, life continued much the same as before. Ruy was busy preparing for his journey to the coronation of Alphonso, Ilena grew more uncomfortable each day with her pregnancy, and Teddy, churlish because Gormaz had proclaimed the chestnut filly not ready to ride, resumed his sulky displeasure with everything and everyone.

The sun-filled days of May were upon them, yellow with sunshine and filled with the scent of newly bloomed flowers. Mirjana still resided in Ruy's chambers, curling herself against him each night as they slept, loving the feel of his arm thrown over her as though he were afraid he would lose her while he slept.

Doña Ysabel had managed to prolong her departure from the *castillo* because of a spring cold that made her eyes watery and red, and produced a bone-racking cough. Mirjana mixed an elixir from a recipe in her physician's text and had Dulcimea bring it to her, warning her not to reveal that she was its source.

The señora spent her days in her private chamber, only attending supper in the great hall in the company of Padre Tomas and her own confessor, the young Padre Juano, who was under the older priest's tutelage. Pietro had already left Bivar weeks ago to return to his own home in Viega, a town many miles east of Bivar. Ruy seemed to prefer the private meals shared in his chamber with Mirjana, but several times he and the princess had attended supper in the great hall. At these times Doña Ysabel was barely civil to Mirjana, but her manner to Ruy was always respectful and humble.

It pained Mirjana to see this haughty, regal woman whose eyes seemed haunted by shadows, and she silently questioned Ruy's assurances that Doña Ysabel would find happiness outside Bivar.

Mirjana liked to keep herself busy while Ruy was attending his duties and overseeing the preparations for his departure. The thought of these idyllic days and nights coming to an end depressed her normally high spirits, and she was careful to keep a cheerful face and lighthearted manner whenever she was around Ruy.

She was returning to the *castillo* by way of the stable yard, carrying a basket of freshly gathered raspberries from the wild bushes just on the other side of the town. Unexpectedly, Ruy had returned early from the wheelwright's forge where he was overseeing the making of new wagon axles. His eyes lighted with the sight of her, hair bright from the sun, skin warm and flushed from her walk.

He took her basket of berries, his hand lingering on hers. "By the time I return you'll be as brown as a gypsy," he chuckled. There was a familiarity, an intimate huskiness in his voice that sent tingles up her spine.

In the bright light of day, Ruy drew her close, feeling the warmth of her and the slight dampness of perspiration through the back of her dress. He also felt her quickened heartbeat and felt it answered by his own.

Mirjana leaned against him, reveling in his lean strength, giving herself over to the tremors of pleasure his nearness always brought. He took her into the comparative darkness of the barn, the sweet fragrance of hay and the dust motes dancing in the shafts of golden light arrowing through it. His hands were in her hair, pulling it from its pins, draping it around her shoulder, curling it around one of her breasts. His eyes bathed her in their sultriness, stirring responsive yearnings within her. He tasted the curve of her throat, the fragile whiteness at the top of her breasts which was revealed by the deeply cut bodice.

"I want you, Mirjana." His voice was a hungry groan. "Here, now!" His touch became urgent, compelling, and she lent herself to it, her own desires soaring, feeling him fill her world with his presence, knowing no other existence than being here, in his arms.

He drew her deeper into the shadows, never taking his eyes from her, as though he could never see her enough, never touch her enough. The trap door in the loft above was open to the sky, and sunlight streamed down onto a bed of hay, warming it, seeping a sweet fragrance of open fields and blue heavens from it.

He had loved her in the darkness of his chamber, by the light of the fireplace, but here, in the shaft of golden sun, she found a certain erotic pleasure in his shadow as he covered her body with his own.

His slow, arousing caresses were becoming fierce and demanding, hurrying to find his pleasure, knowing his pleasure could only be found in hers.

His hands were hungry, parting the fabric of her bodice, caressing her breasts, his mouth following the tender path he traced, nipping at their coral crests, making them stand in provocative peaks that beckoned his lips over and again.

She moved beneath him, rucking up her skirts, parting her thighs, eager for him, hungry to have him enter her and satisfy this passion he aroused. She breathed his name, then cried for his mercy when he seemed to linger too long.

He teased her, gently rubbing her inner thighs, moving upwards, skirting the center of her desires. She writhed and moaned, begging him for her release, feeling as though she were caught in a whirlpool of emotions, eddying in wide circles that became smaller, more closely spaced, until at the center she would find him, whirling with her in the cool green center of passion spent.

He watched her face as he moved within her, feeling her body contract and ripple around his, drawing him into her, making him a part of her. Her eyes were closed, lips parted, her head rolled back and forth as though to deny what she was feeling. And at the end, when her back arched and a deep purr of contentment erupted from her throat, she opened her eyes as though in surprise to find him looking down at her, the sight of her passions enflaming his. He quickened his stroke, seeking his own satisfaction, certain of hers. It was her name he cried as he rushed to his own blazing release, and the sound was a symphony to her ears.

CHAPTER 10

Doña Ysabel poked angrily at a crumb of bread with her thumbnail. She jabbed at it and then crushed it as though it were an ant beneath her shoe. A dark scowl formed between her brows, setting her mouth in a bitter downward line.

Ruy ate quickly, wolfing down his food in his desire to leave the table and his mother's presence. It was early, very early, the sun had not yet begun to shine weakly over the horizon. The great hall, always dark because its only windows faced the west, was feebly lit by an occasional torch and candle to challenge the shadows.

"With Padre Tomas's influence, it could be possible to send the woman to a nunnery," Doña Ysabel broke the uneasy silence, her voice louder and more forceful than she intended. "Surely you can see, Ruy, how this infidel has already interfered with your life! You are a knight of the realm, dedicated to your career. She has affected your judgment, shaken your allegiances . . ." The señora found it difficult to continue speaking to a man who seemed not to have heard her and merely continued to tear at his bread. She tried another tack. "There are convents, Ruy, who for a hefty donation would not be too particular about giving hospice to an Islamic *princesa.* Perhaps they are in a better position than yourself to induce Hassan to accept her back into Seville."

Ruy lifted his head, looked at his mother, and went back to his breakfast.

"Ruy! Are you hearing me? If you sent the *princesa* to an influential convent your problem would be solved!"

"Only your problem, Madre. I was not aware the *princesa* presented a problem to me," he said before biting down on a chunk of cheese.

"Of course we have problems." The señora insisted upon grouping herself with her son. "Teddy is a problem. Poor child, exiled to the stables, of all places, wearing rags, and eating God only knows. The *princesa* is a problem. She does not belong here. She is not one of us! And you have compounded her distress by keeping her in your chambers. You have ruined her reputation, you have sullied and defiled her. Your only recourse is to send her to a nunnery! If her internment there is of length, perhaps her sins and your mischief will be forgotten."

At this, Ruy slammed his fist down on the table, rattling the wooden bowls and shaking the candles, causing wild patterns of light to fall on his face. "The *princesa* is not going to a convent! And how conveniently you make your judgments, Madre. The *princesa*'s sin is merely my mischief! You are a bitter woman, Madre, and if anyone is in need of the nuns' prayers, it is you. I want to hear no more. Teddy, by the way, is doing quite well. I hope to God you have your trunks packed for your journey. I am sick of your meddling."

The señora was shaken. Ruy had never treated her this way, only since the *princesa* had arrived into his life. "No, son, I have not yet prepared to leave. I was praying you would reconsider and permit me to spend my last days here in the *castillo,* in my home. I belong here."

"No, Madre. You will leave tomorrow. You will fill your Christian duty and spread your beneficence through the provinces. I will sit down this very day and write to our family and friends to inform them you will be nearby and expect to avail yourself of their hospitality." Suddenly, Ruy's voice softened. "Madre, regardless of what you believe, this is for your own good. The matter is settled, you leave tomorrow. Teddy stays behind, and shortly thereafter, I leave to mend my differences with Alphonso and attend the coronation. Castile will never accept him as king unless I do this."

Doña Ysabel sat a moment, staring at her son. She had known in her heart it would be useless to try to persuade him to allow her to stay in Bivar. He had changed in these past weeks. She, as his mother, was more aware of it than most. Even more so than his old friends, Pietro and Padre Tomas. Her mind searched for the proper description. Ruy was not softer, nor was he mellow. In his breast still beat the heart of a warrior and politician. No, he was more peaceful. That was it. She didn't care for the change in him, could not cope with it. And it was all due to the influence of the *princesa*. The señora sniffed disdainfully as Ruy rose to leave the table. She watched in disgust as he wiped his mouth with a cloth he insisted be placed at his seat. A napkin, he called it. Before, he had used his sleeve like all the others.

She would leave because the choice was not hers, but there was still one more gambit to be played. She would be long gone before Ruy and his paramour felt its repercussions.

Ruy bent to kiss his mother's cheek. He

saw the expression in her eyes and it was not to his liking. She would not dare to defy him. Tomorrow, he would be relieved of this particular worry when she left. The señora would depart for the provinces and he could put her from his mind. At least, he told himself, Mirjana would not be threatened by Doña Ysabel's plotting and scheming. God knew it was difficult enough for him to keep his mother at bay; Mirjana would find it impossible. Two females at one another's throats was too much even for the strongest of men. Tomorrow would see an end to it all.

At a loss as to how to excuse himself, Ruy reminded his mother that it was nearly time for Padre Juano to say Mass in the tiny *castillo* chapel. "Are you receiving communion this morning, Madre?"

"This morning as every morning!" she answered him angrily. "Why else do you think I abstained from breakfast?" As she spoke, the bell in the chapel sounded, calling the faithful of the *castillo* to Mass. Wearily, Doña Ysabel stood from her chair, smoothing the fullness of her black skirts. "Some day, Ruy, you will live to regret your decision," she said ominously.

Ruy quirked his eyebrow, looking at his mother with curiosity. "And you, Madre, will take great pains to see it is so, I am certain.

Heed me, Madre, no more of your meddling tricks, else you will never be welcome back to Bivar." A sudden chill descended over him, remembering his mother's power and influence and ruthlessness.

"How could an old woman threaten you, Ruy? You are a great warrior, are you not? Do not let the words of your old mother trouble you." She waved her hand, brushing him aside, lifting her chin imperiously, a glimmer of a smile on her face. It pleased her that Ruy could be apprehensive about his decision. In some way it assured her of her remaining powers over him.

The chapel was dim and damp as it always was. Young Padre Juano, dressed in his long brown robe, performed the ritual of the Mass at the altar. The relic in the altar stone was bones from St. Clothilde, brought from Doña Ysabel's home long ago when she had first come to Bivar as a young bride. It was due to her influence that this chapel had been refurbished, that the kneelers and pews had been built.

The stained glass windows over the altar were in the form of a triptych, picturing the Blessed Virgin holding the Infant; St. Clothilde carrying a small cross; and of course, in the center of the three reproductions, a scene from Christ's crucifixion with the holy

Maria weeping near his feet.

A mother always weeps, the señora scorned. The sharpest thorn is an unloving child. A woman flirts with death at the birth of her children and to no reward.

All through Mass Doña Ysabel prayed for strength and the wisdom to protect her son, even from himself. Following the ceremony, when the *castillo* servants returned to their duties, the señora prayed for guidance. Ruy must take a wife! The answer came to her as though an angel had whispered in her ear.

Doña Ysabel walked boldly into the sacristy, hoping against hope that Padre Tomas would be off tending his duties in the village. This was something he rarely did, preferring to allow his subordinates to preside at Christenings and Last Rites. Even preaching sermons to the people of Bivar seemed to be something he wished to avoid.

It depressed him, Padre Tomas had once confided. He had even gone so far as to say there were times he doubted his calling. Of course this confidence came after the Padre had consumed too much wine, and there had been a wicked gleam in his dark, somber eyes. The señora knew he had been a man of the world before taking up the cross, carousing and womanizing, not giving his services to God until much later in life. His misspent youth was something the señora held against him, having no tolerance for the man. No, it was not Tomas Martinez she needed now. It was her own confessor, Padre Juano, with his greedy eyes and pasty skin. Her confessor was a man of discretion, and for a price he would do as she asked and die with the secret.

"Doña Ysabel, what brings you here at this time of day?" Padre Juano asked as he was putting away the sacramental wine. His thin, sunken cheeks delineated the sharpness of his nose and his too closely set eyes. The fine hairs in his nostrils quivered with annoyance at this interruption. He hoped the señora was not seeking confession. She required long and fervent absolutions which he was required to join, praying along with her, seeking forgiveness for her sins. He was hungry and wanted his breakfast. Also, there was nothing more boring than hearing the señora's confession. She had little use for absolution from a priest, excusing her sins as being the cause of other's making. Still, she was his benefactress and was the easiest path to acquiring the bishop's robes he so coveted.

Padre Juano was no fool. He knew his immediate superior, Padre Tomas, used him to suit his needs, caring little if his subordinate was content in his post. As long as Padre

Tomas was in control, there was nothing he could do but suffer in silence. One day, though, his time would come, and there were those in the *castillo* who would answer to him. His dreams were to become abbot of a monastery, secure and comfortable with the donations from the landed rich. And Doña Ysabel was his champion. Little as he liked the woman, he knew her to be influential and valuable in seeing his dreams come true.

The señora smiled coyly, emitting her charm. Immediately, Padre Juano knew she was approaching him with a purpose in mind. "Padre Juano, *por favor,* a moment of your time. A small favor only you can grant."

The señora watched the priest rise to the flattery as she had known he would. "I would like you to write a letter for me to our new king, Alphonso."

The young priest was taken aback. A letter to the king! A thin smile played near his mouth. How fortunate, he thought. Through his favor to Doña Ysabel, he would find the door open to correspond with the most important personage in Spain! Daydreams roiled through his brain. He had sudden images of seeing himself as confessor to the king, living in the elaborate palace, presiding over royal ceremonies, becoming a Cardinal, Pope!

"Padre Juano, do you hear me?" Doña

Ysabel said irritably. "I would like you to write a letter to Alphonso!"

The priest felt the hairs on the back of his neck rise. He knew he would write the letter, but first he would wait for the bribe she would offer him. Whenever the señora implicated him in one of her schemes she always rewarded him. What would her price be this time? A jewel, a few coins, his own horse from the *castillo* stables to replace his humble donkey? Whatever the price, he would know the importance of her request by its value. He waited, and when there was no proffering of any kind, he frowned. "I am rather busy today, Doña Ysabel. Perhaps next week —"

"Next week! There will be no 'next week.' I leave for the provinces tomorrow, and I wish the letter to be delivered to Alphonso by Ruy when he attends the coronation. What can you possibly find more important than writing this letter for me?"

Padre Juano crossed all thought of suitable bribe from his mind. The mere mention of El Cid was all he needed to hear. He must be gracious and do as asked. "Very well, Doña Ysabel. Please be seated. Now, tell me what it is you wish me to write to Alphonso."

The señora seated herself across from the priest, clenching her fists, hating the fact that she, an intelligent woman, had never been taught to read or write. Only men were thought to be quick enough of intellect to accomplish literacy. She sniffed. As though this fanatical dolt who sat before her could be considered more intelligent than she! "Firstly, you will offer my greetings and my regards to Alphonso and Infanta Urraca. Next, you will speak of the unseasonably good weather, and from there you will pledge the allegiance of the Diaz family to our new and worthy king."

Padre Juano felt uneasy, and he did not like the feeling. It seemed a simple enough letter but totally unnecessary since Don Ruy was attending the coronation himself and could convey this affection in person. There had to be another reason for the señora to seek him out this way, he was certain of it. "How do you wish me to sign it?" he asked craftily.

"I have not finished, Padre."

He waited expectantly. His skin was beginning to itch and his palms were moist and clammy. Perhaps there would be a bribe, after all. He leaned back in his chair and made a steeple with his long, white fingers. "What else do you wish me to write?"

"At the end you will include my happiness at having the Diaz family joined with his. A small reminder that since Ruy will be attending the coronation as will no doubt Alphonso's niece, Himena, I expect the nuptials to be arranged. Remind the king that the marriage agreement was signed by Ruy's father when Himena was first born. We will enclose my copy of the agreement should the contract have slipped Alphonso's memory. He is not a tidy person, Padre."

"My dear Doña Ysabel, does my lord know of this letter?" Padre Juano asked anxiously.

"But of course! How dare you question me? Ruy himself is going to deliver the letter to Alphonso and what better opportunity to have royal sanction when Ruy is endorsing Alphonso for king. A much needed endorsement, I might add," she said proudly. "Should you doubt my word, ask my son yourself, but be prepared to suffer the consequences."

Padre Juano was staring her directly in the eyes. It was Doña Ysabel who looked away first.

"For your trouble, since I am aware of how busy you are," she said briskly, as she stripped two rings from her fingers. A large emerald and a glittering topaz lay in the priest's hand for merely an instant before he pocketed them in his surplice.

"When will you have the letter for me?"

"Within the hour. Bring your copy of the marriage agreement if you want it sealed within the letter. Do you wish to use your own seal or would you prefer the official church seal?"

Doña Ysabel pondered. "I think it would be wise to use the church seal since Ruy will be carrying the letter. I would rather he did not poke into my little missive. He would never contemplate toying with a letter bearing the church seal."

On the long walk back to her chambers Doña Ysabel dusted her hands together gleefully. It was done. She might be forced to leave her home, but she would hear the repercussions of her letter for years to come. Short of sending Mirjana to a nunnery, it was a brilliant idea. A plan without fault. It was ordained, planned from the day of Himena's birth. As a mother, she was doing her duty. And Ruy could not refuse without insulting the king himself!

From out the window of their chamber, Mirjana could see the gathering of soldiers and people in the town and in the courtyard. They had been arriving for days now, dressed for the journey to the coronation. She had known this day was to come; she had even encouraged Ruy to proclaim Alphonso as his king. But then, she had known the loneliness of the hours and days without him. She brushed a tear from her cheek. He was not even gone from her yet and already she mourned his loss.

Ruy was fastening his boots when he glanced up and saw her standing at the window, silently looking down at the crowds below. Her thin nightdress was a gossamer veil through which the daylight revealed each lovely curve he had come to know so well. She still had not dressed for the day and would not do so until he had gone. He wanted to think of her here, waiting for his return, he had told her, and it was true. He did not want to lose sight of her face among a throng of faces, and when he was miles out into the distance and could see the last of the *castillo* dipping from sight, he wanted to know she watched from the window.

When he was ready to leave, he went to stand behind her, cupping her shoulders in his hands, feeling her tremble beneath his touch. They had lain awake in each other's arms long into the morning hours. Their pleasure and desire for one another never seemed sated. And this morning, only an hour ago, she had come into his arms, giving and trusting, holding back that rush of desolation he knew she was feeling. There would be no tears to mar this parting, and it was as he wished.

Looking over Mirjana's head into the distance, he saw his column of soldiers making formation. Padre Tomas carried the standard of the church, his tonsured head glowing pinkly in the early light. "I will send word to you of my return, *cara.* Then you will watch through the window and I will find you here as though I had never left." His voice was thick with emotion, and he cursed himself for it. Never did he think he would find it painful to leave a woman.

"I will watch for you," she told him, leaning back against him, allowing him to caress her, feeling her response to his touch even through her misery. They had made love only an hour ago and still her need for him was sharp, hungry, yearning to be near him and give of herself to him.

Her eyes dropped to the small bedside table, and she reached for an ivory white parchment waxed with the church seal. "This letter, Ruy. Do not forget to deliver it to Alphonso."

He took the parchment and tucked it into his tunic. "I leave you in good hands, Mirjana. You have only to go to Gormaz and he will see to your needs. Even since before my mother left the *castillo,* you've wooed the servants into complete obedience." He waited, not wanting to be the first to bid *adiós.*

"Go now, Ruy, your regiment awaits you." It was a cry, a denial, a sob of longing. Quickly, he turned her about in his arm, kissing her, deeply, searchingly, hating to leave her this way, hating even more to deny himself of her.

Mirjana watched from the window. The caterpillar of men rounded the swelling hillocks until she could see them no more. But she knew that before the last of the *castillo* had slipped from his sight, Ruy had turned and offered a loving salute.

In the days that followed Ruy's departure, Mirjana languished in the *castillo,* venturing out only to see Teddy and Gormaz. Even though Ilena was quite close to her time and frightened of childbirth, and had asked for Mirjana often, she hadn't the heart to walk into the village to visit her. The servants in the *castillo* sighed compassionately. The villagers made whispering inquiries. Where was the girl with the sunshine hair? they asked. Had Don Ruy broken her heart? They missed her smile and the softly hummed songs they would hear as she passed their way.

Mirjana spent long days in Ruy's chamber, reading poetry or just lying abed remembering the times she had spent with him. Her loneliness for him was acute, stealing her appetite, and worse, her interest in others.

One particular morning while in search of Tanige who was hanging laundry in the kitchen yard, Mirjana trespassed down the back staircase, again noticing the poor housekeeping in the *castillo.* The chamber she shared with Ruy was by now scrupulously clean due to the efforts of herself and Tanige. But what of the rest of the *castillo?* Something was fired within her. Ruy would be absent weeks, more than likely months, and this was the perfect opportunity to improve living here.

Mirjana threw herself into the many necessary chores, enlisting a bevy of servants. The first thing to be done was have the great hall swept of the old rushes and refuse. Next, the cobwebs, hanging for centuries, it would seem. This seemed to be the exact therapy she needed. By the time she was ready for bed, she was exhausted, only to rise to another day and begin again. While having absolutely no former knowledge of housekeeping techniques, Mirjana followed her instincts, seeing each project through to the finish.

She had already conferred with artisans in the village and with Gormaz, who was invaluable to her. The man was a master of many trades and had an inborn quality for organization. From the storeroom she ordered all her books unpacked and brought to the great hall. In several were written accounts for making tiles, and after conferring with the blacksmith, he assured her he could build a kiln for firing the glaze.

Ancient stone walkways surrounding the *castillo* were repaired, and the kitchen floor was laid with stone, making a smooth surface for walking and ease of cleaning. Trees were brought down from the hillside and replanted in the arbor. In a few years it, too, would be flourishing, helping to restore the area to its former grandeur. Women brought flowers for planting in beds, and potters supplied containers for shrubs to line the walkways. Even the barn roof was repaired under Mirjana's watchful eye.

As the weeks passed, the storehouse containing the contents of the caravan became emptier and emptier as Mirjana helped herself to the goods, reasoning that the treasures belonged to Ruy and he would appreciate having them in the *castillo* for his enjoyment. An itinerant glazier happened to be passing through Bivar, and Mirjana utilized his skill to create windows for the great hall and the master's chamber. His work was rough and lacking the artistry she had known in Seville, but he was thorough and the glass would keep out the insects and the worst of the winter winds.

Fabrics and tapestries from the storehouse found their use in the *castillo*. The largest and most beautiful of the tapestries hung in the great hall over the hearth and along the high stone walls. The rusty armor and cross bows that once hung there were placed in the quickly emptying storehouse.

Everyone worked hard, giving of themselves, enjoying the accomplishments of their efforts. Mirjana was always quick with praise for a job well done, and almost every evening the cooks prepared supper for those who worked that day. When the craftsmen finished laying the tiles in the great hall, it was a day for celebration. This had been the most involved and important of the undertakings. Mirjana had devised a simple pattern with slate blues and shades of gold which when properly placed formed a diamond design with intertwining circles. The tiles had been buffed to a dull gleam, reflecting the light from the fire and bringing an atmosphere of cleanliness and richness to the *castillo*. Ruy's *castillo*. His home.

Once started, she had difficulty stopping, and would not be satisfied until all was to her liking. What could not be changed could at least be cleaned. She threw herself into her decorating tasks as the days wore into months. Each task, large or small, would make her stand back to view her handiwork and wonder how Ruy would like what she had done. The *castillo* was taking on a life of its own. Everywhere the eye could see was beauty and color. On more than one occasion she had heard the workers and servants singing as they hurried through the corridors. Beauty always lightened the heart.

Tanige would smile and call it Mirjana's nesting instinct. Mirjana called it cleaning.

Only in the master's chamber had Mirjana held her excitement in check. Everything was for Ruy's comfort, each color carefully selected for him, bold and masculine, in complete harmony with the man. A tapestry hung over the bed, the deep reds and muted golds echoed in the velvet coverlets. Her own supply of bedding was brought to the chamber: silken sheets and down pillows. Rare and exotic porcelains, collected from when she was a child, were placed in advantageous spots in the chamber, their tiny, polished pedestals bringing murmurs of approval. Each item was in exquisite taste and always with Ruy in mind.

A brazier was installed near the hearth for permanent use, and in an alcove opposite the bed she arranged a setting of a table and two chairs. Everything was in twos, she smiled — two pillows, two chairs, two lamps . . . two, Ruy and Mirjana. She herself had scrubbed the stone floor, scattering brightly woven rugs to bring more color to the huge room. Sconces were hung for lamps. Lengths of sheer cloth hung over the windows, and in the evening they would billow with the gentlest of breezes.

She wondered what Ruy would think when he saw what she had done to the adjoining anteroom. A tub had been installed, along with a trifold screen brought from Seville. In the afternoon the sun streamed through the newly installed amber glass windows and bathed the room in gold. Soft cloths, softer towels, fragrant soaps, and pots of oil poised delicately on a service table. Luxurious lengths of colorful toweling lay stacked on two narrow shelves, and beside them stood an elegant silver-chased chest into which she had placed the spicy soap Ruy was fond of using.

But it was the kitchen that Mirjana felt presented her biggest challenge. Cleanliness in food preparation was a necessity. It had taken her weeks to make the cooks and kitchen maids understand what she wanted and expected. In the end, she had been forced to tie a scarf around her hair and begin the work, shaming them, until they applied their own energies to the arduous task of scrubbing away years of grease and grime. The soot-blackened beams sparkled as though new, and Gormaz, seeing this and anticipating the need for new venting, applied himself to the task. In this area, Tanige was invaluable. Her own mother worked in the kitchens of Mútadid's palace, and she had a good deal more knowledge of how things were done than Mirjana.

Tiles that had not been used for the floor in the great hall were placed on the walls surrounding the work areas. Soap suds and lye scoured the ovens and open pits. Fragrant herbs now hung from the beams, and copper pots and skillets twinkled in the light. Refuse was no longer permitted in the kitchen and was carried away twice a day.

The preparation of fresh foods was what pleased the kitchen staff. No longer were the servants to eat what wasn't fit for the family. Everyone ate the same food, insuring its goodness. Under Tanige's imperious instructions, new methods of cooking were learned, and even Mirjana joined her classes, laughing whenever Tanige became too arrogant with her own importance. The staff became apt pupils, eager to please, and enjoyed themselves, oftentimes offering to work beyond the hours Mirjana set for them.

"What is needed in here is a big old yellow cat, soon to have kittens," she told them. It was a symbol of luck in Seville. "And," she said waving her arm, "we need some colorful flowers for freshness and color. A little greenery near the hearth would be cheerful."

That evening, when Mirjana went to the kitchen, she was stunned to see a huge yellow cat sleeping near the fireplace. Immediately, her eyes circled the huge proportions of the kitchen. Twelve crocks of dry flowers and fresh adorned each shelf. Tubs of fragrant evergreens flanked the doors to the pantry. Amazed, tears stung her eyes. "Who did this?" she asked softly.

"We all did," chirped a rosy-cheeked maid. "Cook said we could take a few hours off to do what you wanted. Does it please you, mistress?"

"Of course it pleases me. But the question is, does it please you? Because you all work so long in here I wanted it to please you. Was I right?"

A babble of voices agreed.

"How wonderful of all of you. Truly, I appreciate what you've done. And wherever did you find a yellow cat?" Mirjana dabbed at her eyes. "Tell me, what is that wonderful smell?" she added.

"Roast lamb with the mint jelly you showed me how to make." The cook smiled. "Roast potatoes and fresh greens for dinner along with wild cherries for a sweet."

"Wonderful, cook. It smells delicious. And what kind of pie is that?"

"Blueberry, mistress, just like you said. See how — how crumbly the crust is."

"Not crumbly. Crumbly means it isn't holding together. Flaky. Flaky means it is light and will melt in our mouths. Flaky."

"Flaky," the cook said dutifully.

"I see that you have learned to time the bread baking to coincide with the evening meal. I'm pleased," Mirjana said, patting the old cook's shoulder. She was rewarded with a wide, toothy ear-to-ear smile. "And the butter, it looks beautiful. Be sure now that you serve the bread in the woven baskets with the colored handles, the flat ones so that the bread can be seen. I'm proud of all of you. Very proud!" And her staff beamed under her approval.

Mirjana sat on a stone bench retrieved from the cellars in the *castillo* and placed in view of the gardens. Soon, evening would fall. Her work was done. There was little more she could do to improve the *castillo,* and she had worked long and hard doing what she thought best. To her eyes, it was beautiful. Compared to the palace in Seville, it left much to be desired, but she knew she would be happy here . . . with Ruy.

Her reflective mood became somber as she mentally counted the days since he had been gone. Too long. Nearly three months had passed and she ached for him. Three months and no word. Soon it would be August, the end of a lovely summer. Autumn would come early here, being so far to the north, and she would like to spend it with Ruy.

Remembered times with Ruy made her heart soar. How close they had become, talking together into the early hours of morning, falling into each other's arms, tasting again the sweet elixir of passion renewed. The tireless chess games they would play, but it was those times he would best her when he could claim his prize and make love to her for long, wonderful hours, shutting out the world. Afterwards, lying together, arms embracing, he would whisper those lovely things she loved to hear, calling her his little miracle.

Mirjana was sometimes homesick for Seville and still grieved for Mútadid, her father. Yet she realized her entire life had prepared her for leaving Seville and home and family. It was a woman's destiny, especially if that woman was a princess. Mirjana smiled. The fates had been kind after all, she thought. Instead of living the rest of her days in Granada as Yusuf's wife, destiny had exchanged a meaningless life for one of adventure and love here in Bivar. Life continued regardless, and one had to move with it and never look back. This Ruy had told her one night when she had told him about her life in the palace and of her father. Life would never stand still for Ruy, Tanige, or herself.

Tanige. Mirjana's eyes widened. How remiss she had become with her friend. They rarely spent time together these days, both of them being so busy. Starting on the morrow, Mirjana vowed to work to bring their relationship back to where it had been when they first arrived in Bivar.

Young Teodoro, a serious, almost reverent, expression on his little face, rode atop the chestnut filly Gormaz had assigned into his care. Firm little legs hugged the animal's sides. His back was straight and his hand on the reins gentle. From the shade of an ancient tree in the stableyard, Mirjana watched Teddy, along with Gormaz, as the boy put the pony through its paces.

"He handles the pony well, Princesa," Gormaz said proudly. "He is not the same child he was. See how lightly he holds the reins and how he talks to her."

Mirjana smiled. It was true, Teddy was hardly the same child. Gormaz's instincts had been correct to make the boy responsible for the pony. He had quickly learned that through responsibility came gentleness and love.

"Mirjana! Mirjana! See what she can do!" Teddy called, waving.

"I see!" she laughed, enjoying his enthusiasm. Not too many weeks ago it had been

"See what *I* can do." Now, because of his love and pride in the animal, it was "See what *she* can do!" Ruy would be so pleased when he returned. From all reports, young Teddy had adjusted beautifully without the overpowering influence of Doña Ysabel, and he hardly missed his mother from all indications. He had found friends among the boys in the village, and was actually telling Gormaz that he looked forward to the time when he would be sent to Don Hernandez's *castillo* for training to become a knight. He wanted to be a man like his brother, he said proudly. And he would be, Mirjana thought; already he sat high and agile in the saddle, becoming one with his steed.

Teddy was handing the filly over to a stable groom and was running toward her, his cheeks flushed with delight. "I'm starving!" he told her, his eyes going expectantly to the basket of food she had brought for their picnic.

Together, they walked to the meadow near the pond where they had shared the celebration of Easter. Once they had found a nice spot, Teddy gobbled his boiled eggs and drank huge quantities of milk until, finally resting back on his elbow, he declared himself stuffed.

"I've brought you something, Teddy. Look in the bottom of the basket." She watched him as he curiously poked beneath the wrappings of bread and cheese and withdrew a book and a slate. He glanced at her quizzically.

"I thought you might like to begin your lessons," she told him, keeping her tone light, not wanting to pressure him. The fact was Teddy should have begun his lessons in reading and writing several years ago, before the age of six. Either Padre Tomas or Padre Juano should have taken the responsibility, but because of Doña Ysabel's determination to keep the boy a baby, she had postponed the child's education.

"You, Mirjana?" Teddy seemed startled — more, astounded. Very few people were literate and hardly ever a woman.

"Yes, me. I learned to read when I was only a little girl, and then it was in Arabic. Now, because of my fine teachers, I can read in Latin as well, and I speak Castilian Spanish, your native tongue. Also, I am quite capable with numbers; something I know you will enjoy."

Teddy appeared doubtful.

"Actually, it was Ruy's idea for me to teach you. What do you think of the idea?"

The boy hung his head and refused to meet her eyes.

"Perhaps you would like to think about it? Think how nice it would be to write Ruy a letter and help him with his duties in the *castillo*. He would be so proud."

Teddy raised his eyes; they were soft and brimming with tears. "Mirjana, I am truly sorry for what I did and how I treated you. I was mean. If it were not for me, you never would have been whipped . . ." His words were choked by tears.

Mirjana put her arms around him, nestling his head against her breast. "Hush, Teddy, what is past is past. It is *now* that is important. We are friends now, truly friends."

He hugged her around the waist, holding fast. It had been a very long time since he had felt a woman's tender touch. He needed someone to mother him, as all boys did. Mirjana was touched by this show of emotions and ruffled her fingers soothingly through his thick, dark hair, thinking how much like Ruy's it was.

"What do you say, Teddy? Are you ready to learn?"

"My — my friend, Antonio, could you . . . would you . . ."

"Teach him alongside of you? Of course, but can he be spared from his duties? This must be done aside of your training."

"Ruy said you would be my friend and he told me I should trust you in all things."

"Your brother told you this?" Mirjana asked in amazement.

"Yes, and he told me other things," Teddy said shyly, "but those are secrets between men. But Ruy said you were the best friend a man could have, but I think it is because he likes to kiss you."

Mirjana blushed, and playfully tousled Teddy's dark hair. "I'll tell you a secret too, Teddy." She cupped her hand to her mouth and whispered in his ear, and when she told him she liked to have Ruy kiss her, he broke out into peals of laughter, saying he would never, never kiss a girl! The chestnut filly was more to his liking.

Tanige fixed a sour expression on her face and stared at Mirjana. "You are in charge of a complete staff of servants, Princess. Must you constantly look for work? Think how your hands look! They will never be soft and white again if you keep on with this. Think what your father would say to see his daughter, a princess, scrubbing like a scullery maid!"

"My hands are my concern," Mirjana snapped. Then, looking at her friend, she asked, "Is something troubling you Tanige?" Was it possible? Was Tanige at last filling out, losing that scrawny, bone-sharp appearance? The thought delighted Mirjana. Aside from Tanige's sour face, she was different, more alive and vibrant. She believed the word she sought was "blooming." Even the bodice of her gown was snug across her bosom. Her sharp, angular features were somehow more rounded, softer. When had this transformation taken place? She had been so wrapped up in the *castillo,* she had paid little attention to Tanige, and here she was, blossoming before her very eyes.

"Actually, there is something troubling me. Ilena invited me to tea today and her brother, Luis, will be there."

"That sounds lovely. You've told me how he adores his newborn nephew. But why are you so disturbed?"

"I have nothing to wear," Tanige blurted.

Mirjana frowned, then smiled. "Ah, I see. Luis is also concerned with your wardrobe."

"No! That is —"

"That is he is quite attentive!"

"Since I only possess two gowns still fit to wear, it is not difficult for him to notice what I am wearing." Was it possible? Was Tanige actually squirming?

"Well, we must do something about it immediately. Help yourself to anything you wish from my wardrobe. And since you are so adept with the needle, find what you like from the bolts of cloth we brought from Seville."

"You mean whatever was saved from decorating the *castillo!* But I accept your offer, Princess, and thank you."

"Hurry now, you must not keep Luis, or Ilena, waiting," Mirjana teased, seeing a fresh flush of color stain Tanige's cheeks. "And send Ilena my regards and kiss the baby for me."

As Tanige left the room, she could hear Mirjana singing a bright tune they had learned as children. Mirjana was quite happy tending her projects to decorate and improve the *castillo,* and she needed Tanige less and less. This thought depressed Tanige somewhat, but then she reasoned that Mirjana needed no help to select fabric and tiles. Of late, it seemed that only Ilena and sometimes Luis valued her opinion. He was so considerate. If she was careful and delayed her visit with Ilena till evening, Luis would offer to escort her back to the *castillo.* He held her arm protectively at these times, and the last time he had pecked her on the cheek. It was all Tanige could do not to fling herself at him and demand more. Much more!

CHAPTER 11

Church bells rang from every part of Zamora, a city famous for its places of worship and bell towers. Spaniards from near and afar had come to the coronation, hailing the regal procession at top voice as it moved slowly through the narrow streets. Alphonso, golden haired and handsome, was the center of everyone's attention and their speculation. Although none would give voice to their suspicions, it ran through the crowd like a fever. Had King Sancho met his death due to Alphonso's covetousness of the throne of Castile? There were already rumors, much later proven true, that poor, weak Garcia, inheritor of the throne of Galicia and brother to Alphonso, was being kept in chains in the dungeons of a remote castle in León.

Ruy took his place with the other eleven men, some warriors, others civil judges, and the remainder Bishops of the Faith, before the white marble altar. He was to issue the oath to Alphonso, and the weight of his deed was heavy on his heart. He knew, beyond reason, that Alphonso and his royal sister, Urraca, were responsible for Sancho's death. Sancho, boyhood friend and his liege, rightful inheritor of Castile. There was no help for Sancho now, only the prevention of an ultimate civil war if he did not recognize Alphonso as king.

Trumpets blared their royal homage, banners waved throwing their brilliant colors back at the sun. The only storm clouds present were in Ruy's head as he solemnly stood at attention, his formal armor polished to a bright gleam. Outside, the peasantry roared their greeting. Inside the cathedral, nobility sat or stood silently watching the pageantry of history. Scanning the faces with his sharp, soldier's eye, Ruy glimpsed Urraca sitting calmly in the front pews assigned for the royal family. Garcia was curiously absent, and Ruy, remembering the rumors of the youngest brother's imprisonment, believed them to be true. Sitting just behind Urraca was a slim, pale girl of perhaps seventeen. She was biting her lip nervously and her hands fidgeted in her lap. Why did it seem she was staring at him, Ruy wondered? Perhaps it was a trick of the light.

The royal procession entered the cathedral and Ruy forced himself to quell the hatred he held for Alphonso. By right deed or not, the man would soon be king. Throughout the high Mass said by the Bishop of Zamora, Ruy recalled the years spent training for the knighthood in his royal household under the reign of old King Ferdinando. He had trained beside the princes Sancho, Alphonso, and Garcia. But of all the sons, Ruy had always thought the Infanta Urraca more fitting to ascend the throne than her brothers. Strong and stubborn, wily of wit, and possessing a better grasp of politics than even the old king, Urraca had often cursed the fates that had declared her a female. No, there was no doubt in Ruy's mind that while Alphonso gained from Sancho's death it was Urraca, with her night-black hair and deep-set, calculating eyes, who had been the force behind the dagger that had spilled Sancho's life's blood.

He glanced at Urraca again, saw her lowered head, her face obscured by the veil from her elaborate headdress. Feeling the tug of a powerful stare, he again looked beyond Urraca to the girl who seemed unable to take her eyes from him. He wondered who this girl was who sat among the royal family, and not for the first time, he wondered why she seemed to hate him. A man like himself made many enemies throughout his career, and he wondered what grudge this pale, nondescript girl held against him. Had he perhaps offended her somehow during the galas Urraca held prior to the coronation? He could not remember seeing her before this, and yet she seemed to know him, of him, and her dislike for him was undeniable.

Mass was over, the chalice and holy wafer put away in the gilt tabernacle over the altar. He had observed Alphonso when Communion was given, had seen his complexion whiten, his tongue take the body and blood of Christ into his mouth, had seen him almost gag, as though he expected to be struck by lightning.

In endless ceremony the prayers continued; Ruy shifted irritably from one foot to the other. Soon now, he himself would declare Alphonso his king, and he could already feel the words sticking in his throat. It is for Castile, for all of Spain, he told himself.

The cathedral became still with a breathless silence. Alphonso was looking at him, doubts and shadows in his eyes. The twelve men, including Ruy, stepped forward, flanking the would-be king. But it was Ruy's voice that rang through the silence, reading from the ancient oath, hearing Alphonso's responses. The moment was a blur, something Ruy would rather forget than remember.

It was after the Bishop of Zamora had placed the crown on Alphonso's light-golden head and all knelt in reverence when it became time for Ruy to lead the others in homage by kissing the hand of the new king. He took Alphonso's hand in his, feeling it tremble, before the man pulled it from his grasp. Pale and shaking, Alphonso refused Ruy's gesture of tribute, and for centuries after, the world would know he had declared his guilt in the death of his brother.

Himena Maria Asturias sat outside the king's council chamber waiting to hear her name called. She sat alongside her Aunt Consuela who kept admonishing her to stop biting her ragged nails. Himena knew why she had been called to this audience with King Alphonso. It concerned her marriage to Don Rodrigo Ruy Diaz. She slunk in her chair, wanting to make herself invisible.

"Sit straight, child," Tía Consuela reprimanded. She jabbed a plump elbow into Himena's ribs. "Remember who you are," the woman hissed, "Himena Maria Asturias, grandniece and goddaughter to the king! And please not to look so forlorn. One would think you expected to spend the rest of your life as a maiden. It is high time the marriage between our House of Asturias and that of Diaz is finally honored. And do not think it was an easy task to forestall this formalization until we could be certain Don Ruy had pledged his allegiance to Alphonso! Doña Ysabel is known to be a calculating and politically minded woman. When we were first told she had sent a letter to Alphonso reminding him of the contract wedding you with her son, I suspected she was attempting to secure favor for Ruy through his marriage to you, despite the fact he would not honor Alphonso as new King of all Castile. Thank God, it was not the case!"

Himena scowled. If she had heard this once, she had heard it one hundred times since arriving in Zamora for the coronation. It was true that since the death of her parents she had much to be grateful for from Tía Consuela and Tío Bernardo. They had watched over her, protected her, been most dutiful and loving. However, they knew nothing about her, what she dreamed of and wished for. As a young woman, it would have been unseemly to complain, but the sudden realization of the marriage contract with Don Ruy was upsetting all her carefully laid plans. She had hoped the contract would be forgotten; she had prayed Don Ruy would protest Alphonso's ascension to the throne. Rebelling against Alphonso would have made Don Ruy an exile, an enemy of the crown, and no one would have expected her to go against king and family to marry him.

All a woman could have or expect to have was what belonged to her husband. But if a woman were abbess of a convent, she could have more, much more! Power, position and even wealth, all a result of her own efforts. And this she could have by royal decree just as easily as her marriage would be recognized by royal decree. She had been close, so close, to realizing her dream. Through the past months she had become quite friendly and close to her grandaunt, the Infanta Urraca who through old King Ferdinando had been bequeathed all the monasteries and nunneries in Spain. This made the princess even more powerful than King Alphonso in many ways, and quite rich. Himena had been on the brink of requesting a position as abbess at a nearby nunnery known for its wealth and influence. Urraca would have given it to her, Himena knew. And now, because of Don Ruy, the dream was lost to her.

She supposed being his wife would be the answer to some girl's prayers, but not to hers! He was rich, that she knew, otherwise the original contract would not have been made shortly after her birth. But it was *his* riches, *his* name, *his* power! All these things she wanted, but in *her own* name, Himena Maria Asturias!

Two days before at the coronation ceremonies was the first time Himena had ever set eyes on Ruy, and she had hated him on sight! All through Mass she had prayed he would refuse to give the oath to Alphonso. Civil war be damned! All that stood in her way was Don Ruy Diaz and his ignorant mother's letter to Alphonso. And now Alphonso, grateful for Ruy's affirmation of his coronation, was prepared to reward him in any way he could. Don Ruy would be rewarded with a wife — herself! And she had no say in the matter whatever!

Tía Consuela had prodded her directly after the ceremonies. Had she noticed Don Ruy? Hadn't she thought him handsome? Wasn't his reputation as a champion romantic? Romantic! What could be romantic about a foolish man riding out ahead of his army to fight the mightiest challenger from an opposing force? Himena was too worldly and too logical to see romance in courting death. Also, why should valor belong to men alone? Like her grandaunt Urraca, Himena, too, aspired to greatness in her own behalf.

The door at the far end of the anteroom opened and Don Ruy entered, tall and handsome. The light from the torches in this dark, cavernous room threw his face into relief against his cloud of dark hair. Tía Consuela jabbed her again with her elbow to prompt her to sit straighter and hide her ugly, bitten fingers.

"Don Ruy Diaz!" Tía Consuela called, her voice ringing loudly from the rafters. "Have you also come for audience with our king? You do remember me, my husband is Don Bernardo Asturias!"

"Certainly, Doña Consuela." Ruy bowed from the waist. Clearly, he did not remember and would not have if she had not prompted his memory. "And Don Bernardo, he is well, I trust." Ruy was suddenly distracted. First, this unsought audience with Alphonso, and secondly, finding Doña Consuela Asturias also waiting for an audience. He had not forgotten it was with the Asturias' niece that a marriage contract had been drawn. Ruy found his gaze being drawn to the pale, ashy-skinned girl sitting beside Doña Consuela. As he answered the older woman's questions concerning his mother, he found himself wondering if this could be the niece, Himena. No, he argued. Certainly not. Himena was merely a babe! Ruy's brows lifted as he recognized this to be the girl from the cathedral who had thrown him such hateful glances and remembered the fact that he himself had been older than ten when the marriage contract was drawn. How old was this girl? Seventeen? Eighteen? A worm of apprehension began nibbling at his innards.

As Doña Consuela spoke she saw Ruy's speculative glances falling on Himena. Misinterpreting the interest she saw there, she was about to introduce him when she heard their names being announced to enter the king's conference chamber. The apprehension that wormed in Ruy's belly coiled into a viper when he realized Doña Consuela, himself, and what he had feared — Himena Maria Asturias — were called in together.

Alphonso sat lazing in a huge, high-backed chair, his brilliant robes falling casually around his feet. He greeted them and called them forward. Don Bernardo Asturias went to Ruy and extended his hand in greeting, clasping him firmly at the elbow, murmuring, "*Saludo,* nephew."

Ruy was astonished. The worst had become reality. How had this happened? How?

"Don Rodrigo Diaz," Alphonso began formally, falling into more familiar tones. "Ruy, I was deeply grateful for your support of my taking the throne of Castile. Even more so, I realized your fealty to me by bringing Doña Ysabel's letter informing me of your wishes to take my niece to wife, thus reinforcing our relationship and guaranteeing your loyalty." Alphonso was smiling fondly at Ruy, his glance also taking in Himena. He wondered at Ruy's sudden interest in taking this pale, unlovely girl to wife. It could only be, he told himself, because of his political ambitions. Whatever the reason, Alphonso was glad of it. As godfather to Himena he had certain duties concerning her, and as a ruler desperately in need of fealty and loyalty from this greatest of champions who would bring the support of all Castile with him, the marriage was as good as consummated.

"Sire," Ruy responded, "I had no idea whatever that my mother had presumed upon you in so humble a matter as my marriage. Also, Doña Ysabel was no doubt ignorant of this child's tender years. I could not, in all conscience, take Señorita Asturias to wife! She is barely fresh from the cradle!"

"*De nada,* Don Ruy. You are too considerate," Alphonso persisted. At least Ruy had a finicky palate when it came to women, he thought. He, too, would have sought the right argument to free him from marrying so pios and dull a woman.

"If I may, Sire," Doña Consuela addressed, shooting irritable looks at her husband who, it seemed, was about to shrink away from his duties to Himena. Consuela was not a stupid woman, and she had raised and married three daughters of her own. Himena, by all prospects, was not ever going to become beautiful. In fact, according to belief, the girl was now, this moment, in her prime. Another year or two and no one, least of all a famous and revered warrior with land and wealth, would take her to wife. "My husband and myself are well up in our years. Naturally, we are concerned about Himena's future. She is a young woman with a large and healthy dowry," she said hoping to tempt Ruy, "and needs a husband to see to her affairs. Naturally, all she owns will become her husband's, and sizable it is!"

Ruy stood by miserably. If this were a battlefield, he would have drawn his sword and finished his adversaries. Mirjana, Mirjana, how could you have sent me off to this? And when he next saw Doña Ysabel, he would be sorely tempted to forget she was his mother. This moment he would see to it she never returned to Bivar and never set her ambitious eyes on young Teddy again. The fires of hell were too good for the likes of her, and he thought he knew why his father had never remained home for more than two months out of a year. God save us all from conniving women!

Himena watched and listened. They were all so determined in their cause. So righteous when it concerned her life, her happiness. And now, this final humiliation, being foisted on a man who cared nothing for her. Why, why? she asked. But there was nothing to do for it. She was a woman who had learned her place in a man's world, and little though she liked it, there was nothing to be done for it.

"Sire!" Ruy was desperate. "Himena is little more than a child. Please rest Doña Consuela's mind that if anything untoward should happen to herself and Don Bernardo, I would see to my duty and guard Señorita Himena with my life, and see to her welfare. Perhaps in a year, two," he sidled, "when the girl reaches a more tolerable age to become a wife."

In the end, there was nothing to be done for it. Alphonso had become angry with Ruy's dissembling. "I will take it as a personal affront, Don Rodrigo, if you persist in refusing to marry and honor the contract drawn between the Asturiases and the Diazes. For your first act of loyalty and obedience to the crown, I decree the marriage shall take place tonight. The time is perfect. All the family have come to Zamora for the coronation, and they will be pleased to save themselves another journey for your marriage!"

Doña Consuela clapped her hands in glee while Himena just glowered. She did not want to marry, and more, she did not want to marry a man who apparently did not want her! Ruy's dark features reddened with anger and helplessness. He had found the one woman in the world who could hold his heart, and now he was to be burdened with another in her place. It mattered little to him that in effect he had been married to Himena since the day the contract was drawn. All that was to be done was finally to consummate it, something he was loath to do. He was trapped and he knew it. In all regards Doña Ysabel had won — except one. She could not tell him whom to love. Himena would never come to Bivar, he swore. She would have no bearing on his life with Mirjana, none at all, except to be known by all as his wife! To Ruy, this was a meaningless title. The woman he loved would warm his bed and walk by his side — Mirjana of Seville.

The long table in the great hall in the *castillo* of Zamora was set for a feast. Breads and cheeses and wines from all over Spain were relished by all. Roast pork and lamb and beef sizzled in their juices and were torn off in chunks by the wedding guests. Himena, her pale yellow hair pulled severely back from her face and hidden under a short veiled wimple, sat beside Don Ruy, now her husband. She picked nervously at her sore and ragged fingertips, making them bleed. Her tunic, new and spotless when she had adorned it for the ceremony, was now wine stained and spotted. Her new husband, well into his cups, had accidentally overturned his goblet onto her as he had excitedly jumped up from his seat to join his friends in a ribald tune unfit for ladies' ears.

Music played, drinks were passed, and all seemed happy, except for Himena who was completely quiet and withdrawn. And if it should seem that the bridegroom was perhaps too exuberant in his appreciation of the wine and for the jokes of the guests, he could be forgiven.

Himena's eyes crawled to the top of the stairs where she would share a chamber with her new husband. Husband! The word itself terrified her. Doña Consuela, having raised and married three daughters of her own, had tried, successfully, to instruct her niece in her duties as a wife. Himena had just stared at her, and in exasperation, Consuela had thrown her hands up in the air. "At least Don Ruy is not a child and he will know what is to be done! Trust yourself into your husband's hands, Himena, and all will go well. Remember, nothing will be asked of you that has not been asked of women since time began. It is a sacrifice we must all make!"

Himena supposed this mystery had something to do with the *morgincap* of which Tío and Tía Asturias proclaimed her to be worthy. In Latin, at the top of the marriage decree, signed by Alphonso VI, were the words *"ob decorem pulchritudinis et federa matrimoni virginalis connubii."* The morgincap was a certificate which referred to the award for beauty and virginity, something coveted and supposed to be held in high esteem by a woman's husband. Nothing, it seemed to Himena, would place her in Ruy's esteem. He had ignored her all evening, not even saying a word to her. While this incensed her she was also grateful for it. What could she possibly have to say to this man on whom she had been foisted? And if he himself had not petitioned this marriage, which she knew to be the case, damn his mother, Doña Ysabel, for standing between her and her ambitions to become an abbess, prioress of a convent, perhaps the one at Coimbra.

Doña Consuela watched her niece sitting silently beside her husband as he joined the men in a ribald song, gesticulating with his arms, waving his wine goblet drunkenly, spilling half its contents over the table and himself. She nudged her husband, Don Bernardo. "Does it seem to you that our newly wedded bridegroom will not be fit to consummate the marriage if he keeps on at this rate?"

Don Bernardo, used to his wife's manipulations, was tempted to assure her Don Ruy was merely an exuberant groom, and in the way of most men, imbibed too much at his wedding feast to mourn the lost freedom of bachelorhood. But duty to Himena came first — she was a meek little thing after all — and he would not want to know she suffered at the inept hands of a drunken husband. As usual, Consuela was correct — again. Clearing his throat as though to gain attention, he stood, holding himself erect by balancing against the edge of the table. Consuela must not know how he himself had imbibed in celebration. "Don Ruy, nephew, is it not time to take your new bride to your chamber?" The old gentleman tried to make a joke of it, not wanting to seem anxious and therefore offend the champion.

"Why?" Ruy challenged drunkenly. "Cannot she find her own way?" he laughed hilariously, others joining him. "My wife has been putting herself to bed alone for enough years, or so the *morgincap* on the marriage contract assures me. Else, I've been duped!" He laughed again at his joke. Only his eyes remained sober of his humor. "Here! Himena, your uncle doubts your virginity! What reason has he?"

Himena flushed red, hating him more than she had ever hated anyone. He had made her the object of filthy whisperings and bad humor, and she would never forgive him. Holding her chin high, her upbringing and natural dignity held her in good stead. "Sir. Even the king has sworn to my chastity. And no doubt even after spending the night in your bed, the same would be true in the morning!"

There was a hushed silence as the wedding guests held their breaths. Himena was saying Ruy was incapable of performing the marriage act. She had insulted her husband of less than four hours. They watched for Ruy's reaction. Had he heard? Was he too drunk to understand?

"Get yourself to bed, wife!" he growled. "If this is your way of making yourself alluring to your husband, you have failed miserably. Now, go! Get yourself from my sight!" His voice thundered, paralyzing her, then prompting her to action. She had overstepped her bounds, tried to defend her dignity but failed. Now she was being sent from the table like a whipped dog. She could not bear to see the look of horror on Tía Consuela's face, nor could she beg Tío Bernardo's protection. He was an old man and no match for El Cid, Compeador.

Himena hid her face in her hands, tripping on her hem and falling into the ready arms of the young knight, Don Diego. "Here, Ruy! Shall I take her upstairs and do your work for you?" he shouted, causing new waves of laughter to rouse among the guests.

"I do my own work!" Ruy said drunkenly. He had no liking for his marriage, but he'd be damned if he'd allow Himena to be subjected to insults.

"Then go and do it!" another of the guests hooted.

"I go when I am ready!"

"Then at least allow me to prepare her for you. I'll get her ready for her husband!" Don Diego's eyes glittered into Himena's, conveying an unspoken message. Ever since arriving in Zamora, he had sought her out, whispering forbidden words and making suggestive gestures, practically beneath Tía Consuela's nose.

Before Ruy could answer, Don Diego sprinted up the stairs, hardly burdened by Himena's slight weight. A blackness seemed to descend over Ruy's face. A bitterness was heard in his voice. "I will be leaving this fiesta," he announced. "There are things that require my attention upstairs!" Saying this, he drained his goblet and left the table on unsteady legs. They all laughed when he stumbled on the first few stairs, and lay odds with one another whether he would ever reach the bridal chamber under his own power.

Ruy kicked open the stout wooden door to his chamber to find Don Diego sitting on the edge of the bed with Himena across his lap. The girl wore a frightened expression and her hands fought with the young knight's. "I said I would see to my own work!" he growled, causing Don Diego to turn in surprise. Never, he would have bet his last dinar, would Don Ruy have been able to make it up the stairs on his own. Guiltily, he jumped up from the bed, sending Himena sprawling.

"And a good job you'll make of it, I am certain," he smiled crookedly, hoping Don Ruy would not see fit to challenge him for Himena's honor.

"Then get out!" The flashing fury and bellow sent Don Diego racing for the door. From the hollers and laughter from downstairs, the young man had gone back to report to the guests.

Kicking the door shut with a bang, Ruy gave his attention to Himena. "Stop looking like a cornered mouse, else I *will* beat you! Help me off with my boots, girl, and let me sleep."

Meekly, Himena did as she was told, fearing to incur his wrath and, perhaps, earn a beating. This man frightened her. He was power itself and she was at his mercy. She had no idea what was expected of her, but she knew she would comply with whatever it may be. It was the way of things and there was no help for it.

Ruy undressed, stripping off his garments, disregarding Himena's presence. His world was spinning in circles from the accursed wine, and he desired sleep more than anything. As for Himena, let the devil take her. She was foisted on him and he had no use for her. There was only one woman in all the world for him, and he had left her back in Bivar. The sooner he could return to her, the better.

Himena tried to cover her eyes. She had never seen a man without a blouse, much less without his chausses. Ruy was throwing his garments about the chamber, tossing his belt and his sword angrily onto the floor, each clatter making her wince with fear. Wide-eyed in terror, Himena backed into a corner, watching, seeing his doublet, his tunic, his chausses follow one another into a heap. She saw the dark thatch of hair upon his broad chest, saw the flatness of his belly and the thickness of his thighs. She almost dared a glance at his manhood, but could not bring herself to do so. There were some terrors that were better unseen and unknown.

Ruy fell onto the bed, pushing the pillow under his head, wishing the world would stop heaving and spinning. He could not remember ever being so drunk, not even that time with Pietro in Toledo . . . Suddenly, his eyes opened and he saw Himena, cowering in a corner, terror on her face. Pity rose for her. "Come over here, child. You cannot sleep on the floor." He hefted his weight with a laborious motion to make room for her beside him. "Come here! I will not touch you! And take off that gown! There's enough of a stink of wine about me without that."

Himena remembered Tía Consuela's words: "Trust yourself into his hands . . ." Slowly, she removed her gown, leaving her kirtle. She stepped out of her shoes and crept to the side of the bed, wondering how she could sleep beside him and not touch him. As she looked down at her new husband, she studied him as he lay with his eyes closed. To say he was handsome was not to say enough. His short dark hair fell over his brow, and in sleep, the lightning bolts in his umber eyes could not strike her. She followed the line of his muscular shoulders down to his arms and his large, capable hands. Hands that would touch her and do mysterious things with her? The flat of his belly was delineated with a narrow strip of hard hair that pointed downward to a thicker, darker patch. Lying on his side, one leg thrown over the other, the mystery of his manhood was kept from her sight, but she knew the tingle of curiosity.

Lightly, she climbed upon the bed, laying down beside him, making every attempt to deny contact between them. Long hours into the night, Himena lay, eyes wide and staring, wondering what ritual of marriage she was being denied.

As Ruy slept, he became conscious of a presence beside him, lightly pressing against him. Still deep in the effects of the wine, he reached out his arm and brought her to him, his hand trailing familiarly over her hip and breast. Even with his eyes closed, even in the blackness of night, he could see her: hair, light titian, springing with life under his fingers; her mouth, one moment sulky and petulant, the next full and smiling, a mouth made for kissing, shaped to fit his lips and to accept the teasings of his tongue and teeth; long and clean of limb, curving where a woman should curve; white skin; dove-gray eyes that could become crystal in certain lights . . . This was his Mirjana.

She danced through his dreams and came to him, yielding her pliant body to his. He could smell the freshness of her skin, the smoothness of her arms, and his hunger swelled to an ache, a yearning. He had been so long without her, weeks since he had held her like this.

He buried his face in her neck, nipping gently at the soft flesh, tracing his fingers over her breasts and arousing the coral tips to attention under his thumb. He wanted her, all of her, needed to show his love for her. In the darkness he held her, loving her, tenderly, slowly, holding his own passions until there was a response from hers. And when he gained entrance to her, it was lovingly, gently, allowing time for her body to adjust to his.

Her arms wrapped around him, holding him, keeping him within her while she came to the center of her passions. She moved against him and she filled his world. His Mirjana.

At last, the morning sun was filtering through the windows, and he could fill his hungry eyes with the sight of her. Mirjana, Mirjana, his mind called, holding off the slake of his desires until he could look into her eyes and see himself reflected there. Too soon passion flooded through him. Too soon she moved in rhythm with him. Too soon he heard her breathe, "I never knew it could be like this!"

The tide of passion could not be reversed and he poured himself into her, uttering his sob of disappointment that too late he had awakened to realize the woman he held was not his love . . . but his wife.

* * *

Himena watched her husband dress, fumbling with the ties on his chausses and belt, seeming to be in a desperate haste to be about his business. She stretched full length on the bed, the covers tangling between her legs. Whatever she had expected to be her duty as his wife had instead become her pleasure. So many things had become clear to her: the whisperings of married women that were hissed into silence whenever a maiden was about; the mysteries of reproduction; the slanted glances of young knights and the hidden meanings of their seductive whispers. The world seemed to have opened up to Himena just as suddenly as her legs had opened, seemingly of their own volition, to admit her husband entrance to that most secret place.

Even now, it was as though she could feel his hands upon her, on her breasts, between her thighs. She felt she might purr like the kitchen cat. She even thought she might become quite fond of her husband if she could look forward to more nights like this one past.

"Where do you go so early this morning?" she asked him. The shared moments between them had loosened her tongue.

"I have business about Zamora. I intend to round up my men and leave for Bivar as soon as possible." He hadn't intended his voice to be so gruff. It surely was not Himena's fault that he had been so drunk and so hungry for Mirjana that he had taken her almost in his sleep.

"Leaving . . . for Bivar? When? I must ready my things —"

"No." He shook his dark head, looking directly at her for the first time since jumping from the bed. "I go alone. I will see to it that your family continues to make a home for you."

"A wife should be at her husband's side." There was a look of pleading in her pale, hazel eyes where only last night there had been hatred. Good God! What had he done?

"No, Himena. I do not want you in Bivar. That is the end of it! I will see to your support as is my duty."

Sudden tears sprang to Himena's eyes. Where had she failed? What had she done wrong? It had all been so beautiful, or so she had thought. Why was he leaving her this way?

As though reading the questions in her eyes, Ruy softened. "It has nothing to do with you, child. It is with me. I have no place in my life for you and I doubt I ever will have."

"So, you will leave me then? Leave me to the jokes and whisperings that I was not able to hold my husband?" Her voice had risen to a shriek and an ugly expression marred her otherwise mild features.

"There is no help for it. I will plead business in Toledo and you will be saved the scorn you fear." He struggled with his boots, disgusted with the stink of wine that permeated his clothes. He could not wait to get to the bath house to steam the last of the wine out of his pores and out of his brain.

Himena climbed from the bed, holding the blanket around her nakedness. She came to stand before him, her voice strident, the hate returning to her eyes. "For this you have taken me to wife? For this you reminded Alphonso of the marriage contract between us?"

"It was not I who reminded Alphonso. It was a trick on my mother's part, and I will see her damned to hell for it! I have no interest in you, Himena. Fate has dealt us an unfair blow. As I said, I will see to your support and do my duty in your behalf."

"No! No! No!" She beat at him with her fists, allowing the blanket to drop to the floor.

Ruy bent to retrieve the blanket, warding off her blows with his arm. Gently, he covered her nakedness and brought her to the bed, holding her as he would a child, soothing her if it was in his power.

"Himena. My leaving is not a verdict on your womanliness. It is of my choosing and has always been. Last night, this mormng, was a mistake, one I deeply regret. If you feel your life is ruined, I am sorry. But I see no reason why you cannot continue to live with your aunt and uncle just as you always have."

Himena stared at him, emotions glittering and jumping out at him. How could she continue just as she always had now that she knew the secret between men and women? Now that she knew what Don Diego had meant when he told her he would like to touch her . . . kiss her . . . Himena railed. "I was better off an innocent child!" she cried. "You have ruined me! You have awakened in me things I had never dreamed!" she blurted, startled at her own honesty and lack of modesty.

Himena jumped from the bed and bent to pick up her hard-heeled shoe, attacking him, screaming curses and epithets she had only heard uttered from the mouths of men. "I am ruined and you leave me! I have been denied a chance to become prioress of the convent in Coimbra!" she exaggerated the truth. "I could have been second only to the Infanta Urraca herself, and you have denied me my chance. If you did not want me, why did you marry me? Was it because you feared to anger Alphonso, because you thought he would take it as an insult that you did not want to join his family? Because of your selfishness, I will never become anything! Any one! I will only be a wife to an insolent *bastardo!* Champion. El Cid! You make me sick! First, you deny me my ambitions and then you take my respectability as your wife to desert me to be the object of scorn and pity! I hate you! I have always hated you! You barbarian!"

Ruy gripped her arm, bringing it down to her side. His eyes shot sparks of fury, his mouth curved downward in a grimace. "Only one woman has earned the right to call me a barbarian!" he thundered, pushing her backwards, escaping her flying shoe.

Ruy's first reaction of pity had turned to anger. Instinctively, he knew Himena would make life hell for any man. She was like those cats who wandered the streets of Zamora — selfish creatures, intent only on their own needs, their own pleasures, without thought or responsibility to any save themselves. She had not even asked why he was leaving her, caring only how it would appear to the others. She had not even considered that he might have needs and wants that went beyond her. She only cared for her destroyed dreams and cared nothing for his. But in one thing she was right: he should have chanced Alphonso's anger and refused to marry her. And he would have if he had not had all of Castile to think about. All he had done — giving Alphonso the oath, paying homage, courting Castile to accept their king's murderer as their ruler — would have been for naught. Lives would have been lost and good men slain, all because he, Ruy, would not honor a marriage contract drawn and decreed almost eighteen years before.

With a rare humility, Ruy hung his head. "Even as a married woman you need not be denied your chance to become a prioress, Himena. If you would like, I will speak to the Infanta myself!"

Sudden panic gripped Himena and she narrowed her eyes to sly slits. "I have no need for you to speak for me. Go! Go to hell, if it pleases you!" She pushed him from the room, throwing his sword after him and slamming the door, locking it behind him.

She paced the chamber like a caged cat. Hatred and the humiliation of rejection bubbled up from her, leaving her spitting and clawing the pillows and bedclothes. As if she could go to a convent now! Knowing what she knew! That she, Himena Maria Asturias Diaz, was a sensual woman who liked the caress of a man's hand! To be shut away in a nunnery! Never!

The steam of hatred oozed out of each pore, leaving her silent, deflated. The memory of how she had felt when Ruy had touched her, availed himself of her, awakened in her passions she had never known existed, prickled her skin and made her feel truly alive for the first time in her life. She was a woman now, no longer a child. Now she knew the meaning of the covert glances and the laughter she had witnessed between couples. Just like when Don Diego had plunged his hand into her bodice only the night before.

Biting down on her lower lip, a speculative expression fell over her face. She wondered if Don Diego would throw himself between her thighs and find that place where he could enter her and bring her to panting submission. He was younger than Ruy and certainly prettier with his carefully clipped mustache and soft white hands.

And then there was Don Santiago, who winked at her whenever he passed in the corridor . . . El Cid, Compeador, be damned!

Later that day, after sending out word to round up his men, Ruy made the announcement that he must attend to business in Toledo, the central Islamic city which was taifa kingdom paying its tribute to Castile. He was careful not to make promises concerning his return in order to save Himena embarrassment when the time came and went. If people were shocked that he would leave his new wife so suddenly, they kept it to themselves, and he did not linger to incur their speculation.

King Alphonso required an audience with Ruy, and it was expected the ruler would chastise his vassal for neglecting his goddaughter. To the contrary, Alphonso appointed Ruy to see to the transference of Toledo's taxes into Castile's treasury.

Ruy was crestfallen that his ruse had not worked. But out of justice to Himena, he said nothing. He would go to Toledo for Alphonso, cursing each day his duty to his king kept him from Mirjana. He would consider himself fortunate if he was able to return to Bivar before summer's end. More likely, it would be mid-September before he held her in his arms, kissed her lips . . .

The hunger and need for her grew within him, and he could not ignore it. Instead of slaking his passions, even temporarily, the time spent with Himena had enflamed them. For Ruy, no other woman existed — only Mirjana.

CHAPTER 12

The early evening air was warm and sultry. Gentle gray shadows cast the dirt road into a fairyland for Tanige. The shadows of the low-hanging trees became graceful dancers, weaving and bending in the soft light. Minuscule dots of perspiration dotted her brow and the small of her back. From time to time a tingle of anticipation raced up and down her arms, making the fine hairs prickle uneasily. This was going to be a night to remember, she was sure of it. Luis walked beside her in companionable silence. He was not a man to say three words when one would do. She liked that and accepted his silence and matched it with her own. It was comfortable.

A blackbird swooped down from the trees and landed almost at her feet. Tanige stopped and watched as the raven beauty daintily plucked a fat, wiggling worm from the soft earth at the side of the road. Luis had slowed too; they both watched the bird take wing as it flew to its nest in the thick trees. Tanige drew in her breath at the sight. That's what she would like to have happen to her, she thought silently, as they continued up the long, winding road — to be plucked from her everyday life into a new world of love and laughter. Laughter and humor were important, and she sensed in Luis these two traits which she knew he was capable of sharing with her. Love was something she knew so little about. With guidance perhaps, Luis would teach her. With repeated interrogations with Ilena it had been decided that Luis was as inexpert as she. Ilena had seemed so certain when she told Tanige that Luis would drag his feet and make excuses, but only because he was inexperienced. After all, Ilena said, there weren't too many available women of Tanige's quality around. Tanige had preened and accepted her new friend's words without question. She would have to take the initiative, Ilena cautioned, and be prepared to follow through.

The tingle raced up both arms again, and Tanige hugged her crossed arms to her chest.

"Cold?" It was a one word question.

"A little," Tanige whispered. Would he offer to put his arms around her and bring her close to his side as they walked down the road? Not likely. This was going to be like the blind leading the blind, Tanige grimaced. What she needed was a plan of action, and Ilena had been no help, merely saying when the time was right she would know. Being shy was one thing, but lack of interest was something else. Luis was shy. He had to be shy. Why else would his face redden when she stared into his eyes. On more than one occasion she had been bold and brazen while she allowed her eyes to travel the length and width of his body. There had been no like interest on his part. Ilena had laughed at her when she mentioned it, saying Luis knew every inch of her because she herself had noticed his close scrutiny when Tanige wasn't looking. Tanige had felt good when she heard that but immediately wondered if he would think her too skinny, not buxom enough, not pretty enough. But, she scolded herself, she must have passed Luis's test because here he was walking her home in the soft twilight of early evening. To protect her. She loved the idea and immediately set about humming a song under her breath. Was it her imagination or had Luis moved a step closer to her side? Tentatively, she reached down for his hand. It felt hot and moist. Her own was scorched and dry. At first the grip had been loose and relaxed. Tanige exerted a small amount of gentle pressure and it was returned. A long, happy sigh escaped her.

"What are you thinking now, this moment, Luis?" she asked boldly.

"You're pretty," he said stiffly.

"Is that what you were thinking? I was thinking you were a handsome man," Tanige blurted. "And I was thinking how glad I am that you're walking me back to the *castillo*. But you will have a long walk back to the farm."

"Si," Luis agreed.

"Perhaps we could rest before you make the long walk back. In the stable," she said brazenly. "Just you and I."

Luis nodded. There was an imperceptible tightening of his hand. Tanige hadn't realized she was holding her breath until it exploded in a loud swoosh. She was halfway there, halfway to becoming a complete woman. A hot flush worked its way through her body beneath the light fabric of her dress.

Their shoulders touched. Luis made no effort to move away. Like a child, she swung both their hands and quickened her steps. Luis matched her, till they were both running down the road toward the stable. He was as eager as she. "Allah, don't fail me now!" Tanige muttered breathlessly as they made their way into the dim interior of the stable.

The warm scent of the hay mixed with the

fragrant aroma of oats assailed her nostrils. It was heady. For a brief moment she felt her head whirl. As they walked deeper into the stable, she noticed the small lanterns that were hung from the rafters. She didn't want too much light. The deep, pungent smell of horse flesh was as good as any perfume or incense she could conjure up on such short notice. This was the time, she was certain of it. The time to become a woman.

"We can rest here in one of the stalls," Tanige said, leading Luis by the hand into a broodmare's stall at the end of the stable. "See, this stall is bigger because the mares require more room." She hated to release his hand, but she had to in order to scatter the sweet smelling straw about the hard ground. She did want to be comfortable. Frantically, her eyes searched the stalls in the shadows for some sign of a blanket. "Wait here," she ordered briskly. She was back in moments with a thick, woven, gray blanket. She spread it out on the straw and then motioned for Luis to sit down.

The moment Luis sat down, Tanige plopped down beside him. "Are you going to kiss me now?" she demanded bluntly.

"I've been thinking about it."

Men! "Don't think about it, do it," she said, offering her lips in a tight pucker. She squeezed her eyes shut in anticipation. She felt a fleeting, featherlike touch and nothing more. Her eyes flew open and she stared at him aghast. "I thought you were going to kiss me."

"I did," came the quivering reply.

Tanige's mind raced. This was going to be harder than she thought. "All right, Luis. You kissed me, now it's my turn." Awkwardly, Tanige strained toward him and then threw her arms around him for balance. She brought her lips crashing down on his. The kiss was wet and more on Luis's chin than on his mouth, but he responded by moving slightly so that she fell into the crook of his arm. Her mouth moved and found its mark. Luis tightened his hold on her as his lips ground pleasurably against hers. It was a hard belly-to-knee embrace, and she could feel him stiffening next to her. Both their movements were frantic and awkward as each of them tried to free the other of clothing, to bring the other closer.

The dress rode high on Tanige's legs as they thrashed about in the sweet-smelling hay. The blanket that she had so carefully spread was bunched in a ball at the side of the stall. The soft pricks of the straw only increased her excitement as they poked at her bare legs and buttocks.

Small, tight animal sounds escaped her

pressed lips while deep groans of pleasure slid from Luis's lips.

"Jesus," he murmured as he released her mouth.

"God Almighty," Tanige panted.

Luis fell back against the mound of straw, his erection stiff and hard. Tanige stared down at the sight, unable to tear her eyes away. She should be saying something, doing something. She had done this, was responsible for the exquisite misery he was suffering. "Are you going to do it?" she whispered.

"Do what?" Luis hedged.

"Take my clothes off and make love to me."

"Oh, Jesus."

"You said that before. Have you ever made love to a woman before?" Suddenly, she had to know. She didn't care what Ilena said, she wanted to hear it from Luis himself.

"No."

"I've never been with a man before. Can you tell?"

"Come here," came the low, hoarse command.

Tanige stood and removed her dress. The soft murmur of clothes on skin brought a groan from Luis. She dropped to her knees and felt his strong hands reach for her. Gone was the fright, the fear of the unknown, as they searched each other's bodies with willing hands. Soft, hungry whispers circled the stall as they devoured each other with clumsy, awkward movements that became sure and practiced. She felt his hands mold her breasts, and a feline growl of pleasure birthed in her, seeking release from her imprisoned mouth. Her hands were feverish as she searched his body, seeking and finding what she wanted, what she needed. She maneuvered her body upward till she was laying on him, her skin glistening with moisture as she moved sensuously against him. Her rhythm was his as her hands tangled in his hair, drawing his head to hers till their lips met.

Almost sobbing, she groaned her pleasure into Luis's ear. Swiftly, she found herself beneath his long, hard body, straining, arching upward, upward . . .

They lay for a long time afterward, their shallow breathing slowly returning to normal. Tanige moved slightly so she could nestle in the crook of his outflung arm. There was no shame, no immodesty, as she gently stroked his chest. "That was wonderful," she said softly.

"Yes, wonderful," Luis agreed hoarsely.

"Did I give you pleasure?" Tanige asked hesitantly.

"Oh, Jesus," Luis muttered.

"Never mind 'Oh, Jesus.' Just give me a

'yes' or 'no,' " Tanige teased.

"More pleasure than a man has a right to know. Did I give you pleasure?"

"I didn't know . . . I had no idea . . . It was something I never . . . I want more," she cried excitedly. "Luis, I want you to make love to me again. Now, right now." Gentle snores were his response. A smile played around the corners of her mouth as she stared down at the sleeping man. How peaceful and contented he looked in the dim, lantern light. And she was responsible for that look, the rest he was feeling now. Gently, she kissed him on the mouth. She lay for a few moments longer, savoring the feel of him next to her. There would be other days, other nights.

Carefully, so as not to wake him, she rose to her feet and slipped into her garments. She blew him a light kiss off her fingertips and raced on winged feet from the stable. She was in love! She, homely Tanige, had found love!

Mirjana awakened to the trill of birds perched outside the narrow stone windows, and she knew a strange expectation rushing through her. Today, she told herself, today Ruy would return. It must be true, she could almost feel his presence. Other mornings she had awakened with the *hope* he would return. Today was different. Today she knew!

Last night she had slept in the bed she had shared with him in the master's chamber. This morning, like all the mornings since he had been gone, she awoke to find her arm stretched rigidly over the place where he would have slept, and her need for him was a tangible curse that would haunt her throughout the day and into the long, lonely hours of the night.

Weeks ago she had received a message from him, written soon after the coronation of Alphonso. He was being sent to Toledo, he wrote, to see to the collection of the taifa, the taxes, and transfer the gold to Castile's treasury. The last line of his letter had fed her soul: "I am finding myself missing you; my eyes are hungry for the sight of you."

Weeks ago. The entire summer gone, now it was mid-September, and here in Bivar on the northern plains of Spain, the leaves were already giving over their glorious green to paint the hillsides with browns and golds. There was a crispness in the air and the pungent aroma of smoke as the outlying farmers burned their fields in anticipation of the following spring's plowing.

Mirjana supposed she was growing more and more melancholy by the day and it showed. Much as she tried to hide her inner desolation, friends like Gormaz and Ilena perceived it and were a comfort to her in helping her pass the long, lonely days. Even Teddy, so quick and sharp with his daily lessons, seemed to take special pains not to test her patience as she heard his lessons. Several times a week, especially if Tanige was off with Luis, the boy would come to the *castillo* for supper and then plead with her to read or tell him tales of mythical creatures and valiant warriors. He particularly loved to hear her repeat the exploits of his brother, El Cid, as they were told in every corner of Seville.

Some afternoons, Mirjana would walk to the little hut of Gormaz and Ilena to play with their robust baby boy, bouncing the child on her knee and chucking him beneath his fat little chins. Sundays after the couple attended church to hear Padre Juano say Mass, they would picnic in the woods, always inviting Mirjana and Teddy, worrying when she declined. They knew she was lonely for Don Ruy; they could see it in her quiet reflectiveness when she thought no one was looking and hear it in her soft voice when she would speak of him.

By midmorning Mirjana was certain this was the day Ruy would return. There was excitement in the air, and she imagined a new lightness in the servants' steps as they attended their duties. It was even in the song of the birds and the slant of the sun. If she could perceive this would be a most important day, surely so must everyone else.

A thought struck her. Perhaps a message had come to Padre Juano and he had not had time to relay it to her. Or perhaps he thought she already knew. She had no liking for the priest, and she was aware that oftentimes he would preach from the pulpit, warning his flock of the "heathen interloper." He disapproved of her and her relationship with Ruy. But surely, he could not refuse to tell her if he knew something, anything, concerning the master's return.

Before she could change her mind about facing the Padre's scorn, Mirjana patted a stray tendril of hair into place and remembered to cover her head with a short veil. She would go to the village church to see the priest, and in deference to Christian traditions, she would wear the headcovering into the place of worship.

Back straight, chin high, she walked the narrow village streets, greeting people and smiling brightly. Her anticipation and happiness radiated from her to them, and as they watched her, they too smiled, although they were not certain why. They only knew that Princesa Mirjana was a kind and goodly woman and that her smile brought warmth and friendship to their lives.

Padre Juano kept his rooms at the back of the stone church, and she hesitated only a second before she rapped on the door. Having committed herself to approaching him, she rapped a second time and then a third. The young priest flung open the door, a scowl on his face. He seemed taken aback when he saw the *princesa* standing there.

"What do you want?" he challenged harshly. He was prepared to defend himself for his attack on her from the pulpit last Sunday. It was his duty to protect the people of Bivar from her heathen influence, and if Padre Tomas was not here to do it, then so must he!

"Padre, I hesitate to take you from your duties. However, I was curious as to whether you had received word from Padre Tomas about his return." Mirjana stood on the doorstep, the young priest standing as though barring her entrance onto church property.

"Why do you wish to know?" the priest snapped rudely. "Are you certain it is my superior you inquire after, or are you looking for information about Don Ruy?"

Mirjana wished she had never come here. This was too humiliating, and the venom and suspicion in the man's eyes seemed to freeze her blood. Deciding to be honest, she said firmly, "Yes, of course I inquire after the lord of the *castillo*. If he is to return, there are preparations to be made."

"Such as preparing your wicked spells to weave over him? To tempt him to live in sin with a devil worshipper? Nay, my lady, I have nothing to tell you!" His small, beady eyes took in Mirjana's appearance. Here stood the infidel, the threat to all Christianity. Here she stood before him with what he imagined was naked lust in her eyes for Don Ruy, and all the while he was married to Doña Himena and had fulfilled the marriage contract between the Asturias' and Diaz'. There was a triumphant gleam in his eye that through Doña Ysabel he had been instrumental in saving Don Ruy's soul.

Mirjana ignored Padre Juano's words. Something else was amiss here. The man was practically rubbing his hands together with glee, and he was making small noises in his throat like a chicken's cackle. She straightened and stared him directly in the eyes, getting small enjoyment when he shrank from her. "I have asked you a question, Padre, and I expect an answer. If it is magic spells you speak of, beware, even this moment I am preparing one for you!"

"I have received only one message from Padre Tomas. It was sent immediately after the wedding, stating his intentions to travel on to Toledo with Don Ruy." He watched her craftily when he mentioned the wedding, waiting for her reaction. Immediately upon learning of Don Ruy's marriage to Doña Himena, he wished he could have raced to the *castillo* to taunt the evil *princesa* with the news. But he had been much too frightened to go against Padre Tomas's orders to keep the information to himself until a proper announcement could be made.

"What wedding? I don't understand. Has the new king taken a bride?" Mirjana was becoming more and more uneasy with this conversation and the glitter of retribution she saw in the priest's eyes.

Padre Juano shot the news at her. "The marriage of Don Rodrigo Ruy Diaz to Señorita Himena Maria Asturias. Did you not know?" he smiled crookedly, meanly, watching the color drain from her face.

Married. Ruy married to someone named Himena. It could not be! It was a lie! Ruy loving another, marrying another . . . She felt faint, lightheaded, as though she had received a physical blow.

"Yes, Princesa," Padre Juano pretended concern. "In actual fact, Don Ruy has been betrothed to Señorita Himena practically since the day of her birth. The Diazes and Asturiases have alliances that go back to the time of the Visigoths. The formal ceremony and royal decree took place only days after the coronation of Alphonso. It is well, don't you think, that Don Ruy has married into the king's family?"

Mirjana barely heard the priest. "*Gracias*, Padre, for telling me the news. I am sorry to have interrupted you. Please, do not let me detain you any longer. I'll . . . I will return to the *castillo*. *Gracias* . . ." She was babbling like an idiot. She had to leave here, go back to the *castillo*, to her room, to hide her shame. Shame. Married. No, it could not be. It could not!

Padre Juano closed the door. Now, he told himself, justice would be done. The wanton would be thrown from the *castillo!* Don Ruy would return with his bride and cast the *princesa* out! Things would return to normal. The *castillo* would be stripped of all its pagan finery, and life would continue. He should be jumping for joy, he knew. But somehow, the total defeat on the *princesa*'s face had touched a spot of pity even in his fanatical heart.

For long, stricken hours Mirjana sat in the intimate little alcove in the master's chamber which she had decorated so lovingly. When Tanige found her, her tears had long since dried. She sat hunched over, arms clasped over her breasts, rocking back and forth, eyes dull and uncaring.

"Princess! What is it? What is wrong? Tell me so I can help you!" Tanige pleaded.

"There is no help for me. I am not even certain I can share my shame with you, Tanige. I am a fool. I should have known, but I buried my head and chose not to see!"

"See what? Tell me? What happened?" Panic rose in Tanige's voice. She had never seen Mirjana this way, not even when she was told she must leave Seville to marry Yusuf!

"Padre Juano told me Ruy was married in Zamora shortly following the coronation of King Alphonso. That is why he has not returned. How can you bear to look at me and see my shame? My foolishness. Go away, let me suffer in silence."

"God Almighty!" Tanige cried, aghast. "It is a lie, a trick of that zealot. It must be."

"Use your brain, Tanige. It is no lie, no trick. I have made myself a fool over a man, and I have only myself to blame. I have lived in a fool's paradise of my own making, but it is a fitting place for me because I am a fool. Tanige" — she suddenly looked up, grasping her handmaiden's hand, clutching it in desperation — "what will I do when he arrives? With his wife? Quickly, please, you must help me remove my clothes from this chamber back to the tower."

"Are you saying you are leaving these beautiful treasures in this chamber for his wife to enjoy? If you do, then you are indeed a fool!"

"The only treasure I leave behind is my heart," Mirjana cried, tears flooding her eyes and rolling down her cheeks. "A wife, Tanige. He brings his wife to sleep in that bed and look from that window . . ." Fresh shudders overcame her, heaving her shoulders, piercing her breast.

"Did Padre Juano tell you he brings her here?"

"No. But I know Ruy; he is not a man to marry a woman and leave her behind."

"I do not believe it," Tanige said firmly. "I will never believe it. Something is amiss here, some kind of mistake. And you, Mirjana, would be making a mistake by acting hastily. Why don't you wait and hear it from Don Ruy himself?"

"Do you think so little of me, Tanige, that you would subject me to further humiliation? Have I not suffered enough? How would it appear to a new wife to come to this chamber and find her husband's mistress, his concubine? Well, answer me!"

"What will you take to the tower room with you," Tanige demanded, suddenly busying herself and gathering Mirjana's belongings together.

"Only my personal things — clothing, toiletries. I cannot stay here a moment longer. I must think! Think! I will go back to the tower room where I should have stayed."

"Thinking again?" Tanige challenged. "We think, but we never do anything constructive. I bleat like a lamb and you sob and cry in shame. Get angry, Mirjana, and do something!"

Mirjana stood upon the ancient brass-studded trunk in order to look out the slit of a window in the tower room. How far away the stars seemed. Millions of leagues away, as far away as she felt from Ruy. Her life was in such turmoil. She was lost, forsaken again. First by her father, and then Hassan, and now, unbelievably, by Ruy. She was betrayed. Both by Ruy and by her own foolish heart. Was it better that she found out from Padre Juano, despite the satisfaction it must have given him, so she could take matters into her own hands, or would it have been better to see Ruy return with his bride? She would have been spared these hours. But, at least now, she could save face and strive to regain her dignity.

Tears gathered in her soft gray eyes. She blinked quickly to ward them off. The time for tears was long past. For now, for Ruy's return, she would fix a smile on her face and try to make a life for herself. If that was possible.

Why had Ruy not mentioned something to her about taking a wife? Why had he ridden off as he had without telling her? It was unfair and he had placed her in a very awkward position. Tongues would wag, remembering how she had overhauled the *castillo* in preparation for his return. The thought stung her. All the hours, all the work, all the weeks, and he had been married to another!

Long, slender fingers pleated the soft silk of her nightdress. Over and over she let the fabric slide between her fingers. It was meant to soothe, like the worry beads Mútadid had carried, but instead, it brought heightened agitation when she remembered the way Ruy had commented on the nightdress, saying he liked the feel of it next to his bare skin. A lone tear escaped to trickle down her cheek. Impatiently, she brushed it away with the back of her hand. If only Ruy was here with her now. When he sensed her unhappiness he would gather her close and murmur soft words to comfort her. She would burrow into his chest and feel content. Now that was stripped from her, Ruy was married to another, and she would be cast aside, torn from him as though her heart had been ripped from her chest.

Dawn was creeping over the foothills and still Mirjana stood near the window. Stood and pondered her fate. Her face was ashen, her features morose, listlessly waiting for Tanige to come to her.

Schooling her face against her reaction to Mirjana's appearance, Tanige quickly noticed the bed which had not been slept in. Anger for Mirjana's situation coursed through her. Men, they were always responsible for a woman's pain. What Mirjana should do was scratch out his eyes. That would teach him not to trifle with her affections. Mirjana might be a fool, but not herself! Men used women to their own purposes and designs, casting them away when they were no longer needed. Nowhere in the world would Don Ruy find a woman more beautiful, more loving than the princess. She gave an elaborate shake to her shoulders and carefully set down a bowl of fresh fruit and warm breakfast cakes fresh from the oven.

Mirjana stared at the food with vacant eyes. She knew she should make an effort to please Tanige, but her legs felt as though tree trunks were tied to them and her arms were useless strands of rope. She nodded her thanks and continued to watch the sunrise.

"Mirjana, perhaps there has been a misunderstanding. Don Ruy would never do anything to make you suffer . . ." Then, seeing the naked pain on Mirjana's face and empathizing, she burst, "Don Ruy is a barbarian! A bastard! Without a heart, without a soul!" She spat viciously.

"He's a man," Mirjana said simply, as though that simple statement exonerated him from all wrong.

"And because he is a man he can disregard everyone? For shame, Mirjana. Since when have you become so tolerant of injustice?"

"Since I have no other choice." There was deadness in her tone, a listlessness that panged Tanige more than seeing Mirjana's tears.

"Where is your spine? Your spirit? This can be no worse than when you were separated from your Persian poet. You survived then, you lived and breathed and ate and slept. This is no different." This is what Tanige hoped was the truth, but even as she spoke, she knew differently. Since being with Luis, since becoming a woman vulnerable to a man, she understood.

"It is different."

"Only because you want it to be so." A note of authority crept into Tanige's voice, a tone that had never been before being with Luis. She thought of the six silk shirts Mirjana had sewn for Don Ruy with her own hands, taking particular pains with the embroidery to trim the collar and cuffs of the wide, billowing sleeves. He would never wear them now, not with a wife to see he wore garments handcrafted by his mistress. Out of her inborn curiosity, Tanige asked if Mirjana knew the name of this woman who had married Don Ruy.

"Himena," Mirjana blurted, the name on the tip of her tongue, having had the long, dark night to become familiar with it.

"What kind of name is that? Already, I detest her!" Tanige sniffed.

By the end of the fourth day, Mirjana believed she was bordering on insanity. Where was Ruy? When would he arrive? According to Padre Juano, he was expected days ago. Had something happened? Was it possible he became involved in a battle and he lay wounded? The thought was so horrible she burst into tears.

She felt so lost, so alone. How had she allowed herself to become so dependent on Ruy? From the beginning she had known he was not a man to be trusted. Hadn't he been the cause preventing her from returning to Seville? She could have been at her father's side when death came to take him instead of being a captive held by El Cid in lieu of ransoms from two kingdoms. Mirjana knew she must act, do something to rid herself of her misery, now, before Ruy returned and she made a fool of herself. How easily it was said: "Do something." What? How could she make herself feel differently? How could she make her heart feel less? How could she will her arms not to ache for his embrace? Would her body ever be purged from the need for him? Would her tears never cease?

So alone, with no one, save Tanige. Homeless and dependent on another's charity. How unjust, how unfair. Omar. A smile tugged at her lips, through her tears. It was almost ludicrous. There had been a time when she thought the sun rose and set upon the Persian teacher. That was an infatuation and had passed. His poetry and teachings would live in her forever, but her feelings for the gaunt, soft-eyed man traveled on the wind. Omar was gone from her thoughts and from her heart by her own choice.

Her glance traveled to the small selection of the books near her bed. Books given to her by Omar. Last night she had thought they might bring comfort and distraction enabling her to fall into a safe, dreamless sleep. Her miserable efforts failed. Instead, she had cried herself to sleep, the rough, coarse pillowcasing clutched in both arms. All through the night she had dreamed of Ruy and herself, riding side by side along the river bank. And she had read in his eyes that he wanted to kiss her, to whisper those strange love words he murmured . . .

She knew she cried during her dream for she would wake to cry out for him, only to find it was her pillow she held in her arms, not the man she loved. Tanige said she should be angry, hateful. Perhaps that would come later, when the raw soreness left her. She felt she was a giant sore, festering, in need of lancing. If only she could do that to herself. One flash of the blade and Ruy Diaz would be sliced from her life. She shuddered. Was that what she wanted? Never to see again the handsome face she had come to love? Never to see his eyes locked with hers the moment passion found its release? Never, ever to feel his arms around her or hear his voice? A second wife, a third, a mistress, a slave — what did it matter as long as he was in her life?

She raised her arms, imploring, "Allah, in your heavens, tell me, when will the hatred come?" The sound filled the tower, lifting through the slitted window to the heavens above. And there was no answer. Silence. The hatred would never come; nothing could be greater than the love she felt for him.

* * *

Shortly after, Tanige came into the room carrying the shirts Mirjana had sewn for Ruy. "Do what you will with them, Tanige. I beg you, leave me. My head pounds, my eyes ache —"

"Bah! There is nothing wrong with you a good tumble between the sheets wouldn't cure, and you know I speak the truth," Tanige scolded boldly, hoping to rouse Mirjana from her listlessness.

"You're a disgusting, vile, loathsome creature and I should punish you for your sharp, wretched tongue, but I don't have the energy. Tell me you are sorry for such a wicked lie and I'll forgive you."

"Lie! I speak the truth and you want me to apologize. You told me I should never lie. I wish you would make up your mind. Lie, don't lie. Which is it to be? This man, this Don Ruy, has warped your thinking. I keep telling you, he's a man. If you put all men into a sack and shake them up, they come out the same. A man is a man," she said loftily.

"Your knowledge overwhelms me, Tanige. One day you must tell me where you discovered the mysteries to life."

"From the kitchen help. They are a wealth of information. I could tell you stories about

Don Ruy and his women that would make your toes curl."

"I'm sure," Mirjana replied tartly.

Tanige waved her thin arms in the air. "He likes women — any woman. You sit here mooning about something you can do nothing about, making yourself miserable and sick. For what? For a smile? For a kind word? For a few moments of pleasure beneath the sheets? And then what? You do the same things all over again. Another smile, another kind word, a few more moments of pleasure. Is that what you want for the rest of your life? Hatred, Princess, hate him and you will be cured."

Mirjana stared at Tanige in disbelief. The kitchen help certainly was a knowing lot. But she was right in many respects. At this moment she would have sold herself into slavery for a smile and a kind word from Don Ruy. She must be sick, sicker than even Tanige suspected to welcome such humiliation.

"You have one day, Princess, to get yourself together. The rumor in the kitchen is Don Ruy and his men are but a day's ride from the *castillo*. They're expected early tomorrow. A day, Princess, to stiffen your backbone and a day to sharpen your dull wits. You can do it. Remember your dignity, remember who and what you are. This is no time to hang your head. What's past is past. Think of today as the first day of your new life."

"We've had so many new lives lately, I'm not sure I can start another new one. I'll try Tanige."

Tanige dropped the shirts on the stone floor and kicked them out of sight. She dusted her hands together and gurgled with laughter. "Now you sound like Princess Mirjana. Come, we'll bathe and dress, and then we'll do whatever it is these damn Christians do to make the day pass. Tomorrow is a new beginning for you."

In spite of herself Mirjana smiled. "Tanige you must tell me what has been going on in your life. I know I've missed your — your coming out, so to speak. I want to know who he is and how it all came about."

Tanige laughed happily. "I'll be glad to share my experiences with you in the bath, but whatever you do, Princess, don't offer me any advice. What I mean is, you aren't . . . you haven't done so well in that area and I am doing just fine. I have no wish to hurt your feelings, but I must insist that you allow me to lead my life. You will mean well, but I'm doing fine on my own."

"I promise," Mirjana said lightly, feeling better than she had in days. What would she do without Tanige? she wondered for the thousandth time.

* * *

An invisible time clock in Mirjana's head woke her an hour before dawn. She lay quietly, stunned that she had actually been asleep. A deep, restful sleep, and dreamless. She felt refreshed and alert. As Tanige had said, this was the first day of another new life.

Her long, lithe body stretched luxuriously in the narrow bed. A wide yawn split her features, making her smile. A warm bath and some clean clothing would be the perfect start for a new day. She rose quickly, tied a cornflower blue wrapper around her and crossed the room to Tanige's narrow cot. "Come, we're going to bathe early so that we can start the day fresh."

"Sometimes you overdo this bathing business, Princess," Tanige grumbled as she climbed from her bed. "And the next time I get an idea, I'll keep it to myself," she continued to mutter sleepily as she followed Mirjana to the empty bathhouse.

"I'm too tired to lather you up this morning, Princess. Bathe yourself. I just want to lay here in the warm water and sleep some more," Tanige grumbled as she lowered herself into the steamy wetness. "For that matter, neither one of us needs any soap. We bathed twice yesterday. Let's just sit here in the water and we'll contemplate your future."

"Oh no, oh no," Mirjana squealed. "This was your idea and you're going to play the game." She slid beneath the water and pulled at Tanige's toes. The sleepy girl slid beneath the water and rose, coughing and sputtering. Playfully, they frolicked in the warm water, squealing and laughing as soap flew one way and wash cloths another. Bubbles and foam rose to the top of the tub, making it impossible to see one another. Their playful water game halted when the blast of a trumpet sliced through the early morning air.

"The Lord of the Manor has returned," Tanige gasped as she wiped bubbles from her face.

"It does sound that way, doesn't it," Mirjana said quietly.

"I wonder what kind of welcome Don Ruy expects?" Tanige said as she grappled for the edge of the wooden tub.

"Probably the kind any man would expect at this time of the morning — nothing." Both women laughed, pearls of laughter bouncing off the steamy walls.

"What are you going to do, Princess?"

"I'm going to get dressed and then I'm going to brush my hair. After that, I'm going to give Teddy his lessons early so you and I can go to Ilena's house."

"How disrespectful of you, Princess. I love

your idea. If you dress yourself, I'll go to the kitchen and get us something to eat. What will you do if Don Ruy seeks you out to welcome his bride?"

"I will be unavailable. You're right, Tanige, I've been humiliated enough."

"I just love it when your backbone shows, Princess. Here's your towel, dry yourself."

Mirjana clenched her teeth at the sounds of thundering hooves. Clanking metal and joyful shouts filled the castle. Pray, Allah, the men didn't ride their horses into the great hall over the new tile.

Her footsteps were light, girlish as she raced back to the *castillo* and down the long corridors that led to her spartan room. Minutes later she was dressed and brushing her hair. The dark smudges beneath her eyes were almost gone. A few dabs of powder and there would be no reminders of the past days.

Minutes later Tanige bounded into the room, spilling the tea and dropping the sweet rolls on the floor. "Princess, wait till you hear," she babbled breathlessly. "You aren't going to believe this. I don't believe it. You know how your ears always get pointy when you hear something that is beyond belief, well they are going to rise soon. Wait till I tell you. I can't bear it. I simply can't bear it. I was stunned, literally stunned, and you know I don't stun easily. I take everything in my stride, which is more than you do, Princess, and you have to admit I'm right. Oh, I don't know if I can get the words out! God Almighty!"

"One more word, just one, and I will throttle you, Tanige. What is it that is going to make my ears grow to a point? And that's a lie and you know it. Tell me," she all but screamed.

"Don Ruy has returned."

"Is that what all this caterwauling is about? We knew that when we heard the trumpet."

"Yes, but you didn't let me finish. Don Ruy has returned but not with a wife. He didn't bring his wife!" Tanige exploded as she jumped from one foot to another.

"A mistake. Padre Juano made a mistake," Mirjana said excitedly. "And all the torment I've gone through. Praise Allah."

"Don't praise Allah, Princess, you're too late. Don Ruy did indeed marry, but he left his wife behind. I can tell you there hasn't been such a scandal in this palace since young Doña Ysabel invaded her husband's room when he was with a wench and saw —"

"I don't want to hear what Doña Ysabel saw. How can this be? Why didn't he bring his wife? Is it possible she died or something happened to her on the journey to Bivar?"

"How should I know. Princess, sometimes you expect too much from me. I told you Don Ruy was a man, and as such, he will keep his wife at a distance and keep you here to amuse himself when he is in residence. A chattel, that's what you are to him."

"Shut up, Tanige," Mirjana said bluntly. "I have to think. Are you certain of your facts?"

"Believe me, Don Ruy did not bring his wife. Nothing was said about death or problems on the journey. Now, what are you going to do?"

"Nothing has changed. He is still married to another. Perhaps his wife will arrive later. There must be much to do when changing a residence. I'm sure that's what will happen. We'll continue with our plans for the day. Is there anything left of the food you brought?"

Tanige shrugged. "The tea is cold and the warm rolls are still fit to eat. I'm not too hungry, are you?"

"No, but we will eat anyway," Mirjana said smoothly, pouring two cups of tea.

"What should I do about these shirts?" Tanige asked as she kicked at the silken fabric with her slippered foot. "If I take them back now, there is no wife to see them. What say you, Mirjana?"

"I say you had best shut your mouth before I take matters into my own hands," Mirjana snapped. "And for Allah's sake, eat!"

It was an iron command and Tanige chewed furiously. She was only trying to help. Why couldn't Mirjana see that? She knew this cool aloofness was a pose devised by the princess to hide her breaking heart. It was a disguise, like a mask, to hide her pain and restore her dignity. Even now, there were shadows in Mirjana's eyes that had deepened at the sound of Don Ruy's name.

CHAPTER 13

A ripe, golden sun of early autumn rode the heavens as majestically as Ruy rode his destrier, Liberte, into his home of Bivar. As always, his people went out to greet him. All of them quickly learned from the soldiers who returned with him that Don Ruy had married Doña Himena. Quizzical glances and speculative looks met puzzlement as the town folk, who had come to think of Mirjana as their Lady, whispered to one another. Many of them were angry that the *princesa* should be put down this way. Especially knowing how hard she had worked in the *castillo* and that special soft expression that dawned in her eyes whenever Don Ruy's name was mentioned. It was already being said that many of them would refuse to take part in a wedding celebration even if the groom was their lord, El Cid, Compeador, himself.

Before midday the soldiers had dispersed; only those who lived or worked in Bivar remained. Ruy himself had been surprised that Mirjana had not run down the road to meet him, or at least waited in the great hall. He decided she must be waiting at the window in his chambers, just as he had left her. There was a quickening in him as he rushed to the bathhouse to bathe, shave, and change into clean garments. He was eager for her, hungry, and he would have her, but first he must make himself presentable.

His steps had taken him at a running pace up the stairs to his chamber. He had seen the work in the gardens, the carefully tended shrubs and flowers, and knew he had Mirjana to thank for making his home hers. He flung open the door, expecting to find her, ready for her to fling herself into his arms. But the chamber was empty, she was not there. Only the faint aroma of her perfume greeted him. Immediately, he noticed the improvements, seeing the window hangings, the silken coverlets, the pottery and figurines. Again, he smiled. Mirjana had kept herself busy while he was away.

Ruy searched for her, yet was too proud to ask after her. Everywhere he looked, he saw her hand — the scrupulously clean corridors, the freshly scrubbed staircases, the tapestries, the tiles in the great hall. She had brought civilization to the home of her barbarian.

A meal was laid for him on the table in the great hall. As he ate, his eyes constantly raked the dark corners, and his ears were sharp for the sound of her footsteps. Disappointment made him edgy and the food tasteless. He chewed methodically, barely tasting the excellently prepared meal. Instead, his eyes followed the line of tapestries hung over the ancient stone walls and then to the newly tiled floor. He hadn't known there was a man in Bivar who knew the technique of making and laying tiles. Mirjana had certainly been busy. Nothing was the same; everything bore the mark of her tender hand. His eyes fell to the elegant lace mat on which the pewter and silver service ware had been placed, to the crystal goblet which held his wine. His palate finally recognized the improvement in the food. She had done it all for him, for the love of him.

Mirjana. Even her name was exotic and rare. He admitted to himself, as he poured from the carafe of wine, that he liked the feel of her, the scent of her as she lay beside him. She satisfied his mind; she tempted his mouth and soothed his body as no other woman ever had. Where in the name of Jesus Christ had the days gone when he took a woman, walked away, and never gave her a second thought? Since Mirjana came into his life he had no thoughts of other women, felt nothing for other women. How he had yearned and longed for this day when he would return to her. And where were the days when he would boast to Pietro of his conquests, regaling him with lurid tales of his prowess with the female sex? Now, he hugged his memories close to him, not wanting to share the long, intimate hours with Mirjana with anyone. Sleeping with her in his arms was rapture. Just to know she was there beside him gave him a peacefulness he had never known.

As Ruy poured from a second carafe of wine he wondered what Mirjana would think of how he had been trapped into marrying Himena. He had followed her sound advice concerning Alphonso, and she would be glad to hear that he thought it was the right decision. No doubt she would be pleased to know that her advice had been so helpful. A frown creased his brow. She hadn't told him to marry anyone. Or had she? The wine seemed to be fogging his brain. What did it matter? Married or not, he was home in Bivar, he had come home to Mirjana.

The tightening in his nether regions was blossoming into something more as his eyes searched for her. Where in hell was she? He roared for the servant standing discreetly out of sight. "Where is Princesa Mirjana?" he demanded.

"I do not know, Don Ruy, perhaps I can ask. Please, allow me to pour the wine for you." With trembling hands the old man poured the red wine generously. "I will return with your answer, my lord."

Ruy continued to drink the wine, his thoughts becoming blacker by the moment. When the old servant returned, his master's eyes were narrowed in anticipation of the reply.

"My lord, the Princesa Mirjana has gone for the day. She left with her servant shortly after your arrival. This, the cook told me. She prepared a basket of food for the *princesa* and told me they could not be expected before dark."

"After my arrival? Is that what you said? She left *after* I arrived home?" Ruy thundered.

"Yes, my lord. That is what the cook said."

"Goddamn women! Do they care for a man's comfort? Not this one! She takes her servant and off she goes without so much as a 'by your leave.' "

He felt foolish. He knew he was being watched by the servants and the staff of the *castillo,* waiting to see what he was going to do. He'd show them what he was going to do. When the princesa returned he was going to wring her neck! "What do you think of that?" he roared into the great hall, his voice echoing back to him from the emptiness. Feeling abandoned and angry, he clutched the carafe of wine and made his way to his chamber.

Once inside he glowered at the change that met his eye. Color ripe and vibrant, made him blink. He teetered one step, then another. She had made the place into a damned harem! That's what she had done!

Unfortunately, Dulcimea peeked into the room. "Here! You! Where in hell has the *princesa* gone?"

Shivering in fright, Dulcimea gasped. "I don't know, my lord. She may be out with Tanige or perhaps at the bathhouse. I only know that I helped her servant remove her belongings and take them to the tower room days ago. Is there anything else, my lord? Would you like to have a bath? Have you seen what the *princesa* has done to the anteroom? See? She's made you a private bath. This way, you won't have to go down to the bathhouse."

"I don't want a bath. I've had a bath. What do you mean you helped the princesa move back to the tower room? When?"

"Don Ruy!" Dulcimea backed against the wall, terrified by this man with the thundering voice. He glowered at her through his dark, piercing eyes, encroaching upon her threateningly.

"Tell me why!"

"Don Ruy," Dulcimea quivered, "I overheard the *princesa* and her servant talking. Padre Juano told the *princesa* you had married and were bringing your wife here to Bivar." Her eyes dropped to the floor, not wanting to look into his face, not wanting him to see the accusation on her own face. "The — the *princesa* felt she should move back to the tower. To — to make room for your wife."

"Well, I want her back here! Now! Fetch her," Ruy clamored. "Call Don Pietro! Call every damn man in this *castillo!* I want the *princesa* found and brought here, to me. Do you understand? *Comprende usted?*"

"Si, si!" Dulcimea backed away from him, turning to run down the corridors shouting for Don Pietro.

Worms of apprehension crawled in Ruy's belly. She had moved out when she heard of his marriage. His gut churned and his heart took on the roll of a drum. A sensation akin to fright settled between his shoulders, making him wince. He had faced battles with more bravery than he could conjure to face Mirjana.

Pietro flew into the room. "Ruy, what is it? You frightened that little servant half to death. She says you want every able-bodied man to come to your chamber? Have you lost your mind?"

"No," Ruy shook his head. "I want the *princesa* found and I want her found now! You tell the men, Pietro. Find her for me."

"You're drunk," Pietro told him with brotherly affection. "There's no need to alert the men and rouse the entire town. I'll find your *princesa* and bring her to you." Pietro hesitated as his eye caught the change in Ruy's chamber. "I see your tastes have improved," he said snidely as he looked around. He had silently condemned Ruy's marriage to Himena as soon as he had heard of it. He even blamed himself. If he hadn't been so drunk, enjoying the festivities following the coronation, he might have been able to talk sense to his friend. "And your own bath. And see this intimate table for quiet suppers alone? The *princesa* must indeed be a remarkable woman if she did all this for the likes of you. You aren't worth it, Ruy." Only long years of close friendship and sharing allowed Pietro to speak this way.

Ruy stumbled and almost fell, but Pietro saved him. "Fetch her back!" he said hoarsely. "Please, bring her back!"

"I'll do my best. Why don't you try to sleep it off till my return? You've had enough wine to fell a regiment."

"Right about needing sleep. Wrong about the wine." Nevertheless, Ruy did not protest when Pietro led him to the bed and settled him on the luxurious coverlet. If he could just close his eyes for a moment, just to clear his head. This was not happening. Mirjana had not left . . .

Don Pietro led his horse from the stables after receiving directions to the house of Gormaz. It was just possible that was where the *princesa* was headed when she had set out that morning, he had been told.

Mirjana sat near the fire holding little Manuel, rocking the babe to sleep while Tanige and Ilena finished the supper dishes. A rap sounded on the door, and when Ilena answered it, there stood burly Pietro, looking and sounding apologetic. "Pardon. Is Princesa Mirjana with you?"

Mirjana's back stiffened, her eyes widened in surprise.

"Princesa, Don Ruy has sent me to find you and bring you back to the *castillo*."

"Did he?" she pretended indifference. "Take a message to Don Ruy. Tell him for me that I am extremely busy and cannot return."

"Princesa, I have my orders from Don Ruy himself," Pietro pleaded. "I cannot return without you."

"I am sorry, Pietro, to have you dragged into this." He could see she was sincere, but then he'd never known her to be otherwise. She looked so small, so fragile, sitting before the firelight, holding a babe. It should be her own babe she dandled on her knee. Pietro found his fury rising. Ruy should never have allowed the marriage between himself and Himena to take place. This was the woman for him, and if he did not know it then from his drunken self-pity, he knew it now.

"Princesa, I must ask you to come with me. Willingly, of course." He hadn't meant his words to sound like a threat that he would use force if necessary. But, obviously, that was the way it was taken, for the women, Ilena, and the *princesa*'s servant stood beside Mirjana, flanking her on either side, their faces set to do battle.

"The princess does not wish to return with you, Don Pietro," Tanige told him coldly.

"You have come to my home uninvited," Ilena said warningly, her eyes drifting pointedly to the poker on the hearth.

Mirjana lifted her hand to stay the women. She turned to Pietro, a glitter of tears in her crystal gray eyes. "Please, Don Pietro, I am not ready to face him yet. *Por favor,* tell Don Ruy I am busy." Despite the torment he saw in her face, there was no bitterness in her voice.

* * *

It had all gone wrong, all of it, and the pain came from the fact that she was not certain that she cared. Mirjana turned over on her narrow cot in the tower room. Shortly after Don Pietro had left Ilena's house, she and Tanige had driven the wagon back to the *castillo,* slipping unnoticed to their rooms.

It was too much effort to keep on with the charade. Her life was a shambles. Her glance took in the circular room and its contents. Move here, move there, decorate and clean, scrub and carry . . . Why? For Ruy's wife to enjoy? If he had not brought his Himena with him, surely would come the day when the woman did arrive.

Ruy had used her to his own advantage and then went off to marry another. Polygamy was a part of the Islamic culture; it was even a part of her religion. If Ruy had been married when she met him, first shared his bed, it would have mattered little to her. But why now? And in Ruy's culture a man was entitled to only one wife at a time, and so he must choose carefully. Why, if he had wanted to marry, had he not chosen her? She would have done anything for him. She would even have adopted Christianity. It had been done before, she knew, and would be done again. Ruy's rejection of her stung, wounded her to the quick. If she had married Yusuf, she would have been a third wife and it would not have mattered. Somehow, it would have been different. Mirjana had no liking to share Ruy with any other woman. She wanted to be the only woman in his life — his only love.

Mirjana's thoughts boiled through her brain. She was devastated, heartbroken. She had meant nothing to Ruy in spite of his hon-eyed, impassioned words. To be honest, he had never spoken of love; she had only assumed it. Now her secret hopes were dashed. She would never be his wife; at best, only his concubine. Coming from her culture, this was not unseemly or the most terrible thing that could happen to a woman. *Not if she could have his love.* Having Ruy love her, truly love her, would be a victory, a triumph. It would erase her rejection and her humiliation, and give her back a sense of her own worth.

Loving Ruy, needing him, and being unable to be loved in return was Allah's punishment for trying to deceive her father. She had begun this adventure by pretending to be a prisoner of El Cid, and the fates had turned the game on her. Now she was Ruy's prisoner in every sense of the word. She could not live with him or without him. She could never speak her heart to him and risk his pity. He already pitied her, she suspected, for being homeless.

This other would be too much to bear. A deep groan of agony swelled in her breast and was born in her throat. The sound, when it emerged from between her clenched teeth, was that of an animal in the throes of death.

Ruy had awakened to find himself atop the bed, his head seeming to swing in wide circles, his temples pounding. Dragging himself from his bed, he did his best to clean himself up before meeting with Mirjana. Doing this quickly, he was left with nothing but his thoughts to occupy him. The longer he waited for Pietro's return and Mirjana's appearance, the more impatient he became until he was storming about the chamber like a caged animal.

Damn the man, Pietro should have returned hours ago. Where in the hell was the brandy he had ordered? "Mikel!" he thundered. "Fetch me the goddamn brandy now! What must I do to be obeyed the first time I give an order?"

An aging servant hastily shuffled in with a bottle on a silver tray. "Sire," he said hesitantly, "I did fetch a bottle; you drank it. See, there it is on the lace cloth."

"Lace cloth, lace cloth," Ruy repeated drunkenly. "Do you know whose lace cloth that is? I wager you do. Everyone in this damn *castillo* knows what's going on but me. Have you seen Pietro?" he roared to the frightened servant.

"No, sir, I have seen no one. The hour is late and everyone is asleep."

"Not everyone, Mikel. *I* am awake. *I am wide awake!* Can you see how wide awake I am?"

"Yes, sir, wide awake, I can see that. Is there anything else?"

Ruy's eyes narrowed. "Do you know where the *princesa* is?"

"No, sir, I do not."

"Go, go, leave me to my misery," Ruy said, waving his arms about wildly. Where was that bastard Pietro? He'd have his head when he returned. And his manhood, too, if he had to make a point.

Ruy stalked the length of his chamber like a caged panther. Thoughts of Mirjana and Pietro crept into his drunken mind. He could almost see them along the darkened roadside, lying naked in each other's arms. The thought set his teeth to rattling. Would Pietro make love to her like a gentleman or like a savage? He imagined he could hear Mirjana's soft moans of pleasure. Suddenly, he wanted to strike out, to bludgeon, to kill, to rape. To torture the man who would dare touch Mirjana. If Pietro dared lay a hand on Mirjana's silken skin, he would show him no mercy. He would slit his throat, friend or no. Would Mirjana cry and weep and wring her hands if he committed such a crime? The picture of her grieving at Pietro's gravesite for all the world to see set him into such a frenzy that he kicked out at the leg of a table that stood in his way. The pain in his foot was so excruciating, he had to clench his teeth to keep from crying out.

Why hadn't she been in the *castillo* waiting for him? Why had she moved her things from his quarters? Why?

Ruy cursed himself for a fool a thousand times over as he brought the brandy bottle to his mouth. Why hadn't he been able to see that she wasn't interested in him as a man but as a means to get back to Seville? She had gladly moved into his quarters, shared her body with him. Shared her body. The words amused him for a second. Rage battled in his chest at the thought. Angrily, he smashed the bottle on the stone floor. He sneered at the spill as it trickled and stained a beautiful Persian carpet — Mirjana's carpet.

Am I to go through life staring at her day by day, he asked himself, remembering the feel of her fast-beating heart, the half-moans she made, the sound of his name on her lips as her passions poured forth? Not once did

Himena enter his mind.

How could he deny that the *princesa* was in his blood? To deny that would be to deny his very next breath.

Sounds of hard heels pounding down the stone corridor made Ruy reel drunkenly toward the open doorway. At last the bastard was back and he damn well better have Mirjana intact and untouched. He tried to focus his blurted eyesight. He saw two figures but both were Pietro. "Where is she?" he roared.

Pietro's dark eyes took in the situation at a glance. He had seen Ruy drunk on many occasions but never quite like this. This was different. As a man, he could read the pain in the dull eyes and see the turmoil that was ripping him apart. Ruy could drink any man in his army under the table and still be aware of what he was saying and doing. He sought for the right words, the right tone to ease his commander's suffering — or what he thought was suffering. "Back at the farm, I think, but I'm not certain," Pietro said as honestly as he could.

"Back at what farm? What have you done with her?" Ruy demanded in a slurred voice. He swung widely, his intention to punch Pietro on the jaw. Pietro backed off and caught Ruy so he wouldn't fall. "If you tell me you touched just one hair, just one, Pietro, I'll kill you. Do you hear me? I'll kill you!"

Pietro sighed. "Ruy, the women ran me off the farm. The last time I saw the *princesa* she was with her servant and the woman called Ilena, Gormaz's wife. The *princesa* said she was busy. I told her you ordered me to fetch her back, and she said she was too busy at the moment."

"Busy doing what? What was more important than coming back to me? Answer me, damn you. What was she doing?" Ruy said, his words slurred and almost unintelligible.

"She was sitting by the fire, holding an infant, and telling me not to bother her. How do I know what women do? They clean, they cook, they have babies. All I know is, she refused to return with me."

"You should have forced her to return with you. I gave you an order, and I expect my orders to be carried out. What manner of soldier are you? I myself decorated you many times for being one of my bravest warriors, and one woman, one small slip of a woman, defeats you."

"If she's so easy to control, why didn't you fetch her yourself instead of sending me?" Pietro spoke with ease born of long friendship. His words were blunt yet kind.

"Because, damn you, I'm the Compeador,

and I don't go traipsing after women. Now fetch her to me. I want her, don't you understand? Send a regiment, an army, but fetch her back!"

"I understand, Ruy. It is the *princesa* who doesn't understand. Your entire army couldn't bring her back if she doesn't want to return. You might as well make up your mind to that fact. The *princesa* does what she wants when she wants to do it. She didn't want to come back with me, so she didn't come back. I returned alone and I'm not taking any damn regiment back for her either. What kind of talk do you think that will inspire among your men?"

"The *princesa* defied an order given by me?" There was awe in Ruy's face as he tried to bring Pietro into his line of vision.

"Yes, that's what she did, she defied you and me," Pietro said glumly as he remembered the three women and how outnumbered and foolish he felt as he rode from the farm. "It's possible she returned to the *castillo* herself after I left. All I know is, she said she was busy and didn't want to return with me."

Ruy clenched his teeth. He hated that word — busy. Women always pretended to be busy, doing this and that and accomplishing nothing. Busy. "Busy! Hanging draperies and smoothing pillows. That's what they mean when they say they're busy, Pietro. We don't have to stand for that kind of thing. We're men! We're strong! We fight battles! We win battles! We win wars! This isn't even a goddamn skirmish. Busy! Busy be damned. I should have her flogged," Ruy said drunkenly. "Flogged for defying my orders."

"You're not thinking clearly right now, Ruy. Your brain is fogged in brandy. Tomorrow will be different. You'll be able to look at all of this objectively and laugh at the fool you made of yourself over the *princesa*."

"When a woman gets the last word with a man, he loses his self-respect. What do I have left? A marriage I detest. A woman whom I cannot abide as my wife." He hiccuped drunkenly.

His eyes were so sad, so humble, so lost, that Pietro reached out a hand to place on Ruy's shoulder. "You must love the *princesa* very much," he said softly.

A burst of harsh laughter grated on Pietro's ears. "Love! Bite your tongue, man, and never speak that word in my presence again!" Ruy straightened his shoulders and made an effort to stare Pietro in the eye. "By first light you will ride to Seville and speak with the *princesa*'s brother, Hassan, and see if arrangements can't be made for her return to Seville. Stay as long as necessary and be prepared to offer whatever is necessary in the way of compensation."

"Can I be spared at this time, Ruy!" Pietro said, not liking the idea of the long ride to Seville and an even longer stay. At this point it would do no good to argue with Ruy in his condition. Besides, it was an order, and in his entire life he had never disobeyed an order given him by Ruy. Something in his gut told him this was not the time to make changes. He would go, for all the good it would do him. He grimaced as he led Ruy to his bed. "Sleep, Ruy. Tomorrow will be another day and you'll have your wits about you."

Ruy imagined he could hear driving, pelting rain. He groaned and rolled over, stretching a long, muscular leg across the bottom of the huge bed. Warily, he let his leg circle the cool expanse of sheeting. Splayed fingers searched for the silken body of which he had been dreaming. His bed was empty. He struggled to a sitting position and was instantly sorry. His head pounded and his stomach heaved. A deep roar of discomfort shot from his clenched teeth. The sound ricocheted around the room, coming back to circle his aching head. He felt vaguely disoriented as he tried to remember the night's happenings. "Pietro," he called loudly. When there was no response, he realized he had been whispering. "Mikel," he croaked.

The aging servant entered the room, his eyes amused. "Yes, sir."

"Send Don Pietro to me. What time is it? How long have I slept? Fetch me something to eat." As his stomach heaved, he thought better of the idea. "Never mind the food, just send Pietro to me at once."

"Sir, Pietro left for Seville at first light. He's been gone many hours now. It's midmorning; you slept for nine hours."

Seville! Memory buzzed in his throbbing head. The old man was right, he had ordered Pietro to Seville. Did he have a premonition last evening or was it a step toward the inevitable? The inevitable meaning Mirjana would eventually return to Seville. The thought made his aching head pound harder and his stomach heave threateningly. He swallowed the sour bile and struggled to his feet. His footing was unsure and he lurched against the small, scattered tables that Mirjana had placed about his room. Angrily, he kicked out with his bare foot and recoiled as if a snake had bit him. "Goddamn claptrap," he shouted as he bent to pick up one of the tiled tables. He sent it crashing against the stone wall. It didn't make him feel better when he saw the splinters and slivers of tile and broken wood that lay on the decorative floor. The lace cloth on the table in the intimate alcove that Mirjana had worked so painstakingly on was ripped off and tossed into a corner. Brilliant scarlet pillows sailed through the air, followed by pots meant to burn incense. The sweet smell of the spilled ashes made him retch.

"Fetch me my clothes and be goddamn quick about it, Mikel. I have no patience this morning. I'm going to the bathhouse."

"Sir, there is no need for you to go to the bathhouse. Princesa Mirjana converted the anteroom to your left as a private bath. If you feel ill, it might help if you bathed here in the privacy of your own room."

"Who said I was ill?" Ruy demanded.

"No one said you were ill, sir. I just thought if you weren't feeling up to your usual self, this private bath might be what you need," Mikel said in a tone that was full of apology.

"Don't think, Mikel. Fetch the water."

Good and loyal servant that he was, Mikel simpered, "The water is in the tub, sir. I took the liberty as you were waking."

"Tell me, Mikel, truthfully — have you seen the *princesa* this morning?" Ruy asked as he slipped down into the steamy water. He hoped his voice was wily and crafty, but he had the feeling it was hopeful and boyish at the same time.

"The *princesa* is in the garden sewing. Would you like me to take a message to her?"

"No need. *This* message I'll deliver myself!"

Each brush stroke against his body set Ruy's teeth on edge. He ignored his torment and scrubbed vigorously. When he finished he sat in the tepid water and looked around at the elaborately appointed bathroom. He had to admit that it was convenient. It pleased his eye. Bright, vibrant color dotted the room by way of pillows, wall hangings, and squares of soft, ankle-deep carpeting. The small porcelain jars and vials containing bath oils and scents that rested on the shelf at the tub's edge were beautiful accents to the restful room. He liked it.

Ruy looked down at his body in the murky water. He felt a warmth in his loins. How was it possible, he wondered, to just think of Mirjana and the room she had decorated for him to have his manhood bloom as it was doing now this minute? If only she were here, now, in his arms trembling for the feel of him, wanting him as he wanted her.

Such thoughts would do him no good. Angrily, he sloshed from the tub, leaving a trail of wet footprints. Purposefully, he strode into his room to dress. His breath was coming in short, ragged gasps as he buttoned his shirt. He blinked as his eyes dropped to the meticulous needlework. More of Mirjana's handiwork. His jaw tensed so hard, he thought his teeth would shatter. By God, he would find her and drag her back here by her long, silken hair if he had to. Enough was enough.

Ruy's eyes were black and hard as he strode down one corridor after another. He took the stone steps three at a time in his quest to find Mirjana. He came to an abrupt halt at the entrance to the walled-in garden. He took a moment to let his eyes drink in the sight of her, a book open on her lap. He watched as she read, her lips moving as though savoring each word. The bright, yellow ball in the sky seemed to cast a nimbus of gold around her head. He wondered if she was aware of the halo surrounding her head. Probably not, he told himself. This must be what an angel looked like, he thought inanely. Immediately, he felt foolish that such a thought should ever enter his mind.

He waited, hoping she would notice him before he had to speak. His shadow fell over her, casting her face and the book she held in her lap into a dim light. Mirjana raised her eyes to see if the sun had slipped behind the puffy white clouds. She saw him.

Mirjana's heart fluttered wildly. He had

sought her out. It cost her dearly, but she managed to speak. "*Buenos días,* Don Ruy."

Ruy hadn't known what exactly to expect, but her cool aloofness was not it. He fought the urge to reach down and bring her into his arms. Arms that ached to hold her next to him. He couldn't just stand here, looking foolish; he had to say something. "*Buenos días,* Princesa."

Mirjana carefully closed her book and placed it on the bench next to her. It was her way of telling him there was no room on the bench for the two of them. She folded her hands primly in her lap and stared up at the tall man. How wonderful he looked. If only she had the courage to stand up and reach for him so he would gather her close to his chest. "Have you ever seen such a beautiful day?" she inquired softly.

How beautiful she was, how serene. If only she would make some move, give him some indication of how she felt what she was thinking. "Not since the day I left for Zamora. The sun was shining much like now. Do you remember?" he asked hoarsely.

How deep his voice was, so full of feeling. "I remember. It was a day such as this." Why couldn't she say what she was feeling? Why couldn't she ask the questions she wanted to ask: Why, why, did you marry another? Why?

Where is your wife? What do you plan for me, for *us?*

Her voice was soft as silk. It caressed his bruised heart like a healing ointment. He wanted to know what she was feeling. He wanted her to tell him why she refused to return with Pietro. Were all those soft whispers in the night lies? He wanted to know, needed to know. But he couldn't ask. He wouldn't ask. He shifted his weight from one foot to the other. "It was a long trip home." He had to say something else, something to jar her, move her from her indifference.

She wanted him to make mention of his wife. She needed an explanation, even to have him lie to spare her. No, no, that was wrong. She didn't need his lies — she needed his love.

Ruy shifted his weight a second time. Mirjana was nothing like Himena. Nothing at all like Himena. The familiar ache was growing again as he stared down at her, willing her to say something, anything, to show she had not forsaken him. His teeth clenched. Why wouldn't she make some mention of why she moved out of his chamber? A core of anger was vying with the ache, making him uneasy. He felt his hands ball into fists. He wanted to shock her, make her react to him. She seemed so far removed from him. She was being polite, like a guest at a wedding. Wedding. That goddamn farce! He made a vow never to think of his wedding day again. Never!

Grieving inwardly, Mirjana lowered her eyes. It was over, whatever they had shared. He was standing here being polite because she was a guest, forced upon him, and nothing more. He was annoyed, she could tell the way he was clenching and unclenching his fists, as though he wanted to be rid of her but didn't quite know the words that would make it possible. She could feel tears prick at her eyelids. This was no time to weaken, no time to show how badly wounded she was. She swallowed past the lump in her throat. "It was considerate of you to stop and pass these few moments with me. I know how busy you must be. You've been away a long time. If you'll excuse me, I must find Tanige. It was so nice to talk to you again, Don Ruy," she said formally.

With a swish of her skirts, she picked up her book and quickly walked from the garden. The moment she was out of sight, her shoulders slumped and the tears rolled down her cheeks. Escaping into the *castillo,* she sprinted down the long corridors ending up in a small chapel. She dropped into one of the pews and sobbed, her heart breaking with each tortured cry.

He watched her leave, unable to stop her. Don Ruy! She had actually called him Don Ruy. So cool and formal. So reserved. So indifferent. What in the name of God had happened to change her? He had left her to journey to Zamora on her own advice months ago. While her eyes had been sad, they had been filled with love. Where had that love gone? Where? She told him she would count the days until his return. Was her love so fragile, so temporary? Not once did his marriage enter into Ruy's thoughts. His balled fist lashed out at the acacia tree. His eyes widened with the shock of the pain. A cold chill snaked down his back as he brought his clenched fist to his lips.

Between the rocketing pain in his head and the searing pain in his fist, Ruy felt as though he had ridden headlong into battle and had come out the loser. Women! First it was his mother with her demands, her ideas and the goddamn letter to Alphonso. Then it was Himena with her layers of clothing and pale ashy skin. Now it was Mirjana with her cool indifference. When he was bedding whores, he never had these problems.

Stomping his way to the stable in search of Teddy, Ruy nursed his injured hand, cursing aloud for any and all to hear. He thought he heard titters of laughter from the kitchen area as he strode by. Were they laughing at him? Did they know of the cool reception the *princesa* had given him? Most likely, they knew everything within the hour of its happening. Nothing was sacred or secret in this damnable *castillo*.

It was a black, silken night, a night for lovers' whispers and even softer caresses. Mirjana lay in her bed, remembering other such nights when she had lain in Ruy's arms. How blissful and contented she had been. How happy. By all that was holy, she had thought Ruy had been as happy, as contented. How wrong she had been. She longed to know what his wife looked like. She ached to know how Ruy felt about her. Did he and Himena talk for long hours about everything and nothing? Was their lovemaking slow and sensual and full of contentment? Had they a total communion as Ruy had said he and Mirjana shared? Did she love Ruy? Did she love him deeply, with all her heart as she, Mirjana, did?

How wretched she felt, how tired and depressed. She wanted nothing more than to dress and run down the corridor to Ruy's chamber and beg him to take her in his arms, to love her, just for now, for this night. She sighed wearily. Where was her self-respect, where was her pride? There was nothing to be gained by remembering.

Mirjana sat up in bed, her heart thundering in her chest. What was that noise? It was her door. Her eyes flew to the stout bolt. Safe. She sighed and closed her eyes. Maybe it was a bad dream again. She tensed, waiting for the sound to be repeated. Her name was being called through the thickness of the door. Ruy? Ruy was calling her name. In the middle of the night Ruy was calling her name. Should she answer or pretend she was asleep? Why was he tormenting her like this? He had a wife, why did he need her? A conquest? To humiliate her further?

The slim, tapered candle beside her bed illuminated the small room just enough for her to see the latch on the door being tried. Then came the bone-jarring sound of wood splintering beneath his boot. She held her breath, not daring to look. More banging, more thudding, until she believed the hounds of hell or the devil himself was breaking through to reach her, to get her. When the door slammed inward and splintered into the stone walls with an ear-splitting crack, he was standing there, hands on his hips, dark hair curling over his brow, his eyes flashing lightning.

"Why didn't you open the door?" he demanded. "You heard me call you, I know you did. Don't you know, Mirjana, that hell itself will never stand between me and what I want?" His voice was a growl, barely human. He panted with exertion, his chest heaving, his fists clenching. In two long strides he was standing over her, breathing down upon her.

"And you want your whore, is that it?" she sneered bitterly.

Quicker than light, his hand lashed out to cross her cheek, making her cower away against the damp, cold wall in shock. Her eyes were wide with terror. Blood smeared a stain across her mouth.

Ruy could feel the power in his arm, could still hear the result of the blow, sharp and cracking in his ears, and a muscle in his cheek jerked as though he had received the blow rather than dealt it. He had never meant to hit her, but she had called herself his whore! Deprecated herself. And this he could not tolerate, not even from her. How could she think herself his whore when she must know she was more, so much more, than any woman had ever been to him? Reflexively, his arms opened to her, wanting to hold her, needing to give her refuge even from his own furies.

Mirjana leaned into his embrace, obedient to his will. He felt the stiffness of her body, the shock of his deed, felt her trembling and quivering. If there were tears in her eyes, he could not see for the tears that were in his. She had come into his arms because of her fright, because of his will. It was not obedience to his commands that he wanted, and the pain of it was heavy in his chest. She was such a mystery, this *princesa* from another world so different from his own. She aroused emotions in him that he could not name.

As though lifting a child, he took her into his arms, carrying her across the room and down the tower stairs. She hid her face in the hollow of his neck, limp and lifeless, offering no resistance. He wished she would fight him, scratch and kick and curse him. This meekness, this helplessness was like a stone on his heart. He had never before struck a woman, and he hated himself for hitting Mirjana, of all women.

Through the corridors he carried her, listening for the cries that never came. When he kicked the door to his own chamber open, he felt her body stiffen in sharp tremors of fright. He lay her down upon his bed, leaning over her, stretching himself out beside her curled, unresponsive form.

In the light of the candles and the glowing fire in the hearth, he saw the ravages of his deed. A smear of blood stained her lips, a fresh rivulet trickled from her inner lip. The bruise on her cheek was scarlet, already swelling along her jaw. Tenderly, he wiped the blood; gently, he kissed the bruise he had put there. She came into his arms woodenly, allowing him to hold her, to comfort her.

"Forgive me, Mirjana, I never meant to hurt you. Do you forgive me?" Almost timidly, he lifted her chin to look into her eyes.

Mirjana could not speak, only nod her head. There was such pain on his face, a pain much deeper than what he had dealt with his sudden blow. She would say anything, do anything, to remove that pain from him, wanting to take it into her own heart and suffer it for him.

His mouth touched hers, bathing the spot where her lip had been cut against her teeth. His hands were in her hair, along her throat. Ruy was giving, not taking, this comfort, this tenderness. Hands that could crush and maim were caressing the plains of her back, cradling her, soothing her wounded spirit. The closeness of him, his caring, told her more than words could say. He made the blood rush through her veins, made her weak with her need for him.

His kisses covered her where his hands disrobed her. Her shoulders, her breasts, her middle. Everywhere she felt his touch, giving herself up to it. She watched him undress in the golden light, her eyes touching him, filling with the adored sight of him. And when he came to her she took him into her embrace, a gasp of pleasure sounding from her, that he was at last in her arms again.

The moon and sun were at her center as he made love to her, covering her with his kisses, worshipping her with his hands, calling her name over and over. Beckoning waves carried her adrift in a sea of their passions. And when he covered her body with his own, she guided him into her, surrounding him with her incredible warmth, rocking beneath him.

He felt himself fill her, and he knew a sense of coming home. She drove him onward with her desires, having them echo in his own. She trembled beneath him as he brought her to the edge of ecstasy and knew she waited until they could cross that threshold together. He held himself motionless, fighting for control. He had dreamed this and now it was true. He wanted, needed, to hear her say his name. To cry his name as she brought them both to the relief of this undulating torment. "Say it!" he whispered as he had so many other nights. "Say it!"

The heavens broke with the sound of her voice, shattering the stillness that engulfed them. And as she cried his name, she heard the echo of her own. "Mirjana. Mirjana!"

CHAPTER 14

Mirjana and Ruy were careful to keep this delicate balance between them. In an unspoken bargain, they chose to ignore the doubts and demons which had come between them and keep them at bay. They never discussed Ruy's attendance at the coronation of the new king of Castile or his resulting marriage to Himena. Nor did they discuss the night Ruy had come to break down Mirjana's door and carry her back to his chamber. These things were too painful, like a raw sore that would not heal.

Instinctively, they knew how threatening this tentative, unspoken bargain was to them, looming far overhead on a shelf that could topple onto them at any time. Still, it was far more threatening to this precarious relationship to face their misgivings and mistrust.

The days passed quickly with hundreds of duties and details to prepare for the coming winter. Harvest was upon them, and from every indication, it would be fruitful. Ruy was a beneficent lord, making certain his people profited from their labors, only taking in tithe what was necessary for the security of Bivar, unlike so many other landlords who gouged their people leaving them in near starvation while they filled their treasuries. There was a vast market for grain and foodstuffs in the cities, both Islamic and Christian. Under the law, landlords were entitled to more than half of what their peasants produced. Ruy was far more equitable to his people and they loved him for it. He took only what was necessary to improve his town, to pay for the construction of new granaries, and to cobble the streets. Rightly, he believed that to take the profits from a man's labor was unjust, merely inducing the people to reduce their productivity and render a town to poverty. In Bivar, all men profited.

Alphonso, in further gratitude to Ruy, had commissioned a vast supply of arms to be forged and was willing to pay well into the coffers of Bivar. The town was burgeoning with new faces, new families — blacksmiths and armorers, miners to extract the precious iron ore from the foothills that were rich with it. In the outlying fields surrounding the town, new huts and streets were being built. New faces and population brought prosperity to the existing shops.

It was Mirjana who one day frowned at the muddy trails and hastily erected huts. While the town was excitedly profiting from this new influx of people and their ready purses, it was also suffering from the transient migration. Bivar was being threatened with becoming a border town, ugly and miskept, and very temporary. One day she approached Ruy, a frown wrinkling her brow.

"What is it, Mirjana? You look as though you might lose your best friend?" He had laughed, but there was a mark of concern in his eyes and the faintest catch in his voice. He lived in dread of the day when she would implore him to set her free to leave him, to return to her own people and civilization.

"I am disturbed by what is becoming of Bivar," she told him, relieving his fears. "It is changing, Ruy. It's only been weeks since the first miners and craftsmen have come and already it is not the same." She pointed out the muddied roads, the leaning shacks, the littered streets. It was now in danger of becoming an untidy, industrial town with little care for beauty or hygiene. The rainy season was soon to be upon them, and disease and pestilence would thrive if something was not done immediately. Also, there had been reports of looting and crime that had never occurred before in the little town.

Ruy frowned. He knew only too well the filth and evil of cities. Even Zamora, with its many churches, was a sinpot of decadence where people lived in slums and in their own offal. He, too, had seen what was becoming of Bivar and did not like it.

"Would it be possible to plan for the expansion of Bivar?" Mirjana wanted to know. "People should not be allowed to come here and build barely habitable mud huts on the first purchase of land they find. Your people, who have lived here for generations and generations, do not like what they see becoming of their home."

"Yes," Ruy agreed. "And the situation can only worsen. As long as the deposits of iron ore in the hills remain accessible to the miners' picks they will come to live and work here."

"Then it is up to you, Ruy, to protect Bivar and your people." She told him of a book she had in her possession, containing the plans for the city of Seville and the designs of the city's engineers that looked to the future and protected portions of the city for parks and gardens and for the removal of wastes and refuse. "Of course, it is all on a very grand scale, but couldn't some of the ideas be applied here?"

Seeing her eagerness and concern for his

home, he insisted on seeing this book. "And to think I thought you a fool to burden yourself with a wagon load of useless books!"

"You were only interested in the sweetmeats you could find," she teased.

Ruy put his arm around her shoulders, bringing her close against him, his lips nuzzling her ear. "The only sweetmeat I was ever hungry for was this." He lightly caressed her breast, sliding his hand down over her belly. "And this."

"You are much too brash, sir!" Mirjana giggled, her pulses quickening. Her cheeks flushed with color, and he found this amazing that after all they had shared, the intimacies, the total knowledge of one another's bodies, she could still blush at a little randy teasing. "Now let us get back to the book, sir. Else all of Bivar will be in ruins before you sate your wicked desires."

He watched her as she thumbed through the pages, reading the scratchy and obscure Arabic writing. As he watched her he thought he would never have enough of her, never be sated in her. And he was saddened that for all she gave him of herself, she held back twice again of what he knew she was capable of giving.

For days, Ruy and Mirjana pored over books, drawing up plans for the growth of

Bivar. They sketched and made notes, and drew up a list of town regulations concerning the disposal of wastes and refuse and building codes, and a list of laws and edicts to protect the citizens. They hoped their stringent and watchful concern would make the town unattractive to criminals and wastrels. When they were done, Ruy held meetings with his soldiers who were appointed marshalls to uphold the law.

At first, it was held in astonishment that a woman had a hand in Don Ruy's business and his plans for Bivar. Their speculations and amusements were obliterated when the first results were proven. Vagrants and beggars vanished from the streets just as quickly as they had appeared. The roads and streets were clean of litter, and drunken loitering was prohibited. But most of all, the crooked shacks and hastily erected huts on the outskirts of the town were torn down, and in their place neat rows of thatched-roof houses that depicted a permanency of residence were built, each with its own plot for a garden and a cobbled walk. Hedgerows were planted, and promised to bloom even this late in the year. Trees which had been standing since Christ was a child were saved from the cutter's axe and others, younger and fruitful, were also spared.

Hygiene and health were protected by a system of outhouses and regular disposal and burial in fallow fields that had seen their productiveness. Within five years' time the soil would be replenished by this natural compost and would again yield a crop.

Ruy and Mirjana spent most days together, overseeing the changes in the town, carefully delegating responsibilities and duties. Several hours each day, Mirjana would personally see to young Teddy's lessons, and Ruy was impressed with his little brother's progress. There was new respect in him for Teddy, and he considered the removal of their mother's influence a wise move. Doña Ysabel would have kept Teddy from the challenges life had to offer, and he never would have changed from that sulky, mischievous child to this strong and secure youngster.

Teddy himself basked in the glow of his accomplishments and reveled in the attentions of his warrior brother. But it was to Mirjana that he looked for approval and confidence with such fervor that at times Ruy found himself actually jealous of the rapport that had sprung between them.

Ruy was discovering so much about Mirjana — her strengths and weaknesses and her capacity for joy. But there was a dark and mysterious side to her, he knew, and it was an area where he was not welcome. There were times when her eyes would lose their clarity and become haunted by shadows. She would become pensive, introspective, casting him out of her thoughts, perpetuating the mystery. Her mysteriousness puzzled and angered him, yet touched him most of all. When she should be the happiest, there seemed to be a part of her that held itself away, refusing to find joy, giving herself over to whatever demon haunted her. He believed it was because she was homeless, and sensitive to her feelings, he realized she thought herself a prisoner and a displaced person, exiled from Seville and abandoned by her family.

Especially at night, as they slept in the bed in the chamber they shared, there were times when he would awaken to find her thrashing between the sheets and crying inconsolably. He would take her into his arms and croon to her, stroking her back to comfort her.

She would tremble in his embrace. He could feel the damp, cold sweat that made her shiver. And at these times she would awaken, holding to him fiercely, pressing herself closer, closer, trying to find safety from her nightmares. Purposely, she would arouse him, kissing and nipping, stroking him and urging him to make love to her. In her desperation and despondency she would become demanding, a heated writhing wanton, seeking him, famished for him, seeking relief from her night terrors in his touch, in his embrace, in his quick and hard riding of her. Using him to conquer her fears.

When the day's light would come through the sheer curtains on the windows, she would turn to him, restored, taking him into her gentle embrace. No mention of what had occurred during the black hours before dawn would be made, but the ravages were there to be seen in the smudges beneath her eyes. Tenderly, considerately, Ruy would take her, using her gently, willing her to find the safety and security he offered.

When the letter came to Ruy he was in one of the spare chambers which Mirjana and he had converted into small a small office. He liked the atmosphere in here — bright for the windows facing the east, colorful for the assorted Persian carpets littering the floor, masculine with its faint scent of aged leather and old wood paneling.

He was glad Mirjana had taken herself off into town to commission the weaving of new household linens when he saw the waxed seal of the Asturias's family crest on the parchment. He wanted no reminders of his marriage to Himena to present themselves to Mirjana.

He knew she had not truly accepted the fact he had married while in Zamora.

While slipping his thumb under the sealed flap, he wondered why Don Bernardo would be writing him. He had paid the Asturiases a healthy sum to keep Himena under their protection and shelter, and would again send for her support at the first of the year.

The news, when he read it, left him shaking. Doña Himena Maria Asturias Diaz was with child. Ruy smacked his fist on the desk, enjoying the shooting stab of pain that traveled to above his elbow. Himena with child? Had that one night in June when he had drunkenly dreamed he was lying beside Mirjana produced a child? Was that pale, ashen-skinned girl so fertile that his seed had taken root and sprouted to a new life?

With everything that was in him, Ruy doubted this could be so. But the ways of women were dark and mysterious, and he knew it could be possible. A child. He cursed his fates. Why then must it be born of a woman who barely existed for him? This child should be growing in Mirjana's belly and he would know jubilant elation.

Ruy sat for a long time thinking, remembering. He knew that at the final moment, when he realized it was not Mirjana's body he was covering with his own, he had tried to pull away, to withdraw, to escape Himena's greedy body. Had he spilled his seed into her or had he not? For the life of him he could not remember. But he had remembered the date. He would send his regards to Himena but promise her nothing. It would be interesting to see when this child would be born. Even an idiot could count on his fingers.

The weather was turning wet and raw, the November days cold and blustery. Just when it seemed eternal gloom had settled over these northern plains of Spain, a sudden golden glow of winter sunshine would spill molten from the heavens and give promise that spring would again return. Winter robes and furs were extracted from their hiding places, aired and placed on the beds. Ruy declared the window glazing in the great hall and in their chambers a marvel, and determined to have each and every window in the entire *castillo* leaded and paned by next spring. When the rain seemed as though it would never stop, he declared he was escaping to the south of Spain where the sun always shone. Everyone in Bivar seemed to be settling in for the long, dark spell, and they groaned and complained with the cold. All except Mirjana. She was warm and content whenever she was within sound of Ruy's voice.

Together they would venture out into the rain, laughing and skipping through puddles. One day she awakened to find the entire world blanketed in a cover of white. Snow! Something Seville could never boast. And she had discovered it and experienced it here, with Ruy. Giggling like a little girl, she tasted her first snowflake on her tongue. Ruy pelted her with her first snowball and tumbled her to the ground to rub her face in a handful of the white, fluffy substance that turned her cheeks to red roses and made her eyes dance. She had laughed, giggled, fought him off to no avail. And suddenly, he replaced the icy snow with the warmth of his mouth, licking the droplets from her chin and nuzzling her face into the warmth of his neck.

To Mirjana and Ruy, each day was a precious gift, and as they played together, they also pretended together that this idyll would never end.

Gloomy afternoons were spent in the privacy of their chamber before the roaring fireplace, nibbling on sweets or cheeses and drinking strong, hot tea. Oftentimes, Mirjana would lose herself in her books, reading until sleep claimed her eyes. It was one of these afternoons that she lay abed, covered only by a fur robe, sleeping with her cheek pressed into the book she had been reading.

Realizing he had been so long over his correspondence that he had not heard from her in more than an hour, he glanced up to find her this way. She was so beautiful, so irresistible.

Her cheeks were flushed with color and her mouth, petulant and rosy, tempted his own. Unable to resist, he lay down beside her, cradling her to him, feeling her warm and yielding softness turn to him even in sleep. His hands caressed her tenderly, tracing the curve of her neck and the satiny globes of her firm breasts. The coral crests rose, tautening to delicious peaks, and his hands moved slowly lower, touching the pliant curve of her waist to the fuller width of her slender hips. He relished her, adored her, touching the sleekness of her thighs and finding the soft down and warm valley between them.

Mirjana stretched, awakening to his loving caresses, a smile playing on her gentle mouth. Purring with catlike contentment, she arched against his fingers, moving against them, and her satisfaction deepened when his mouth followed the trail his fingers had made, delicately, sensually, finding the soft mound and warm valley.

Seeing her pleasure awakened his. He had long ago discovered that his pleasure lay only in hers. He brought his mouth to hers and she could taste herself there. He filled her world as he filled her body, urgently, tenderly.

He watched her eyes, heavy lidded, drugged with desire. Her lips parted, little pants emitting from them. Her body accepted his, fitting like a hand and a glove. Her rhythm matched his, slowly at first, undulating, meeting his thrusts, taking him inside her, deeper, deeper. He groaned his pleasure, sighed his delight, the sound coming from down in his chest and rippling over her in waves of ever-widening circles of which she was the center.

His name erupted from her lips in a cascading spill of symphony. Together they joined and met upon their well-traveled crystal starship to the back of the moon where the passions of the flesh gave way to the joining of their souls.

The gray days of December were upon them when Don Pietro arrived in Bivar. Mirjana had not seen him since the night he had come to Ilena's to bring her to Ruy. She liked the man and would have enjoyed talking with him, but she sensed an urgency about him when he inquired for his commander, Ruy.

Mirjana sent him upstairs to Ruy's office with Mikel, the old servant. She watched him as he climbed the stairs, still in full armor, dirty and dusty from his travels. Whatever it was he was anxious to tell Ruy. It must be important, Mirjana told herself. A new fear struck her heart. What if fighting had broken out somewhere and Alphonso required Ruy's services? Would she be able to sit through the days and sleep through the long nights worrying about him? What if something should happen to him? She was grateful to escape this sudden turn of thought when Tanige called to her from the kitchens.

Ruy looked up from his accounts when the door opened. Pietro saw the almost instantaneous grief fill his eyes. All the while Ruy poured him a goblet of wine and offered other hospitalities, he felt his eyes upon him, waiting for the news, dreading it, whatever it may be.

Seated once more behind the desk, Ruy gave Pietro his full attention. "What do you say, man? Have you talked with Hassan?"

"*Si*. And the man has agreed to accept his sister, Princesa Mirjana, back into the household. Of course, there will be a price, you understand. I have the terms written here." Pietro withdrew a parchment wrapped in leather from inside his tunic and threw it on the desk in front of Ruy. "The man's a devil, I tell you. He wasn't even interested in Mirjana's welfare, only in the price he could extort from you. It would seem the situation between Yusuf of Granada and Hassan is quite stable. Each has gained from the betrothal of the *princesa* to Yusuf, and they have also gained by the marriage never taking place. Yusuf has already allied himself with the taifa of Cartagena and arranged a marriage for himself there. Now Hassan will gain by accepting her back to Seville."

Ruy's shoulders slumped and a despondent expression marred his face. "So. Hassan will have her back," he said quietly, his voice harsh and thick.

"That is as you wished, is it not?" Pietro asked, a knowing expression in his eyes.

"Yes. I mean, no! Yes, it is what Mirjana wants."

"When will you tell her? Will you be wanting me to bring her back to Seville?" Pietro prompted.

"Yes! No! No, dammit! I need time to think!"

"Think about what? Is this or is it not what you wished?" he asked cagily.

"Yes," Ruy finally said firmly. "It is as I wish. She pines for her own people, for her own land. It is cruel of me to keep her here. It was cruel of me to trick her as I did by attempting to ransom her."

"That certainly fell afoul. Wait until you

see the price Hassan demands to have her back!"

A sick look came over Ruy; he felt as though he'd been kicked by Liberte. "Traveling conditions are poor at this time of year. I will tell her at the first sign of spring."

"Spring, is it?" Pietro queried, drinking his wine, pretending not to see Ruy's naked pain.

"Yes, spring, dammit!" Ruy jumped up from his chair and pounded his fists on the desk. "If I tell her now, she'll devil me until I give her leave to go! I don't want her traveling in this weather. The roads will practically be impassable and you know it!"

"*Si,* this I know." Pietro took in his own filthy and mud-spattered appearance. "You are right, my lord. Send her back to that devil in the spring. It matters little to Hassan, believe my truth. Of course, if you postpone sending the *princesa* now, it is possible Hassan's price will be twice that by spring."

Ruy was enraged by his friend's goading. He swept his hand across the desk, sending papers and accounts flying in all directions. He leaned until his face was only inches away from Pietro's. "Little I care what Hassan's price will be by spring. I would give him my entire holdings if he will have her back!" The words were strong, the tone vicious, but Pietro thought he heard the start of a sob before Ruy swallowed it along with a long gulp of wine.

It was on a gray day with only brief glimpses of the thin, watery sunshine of winter when the missive arrived: Doña Ysabel had fallen ill. So ill, the prioress of the nunnery she was visiting thought her to be near death. Although the señora was critically ill, she had insisted upon being returned to Bivar; if she was to die, it would be among her own people with her sons at her side and her confessor administering the Last Rites.

When Ruy received the letter, he went to Mirjana immediately, telling her of his mother's condition. His voice had been somber, his broad shoulders carrying the weight of his misery. He was not an unloving son — he knew his duties to his mother — and Mirjana could see the guilt he bore that he had been the one who had sent Doña Ysabel away, breaking her heart by separating her from her darling Teodoro.

The letter from the prioress arrived only hours before Doña Ysabel herself. Horsemen escorted the wagon bearing her prone form. A habited nun sat beside her, tending to her, attempting to cushion the benefactress from the jolts and jars the rutted roads afforded.

When the procession arrived at the *castillo*, a light, freezing rain was falling. Mirjana had seen to having Doña Ysabel's chamber in readiness and had commissioned a woman from the village who was known to be wise in the ways of tending the sick and infirm. She instinctively knew that the señora would only be upset and demeaned if she was left to the ministrations of Mirjana, whom she considered to be her enemy.

Ruy went out into the courtyard to his mother, anxiety and remorse making strange new hollows in his face. Nothing could have prepared him for what he saw. Doña Ysabel, a hearty woman of incredible strength and determination, had been reduced to a frail, old woman with sorrow in her eyes. The skin was pale, deathly; streaks of white glossed through the black hair. Mirjana hung in the background, careful to keep from sight. She, too, was horrified to see what had become of Ruy's mother.

It was Ruy who pushed away the interceding hands and lifted his mother into his own arms, carrying her through the great hall to the stone staircase, bringing her up to her room. Mirjana saw the woman's hand feebly reach up to pat Ruy's cheek, saw the whiteness of the skin, the blue veins on the back of the hand, the fingers thin and bony. It was the hand of an old woman, fragile, useless.

At the top of the stairs, Doña Ysabel opened

her eyes, looking down over Ruy's shoulder to see Mirjana at the bottom of the stairs, wringing her hands with anxiety. "Wait," she murmured, halting Ruy in his steps. Pointing a cronelike finger down at Mirjana, she beckoned her. "You." Her lips formed the word almost soundlessly. "I want you to take care of me. The others will let me die; *you* will make me live. You hate me too much to give me the solace of death." The effort left Doña Ysabel panting from exertion and her head dropped back onto Ruy's shoulder. He felt her cheek against his own, the skin dry and thin like an old parchment. Pity for the woman and self-contempt to have brought her to this struck opposing chords. He swung around, his mother still in his arms, and looked to Mirjana with a plea in his eyes.

Silently, Mirjana started up the stairs behind him. She would tend to the señora and save her, if she could, from the hands of death. This she must do for Ruy. Doña Ysabel had been wrong again. Mirjana would not try to save the woman because she hated her too much to give her the peace death would bring. Mirjana loved Ruy too much to burden him with the misplaced guilt of his mother. It would be for Ruy.

Mirjana lived within the sound of Doña Ysabel's enfeebled voice for the next two days.

Tending her, silently encouraging her to sip the hearty broth Tanige prepared, cooling her fevered brow and holding her head when the broth or anything else that passed the señora's lips violently erupted from her stomach. When the señora slept, Ruy would come and take Mirjana to their chamber, insisting she rest herself, watching over her to be certain no one disturbed her unnecessarily.

On the third day Ruy and Mirjana stood outside the señora's chamber, each of them dreading the coming hour. Teodoro wanted to see his mother, and while they understood, they would have preferred to postpone it a little longer. Under Mirjana's sympathies, Teddy had been allowed to peek into the darkened room to see his mother sleeping, to assure him she still lived. Today, they knew how shocked Teodoro would be when the sudden change in his mother's appearance became evident to him. Ruy had made the decision. Teddy was her son and he had the right to see her before she died.

Doña Ysabel herself kept asking to see her youngest son. Today she had begged, her eyes watery and unseeing, her lips trembling with her plea.

It was cruel and inhuman to keep a son from his mother at such a time, and Mirjana was grateful for Ruy's decision.

When Teddy arrived, Ruy put his arm around the boy's shoulders in a protective gesture of brotherly love. "Five minutes, Teddy, no more. I have already told you Madre is very ill and very weak. Everything possible is being done for her, and we are all hopeful she will recover soon. This is the reason you must not tire her, must not excite her. *Comprendes tu?*" The boy nodded, his eyes deep and fearful, his attitude somber and dreading. Ruy urged him forward into the room with a gentle push. Mirjana met Ruy's glance and she tried to smile reassuringly, tried to tell him all would be well. They both knew the boy would be shattered.

"Madre," Teddy gasped as he leaned over the bed, feeling the heat radiating from his mother. "Madre, Madre," he cried softly over and over again. He touched his mother's hand, staring down at her, unbelieving this change from the strong, supportive woman in his life to this enfeebled stranger.

"*Mi hijo,* my son," Doña Ysabel breathed weakly. "*Mi querido,* Teodoro." Her hand sought to touch him and Teddy leaned his face into the palm of his mother's hand. The words seemed to rattle from deep inside the señora's chest, leaving her gasping with the effort. Her eyes drank in the sight of her beloved son, touching him with maternal love, committing him to memory as though she thought she would never see him again. Doña Ysabel closed her eyes wearily, her hand falling back onto the bed.

Teddy raised his glance to stare at Mirjana, his eyes so much like Ruy's, asking silent questions. Then, touching his mother's hand, he bent to kiss it, his slim shoulders straightening almost imperceptibly as he turned away, dry-eyed. He looked neither at Ruy nor Mirjana as he left the room.

Ruy seemed helpless to reassure his younger brother, and he followed the boy's stooped shoulders to the top of the stairs with his eyes. "Teodoro, where are you going?"

Without turning, Teddy answered, "I — I thought I might take my pony out for exercise." He was making a great effort to choke back his tears.

"Ride her carefully, the ground is slick," Ruy cautioned, his voice soft with sympathy.

Like Teddy's eyes, Ruy's questioned Mirjana's. She shook her head to tell him there was no noticeable change in his mother's condition. Understanding, he reached out to brush a stray lock of red-gold hair from her perspiring brow. "Why don't you have Tanige bring you something to eat. I will sit and watch over my mother."

"Tanige will bring me something later. I

would prefer to stay here. You must have things that need your attention."

Apparently, Ruy could think of nothing except his mother's condition and his brother's grief, for he looked at her blankly, helplessly.

"Perhaps you should be with Teodoro. He might need you. And you look as though you could use a respite from haunting the sick room," she said gently.

He appeared to debate the wisdom of leaving his mother, but he did need to be away from the *castillo,* away from the stench of sickness. Touching Mirjana's cheek with gratitude, he turned and followed behind Teddy to the stable yard. A ride in the cold air would clear his head, and if he hurried, he might catch Teddy and they could ride together.

Ruy saddled Liberte himself. He had called to Teddy as he rode the chestnut filly out of the yard to wait for him, but apparently the boy had not heard. Atop Liberte's broad back he headed out after the boy, frigid air rushing through his hair and stinging his cheeks. Through the stable yard and out the gates of the *castillo* he rode, over the wide, trenched moat which was frozen over with thick blue ice. He caught sight of Teddy on the chestnut pony, skirting the main road through the village onto the pastures and the woods beyond. Ruy dug his heels hard into Liberte's flanks, prodding the beast to a faster pace. Teddy was riding the young chestnut too fast, dangerously fast, on the treacherous, slick ground. He shouted for the boy to slow, to stop, to wait, but Teddy pounded forward. A lump was growing in the pit of Ruy's stomach as he realized the boy was heading into the ancient remains of the quarry from which the stones for the *castillo* had been cut. In summer underground springs fed the place, putting it almost completely under water. But now, at this time of year, it was a dangerous bog of soft ground, shallow holes and boulders. Again and again he shouted, fearing for both the boy and the inexperienced pony.

Sudden fear trapped Ruy in its grip. Had he made a wise choice in allowing the boy to see the señora so close to death? He had been so close to her for so many years. No, he told himself, it would have been inhuman to keep him from their mother, and should she die, he would never forgive himself. Death was something Teddy had never had to deal with; death had never touched him. Their father had never really existed for Teddy, and he was too young to know his loss.

Ruy saw the outcropping boulders ahead of him. If Teddy was blinded by his tears, he might not see them. "Teddy!" he thundered, the name tearing from his throat, ripping from his innards. The pony tried to halt the wild stampede against the pummeling and proddings of her young rider. Rear hooves dug deeply into the spongy ground, her forelegs rose, pawing the air, equine shrieks and snorts of terror sounding across the forbidding terrain, while Teddy clung fiercely to the saddle. It took an eternity, yet was quicker than a flash. Ruy would live with the nightmare vision the rest of his life. Again and again, the pony reared, pawing the air with her front quarter, toppling Teddy into a more precarious hold on the saddle. In a last, terrified moment, the boy was flung from her back, falling against the outcropping, lying there so still, his head at an awkward angle.

It was an age of saints that passed before Ruy could hold the boy in his arms. Countless centuries passed, it seemed, before he could scramble over the rock-strewn field to run to his brother. Harsh, guttural sounds forced their way between his compressed lips. Again and again he heard the bone-cracking sound that ended Teddy's too short life.

Ruy's movements were tender as he took the boy into his arms, carrying him as he picked his way over the uneven field. Liberte followed behind him, the destrier's black head hanging as though in sympathy with his master's grief. As Ruy looked down at his grim burden, he realized he had barely known his brother and he would bury him still not knowing him. The boy had died before he had even begun to taste life. Ruy knew a choking sensation in his throat that would not clear. Grief and guilt could not be coughed away.

Back to the *castillo* he walked, his burden firm in his arms, the small dark head nestled peacefully against his chest. Where to go, what to do? To Mirjana. Always Mirjana.

He stood framed in the doorway waiting for her to see him. Her eyes registered everything with one glance. "Poor Ruy," was all she said.

Teddy was safely in Tanige's hands when Mirjana took Ruy back to their chamber. "He was my brother and I barely knew him," he muttered. "Mirjana, I barely knew him! I only know he loved our mother and I took him from her!" The words were anguished but they were not an appeal for sympathy.

"The years put distance between you and your brother. He was a babe and you already a man." She was stirring something into a goblet of water. "Here, drink this."

Ruy shook his head. "No, I don't want to sleep. I want to sit here and think of my sins."

"Trust me. This will not bring sleep if you do not want it. Lean back, *querido,*" she soothed, putting pillows behind his head and letting her fingers stray to the hair that fell over his brow. "I must leave you now, you understand." He nodded, his brow furrowed with grief. She knew he needed to be alone, to work this through for himself. He would know when he needed her again.

Tanige was bustling down the corridor to meet Mirjana. "It's that priest!" she whispered. "He's heard of Teddy's death and he's gone into Doña Ysabel."

Mirjana stiffened. "Who? Padre Tomas?" she asked hopefully, praying it wasn't the crass, unsympathetic Padre Juano. The look that crossed Tanige's face told her praying was useless. Padre Juano was already with the señora.

"Tanige, he would not . . . could not tell her about —"

"The padre seems confident in the power of prayer," Tanige grimaced.

Mirjana rushed through the corridors, hoping to interrupt the padre before he would shock the señora with the news that could bring her death. She burst into Doña Ysabel's room to find the padre on his knees at the bedside, his head bent in prayer, his body shielding Doña Ysabel's inert form from her eyes. She could hear the dull drone of the prayers he was offering for the saving of Teddy's soul, but there was no response from the bed.

Hastily, Mirjana walked across the room to the far side of the bed. Her mouth opened in alarm when she noticed the woman's awkward position and foam dribbling down her chin. Mirjana's glance flew to the señora's face — one eye was open in wide, staring horror while the other was squeezed shut, the mouth pulled downward into an ugly grimace.

"She goes to her holy Father," Padre Juano murmured.

"Not yet!" Mirjana retorted, already moving Doña Ysabel's arms and legs into a more natural position and raising her up onto pillows to make breathing easier.

"There is no hope," the young priest offered, reaching out to stay Mirjana's hand from wiping the señora's mouth with a fresh square of linen. "I have seen this many times among the aged. When God calls, there is no refusing Him!"

"*I* refuse him!" Mirjana hissed. "*I* will not give her up!"

Clearly, the padre was shocked. He narrowed his eyes in scorn, hatred spewing out of them. "You will not touch her, adulteress! Heathen! Woman of a pagan god!"

Mirjana shrank back from the venom in his voice, from the hatred in his eyes. He advanced on her, his arm raised to strike her down. She saw that Doña Ysabel's eyes followed her, believed she could read the resignation in them. Shoving the young priest away from her, Mirjana ran to the bedside, leaning over the woman, her face only inches away. "I will not let you die! You still have one son living and he carries a terrible burden. You must get well! You must help him carry that burden!"

"She cannot hear you. Soon her heart will give out and that will be the end." The young priest chortled, certain that he would be proved right.

"Señora!" Mirjana cried frantically. "You must think of Ruy. You are his mother and he needs you!" She watched, hardly daring to breathe. Slowly, the señora's eyelids closed and then opened again, giving her answer.

Like fury, Mirjana turned on the priest. "Now, get out! Get out and do not return until the señora herself can ask for you! Out!"

Teddy's burial was a sad affair. The entire village turned out for the Mass and ceremony. They would miss the little boy who raced through the fields on his pony, shouting cheerful greetings to one and all, and who would always stop to ask questions about how this was done or how that was made. Many tears were shed for the lost life of one so young, and mothers placed tender hands on their children knowing how fortunate they were to have them with them.

Mirjana refused to cry. Tears were for the living. Ruy stood at the service, his expression sorrowful and somber. If tears were to be shed, she would shed them for Ruy.

That night, while all the world slept, Mirjana held Ruy in her arms as they lay together in their bed. Tonight he needed her, could not be without her. In her arms the demons were kept at bay and he could hide himself from his self-condemned guilt. He had taken her quickly, roughly, as though proving to himself that life and its pleasures could still exist for him. And when he had lain against her, his mouth buried in the hollow of her throat, she felt such a rush of tenderness for him that it left her shaken. He had whispered he was sorry, asked for forgiveness for this rough use of her.

"Hush," she told him soothingly, gently, turning him onto his back and following with her body. She tasted the salt of a tear on his lips and realized it was her own. She enfolded him in her embrace, caressing him, loving him, showing him that goodness and love still existed in a world seemed to have gone insane.

She stroked warmth back into his limbs

gone cold, kissing, nibbling tenderly, oh so tenderly, demanding nothing, giving everything. She waited for him to reawaken to her touch and took him into her, bathing him with her gentleness and caring. This time there were no demons to hide from, no self-recriminations and guilt to hurry him and find him undeserving of this proof that he still lived, breathed, could couple. Slowly, ever so slowly, he took command, covering her with his body, finding the center of her and inhabiting it with himself. Her body rippled and sang around him, welcoming him, pulsing with his. She stroked his thick hair, searched for his mouth with her own, tasting the salt of tears that this time were for the joy of life and not the pain of death.

CHAPTER 15

Padre Juano would not have believed it, but Doña Ysabel had no intention of dying. She lay in her chamber which overlooked the woods beyond the *castillo,* paralyzed on her left side, unable to speak and furious about it. It was intolerable that she could not speak when her mind was so clear. And none but Mirjana seemed to understand this. The señora's bright little eyes glittered with anger and frustration as the servants fussed over her and crept into her chamber reverently, as though she were already dead. Her chagrin was absolute and rendered her determined to become well.

The most difficult and certainly most humiliating feature of her infirmity was to subject herself to Mirjana's hands. When Ruy had carried her up to this room when she had first arrived at the *castillo,* Doña Ysabel had insisted Mirjana take charge of her, truly believing that this woman would do all in her power to save the señora from death. It wasn't as she had accused that Mirjana hated her too much to allow the señora the peace of death. It was, rather, that she knew the *princesa* loved Ruy, and in loving him, she would try to protect him from the loss of his mother, to save him from the guilt of having sent her from the *castillo*.

If Doña Ysabel's frog features could have smiled, she would have. She had been proven right. Mirjana was most attentive, seeing to her every need and more, fighting against the illness when the señora herself was too exhausted to fight any longer. Each day Mirjana would come to attend her, ministering unto her, patiently, carefully, almost lovingly. Yet, there was a core of strength in the woman that Doña Ysabel believed was curiously similar to her own. A kind of blind determination that would broach no interference and would accept no refusal. As the days wore on, it was to Mirjana that Doña Ysabel turned for comfort, strength, and assurance. When it would seem the woman was half mad with assisting and insisting upon exercising the useless limbs and regaining the use of speech, it was then that progress would be noted.

Long, bone-wearying days passed into weeks. Mirjana worked tirelessly, never resigning, as she tended her patient. She consulted her medical texts time and again, going to the señora with her newfound methods, prompting Doña Ysabel's conviction that she could become well, goading her into cooperating.

Shortly before the end of the Christian year, the days became bitter and cold. Huge fires were built to chase the damp. Concerned with her patient's comfort, Mirjana ordered hot bricks to be wrapped in soft flannel and placed in Doña Ysabel's bed. Small braziers were kept burning to ward off drafts and sudden chills.

As the days crept along, there seemed to be a change in the mood of the *castillo* and in the village of Bivar. There seemed to be a sense of excitement, and people smiled more warmly than before. Servants decorated the great hall with evergreen boughs and candles. According to Tanige, preparations were underway in the kitchens for the feast of Christmas. It was Mirjana's fervent wish that Doña Ysabel might somehow attend. Because of Teodoro's death the celebration would be subdued compared to other years, she was told, but the *castillo* would nevertheless celebrate the birth of Christ.

The señora was still in mourning, and often Mirjana would come into her room and find her cheeks tear stained. She was thinking of Teddy, Mirjana knew, and would sit near her just holding her hand and reminiscing about the boy. She told her of Teodoro's new friend from the village, Antony, and how Ruy said he and Pietro had become friends at a similar age. Ilena and Gormaz's baby, Manuel, had been a particular favorite of young Teddy's. She believed Doña Ysabel was laughing when she recounted how the boy had been so frightened to hold the infant, and how just when he'd gained confidence and was so proud of it, Manuel rewarded him by leaving a dark, wet patch on the knee of his chausses.

Ruy's mother seemed to take comfort in hearing about Teddy, and Mirjana understood. Not to talk of him would seem almost as though the boy had never existed, and Doña Ysabel would have been left adrift in a sea of lonely grief. To know that grief was shared by others who had loved the boy was to make it easier to bear.

Mirjana did not speak of the festivities being planned because she did not want to rush the señora into something she was not ready to meet. However, the señora was awake for longer periods of time, and her facial muscles had relaxed somewhat. She had regained the use of her forearm and three fingers on her hand. While slight, it proved the señora was indeed on the mend, and while she might never regain full use of her faculties, she was not going to die like a vegetable left too long on the vine. Her vocabulary had increased to several words spoken clearly, while others were still muddled, and most frustrating of all, often the correct word she was seeking just would not come to her.

"Princess, have you given any thought to your Christmas gifts?" Tanige asked one afternoon as she was bringing fresh laundry into the chamber Mirjana shared with Ruy. "It is custom, signifying the gifts of the three kings brought to the Christ child." Although children of Islam, Tanige and Mirjana recognized Christ as being a prophet of God just as Mohammed was a prophet of Allah. "I thought you would like to give something to Don Ruy and something to Doña Ysabel. I wonder what Luis will give me," Tanige rushed on. "I never received a gift from a man!"

"Especially a man like Luis?" Mirjana teased. The change in Tanige was remarkable and she wondered what had become of that surly-tongued, too-skinny girl whose features had always been pinched into a scowl. She certainly had bloomed, and this inner glow she carried with her had brought her very close to a beauty all her own. Satisfied at seeing Tanige blush prettily, Mirjana asked curiously, "What manner of gifts do they exchange? Do you know?"

"Oranges from the Holy Land and the south of Spain. You remember the fruits we so took for granted in Seville? Here, so far to the north, they are a luxury. Cook tells me Don Ruy and Doña Ysabel always give oranges and nuts and a gold coin to each member of the *castillo* staff. They seem to think this is more than generous. I am making a shirt for Luis," Tanige added proudly.

"A shirt to be married in, eh Tanige?" Mirjana teased but knew a sense of loss at her own words. It would be wonderful for Tanige and she would gladly give her her freedom. But she would miss her and her acid tongue terribly.

The days moved quickly as the feast of Christmas approached. Before Mirjana knew it, Christmas Eve was upon them. Doña Ysabel asked for her rosary to pray with Padre Tomas. At her own insistence, Padre Juano had been asked to stay in the village, away from the *castillo*. The señora continued to gain strength and Mirjana and Ruy were both pleased.

Aromas from the kitchen filled the *castillo*. Breads and cakes, liberally spiced with precious cinnamon and cloves from Mirjana's caravan, tempted the tongue and pleased the nostril. Roast lamb and freshly killed chickens were done to a golden brown, and complemented the mint jelly and sweet, glazed oranges. Because the *castillo* was still in mourning for Teddy, festivities were kept to a minimum, but friends were invited to call — Pietro and Padre Tomas, Luis and Tanige, Gormaz and Ilena, and of course, the wide-eyed Manuel who screeched with delight at the wondrous sight of hundreds of candles and his first taste of orange.

Holding Manuel on her lap, Mirjana nuzzled him behind the ear, relishing the sweet baby fragrance of him. A thought occurred to her as she remembered Doña Ysabel upstairs alone in her chamber. She signaled for Ilena to follow her and carried Manuel up the long, stone staircase to the señora's room. Just outside the door she bit her lip, wondering if she was doing the woman kindly. Teddy's death had been less than two months before. Quickly, she rapped on the door, opening it and peeking in.

"Doña Ysabel . . . are you sleeping?" Cautiously, she stepped into the room, finding the señora propped up on her pillows, rosary in hand. "I've brought someone to visit with you."

Doña Ysabel's heart was on her face as she noticed the baby. Her lips quivered and sadness filled her eyes. Immediately, Mirjana regretted her impulse until the señora stretched out her arms, beckoning.

Mirjana placed the sleepy Manuel in Doña Ysabel's arms, standing close should she tire. Looking down at Manuel, a tear dropped from her eye, and Doña Ysabel clasped the baby close to her, lowering her eyelids, remembering perhaps the day when little Teddy had been brought to her this way.

Tears of grief and shuddering sobs quickly abated into long sighs of acceptance. Manuel had released the imprisoned emotions the señora had been unable to express. She fondled the babe's cheeks, kissing the top of his curly head and making cooing sounds. Manuel looked up at her with round, dark eyes, pursing his tiny mouth into a round "O" and then yawning. Slowly, his eyes closed, feeling completely safe and adored in these strange arms.

Doña Ysabel looked up at Mirjana with gratitude. "You always think of me. Always know what I need." The words were simple but the emotions behind them were so deep. The look, the words, were both expressions of a kind of love the señora was as yet unable to express. And there was a promise there that some day soon, she would be able to tell this peaceful woman whom her son had brought to the *castillo* that she loved her and was grateful to her and knew herself to be undeserving of this dedication Mirjana so willingly gave.

* * *

It was well past the witching hour when Ruy and Mirjana bade their guests farewell and climbed the stairs to their chamber. A soft, light snow had begun to fall and the earth seemed hushed and solemn. After making certain that Doña Ysabel slept peacefully, Ruy smiled down at Mirjana and lightly touched her hand.

In their chamber the fire in the hearth glowed cheerily, throwing golden light into the room. Mirjana prepared for bed, slipping into one of her gossamer sheer nightdresses, and sat on the edge of the bed brushing her thick, light titian hair into a silky sheen. It was then Ruy handed her a small parcel. "I wanted to give you something that would have some meaning. Something that holds special meaning for me . . ." he stammered. "I know you are not of my faith and . . ." The words were awkward, terribly difficult for him, and Mirjana silenced his shyness with a kiss.

"Hush," she told him. Carefully, she unwrapped the tiny parcel and stared down at the shiny object in her hand. She knew immediately what it was and what it meant for Ruy to part with it. Teddy's gold cross. Tears blurred her eyes. "Truly, you could not have chosen better. I will treasure it always. Although, I fear my gift to you is less than grand. Selfish, even." She reached beneath the pillow and withdrew a tiny carved box, and watched with anxious eyes as he opened the gift.

Ruy seemed astonished. His breath seemed to rush from his chest. "Who did this?" he whispered.

"My father had it commissioned when I was sixteen. I had no idea what to give you."

Ruy held the disc-shaped medallion of gold which was minted in Mirjana's likeness. He had never seen anything more beautiful. Every line, every nuance of her face was etched into the gleaming surface.

"My father, Mútadid, had these commissioned for each of his children. One for the child and one for himself. I prayed you would like it."

"Like it, Mirjana, it is exquisite. Just as you are." His voice was hushed, barely audible.

Later, in bed beside him, Mirjana nestled against his warmth and murmured softly, "This is all I will ever want."

They loved one another with tender care, deliberately prolonging these precious moments and giving themselves over to the glorious waves of pleasure they created. They touched and knew each turn and curve of each other's bodies, knew where the pleasure centers were to be found, and yet they explored and tasted each one as though for the first time. The familiarity between them increased rather than diminished their delight and hunger for each other. Their passions were deep and fiery, and their tenderness was created out of beauty and caring. In the half light of the room they touched, kissed, and caressed, watching the responses of the other. Together they boarded their own crystal starship and rode the heavens beneath the silvery sails. Their room was a launching place where they began their journey in each other's arms before flying off to those elating heights where only lovers are welcomed.

Ruy lay awake long after Mirjana nestled herself to sleep in the crook of his arm. In those long hours before the winter dawn Ruy looked down into his clenched hand. Slowly, he opened his fingers and saw the medallion she had given him. Mirjana slept peacefully, unaware of the tautening of his muscles.

He felt his teeth clench and an alien sensation in the pit of his belly, a feeling of ill boding.

A primal savageness to protect swept through him as, with a pantherlike movement, he turned and brought Mirjana to rest against the full length of his body, waking her. Startled, she gasped, "What is it? What's happened?"

"It is nothing. A foolish dream. Go to sleep, little one," he said huskily, straining to keep the alarm from his voice.

Making little kitten noises, Mirjana settled again into sleep even as Ruy watched her. His thoughts throbbed through his head, his jaw ached from clenching his teeth. You are mine, Mirjana, and none in this world could love you as I do. These were the words he could never speak aloud, could not dare to utter. Even as he held her in his arms he had no illusions of where she would rather be if given the choice. Home, among her own, in Seville. He had taken her by default and had come to love her. She began as his captive, his prisoner, and he had become hers instead. Even while he made love to her, felt her receive and give in return, he knew she was not truly his. Soon now, he would tell her she was free to go back to her home, no longer to be abandoned by her family, no longer unwanted and displaced. How he would part with her he did not know. But he would have these cold winter months before the burst of spring to ready himself. Suppressing an aching urge to awaken her, to take her again, to will her to feel his love for her, Ruy forced his eyes shut to tempt sleep.

The next morning when Mirjana straightened the bed covers and the fur throws, she was stunned to find the medallion beneath Ruy's pillow. She smiled as she put the gold cross beneath her own pillow, patting it into place. The smile stayed in her heart for the remainder of the day. To deny she was happy would be to deny her next breath. She wanted more, much more, she knew. Paradise would be complete if only she could tell him how she loved him. If only she could hope one day he could love her in return. So often, while lying in his arms, feeling him come to the center of her, invading her and possessing her with himself, she had had to bite back the words that threatened to spill from her lips. She would not torment herself with these thoughts. For now, they were together, and that was all that mattered.

Winter gave itself over to spring. A new, warmer sun shone on the land and the rains seemed to nourish the earth rather than to sap it. Planting was under way and new people were passing through Bivar, urged by the promise of kinder weather to make the journey from their homes to do business in this new and burgeoning town. It was a time for growth, both for the earth and for Mirjana.

On those first warm days at the beginning of May, Doña Ysabel was able to be brought down to the garden. She would sit for hours praying her rosary or visiting with new friends from the village. She damned those long and lonely years when propriety prevented her from seeking companionship. Her pride in her station and breeding had prevented her from associating with "peasants." Now, those same women proved to be her greatest friends, and Doña Ysabel realized that being a woman brought its own kind of sisterhood that could not be barred by rank and pride.

When she prayed, Doña Ysabel always included Mirjana in her prayers. Padre Juano would have said it highly unlikely that the Heavenly Father would bless the heathen *princesa,* but Doña Ysabel knew differently. Hadn't Mirjana's own prayers been answered to save the señora's life and make her well? Doña Ysabel quickly disregarded Padre Juano, now thinking him a vicious zealot. How could she have approved of the young priest for her own confessor? Worse, how could she have betrayed both Ruy and Mirjana by arranging that farce of a marriage with Himena? Although Ruy never mentioned it, she knew he was aware of what she had done. For Ruy, it had been bad enough to betray her own son, but what she had done to Mirjana would never be forgiven, most of all by herself. If there was ever a love so pure and deep as Mirjana's for Ruy, Doña Ysabel could not believe it. The *princesa*'s caring and tenderness for Ruy and for everyone connected with him were given unselfishly and without reservation.

No flesh-and-blood daughter could have done more for the señora than Mirjana. She knew how ill she had been and how Mirjana had fought to bring her back from the grip of death. For her reprieve here on earth she had to make amends for her wretched treatment of the *princesa*. The señora hurried with her prayers so she would be ready when Mirjana brought Ilena and the babe, Manuel, to see her. For a brief time she would hold the babe who was growing stronger and bigger every day and remember her own boys when they were babes. There were still shadows of grief in her heart for Teddy; there always would be. No mother could lose a child and not grieve. But she knew that life must go on and with Mirjana's help she seemed to be able to find some joy in each day.

Mirjana went down to the stable yard to wait for Gormaz to bring Ilena and Manuel in the cart. How warm and wonderful the sun felt after the brutal winter. Life was good. Tanige was in love and anticipating marriage. Doña Ysabel was recovering more rapidly than she ever dared hope. And a niggling voice prompted, as Mirjana smiled to herself, I think there is a new life growing within me. A child. Ruy's child. So far it was only a suspicion, a hope that she dare not mention. Soon, soon she would know.

Looking up at the position of the sun, she realized she was early. Gormaz could not possibly bring Ilena and the babe so soon after midday. Sighing with disappointment, she walked to the back side of the stables, carefully lifting the hem of her skirt to keep it from the dust. It would be cooler back here, out of the sun. Settling herself on a long, rough bench placed against the cool, stone wall of the stable, she noticed the wooden shutters had been opened to admit the spring breezes. Voices were sounding from inside the structure and she heard her name mentioned.

"Have you told the *princesa?*" Pietro asked.

"What kind of fool question is that?" Ruy demanded. "You saw how she was when she learned I had married Himena!"

"It is an honest question. If you have not told her, I suppose I should have asked if you plan to tell her?"

"There's no need," came the gruff reply.

"You can hardly keep it a secret, Ruy. It is not every day that El Cid, Compeador, becomes a father. Pity the child was a girl, perhaps a son would give you reason for pride." Pietro's voice was cutting, almost malicious, but Mirjana was not aware of the sarcasm he spewed. She only heard that

Himena had given birth — to Ruy's child!

Stumbling, Mirjana retraced her steps, wanting to be as far away from Ruy as possible. She didn't think it possible to be so shattered. Her world was crumbling about her. Whatever Ruy had replaced had been lost to her. Ruy and Himena had a child. Hardly aware of herself, she covered her stomach protectively. There were no tears. None would come. She was dead. As dead as Teddy.

Unknown to Ruy and Pietro that Mirjana had overheard, they continued their conversation in the dim of the stable while Ruy curried Liberte.

"A son would certainly have changed these circumstances," Ruy sneered, his mouth turning down into an ugly line. "If the child had been a son, I would have had to expose Himena for the adulteress she is. Do not think for one moment this child is mine. I may be a fool, my friend, but I can count as well as any man. I have already inquired as to this child's birth date, and even one as ignorant as myself knows no woman is pregnant for eleven months. Bah! Since Himena has given birth to a daughter it makes little difference to me that the child carry the name Diaz. If she lives to marry, I will make a proper dowry for her and be done with it. If it were a son, he would be my heir and that I would never allow."

Pietro blinked. "You will allow yourself to be cuckolded?"

"What choice have I? You forget, Himena is godchild to Alphonso. To bring scandal upon her is to dishonor the royal family. My relationship with the king is strained as it is, and to bring a mark against his house would bode ill not only for me but for all of Bivar and everyone I love. No, it is better to leave it this way. And I tell you again, Pietro, that child is none of mine!"

"And you are not going to tell Mirjana; you will let her discover for herself there is a child who is not yours yet was born of your marriage nonetheless?"

Ruy clapped the curry brush onto Liberte's hide with such force, the animal balked. "Mirjana will never know!" Ruy exploded. "You forget, spring is upon us and Hassan has agreed to take her back. The weather warms and promises to hold. She'll soon be on her way back to Seville."

"I see. And is the *princesa* aware of this? Have you told her Hassan will have her back?" A speculative look came into Pietro's eyes.

"Soon, I will tell her. Stop plaguing me, you bastard! Leave me to my own life and stay out of it!"

Pietro smiled as he left the stable. He wondered if Ruy was aware of how deeply he loved Mirjana, and Pietro had a sack of dinars that said Ruy would never permit Mirjana to leave.

In the cool dim of the stable, Ruy pressed his brow against Liberte's arching neck. It had never left his mind that he owed it to Mirjana to tell her Hassan would welcome her back to Seville. He had thought of it constantly and his head ached from the weight of it. Plans were being made for a birthday celebration for him, and he must tell her before then. He could not allow her to make another kind and loving gesture while she still thought herself homeless and at Ruy's mercy. She shared his bed, made his house a home, and tenderly cared for him and his own. And she thought herself his prisoner when, in truth, everyone who felt her touch of kindness became her captive — and none more than himself.

She sat propped in bed, watching Tía Consuela tend her newborn daughter. It was a pretty child, or so everyone told her, but she had little affection for it. The pregnancy had been so long, eternal, bloating her almost from the beginning of it, making her sick each and every day. She had been so clumsy, she who had always been so slim and wraithlike. In the beginning when Himena had first discovered she was with child she had panicked, not knowing what to do. She knew, without a doubt, this was not a child of Don Rodrigo Ruy Diaz, but a product of Don Diego's hastily planted seed. Since the night of her wedding she had had two monthly fluxes and was probably into a third when the bleeding ceased, never to come again till now, after the birth of the babe.

While she had cursed her sudden, huge burgeoning, it had been a blessing all the same. Tía Consuela had looked at her swelling midriff and counted on her fingers, deciding that Himena was correctly blossoming for her sixth month of pregnancy. In truth, it had only been the fourth month. No, this was not a child of Ruy, but to declare this fact would be to ostracize herself from society. When the nine months had passed since the wedding and she was into her seventh month, Himena had tried everything she knew to produce labor. If she had been warned to stay off her feet, she practiced running up and down the stairs when no one was looking. When she had been told not to lift anything larger than a loaf of bread, she spent long hours in her chamber straining to lift the foot of her huge, wooden bed. And still the brat had not come! Treacherous fate!

Still, no one had approached her with questions. For that, at least, she was thankful. It was well-known that she had not shared a bed with her husband since the beginning of June the year before, and a pregnancy to last into the eleventh month was unheard of, or so she was told. However, it was not up to her family to pronounce a verdict. No one could condemn her before Ruy, and so far, she had heard nothing. She knew he was told of the birth; Tío Bernardo had written the letter himself.

Now, all she could do was wait. Perhaps Ruy Diaz, El Cid, Compeador, was not quite as smart as he looked. Or perhaps he was forgetful of dates. Or perhaps, by writing the letter immediately, he had assumed the child was older than she was, since it was the custom not to announce a birth until it was fairly certain the child was sound and would live. There had been time enough for Ruy to make his intentions known. But she had heard nothing aside from a vague missive from him, saying he wished both she and *her* child well. Bah! It was as formal and indifferent as anything she might receive from a distant relative.

Tía Consuela coddled the baby, offering the infant a cossette of honeycomb wrapped in clean linen. The wet nurse had not arrived for the feeding and the babe was fretful. Himena's milk, if she had ever had any, had long since dried.

An anxious unsettling was descending upon her. Even should Ruy believe this child to be his, a daughter was no accomplishment. If she had only had a son, an heir. That would have put him in her debt, at least. It would have assured her of his continued support, and perhaps, to have his son close to him, he would have brought both of them to the *castillo* on the outlands in the peasant town of Bivar. She would not have liked living away from the city, away from the pleasantries of society, but sleeping each night with her husband would be ample compensation.

Another thought had been plaguing her, one more dire and dangerous. Mayhaps it was a blessing the child was a girl. If the babe had been a son, Ruy might be more rigorous in determining whether or not the child was his. A son would inherit the lands in Bivar and Ruy's title, not something a man took lightly. It was just possible that Ruy suspected this was not his product, but cared to spare himself and his family the scandal of declaring the child a bastard and exposing his wife's adultery. Yes, it was just as well the child was a girl, Himena decided, knowing the power of the man with whom she trifled.

Yet, it was his own fault! Even now, just thinking about him, she could feel the heat in her blood rise. She had never known a man like him, and now, considering her adventures and experience, was doubting she ever would. Was she then destined to go from man to man as she had immediately following her disastrous wedding, hoping to find one who could make her feel what Ruy had?

The babe screamed in hunger, the sound irritating Himena. In a sense she commiserated with the child. She was learning what it was to be denied something that she hungered for. With the babe it was the breast; with Himena it was Ruy.

Mirjana had gone about her duties, talking, smiling, pretending her heart had not broken. Only Doña Ysabel was aware of this change in her, in the sudden shadows in her soft, gray eyes, in the slight lowering of her chin. It was growing late and Doña Ysabel listened to Mirjana read from her book of poems. Tonight, it was several quatrains from Omar Khayyám. It was from the *Rubaiyát* and the señora loved to hear Mirjana read it. But tonight, there was a strange tremor in her voice and a heavy sadness seemed to overlay the reading.

There was the Door to which I found
  no Key;
There was the Veil through which I might
  not see:

Some little talk awhile of ME and
THEE
There was — and then no more of
THEE and ME.

Yet Ah, that Spring should vanish with
the Rose!
That Youth's sweet-scented manuscript
should close!
The Nightingale that in the branches
sang,
Ah whence, and whither frown again,
who knows!

"What troubles you child?" Doña Ysabel asked quietly, measuring Mirjana with her eyes, waiting for her answer, seeing her tremble instead. "Why do you sit here with me when you should be with Ruy? Surely, he waits for you?"

It was true. Mirjana had prolonged this evening with the señora. She would have done anything to save herself from being alone with Ruy. More than anything, she feared she could not keep what she had overheard a secret, afraid she would condemn him with the birth of his first child. Worse, she did not want his pity or to have him see how painful it was to her that his child had not been birthed by her.

"Go to bed, Mirjana. You need your sleep," Doña Ysabel told her fondly, reaching out to pat her hand. She wanted to take Mirjana into her arms, to hold her head against her breast and let her cry until she could cry no more. But it would do the girl a disservice when she was obviously straining to keep her composure. When the door closed behind Mirjana, the señora leaned back onto her pillows and closed her eyes. Another quatrain from Kayyám came to her mind and she brushed away a regretful tear.

> The Moving Finger writes; and, having writ,
> Moves on: nor all your Piety nor Wit
> Shall lure it back to cancel half a Line,
> Nor all your Tears wash out a Word of it.

What was done was done, and there was no help for it. The señora would pay for her cruelties with the sharp pangs of conscience. But it was only the tomorrows that ever really counted for anything. She hoped that Ruy would know this and follow his heart and believe in Mirjana's.

Mirjana slipped into the chamber, grateful to find Ruy asleep. She could hear his soft, even breathing as she slipped off her robe and climbed into the bed, careful not to waken him. She had thought of moving once again to the tower room, but it would require an explanation to Ruy, and she feared that once pressed, she would not be able to keep her counsel. As she lay back against the pillows, he sensed her presence, reaching for her to bring her against him. Involuntarily, she shuddered.

"Are you cold?" he asked, startling her, dashing her hopes that he would sleep.

"A little," she answered, knowing the truth in her words. She was cold, cold as death, and no fire would ever warm her again.

As his hands found her breasts and his lips sought her mouth, Mirjana felt herself withdraw from him, not by movement of body nor by shrinking of flesh, but deeper, so deep that her breath caught in her chest and an ache in her heart deadened her to all other sensation.

Ruy sank back onto the bed. Something was wrong, terribly wrong. He had taken her into his arms, made love to her, desperately tried to evoke her responses to no avail. She had withdrawn from him totally, giving only the use of her body, withholding her emotions. Her movements had been wooden, like a puppet's, reacting only in reflex. His hand reached under his pillow to grasp the medallion with her likeness engraved on it. She had been as lifeless as this, he thought. Beautiful, golden, but unlike the medallion, she had not warmed under his touch. So, at last the time had come. At last, she had had enough of him and she was homesick for her people and her rightful place to belong.

Mirjana lay with her back turned to Ruy. His lovemaking had been as tender and artful as ever, but something in her, some part of her defenses, refused to allow her to respond. It will be better, she told herself, squeezing back a tear. I learned to live with his marriage, and I will learn to live with the existence of Himena's child.

CHAPTER 16

Because Doña Ysabel was on the mend and Mirjana was able to spend more time doing other things, Tanige was free to spend all of her free time with Gormaz's family and Luis. If she sensed a mood swing, a depression in Mirjana, she put it down to overwork and worry about the señora. Even Doña Ysabel had cautioned Mirjana to rest more, eat better, and at one point had even accused her of burning the candle at both ends. Tanige was certain the princess would snap out of it now that the lovely weather was here to stay. It was hard to believe that she and Mirjana had arrived in Bivar more than a year ago. So much had happened, so much had changed. The month of June was just around the bend, and it was only this time last year Don Ruy was preparing for his attendance at King Alphonso's coronation. Soon, it would be one year since he had married that woman named Himena. Tanige scowled. There were times she would have cheerfully killed Ruy for the pain he had brought to Mirjana, and she did not like to remember.

Tanige felt she could see signs that Luis was about to ask her to marry him. Delirious with joy, she had confided in Ilena who had smiled and rocked her baby. The princess would not stand in her way, refusing to release Tanige from her service. On the contrary, Mirjana would hug her and wish her all the happiness in the world. A pity that Don Ruy could not marry Mirjana because, unlike the men of Islam, he could not go against the laws and faith of Spain. Tanige frowned and tried to recall when it was she had noticed Mirjana's low spirits. Shame washed over her. Here she had been so caught up in her own affairs, she had not really noticed. Perhaps a word in confidence to Doña Ysabel to have a word with Don Ruy, saying the princess seemed tired, out of sorts, looking drawn. A mother could say these things to a son. Another frown, this one deeper, drawing deep lines across Tanige's forehead, as she gasped, "Impossible!" She refused to put a name to her dread for Mirjana. Yes, there was something definitely amiss. Lately, whenever the princess smiled, it was with her lips, never her eyes.

It irked Tanige that only moments ago she had been so happy, and now, thinking about

Mirjana, she felt out of sorts and guilty — guilty about leaving the *castillo* and Mirjana to spend a wonderful afternoon with Luis. How could she enjoy the baby and Ilena's company now that she was worried? Dejected, she plopped down in an unladylike position onto a bench and contemplated her feet. Sighing wearily, she picked at the fabric of her dress. What could she do? Of late, Mirjana had held her own counsel, not seeming to want to discuss anything, save Doña Ysabel and her recovery. She was not happy, of that Tanige was certain. What to do? First, she would approach Doña Ysabel. Then, and only then, would she go off to Ilena's. She must go, Tanige told herself, soothing her guilt. After all, she must invite them to the banquet Doña Ysabel was planning for Don Ruy's birthday.

Later that afternoon, Ruy paced the length and breadth of his office. Angrily, he kicked and lashed out at the base of his desk. When the pain ripped up his leg and thigh, he smacked one fist into the other. As if he needed his mother to call him to her chamber to tell him Mirjana seemed unhappy. Of course she was unhappy! Certainly, she was unhappy! Did he not know this? Did it not tear at his heart each night in bed when he took her into his arms, and he felt that hesitant withdrawal? Not of her body, never with her body. She repaid him for her keep with her body! It was an inner withdrawal, something intangible, and it was tearing him to pieces.

Pietro entered Ruy's office and waited to be acknowledged. He saw the tightness around his friend's mouth and the pain in his narrowed eyes. It had been days, weeks really, since a smile had crossed Ruy's face.

"I've made up my mind, Pietro. Send a messenger to Hassan telling him she will begin her journey back to Seville before the week is out."

Shock marked Pietro's burly features. How haunted Ruy was, how desolate he appeared. "Have you thought this through, friend? Are you certain this is the wise course of action?" Seeing Ruy's sudden anger, Pietro stood his ground. "You aren't thinking clearly, Ruy. You know as well as I you want Mirjana here with you and not on the other side of Spain. Ruy, I beg you, spare yourself a rash decision." Pietro's tone was brotherly and concerned for his boyhood friend. It wounded him to see Ruy so tormented.

"I have made the decision and it is final." Ruy seemed to gulp back a lump in his throat before addressing Pietro again. "Now, have you come here for a reason? And if you mention Mirjana's name to me, I swear I'll choke the life out of your body!"

"What else is there to discuss?" Pietro snarled. "Nothing else occupies your mind, nothing and no one else matters! I have been following your every command, seeing to your every wish, and I am sick of it. I have my own life to attend. I am only too happy to hand your affairs back to you. Get yourself in hand and then we will talk."

"I think you are forgetting whom you are addressing, Pietro," Ruy stormed arrogantly.

"On the contrary, I remember only too well. It has been too long since you've carried out your duties instead of delegating me to do them for you. Bivar has grown, or have you not noticed? Life moves on, Ruy, and there are many things that need your attention. I've done my best, but I cannot walk in your shoes. If you are jackass enough to send Mirjana away, then do it and spare me your self-pity!"

Ruy glowered at Pietro, his fists itching to beat him, to crack his face into fragments, but he knew his friend was always his friend and only spoke the truth. Self-pitying fool, he had called him, and he was right. Without another word to his defense, Ruy strode from the room without a backward glance. He could not meet Pietro's eyes until he had indeed taken himself in hand, and the sooner the better.

His heels pounded the corridor like the beats of a drum. What he wanted no longer mattered. It was what Mirjana wanted, needed, that mattered and only that. If returning to Seville was what would make her happy and what she had wanted all along, he would not stand in her way. She would hate him if she learned she could have returned months ago, and he had kept her for his own selfish purposes. He would free her, stand aside and watch her go.

Tomorrow was the birthday celebration Doña Ysabel planned for him. It was as good a place as any to make his announcement. There would be people around, and he would be forced to hold himself back from begging Mirjana to stay with him. It would be all he could do to handle the happiness on Mirjana's beloved face when she heard the news. She would have a week to leave, one last week with her, his heart mourned. It would take that long, at least, to strip the *castillo* of all she had brought into it. He intended, as far as was possible, that she return to Seville with everything she had brought.

Now, he would go to work. Pietro was right. Too long he had wallowed in self-pity. Throwing himself into his affairs was what he needed. He had decided what was best for

Mirjana. But never, never for him!

Mirjana heard Ruy creep into their room. He had stayed far too late over his accounts, and she could smell the sourness of too many goblets of wine as he entered. She wondered, not for the first time, if his depression was an imagined echo of her own or was one of his own making. He slipped into the anteroom she had made into a bath, and she heard him washing and rinsing his mouth. When he returned, she was aware of the scent of her own perfumed soap on his skin.

Tonight will be better, she told herself. Tonight she would fight this demon, this foolish pride, and give herself to him, totally as she always had. Enough of false pride.

Even before Ruy slid into bed, she was in his arms, holding him, nuzzling her lips against his chest. All would be well again, she told herself; if Ruy needed her, she would be here for him. Always. Until he sent her away. This last sudden thought had occurred with such surprise it left her shaking.

"Here, sweet, are you cold?" he asked solicitously, wrapping his arms around her.

She had no words, only a deep-rooted need for him. Her insecurity made her the aggressor, willing him with every fiber of her body to know how deeply she loved him, begging him with her kisses, never, ever to send her away.

She brought him down onto the bed, pressing him back against the sweet-scented pillows, kneeling over him. Her hands followed the sinewy lines of his broad chest to the slimmer, cat-like sleekness of his narrow hips and flat belly. She thought him magnificent and told him so, whispering in a throaty voice that invited his passions. She caressed him, fondled him, bringing him to full arousal. In the half light of the room she appreciated the sight of him, the dark, soft patches of hair leading the eye to the power of his manhood. She loved him, kissing him in the most intimate places, in the pits of his arms, in the hollows where thigh joined hip, in the valley beneath his belly where the hair was coarser and more erotic to her lips. She grazed his chest with her breasts, awakening their tips to hard points that teased his hands and enticed his tongue. She covered him with herself, rubbing against him in a silent plea that he take her, that she could wait no longer.

When she began to lay down, taking him with her, he protested, again pulling her atop of him, rendering himself up to her delicious mouth as it moved over his flesh, tantalizing him until he groaned, "Love me, Mirjana. You take me!"

She took him into her, feeling him enter her all at once, not in tender gradual stages as when he was atop her. Her knees bent, kneeling over him, lowering herself onto him, taking him deep, moving against him.

He kissed her breasts, her mouth. His hands were in her hair, on her face, touching, kissing. He held her with his eyes, kissed her with his eyes, watching her, fascinated by her, losing himself in her, unaware of anything except the hot caress of her engulfing his flesh. His irreversible response dictated the driving thrust of his sex, the motion of his hips under her, the fullness of her weight atop him. Desperately, he drew her to him, molding her body to his own. This was the last time he would hold her, love her. And when she heard his sob she thought it was a sound of passion spent.

Mirjana hurried up the staircase from the great hall to the long and winding corridor leading to the master chamber to bathe and dress for Ruy's birthday celebration. Even Doña Ysabel was primping and preening with Dulcimea's help. The year's mourning for Teddy was not yet over, and so it would be a small gala with only the closest of friends.

So busy with her preparations, Mirjana was unaware of any difference in the room. But as she bathed and laid out her garments, she began to notice small changes. The shock, when it hit her, was like a blow to her middle. Her indrawn breath exploded into a long, tortured sigh. Ruy's shaving materials had been removed. Ruy's boots were gone. His clothes had been taken away. Hastily, she wrapped herself in a long towel and raced into the bedroom. In a frenzy of panic, she ripped back the coverlet and pillows. The medallion was gone.

She sank onto the edge of the bed. So, it had come, at last. Ruy was done with her. Her head dropped to her hands, her back curved in an expression of deepest sorrow. Ruy was done with her.

All the energy was driven from her, and she thought it would be impossible to move, to even breathe. Still, she knew she must dress, must make an appearance at the birthday celebration. Because of Doña Ysabel's eager anticipation it would be necessary for her to behave normally. Normally! What could ever be normal after this?

Last night, Mirjana thought as her hand reached to stroke the pillow where Ruy slept, only last night she had brought herself to overcome the withdrawal, the rejection she was feeling. She remembered the sudden, unexpected thought of Ruy sending her away, of leaving her, and how she had shuddered. But she also remembered what she had believed was love, hoped was love. And now she knew. The news that Ruy was now a father brought out his paternal instincts. It was natural, after all, that he would want to make a home for the child, a home including both himself and Himena. In that home there was no place for her. A chill settled over her with the knowledge that she was homeless and abandoned once again. Only this time it was worse, much worse. She was being abandoned by Ruy, the only man she ever really loved, and the father of the child growing in her womb.

The guests were already gathering in the great hall below — Gormaz, Ilena, and little Manuel, Luis and Tanige. Padres Tomas and Juano were present as was Pietro; and, of course, Doña Ysabel. Mirjana immediately went to stand behind the señora's chair. Ruy was already at the head of the table, and Mirjana wondered if it was her imagination or if he really was avoiding her questioning gaze.

Everyone chattered happily, congratulating Ruy on his birthday and presenting him with small gifts which he accepted with obvious embarrassment. The entire scene seemed to pass before Mirjana as though seen through a veil. While she conversed and smiled and made attempts to taste the food put before her, her soul and consciousness were trapped in a world of disbelief.

Ruy rose, his goblet of mead held high, to make the first toast to his mother. Doña Ysabel nodded graciously, smiling proudly at her son.

How haggard he looked, Mirjana thought. His smile appeared to be pasted onto his face. Still, he had not met her eyes. Doña Ysabel seemed to be the only one to notice this change in Ruy, and she covered Mirjana's trembling hand with her own beneath the table.

Ruy was speaking. She must give him her attention. "This is a day for twofold celebration. Doña Ysabel has complimented me with this fiesta, and I wish to thank her for her love and the honor she gives me." He bowed slightly in the señora's direction. Goblets were raised in Doña Ysabel's honor.

"And now for the second reason for celebration. It is now possible for Princesa Mirjana to return to Seville with her bother Hassan's blessings. She will be leaving in less than a week. In a manner of speaking, this is farewell."

Mirjana was frozen as though carved from stone. Doña Ysabel and Ilena gasped aloud, the señora's face going from purple to white and back to mottled purple. Her breathing was ragged, uneven, and she stared at her son, not believing him capable of this cruelty.

It was out of concern for the señora that Mirjana was propelled to action. A gentle hand was placed on Doña Ysabel's shoulder, warning her to calm herself. No words were spoken as the women locked eyes.

Mirjana called on every shred of strength to support herself while answering questions and hearing her friends' regrets that she should leave them and Bivar. The most she could say was that it had been too long since she had been among her own people, her own family. When asked about her plans to return to Bivar, she merely smiled, blinking back tears, giving some vagary that seemed to satisfy. Only Doña Ysabel's firm grip under the table gave her the strength to lie this way, to keep her composure and not to run upstairs to cry out her misery.

When the initial shock of the announcement had abated and Mirjana was able to gather her thoughts, she was stricken by the cruelty Ruy displayed in choosing this method to inform her he no longer wanted her. But as she listened to his voice as he spoke with Gormaz and Pietro, she heard his unconvincing laughter, his forced jubilance, and the distracted way he answered questions. It was as though he were missing a beat, hesitating slightly as though not really hearing what was asked. He pitied her, Mirjana realized. His method had been cruel, but it also saved her from humiliation. Here, among all these people, he had given her time to absorb his decision, rather than telling her while they were alone when she would have degraded herself by begging him to allow her to stay.

Ruy had purposely avoided looking at Mirjana as he made his announcement. Though he be a man, a fearless warrior, he could not bring himself to see the suffusion of her happiness when she heard. Even afterwards, he could hardly bring himself to glance at her as she answered various questions. But he had heard her vague answers concerning her return to Bivar. He had not actually expected her to applaud — she was much too kind for that type of display — but her eyes seemed to shine and she was smiling. It was done. Good. And he had not cracked and shattered. Here in public, among friends and servants, he had been restrained from pleading, begging her not to leave him. The vast hall seemed to be closing in on him. He wanted to run, to hide, to be alone with his grief. He could not remain here in the *castillo* with Mirjana. He would plead business in a nearby village. Like a coward he would run, knowing he would be unable to say good-bye.

* * *

Mirjana stood alone near the window in her chamber watching Ruy ride off into the distance. Once before she had stood here, at his request, watching him ride away. Then, he had gone to marry Himena. Now, he was probably going to see their child. Her eyes ached for the sight of him, her heart yearned for the sound of his voice. Dead. She might as well be dead. She would never see him again, and the sun had been stolen from her life. She wished she could fall asleep, never to awaken. A taste of deadly nightshade. A taste of oblivion. An end to pain, to torment, to this dreadful beating of her heart which refused to die although she was already dead. Had she ever lived? Laughed? Or was she a spectre, walking this earth and knowing her doom? Had she already died and no one had had the grace to bury her?

An overwhelming desire to destroy herself attacked her. Her fingers raked through her thick, lustrous hair. Ruy had once said it was like a curtain of sunshine that draped them from the world. She bit back a sob; trembling hands reached for the scissors in her mending box. Like women from ancient civilizations when in mourning for the dead, she hacked at her hair, mercilessly cutting, pulling, the red-gold curls falling about her shoulders and at her feet. If her hair be a woman's glory, then Mirjana would have none of it!

Holding her tremorous fingers out before her, she stared at them as though they were her enemy. Beautiful hands, sensitive hands, made for touching, for caressing. Ruy had told her they were gentle and fierce, all at the same time. Demanding hands. She found the scissors again, cutting the nails, digging into the soft fingertips, leaving hard, jagged, bleeding edges. She ripped her gown from her body, pulling the fabric, shredding it, leaving her gasping and panting from the exertion. There was little that could be done to satisfy her wish to no longer exist. Regardless of what she inflicted on herself, of how she tried to cause her own destruction, she still lived, still breathed. Total destruction was within her grip and she denied it. To kill herself would be to kill Ruy's child and this she would never do.

An inner voice pleaded, fought to be heard: If you tell Ruy about the child, things will be different. No! No! He would keep her out of a sense of obligation. She detested the thought. If she could not have his love, then she wanted nothing. She would have Ruy's child, a part of him, to hold and to love. Always.

The *castillo* was in an uproar, from Doña

Ysabel down to the kitchen cat. Five days and nights had passed since Don Ruy had made the announcement of Mirjana's return to Seville. Since that time, Mirjana had refused to come out of her room and Ruy had ridden off somewhere.

Several times Doña Ysabel had gone to speak with Mirjana, her heart aching for the girl who had taken such loving care of her, a girl she had come to think of as her daughter. Differences were dissolved. Religion and heritage counted for nothing. This girl, Mirjana, was deeply loved by the señora, and she cursed her son for his foolishness and stupidity.

When the señora had seen what Mirjana had done to her hands and her beautiful hair, she held open her arms and brought the girl into them, holding her, soothing her. She had no answers, only a silent sympathy. Tanige was sent for to try to rectify the damage done. Crying, the *princesa*'s serving girl had taken up the scissors to even out the shorn hair, and trim and bandage the wounded fingers. Mirjana allowed herself to be ministered unto, silently miserable. And now the time had come for her to leave. The wagons and escort were ready and all hope was gone.

With a heavy step and heavier heart, Tanige went to Mirjana. She knew she would find her sitting silently near the window, staring dully into the distance. There was a heart-stopping fragility about Mirjana that was accentuated by her severely shorn locks that curled about her face and at the nape of her neck in glossy ringlets. She looked like a tragic child, eyes vacant, unaware of her own worth or beauty.

Throwing open the door, Tanige made her voice sound cheerful. "Princess, at last the escort is ready. We must make ready to leave." Nothing in the world could bring her to tell Mirjana that every single item in the storehouse and from the *castillo* itself that had been a part of the bridal caravan to Granada had also been packed for the return trip. "I, for one, cannot wait to leave this place. Think, just think, how wonderful it will be to be home again. Please, Princess, come and see that I am doing everything the way you like. I am certain we will have a good journey. The weather promises to hold."

"*I* will have a good journey. You, Tanige, are staying here. Do you think I would ask you to return with me when Luis is here and your life is here?" Even while she spoke, her eyes implored Tanige for answers.

"No, Mirjana. There has been no word from Don Ruy." Tanige would have cried for the injustice of it all, but Mirjana would not abide her tears.

"No word," Mirjana repeated. "Yet there are enough tears to fill the sea."

Tanige bent before an open trunk, packing Mirjana's clothes. "Luis has already received permission from Doña Ysabel to come to Seville with us," she told Mirjana quietly. "I would not leave you, Princess, and Luis said it is time he saw more of the world." There was no response, and in frustration, Tanige tried a subject she had been avoiding. "If your child is a girl, what will you name her?"

Mirjana's eyes widened. "How long have you known?" Then, desperately, "Does Doña Ysabel know?"

"Calm yourself, it is neither good for you nor the child. No, I don't think the señora knows for certain, but I think she suspects. I asked you," Tanige said again, trying for a happier subject like the birth of Mirjana's child, "what will you name the child if it is a girl?"

"Ysabel Tanige," Mirjana said quietly, the faintest touch of pride and expectation penetrating her sorrow.

"And a boy?"

"Only one name will do." She glanced again out the window. "Rodrigo. His father's name and his grandfather's name. There is no other."

Mirjana leaned back in her chair, her hand

placed protectively on her stomach. How relieved she was that Tanige and Luis were going with her. How wonderful to speak to someone of the child. It made the babe more real somehow, bringing her comfort.

Early the next morning there were tears, embraces, and promises that would never be kept. There was one last fond embrace for Doña Ysabel. "*Vaya con Dios,*" the señora whispered bravely. Mirjana motioned for Tanige and Luis to go ahead to the carriage. There was one last thing to do. She walked back into the great hall and up the stairs to the room where Ruy's belongings had been moved. The bed was made, looking as though it had never been slept in. It hadn't, she remembered. The same day he had moved his possessions, he had left the *castillo.* An eternity ago. Pulling down the pillow, she saw it there. The medallion. Before she could change her mind, she quickly laid Teddy's gold cross beside it. It was over. All of it. All the glory and the pain and the love that would never be.

In the dark hours before dawn, Ruy rode into the courtyard of the *castillo,* avoiding the inquiring eyes of the guardsmen on duty. Even before letting himself into the great hall he could feel the desolation from within. Mirjana was gone. And the world had gone mad. He had seen her leave earlier that morning, watching from a hilltop as the escort led her carriage and the wagons out of the village of Bivar. It had been all he could do not to call her name, to keep from riding Liberte at breakneck speed to catch her, to beg her to stay. All that long day he had sat on that same hilltop, looking off into the distance, wondering what would become of him now that his reason for existing was gone.

He could not find it in him to climb the stairs. Where would he go? To the master chamber, where so many memories haunted the corners? To the room where he had had himself installed on his birthday? That, too, was so empty, so meaningless, merely a place in this vast world where he would find a spare pair of boots or his lonely, empty bed. Wearily, he sat near the table, throwing his long legs out before him, waiting for the start of the new day. A day without Mirjana.

Doña Ysabel came down early that morning, suspecting she might find Ruy had returned during the night. She found him before the hearth in the great hall, ignoring the meal the kitchen staff had silently placed before him. Immediately after, Padre Tomas joined them for his own morning meal, quickly followed by Pietro.

The atmosphere in the hall was like a wake for the dead. Doña Ysabel would not look up from her place, except to send him black scowls that made Ruy wish he were somewhere else. Padres Tomas and Pietro seemed to form a silent conspiracy and spoke in low tones only to one another. Even when Ruy addressed them by name, they pretended not to hear, keeping their eyes downcast.

It was Pietro who finally broke the silence and stared at him a moment before announcing that he had never numbered fools among his friends. He then stood and stalked out of the hall, his shoulders hunched, his head bowed low.

Doña Ysabel watched him leave and then turned to Ruy. She pointed a long, bony finger and accused, "You have become a wretched son, Ruy. I mean to pray to God that you be punished for what you have done. I will never forgive you. Never!" The word vibrated in the cavernous hall, echoing from the vaulted ceiling. "Bah! Take me out of here," she called to Dulcimea. "I cannot bear to look upon my son a minute longer!"

Ruy pounded his fist on the table, and Padre Tomas and the servants scuttled away like rats leaving a sinking ship. He was alone. He would always be alone. Without Mirjana there was nothing but loneliness.

Ruy leaped from the table and stormed to his chamber. How neat and spartan it was. Gone were all traces of Mirjana. Everything was gone, even the silken pillow on which she had slept. Something grabbed his throat, making it impossible to swallow. Angrily, he ran his hands through his hair. It was impossible to remove every trace of someone's existence but Mirjana had done it. He could not stay here, ever again. It was haunted by her, by his love for her.

Banging out the door, he raced through the corridors until coming to the room he had taken after moving from the master chamber. His quick eye saw the pillows tumbled and disturbed. Like a madman he raced to the bed and ripped away the cover. There, beside the medallion he had left, lay the little gold cross. A gut roar of pain thundered through him.

She was out of his life. Gone. Memories of her kept flooding his brain and cut like a knife — the color of her hair in the sun, the softness of it as it brushed his cheek. Biting on his fist to quell the explosion of sound that threatened to rip into the silence, he knew not whether to live or to die. She was out of his hands. She had come and left him, had slipped through his grasp like the sands of time. Out of his life, leaving him bereft and hollow. Gone!

Anger and pain charged through him, whirling him about like a mindless leaf in the autumn wind. He smashed about the room, beating his fists against the stone walls until his hands were broken and bleeding. Bellow after bellow poured from him in a voice he did not recognize as his own.

He loved her! Loved her! And he had sent her away! What matter would it have been if he had begged for her to stay? Did it make him more of a man to hide his feelings from the one person who was more important to him on this earth than any other? Love did not exist of its own sake! Love needs expression, words and feelings that he had kept buried deep inside.

Mirjana! Mirjana! The name kept sounding in his head. He heard it as he had whispered it as she had lain in his arms. Then it became a call, to bring her back, and finally a cry of desolation.

Mirjana. The loveliest of melodies, and together they had danced to the moon. She had come to him soundlessly, softly, taking his heart by surprise. He knew her voice and had heard her words, but he had let their true meaning go past, never really knowing her, always making assumptions. He loved her. Loved her and wished he'd found a reason to make her stay. All the loving, all the god-damned loving. The tears and the touching, all the caring. Perhaps it was not her words he should have waited to hear. Perhaps it was her heart he should have listened to.

Pietro found him hours later, lying on the sterile bed, staring at the medallion and the tiny cross. He dropped to his knees, putting himself on eye level with Ruy. "I told you this morning I had no fools among my friends. Go after her, Ruy. Do you think she is capable of such tenderness and kindness if she did not love you? For a woman like Mirjana a man would travel the world a thousand times over to be closer to her. Go, Ruy. But first let me see your hands." There was awe in his voice when next he spoke. "The pain must be more than you can bear. You've broken your hands."

There was a puzzled expression on Ruy's tormented face. "Pain?" Even he was astounded to see what he had done to himself. "I cannot feel it."

"You will, friend. Take my word for it. Gormaz and I will wrap them for you. Tell me, have you come to your senses? Will you go after her?"

"I will not force her to stay with me. I have no liking to be her jailor and have her come to me out of duty, out of punishment, or payment for her keep! She wants to return to Seville." His tone was pleading, begging Pietro to tell him all he had said was a lie.

"I saw nothing of this. I saw a woman whose eyes followed a man whenever he was in sight. I knew a woman who cared for an old woman to spare the son the pain of his mother's death. I heard a woman's voice soft and tender whenever she spoke your name. Am I deaf? Am I blind? Or did you see and hear this too?"

"I saw, I heard. I also know how lonely she was, how desperately she had wanted to go back to Seville . . ." Ruy's words hesitated, trying to recall when it was Mirjana last spoke of Seville. It had been so long ago he could not remember. "Pietro, what if Mirjana refuses to come back with me?"

Pietro sighed. "It is up to you to whisper the honeyed words that will bring her back. Use your head and listen to your heart, man! Tell her what you feel. Tell her why you broke your hands. She will understand."

When you are not alive, the world as you knew it ceases to exist. Though the blood pulsed through Mirjana's veins with each beat of her heart and her limbs moved and her ears heard, she could not think of herself as being alive. Alive, life, *vita* in Latin. Vital. No, she was none of these things.

Vital was being with Ruy, feeling his gaze

warm her. Alive was feeling the touch of his hand upon her cheek or the sound of his voice laughing. Life was Ruy.

She walked slowly along beside the carriage, traveling the same roads which had brought her to Bivar an eternity ago. She had only to look over her shoulder, and she would see him, riding toward her, wolfskins ruffling in the breeze, Liberte's proud black head lifting, the flash of the sun glinting off his breastplate armor. As though to tempt both fate and her dream, and to defy the gods, Mirjana turned to look at the crest of the hill and blinked her eyes — blinking again, thinking she was indeed going mad.

Ruy rode atop Liberte, faster now that the line of wagons was in sight. He had ridden for almost three days to find her, and now, faced with seeing her again, he felt the blood rush through him, his pulses pounding with anticipation. Even if she would not have him, he would speak his heart, at last. Even though she might refuse to go back with him, he would tell her of his love for her, only her. There were things she did not know, did not understand: Himena, the circumstances of his marriage, and then the child who carried his name. Even though she had never asked, he would tell her.

He was a god, dark-haired and fierce, a warrior in armor, his destrier churning the turf beneath its hooves as they thundered toward her. She could see his face, each line and feature so dear to her and engraved forever on her memory. She would become an old woman, and this is how she would always see him — strong, tall, eyes blazing and arms reaching for her.

In the space of a minute he was beside her, pulling hard on Liberte's reins, hooves digging into the earth. She had only to look at his face, to hear the sound of her name on his lips, and she knew he had come for her, to keep her to himself and never to let her leave him again. With the quickness of a breath, she was in his arms, across his lap and atop Liberte, riding off with him. He had swooped down like an eagle capturing his prey, flying off with her to take her to his aerie.

Beneath a copse of trees he drew rein and wrapped his arms around her, holding her close to him as though he would never let her go.

Taking her face in his bandaged hands, he looked down into her radiant face, seeing her beauty and boundless love. The tips of his fingers touched the unfamiliar softly cropped ringlets of her titian-gold hair. Ruy's eyes seared her face, searching and discovering the changes in her.

Violet smudges stained the translucent skin beneath her eyes. Her mouth, so full and tempting, trembled with vulnerability. Her long, glorious hair was shorn like a boy's and he saw the pitifully bloodied and scabbed fingertips where she had cruelly cut the nails back beyond the quick.

A cry of pain which could find no escape or release engulfed him as he crushed her to him. She had ravaged herself, disfigured herself, and the sin was on his soul. Her hair would grow, the flesh of her fingers would heal but never the wound to her spirit, and the fault was his alone. She was in his arms, leaning against him, small and fragile like a child, and he could feel the deep spine-wrenching sobs shuddering through her. There could be no forgiveness for the beast who had crushed this fragile heart; yet her arms wound around him, yielding herself up to him, offering herself for his love. Giving, always giving.

A blunt-edged axe carved from within and rendered him helpless to his misery. There was no need to ask her why, he knew with an agonizing scourge of recognition. She was his love and he had made her his victim. The reality of his cruelty and stupidity convulsed and punished to the core of his being. He had broken his hands, and with the same kind of self-contempt she had robbed herself of the symbol of her femininity by ruthlessly cutting her hair.

His lips were in her hair, on her face, against her mouth. Over and over he begged her forgiveness, murmuring his love for her, his need for her, telling her life meant nothing unless she shared it with him.

Mirjana's heart sang and sunlight burst into her soul. She answered his kiss, crying her love for him. Her hand caressed his cheek, finding it damp with tears. Surely, they were her own. He was El Cid, Compeador, and warriors did not cry.

Lifting her face to his, she saw his eyes, dark and pensive, brimming with love and overflowing with tenderness. As her lips found his in a promise she knew that for all his power, for all his strength, he would always be her tender warrior.

The employees of THORNDIKE PRESS hope you have enjoyed this Large Print book. All our Large Print books are designed for easy reading — and they're made to last.

Other Thorndike Large Print books are available at your library, through selected bookstores, or directly from us. Suggestions for books you would like to see in Large Print are always welcome.

For more information about current and upcoming titles, please call or mail your name and address to:

THORNDIKE PRESS
PO Box 159
Thorndike, Maine 04986
800/223-6121
207/948-2962